LIFELINE

Author: Christopher Keith
Title: Lifeline
www.christopherkeithauthor.com

ISBN: 9780648241409
ISBN: 0648241408

Published by Pagetrim Book Services
www.pagetrimservices.com
info@pagetrimservices.com

LIFELINE

CHRISTOPHER KEITH

PAGETRIM
BOOK EDIT &
DESIGN SERVICES

Death is a process, not an event

OTHER BOOKS
BY CHRISTOPHER KEITH

1

"It's time," Dr. Huber murmured, leaning over the bed that held the facility's only patient under primary care of Europe's finest surgeons and biologists. Though equipped with break-through technology and cutting-edge instruments, the facility felt more like an abandoned clinic than a hub of innovation. The walls were a faded yellow with concrete blocks visible beneath the peeling paint, and the linoleum floor was streaked with stains from years of neglect. Along one side of the room, uneven stacks of flimsy plastic chairs lined a wall composed of grimy, square-shaped windows. The harsh glare of artificial light spilled through the glass, casting a sterile glow over the forty-six-year-old patient, hooked up to machines and lying motionless in his bed.

Still in his mid-twenties, Dr. Huber had already gained a reputation as a prodigy in the fields of biochemistry, human biology, and neuroscience. Admired and respected by all his peers, Huber's deep, raspy voice held a natural authority that could silence any room. His lack of sleep had become a signature trait, visible in the dark circles beneath his eyes, and his small, slightly hunched shoulders gave him an almost fragile, deformed appearance.

Dr. Huber's sharp eyes assessed the patient as he leaned over the bed. He parted the patient's lid and shone a penlight into his left eye. "The pupil dilates."

On the other side of the bed, the eight medical specialists nodded in unison, as if controlled by a single mind, all eager to learn whether the procedure to remove the right eye, along with the necessary blood vessels, muscles, and optic nerve, had proved successful. While the surgery was a success, the post-operative risks remained high, making the next few days of recovery crucial.

"Brain activity?" asked Dr. Steinhart.

Dr. Huber shook his head. "Too early to know." He then leaned forward, close to the patient's ear. "You can hear me, Herr Smolensk?"

At first, Smolensk remained still and silent, showing no signs of a cognitive return.

"Herr Smolensk, you can hear me? My name is Dr. Huber. The year is 1968. You're in the underground facility in Vaduz, Liechtenstein. Do you know why you are here?"

The atmosphere in the room was quiet and tense. Arms folded, nerves frayed, the medical team exchanged words in hushed voices, waiting for Mr. Smolensk to regain a waking state.

It happened after almost thirty minutes, at ten past four in the morning. His left eye struggled to open. For two full minutes, he existed in a conscious void, as if he had come into existence from nothingness. Gradually, as the darkness faded into light and his vision improved, he focussed on the blurry outline of a fly relentlessly striking the tube bulb on the ceiling until the cold, clinical glow forced his eye to close.

Reaching a third minute of consciousness, his memories flashed and sparked as he slowly pieced his life together. All his muscles were numb, he noticed with primitive fear. For some reason, he couldn't swallow. His tongue tasted of metal. A chemical scent lingered in his nostrils. He realised he could only see out of one eye, an eye that had long been shielded from the world by a dome of skin. Through blurred vision, he noticed wires curving out of his body like slimy feeding tentacles.

Where was he? What had happened to him?

Eight minutes ticked by. He had no colour in his cheeks. His lips were white, as if all the blood had been leached out of them. His mouth opened with a gummy pop. He rolled his head to one side and whispered to Dr. Huber, "Am I alive?" in a voice he barely recognised as his own.

"Yah," said Dr. Huber. "Gratulation, you just made the history!"

Cheers and applause erupted with a loud cacophony. Dr. Steinhart yelled into the corridor, and a dozen more doctors and biologists filed into the room, bringing champagne and glass flutes.

Dr. Huber popped the cork and white foam drizzled over the bed. He raised the green bottle above his head and toasted, "Gratulation! Ich möchte einen Toast auf Herrn Thomas Smolensk aussprechen!" The celebrations echoed around the room and along the barren labyrinth of corridors.

One month later, after his recovery and rehabilitation, Smolensk was taken to a limousine by a chauffeur, who gently helped him into the back seat.

The chauffeur engaged first gear and drove slowly out of the car park, away from the secret facility. "How does it feel?" he asked, craning his neck to view his passenger.

Smolensk turned to observe the dramatic forest in the undulating landscape unspool in the rear window, captivated by the low valley and majestic alpine peaks, his first taste of freedom. Sunrise planted spectacular orange shades on the Alps, but the harsh light brought a sharp pain to his left eye. Equally unpleasant was the patch over his right eye, now a permanent fixture on his face.

"How does what feel?" he asked in a cold tone.

"You are gone for a very long time. Now you go home to a new life."

"Home? I don't know what that is anymore. As you say, it's been a very long time."

Liechtenstein, situated on the east side of the Rhine River, was smaller than London, and he watched the scenery glide by, making connections, weaving his past life into his present, digging through old memories.

"How's my son?" he asked.

The chauffeur swallowed nervously. "He's alive and waits a long time for your return."

"Thank you." Smolensk stared out through the window. "Now stop talking!"

The chauffeur nodded and raised the window separating the front and rear compartments. He didn't say another word until they reached the airport, where Smolensk boarded a private jet for London.

By midday, he was inside another limousine, heading west along the familiar country road, passing villages, forests, and fields patterning the land in irregular quadrilaterals.

The sandstone walls of Windermere House, an eighteenth-century mansion tucked deep within the English countryside, loomed on the left side of the road like a forbidding fortress. The mansion, with its ninety-five rooms, was surrounded by 350 acres of fields and forest. The chauffeur drove through the wrought-iron gates and followed the winding driveway that dipped and curved, terminating outside the mansion in a gravel circle with a water fountain in the middle.

A young butler in a black tailcoat and bow tie opened the car door. Smolensk stepped out, inhaling deeply as he took in the familiar essence of his home. Feeling suddenly dizzy, he steadied himself against the limousine. His monocular vision would require some getting used to. He had lost depth in his sight and the ability to triangulate on an object, near or far. Moreover, his peripheral vision had been reduced by twenty per cent. He needed time to adjust to this new reality. Time was the great healer and would make him whole again.

For now, he was just grateful to be alive. And home.

When the dizzy spell passed, he studied the old mansion while the butler retrieved his luggage. The entrance had been redesigned in gothic revival architecture with a symmetrical façade and a steeply pitched red slate roof after a deadly fire had gutted the original structure, he had learned on the flight home. He had also learned his son was on his deathbed.

"This way, Sir," said the butler, leading him along a pine-panelled hallway with a cold, marble floor. They passed the drawing-room and study and the many landscape and portrait paintings adorning the walls. He remembered painting each one, and to see them all still intact and on display gave him nostalgic pleasure.

They ascended the marble staircase, which spiralled near the summit, and made their way towards the square-shaped master bedroom.

The butler stopped him at the door. "I must warn you, before you go in. He can no longer speak."

Smolensk brushed past the butler and marched up to the bed. An elderly man lay beneath the duvet, his head sunken into the pillow, his pale face unfamiliar with the passage of time. The veins in his arms were a vivid purple, and bulging arteries webbed the back of his wrinkly hands. The stench of a sickbed lain in around the clock accompanied the miserable scene.

The old man came around; a sparkle of delight lit up in his grey eyes.

"Yes, it's me, son," said Smolensk, smiling down on the elderly man. "Your father!"

2

Bryan's mother had passed away one day before Christmas in 1972, in the very hospital where she had spent her life as a surgeon saving others. Only fourteen at the time, he had sat in stunned silence as his father, with a cold, detached tone, told him she wasn't coming home. The words had barely sunk in, as if his father's emotionless delivery made them less real. Bryan had clung to some faint hope that maybe this wasn't the end, that she would walk through the door once more. But after the funeral, all illusions shattered. His father, never one for warmth, threw himself into his RAF career, leaving Bryan, his only child, to fend for himself, abandoned in a house that suddenly felt far too big and unbearably empty.

Now thirty-five, but Bryan could still feel the young, hurt version of himself inside. He blinked to hold back the tears, but a few slipped through, trailing down his cheeks as he put on his motorcycle helmet and flipped the visor. "I have to go, Mum."

He rose from the bench and squatted beside her cheap headstone. Some words had faded over time, including her name, but he knew the inscription by heart. He had come to visit her grave for two decades, no more able to conquer his grief than prevent the sun from rising every morning. He never missed her birthday or the anniversary of her death. He visited every month, rain or shine. Out of respect, he always dressed in black from head to toe, which wasn't difficult since his motorcycle gear was all black. He kept her photo tucked away in his wallet. He hardly ever looked at it. He couldn't. But he wanted to always have it with him as a reminder of the blessing he once had.

The damp, earthy smell of early autumn hung in the air. The cemetery lawns and flowerbeds had received minimal landscaping during the summer. Ranks of headstones stood decrepit, and a maze of larger tombstones and mausoleums were like a shantytown. It used to be a thriving memorial park. These days, it seldom attracted visitors, save for the tramps seeking asylum on the park benches or occasional relatives paying their respects to people once good to them.

A van backfired just outside the cemetery gates, startling Bryan and a flock of pigeons that scattered into the sky. He slipped his freezing hands into his leather jacket pockets and stood up, spotting the caretakers arriving to lock the cemetery gates for the night. It was much later than he thought, and darkness had crept in unnoticed.

He also failed to notice the two men wearing black suits sitting inside their parked Land Rover outside the cemetery, watching him through their binoculars. They remained still, studying his every move as Bryan stood over the grave. His mind had been elsewhere, drifting through memories of his childhood, the familiar ache in his chest growing heavier.

Unaware of the watchful eyes upon him, he kissed his hand and touched the gravestone, then whispered, "Happy Birthday, Mum."

Julia approached the door cautiously, convinced she'd heard a noise outside. She double-checked the bolt and chain-lock, then pressed her eye onto the peephole, scanning for signs of movement. Assured all was quiet, she returned to the lounge and curled up on the sofa. But not twenty seconds later, the telephone rang, startling her upright. She grabbed the receiver. "Julia speaking."

She heard someone breathing over the mouthpiece.

"Who is this?"

The line cut off.

Someone entered the kitchen through the rear door. Julia stood slowly and hesitantly. "Bryan? Is that you?"

Bryan walked into the room and hung his keys on the rack. He placed his helmet on the table and took off his backpack and black leather jacket.

"Hey," he said. "You look like you've seen a ghost."

Julia fixed him with an icy stare, her face make-up free, her long, brown hair still wet after her shower.

Something was bothering her, and Bryan had a reasonable idea what it was. He let the silence stretch, giving her a chance to speak her mind.

"Where have you been? I've been trying to reach you."

"I was with Mum."

"All day?"

"It's her birthday."

"She's dead, Bryan! She's been dead for twenty years."

He shot her a sharp look but aborted an angry response and raised his hands in conciliation.

He spotted a bottle of brandy on the kitchen worktop and poured a generous measure into a crystal glass, conscious of his wife's eyes upon him.

"Drinking again?"

He ignored her and knocked back the brandy, exhaling a cloud of warm breath. "Why is it so cold in here?"

"The gas has been disconnected because we haven't paid the last three bills. That's why I've been calling around, trying to reach you." She put her hands on her hips. "It gets worse."

"Worse? How so?"

"The bank's applied to the courts for a repossession order on our house as we're now several months behind with the mortgage. I received a telephone call about it this morning."

Their financial crisis was entirely his fault, beginning with a series of bad investments and ending with him quitting his job. He had no issues accepting full responsibility. "I can fix this. I'll fix this. I promise."

"You'll need to fix it quickly. We can expect an eviction notice any day now."

He raised a weak smile. "That's not such a bad thing. We both want out of here!"

"Not funny, Bryan! If we get evicted, we'll have nowhere to go, and a black mark against our name will make renting or buying elsewhere extremely difficult. Just find a job! It's been more than three months. You know I can't support two of us on my salary."

Bryan lowered his head. "Okay."

Jodie's tone softened. "I know it's been an awful time for you. Witnessing one of your patients commit suicide in your office is as traumatic as it gets. I do understand. But you know you can't hide your face forever."

"It's not that simple, Julia."

She put her hand on his neck. "I know. What happened with the police and all the media attention was stressful and unfair. But you can't let it ruin your life. Look what it's doing to us. We can't go on living like this. I really want to leave this neighbourhood, but under the right circumstances."

Bryan nodded. "Me too. Now is not a good time to sell with the current state of the market."

"I'm willing to cut our losses."

"No, we won't do that."

"We might not have a choice. I can't take much more of this, Bryan. It's been six months since the break-in here, and I'm still a nervous wreck. I shouldn't have to feel on edge in my own home. Either you sort yourself out or…"

"Or what?"

She pushed past him, sprinted up the stairs, and slammed the bedroom door.

Massaging his temples, Bryan's eyes were drawn to the bottle of brandy.

The following morning, he awoke with a hacking cough, finding himself ensconced on the sofa. Sunlight cut through the curtains, and he heard activity out in the street. He sat up, loosening his grip on the empty brandy bottle he had been cradling, which dropped to the floor with a thud. Yawning loudly, he then rubbed his reddish-brown hair into a mess.

At the kitchen sink, he popped an aspirin and downed two glasses of water to appease his headache. He opened the front door to collect the milk from his doorstep, inhaling the fresh morning air. He saw a skinhead teen dressed in a green tracksuit kicking a patch of grass that had overtaken a kerb. A car of youths blasting jungle music pulled up to collect him. If it weren't boy-racers tearing down the streets or teenage gangs loitering on corners, it was junkies skulking along the pavement, their eyes glazed over, or young kids pretending to be drug dealers, mimicking what they saw around them. The nights were a cacophony of revved engines and screeching tyres from burnouts, making sleep impossible. By morning, fresh graffiti stained the walls, and shattered glass littered the ground. In the space of two years, the suburb had become a playground for bored kids.

An abandoned housing project of half-built homes stood opposite their house. Gardens were overrun with brambles and leftover building materials. Windowpanes were smashed or barricaded with plywood sheets full of gaping holes, as if they had been blasted with a shotgun. Squatters lived in half of them. Bryan used to love the neighbourhood. It had once been an exclusive London suburb, a peaceful oasis where tree-lined streets and well-kept gardens made it a hidden gem in the bustling city. When he and his wife had bought their dream house, it felt like the perfect place to build their future. The home was spacious, with large bay windows overlooking the quiet street, and the neighbours were friendly, a mix of young families and retired couples who had been there for years. It had all the charm and promise they had been looking for. But in recent years, that idealised vision had crumbled, and the feeling of safety Bryan had cherished was gone. Now, the very place that had once been their refuge felt more like a trap, filled with rough gangs, drug-users, and troublemakers, colonising the street one house at a time. He was convinced one of the local thugs had broken into his home, looking for something of value to steal. At times, he felt as if he was being watched or followed. Even then, standing on the doorstep and holding the milk, he sensed he was within the scope of prying eyes.

He closed the door, put the milk away, and went upstairs. He crept into the bedroom, careful not to wake up his wife cocooned in the covers, and changed into his golfing gear. He applied some gel to his dishevelled hair at the bathroom sink, so long now it hid his ears. He brushed his teeth and stroked his stubble, in no mood to shave.

Leaving the bathroom, he stopped at the door and stared at Julia's pretty face. He wanted to fix things in his marriage. She deserved better than this. She was right, she talked sense. He had to get himself back into the workforce. He did miss counselling patients through their turmoil. It was in his blood. He was the son, the grandson, and great-grandson of medical professionals in one field or another. But after the incident in his office and what followed, he carried a burden. Every time he closed his eyes, he saw Michelle Locke, the patient who'd unceremoniously killed herself when–

The telephone rang.

Bryan ignored it, picked up his helmet, and left the house.

The answering machine kicked in and invited the caller to leave a message. *"Bryan, it's your father. I know you don't want to talk to me after all these years. Who can blame you? But it's important you do. It's about your mother."*

3

The new golf complex featured exclusively designed greens complemented by top-notch clubhouse facilities, set to host two major opens on the European Tour. Recently opened, it was hailed as one of the finest in Europe.

With a rented golf bag slung over his shoulder, courtesy of Flymo, who loved to flaunt his wealth, Bryan made his way to the West course, comparable in quality to the East course but slightly longer, promising an enjoyable round of golf.

He found his old friend waiting at the first hole. He had known Flymo since the Falklands War when their paths had crossed during a ferocious battle on a mountain in freezing conditions. An almost unbroken line of machine gunfire had ripped through the air. Two bullets had struck Flymo's thigh, and Bryan had fought to restrain him to administer painkilling medication, apply makeshift dressings in the heat of battle, and assist him back to base for treatment. His fieldwork had saved Flymo's life, forging a bond between them that would last long after the war. What you saw with Flymo was what you got. And what you got was an overconfident man who thought his solid build, towering height, and commanding presence granted him a free pass in life. As a teenager, Flymo had caused his parents all sorts of headaches. He often broke curfew, went to parties he was forbidden to attend, lost his virginity at thirteen, and sometimes found himself locked up overnight for drunken-related behaviour. Bryan, on the other hand, never got in trouble and had his first sexual encounter at eighteen with Julia, now his wife.

Flymo was fit for his age, prominent across the shoulders with a large, rounded chest—the build of a man who worked out regularly but who also loved his food. He woke early each day to run six miles to the park and back. He had spent almost two decades in the army and had just returned from the Gulf War with a promotion to staff sergeant. To celebrate, he bought a Dodge Viper, which satisfied his love of loud, brash sports cars and speed.

Flymo wore bright, yellow-checked trousers paired with a black Ralph Lauren polo shirt. He always dressed smartly, whatever the occasion, and took great pride in his appearance. Unlike Bryan, who only made an effort when the situation demanded it.

"Saw you a mile off in those trousers," said Bryan.

Flymo spun on his heel. "About time. I thought you had fallen off the planet."

"Woke up late."

Flymo shook his head. "You look like shite."

"I had a late night."

"Yeah, I can smell it," he said, waving his hand in front of his nose. "When are you going to sort yourself out, mate? You can't go on like this."

Bryan raised his eyebrows. "Let's just play. Nice car, by the way."

"Isn't it? Gash magnet."

"Flashy, tasteless, and totally pretentious. I noticed you parked it in a disabled spot."

"Do you see any cripples around?"

"Don't call them that!"

"Why?"

"How many soldiers do we know in a wheelchair?"

"Okay, Mr. fucking sensitive."

Bryan took up his striking pose, eyed the green, and gave the ball a whack.

Flymo stuck out his bottom lip. "Not bad. For you. Now, step aside and let me show you how the pros do it."

"This I've got to see."

Clenching the driver with his large, powerful hands, he stepped up. He glanced back at Bryan and grinned. "Watch and learn, mate."

"Let me write you out a prescription for your delusion."

Flymo struck the ball and watched it soar towards the first hole. Bouncing twice, it missed the bunker and stopped just shy of the green.

Bryan laughed. "Unlucky."

"Are we watching the same game?"

"You didn't kiss the ball for good luck before you hit it."

"You forget I don't follow your bullshit superstitions."

"Superstitious beliefs promote a positive mental attitude. That's a fact."

"I didn't see you kiss *your* ball."

"But I did."

"What toss. I told you about that guy I once served with, right? The bloke who wouldn't fly to Europe on Friday the thirteenth?"

"A hundred times. He died on Thursday the twelfth in an accident on the way to the airport. That means nothing."

"Superstitions are like ghosts and monsters. They don't exist. We humans just like to make shit up. Superstitions are your mechanism to explain bad shit. Like this losing streak. When was the last time you beat me?"

"I've had a lot on my mind lately."

"Oh, a lot on your mind! Huh. Not because of magpies or crows or… or the fucking bird that shat on your head on your way to work? Or the ladder you walked under?"

"I never walk under ladders."

"You get my point. I'm simply a better golfer than you."

"Beginner's luck."

Flymo laughed. "Beginner's luck? Okay, whatever helps you sleep at night." He glanced at the dark clouds rolling nearer and noticed the wind agitating the trees, knocking off leaves. Most golfers had retired to the clubhouse to avoid the incoming storm. "Let's try and finish the first hole before it pisses down. Unless you've got some ridiculous reason not to continue?"

Bryan hadn't heard. He wasn't listening. He looked at the clubhouse where golfers seemed to be heading in droves.

Flymo watched his friend with an increasing frown and snapped his fingers. "What the hell's wrong with you?"

Bryan swung his head back to Flymo. "Nothing."

"Something's up, what is it?"

"I think someone's following me."

Flymo scanned the trees and clubhouse. "Who?"

"I don't know. The police? Ever since that suicide at my work, I've been on edge. Everywhere I go, I get this feeling I'm being followed."

"The police have no reason to suspect you, do they?"

"Of course not. I didn't kill her."

"You're just acting paranoid, mate. Nobody's following you. You're not that interesting."

Bryan felt raindrops on the back of his hand and looked up at the clouds. "I think we're done here."

When he turned, Flymo was gone. True to his rebellious nature, he'd wandered off the green to relieve himself among the trees, leaving Bryan's cheeks flushed with embarrassment. This was a first-class golf complex; only Flymo would dare to do behave so brazenly.

He wandered back, nonchalantly zipping up his fly and looking up at the sky. "I guess that's game over."

Bryan frowned. "I'm not in the mood, anyway. Why don't we get an early lunch? This time I'm paying."

Retreating to the clubhouse, warmed by a large fire and filled with the residual aromas of hot meat and thick gravy, they claimed a table by the window.

Flymo clicked his fingers, summoning a waiter. "Roast of the day, what is it?"

"Chicken," said the waiter, looking displeased.

"Two of those."

Bryan shielded his eyes to hide his embarrassment.

Flymo launched into one of his op-eds. "This country has lost its sense of tradition, you know. Roast lunch used to be the most anticipated meal of the week. Now you see families feeding their kids cheap microwave dinners and fast food I wouldn't even give to a pig. No wonder this country has such high cholesterol. These people wouldn't last ten seconds on the battlefield."

Bryan wasn't really listening. He thought about Julia and what she'd told him yesterday. He had to change his attitude, stop revisiting the past, and look ahead to the future. After all, it was advice he had often bestowed on his patients.

"What's really on your mind?" asked Flymo.

"Julia and I had another fight. She more or less threatened to leave me."

"Why?"

He filled his lungs and emptied them with a loud sigh. "I need to find a job."

He had taken a huge risk resigning on the back of a major economic downturn, joining roughly two million others also out of work.

"I don't think I can face working in the public eye again. My face was all over the news until I was acquitted of any involvement and her death was confirmed as suicide."

Different theories had been espoused in the local papers, mostly cruel and defamatory. Every time he had opened his front door, a camera was thrust in his face. The telephone had trilled every five minutes for the best part of a week. That a reporter had broken into his house to snoop around in the hope of finding a story had crossed his mind.

"Mate, you've had long enough to get over it."

"Get over it? It's not the flu. Michelle was my patient. My responsibility."

"She's the woman who jumped from your office window, right?"

"I had only been gone a few minutes. When I came back, I found the window wide open, and when I looked out into the car park, there she was, all—"

"It wasn't your fault. There's nothing you could've done to save her. She obviously wanted to end her life."

"I left the army to get away from death. But after she died, I was forced to quit my job, and now it's ruining my marriage. I dread to think what comes next."

"What do you mean?"

"All bad things come in threes!"

As Bryan rode home, he saw a Land Rover with darkly tinted windows parked on the hard shoulder with its hazard lights flashing. He steered his motorcycle in front, came to a stop, and kicked down the stand. Removing his helmet, he walked to the vehicle and saw the bonnet propped open, revealing a short, balding businessman hunched over the engine.

"Do you need some help there?" he asked.

The man removed his hand from the engine. The tips of his fingers were smudged with oil. He took a rag from a side groove and wiped them. "All good, thanks, Dr. Morgan."

Bryan froze. "How do you know my name?"

"Let's talk inside the car."

Bryan's eyebrows went up. "Who are you? Police?"

The man walked to the driver's side. "Let's talk inside. I will explain."

But Bryan hesitated, unsure what to make of the strange encounter. "How did you know I would stop?"

"I know a lot about you. I have a detailed profile. Your likes, dislikes, your superstitious nature, which Flymo likes to mock. I know about your childhood, teenage years, and life before and after your marriage to Julia. I know your mother died and why you lost contact with your father. I knew you were going to stop because that's what you do. You help people. That's why you became a medic in the Royal Army Medical Corps, serving in the Falklands, and why you have spent the last seven years as a counselling psychologist. Please, if you would join me in the car, we have a lot to discuss."

4

Following a long, uncertain pause, Bryan joined the business-man inside the Land Rover and shut the door. "Why are you following me?"

The man reached into the glove box and retrieved an A4 envelope, setting it carefully on the dashboard in front of him. His attire was deliberately black: crisp suit, shirt, tie. Even his polished shoes gleamed with the same dark intensity. Black wasn't just a colour; it was a message. It symbolised power, authority, strength, and intelligence. Unless he had just come from a funeral, his wardrobe choice suggested he wanted to make a statement that demanded attention without a word spoken.

Bryan allowed himself a brief moment of satisfaction. If one thing could be deduced from this bizarre encounter, it was that his intuition had, once again, not deceived him.

The man reached into the inner pocket of his jacket.

Bryan stiffened in his seat, fearing he was about to pull a weapon on him.

"Cigarette?" He held out a packet and shook one loose. "Oh, that's right, you wear those nicotine patches on your left arm, and you're still getting shot of your smoker's cough."

Bryan frowned. "Very good. Would you mind getting to the point?"

The man lit his cigarette and exhaled a steady stream of smoke from his nostrils, filling the interior. The tantalising smell distracted Bryan. How he missed that bitter tobacco taste, the tickly rush on the back of his throat and tongue, the chemical release in the brain. Just the simple act of securing one between two fingers, something his hand often did on autopilot around an invisible cigarette.

The man took another drag. "I am a CI agent. You don't need to know my name. I'm not important. I'm only here to offer you a job."

"A job?"

The agent nodded and blew a long stream of smoke from his nose.

"What makes you think I'd be interested?"

The agent took a stapled document out of the envelope. "Take a few minutes to browse the contract, tell me what you think."

He accepted the document with reservations.

"Please, take your time."

Bryan read the details, conscious of the agent by his side and the smoke encompassing him. The six-digit salary was enough to immediately pique his curiosity and engage his full attention. "Is this for real?"

"Absolutely."

He skimmed through the fine print, reading the clauses and conditions, absorbing the duty statement and company expectations outlined in the dense contract. He scanned over the legal jargon with growing curiosity. So engrossed was he in deciphering the details that the rumble of thunder outside went unnoticed. It was only when he reached the final page that something felt off.

"There's no job title."

"It's not included."

"There's no mention of the company or location."

"If you're interested, you'll be invited for an interview."

"How can I be interested if I don't know what the job is or where it is?"

"For now, I just need to know if you're interested."

"Interested in what?"

"You'll have to trust me."

"Trust you? I don't even know you! And yet you act like you've got me all figured out." He held up the contract. "Is this some kind of illegal operation? A bank heist, maybe? You need a getaway driver, or am I supposed to take out the prime minister? Is that it? Or are we talking drug trafficking? Does CI stand for Cocaine Importer? Am I getting warm yet?" He threw the contract onto the dashboard.

The agent laughed. "Right now, you're unemployed and on the verge of losing your house. Your wife, well, let's just say she can't even stand to look at you anymore, can she? The stress from your old job has chewed you up and spat you out, giving you anxiety, high blood pressure, the whole package. And now you're here, back at square one, wondering what went wrong."

He gestured casually to the contract on the dashboard. "This job is different from anything you've ever known. It's still working *with* the public, but not *in* public. It's behind the scenes, but still something you're already used to. Something you're good at, and something you care about. And let's not forget the money." He gave Bryan a sly smile. "The financial gain is not something to ignore. This could save your house, your marriage, your pride. All of it."

Bryan was put out by the agent's remark about Julia but accepted the rebuke without any reaction at first. He was right. Their marriage had been shaky for some time. He still loved his wife, and this stranger had no right to offer his assessment on a relationship he knew nothing about. Before he could express his discontentment, the agent continued.

"I don't want to harp on about your situation, but I know you want to continue your work as a psychologist and even miss providing medical aid to people, though not in any war scenario. You've defaulted on your mortgage and are behind with bills, I understand. Your wife works hard as a secretary for a small biotechnology firm in London, and it's my guess that—"

"Stop! Just stop!"

The agent finished his cigarette and flicked the butt out of the window. Cool air knifed in, clearing some of the smoke and humidity and a good deal of tension.

"The organisation I represent is offering a generous salary, and what I *can* tell you is that it requires your expertise and experience, both in counselling psychology and medical care, which is why you've been chosen. All you have to do is agree to an interview and see where you stand afterwards. You have nothing to lose."

The man had a point; he raised a good argument. While Bryan considered the offer, the rain came down hard on the Land Rover, sounding like a thousand spoons tapping on the roof simultaneously. The rainwater on the windshield masked his motorcycle in front, already soaked. His mind switched to the long ride home. He would need to exercise caution on the roads.

He circled back to the proposition and the huge salary tag. *Generous* was an understatement. It would fast-track them to financial recovery. And he missed having a workplace. Not for one minute did he enjoy unemployment. One could go crazy spending time at home all day. It was counterproductive to all other aspects of life. It was also unfair on his wife, who worked hard at her job in London only to find herself living in financial hardship.

"Okay, what do I have to do?"

The agent reached across to the back seat and retrieved an aluminium Halliburton briefcase, one of the world's most durable brands. The buckles were sealed by a combination lock.

"Keep this case on you at all times. Inside are important documents and the full contract. There's also thirty grand in cash inside. Consider it a sign-on bonus, whether you join the company or not. It will give you some breathing space. You can keep the money providing you show up to the interview. Bring the case. The interviewer will give you the combination pin as soon as the interview has concluded."

"That's it? All I have to do is show up for the interview?"

"Exactly. There are rules, mind you."

Bryan leaned back, eyeing the man with suspicion. "What rules?"

"As I said, you must keep the case with you all the time; in the house, on the bike when you're riding, whenever you're playing golf with Flymo, even when you take a leak. You must not tell anyone about the offer or our encounter, the money in the briefcase, the interview, or talk to anybody about the contract. If you do, the bonus will be retracted. We will be watching you closely. Follow the rules, and the bonus is yours. You even get to keep the briefcase. Any questions?"

"When's the interview?"

"Friday evening, six o'clock inside the Beaufort Hotel in Knightsbridge, London."

The agent extended his right arm.

Bryan shook his hand half-heartedly.

"You won't see me again. Remember, *mum's* the word."

Bryan half-expected him to tap his nose like some cliché character from an old spy film. But the phrase stuck with him, twisting the words in his head and arousing his superstitious nature. *Mum's the word*: was it just a harmless expression, or was there something more to it? Was it some veiled reference to his own mother? Was there a deeper connection, or was it merely his mind racing to fit pieces where they didn't belong?

Bryan slipped on his helmet and walked to his motorcycle. The briefcase fitted snugly into his side pannier. Questions nibbled at the frayed corners of his mind. Should he trust the man and attend the interview? CI agent? What did that stand for? Was he CIA? Why him? What made him so special? How long had these people been studying him? And how could he possibly turn down such a lucrative salary?

Intrigued by the briefcase and driven by the financial incentive to show up at the Beaufort Hotel, he made up his mind, quickly and easily.

Starting up his motorcycle, he glanced into his side-view mirror at the CI agent inside the Land Rover and sped off.

A squawk sounded in the agent's handset as Bryan rode off into the rain, vanishing into the grey blur.

"Looks as though he can be persuaded?" said Kane on the car phone.

The agent cleared his throat and opened the window for some fresh air. "Yes. Have you checked the live feed from the briefcase? Is it streaming?"

"Yes. We have both volume and visual. He has six days to prove himself."

"Do you think he'll suspect we've lied about what's really inside the briefcase?" asked the agent.

"It doesn't matter. He doesn't have the pin. All the while he believes there's money in there, he'll keep it close by."

The agent laughed softly. "So, what do you want me to do now? Do you want me to follow him?"

"No, I have agents assigned to him already."

"I'll head back, then."

The agent stowed the handset and started the engine. The wipers sprang to life, swiping the water off the windshield. He switched off the hazard lights and swung the Land Rover around. A break in the clouds hinted that the rain might ease up soon, though it was still pouring heavily at the airport, where a private jet awaited his arrival.

5

Dr. Heath Fletcher finished reading the logbook and closed the cover, sickened to his core. The realisation churned in his stomach as he understood the power the book held, not only to bring down careers but to potentially destroy lives. Full of irrefutable evidence that exposed the foundation's dealings, its pages detailed illegal activities that went far beyond simple corruption; they revealed a carefully orchestrated network of lies, manipulation, and exploitation, constructing a horrifying picture of a place he'd trusted for many years. He could feel its weight, not just in his hands, but in his chest, as it sank in. It wasn't merely a scandal but a dangerous, criminal enterprise he was entangled in. With this knowledge, he found himself at a crossroads, knowing whatever step he took next would change everything. In fact, the logbook would unravel the entire foundation.

Sitting at his desk in the safety of his private room, the fifty-three-year-old psychologist stared at the leather-bound logbook, its contents still burning in his mind. He had read every page, uncovered every secret, and had learned about the unspeakable harm done in the name of progress, leaving him saddened, vulnerable, and deeply shaken. He couldn't allow it to continue. He had to end it. Now. But how?

He was deep inside the foundation, surrounded by state-of-the-art surveillance and top-level security. Every move was tracked, every corner watched. Taking the logbook outside without being caught seemed nearly impossible. How could he slip past the cameras, the guards, and encrypted systems designed to protect the very secrets he now held in his hands? One wrong move, and he'd be exposed. Failure wasn't an option; the stakes were far too high. But then he *had* managed to steal the logbook from the president's office the day before, somehow undetected, instilling him with confidence.

The puzzle book on his desk lay open on the cryptic word finder page. It gave him an idea. He grabbed his black marker from the drawer and went to his sleeping booth, a rectangular dugout in the wall. Removing the lid from his marker, he leaned up and scrawled a message across the concrete ceiling above his bed. If his escape failed, the message would serve as his backup plan—a set of coordinates that would lead the next occupant to his secret hiding place. Once finished, he replaced the lid and sat back, looking at his hidden insurance.

A loud, persistent knock sounded at the door.

Dr. Fletcher jumped up from the bed. He palmed his long, white hair off his face as he approached the door and opened it to an agent he didn't recognise.

"The president wants to talk to you."

He scrutinised the man's body language; the subtle shift in his stance, the way his fingers twitched by his side. There was a coldness in the agent's expression, a forced calm that masked the suspicion materialising underneath. His voice was clipped, with a sharpness that hinted at growing impatience. But what mattered most was the firearm. Dr. Fletcher's eyes darted to the agent's hip, tracking the weapon with a mixture of fear and calculation. The holster was secured, but the agent's hand lingered close. Things could quickly spiral out of control if Fletcher made even one wrong move. If he wanted to get out of this foundation alive, he had to stay sharp and read the agent's movement as if his life depended on it— because it did.

"What about?"

The agent frowned. "He's waiting."

"Give me a moment, please. I need to… tell him I'll be there in five minutes."

He closed the door and pressed his back against the wood. He had already broken the code of conduct by trespassing in a restricted lab and taking forbidden photographs. The fact he had snuck inside the president's office and had stolen the logbook, discovering a series of terrible truths, now put his life in jeopardy.

He dropped the logbook in a transparent plastic bag, tied it around his belt, and slipped it into his trousers. To conceal the bulge and the logbook's outline, he threw his lab coat on. Reassured with the cover, he slipped his passport and wallet into his pockets, essentials for the daring escape he now faced. He knew once he made his move, there would be no turning back. The only way out of this dangerous predicament now was to leave the country.

He left his apartment, looking down but not back as he paced along the wide corridor that spanned the east wing. The agent was no longer around. But Dr. Fletcher was in range of the security cameras now. No matter how hard he tried to act casual, his lack of eye contact with those he passed gave him away.

In no time, he was at the lifts. He tried his swipe card on the authentication device. Nothing happened.

He swiped it again. The red light flashed.

Sweat broke on his forehead as he realised it could only mean one thing: they knew about the logbook. He anxiously scanned the corridor in both directions, expecting an ambush at any moment. To his surprise, the lift doors slid open, and a team of biologists stepped out, chatting among themselves. Without hesitation, he slipped inside and jabbed the ground-floor button with his trembling fingers.

The doors sealed shut, and the lift lurched into motion, climbing slowly. When it finally reached the top, he stepped out and approached the checkpoint in the passageway. Ahead, two security guards sat at their post.

Dr. Fletcher held up his ID badge. "Just popping out for some fresh air. Been a long day."

The guards nodded.

Following the passageway to the end, he climbed a steep staircase, gripping the handrail as he took the stairs two at a time. At the top, he marched through a large, dark hall that was eerily quiet. The exit door stood ahead, a barrier between him and freedom. He stood still at the brow of the steps, overlooking a dark line of trees in the distance.

A thick, pernicious fog enveloped the terrain, but it did not deter him and would in fact aid in his escape. He set out towards the trees, his thumping heart accompanied by rustling leaves and the all-pervasive sounds of owls hooting and foxes howling, a solid background noise.

Pausing to catch his breath, he glanced behind him at the foundation with instant regret. Within the foggy blur, human shapes materialised into agents, and they had dogs on leashes. He watched with growing fear, but when they stopped, their hesitation gave him hope until they turned in his direction, and the leashes were unclasped.

With little time to reach the field and locate the Polaroid he had hidden inside the firepit a fortnight back, which had prompted his search for more evidence and had ultimately led him to the logbook, he sprinted without a single rear glance. Low-hanging branches impeded his escape like angry talons clawing at his skin, but he kept moving.

He heard the agents behind him. Their taunting shouts were aimed at scaring him, but he didn't think he could be more frightened than he already was.

"Keep going!" he said under his breath. "Keep going!"

His determination gave him renewed speed as a string of oaths flowed perpetually from the agents' mouths.

Heading deeper into the forest, tripping and fighting his way through the undergrowth that rustled and snapped under his feet, he arrived at the small, circular field surrounded by trees. The brickwork firepit stood in a sea of stone ruins at the edge of the field.

Zigzagging between the brambles and broken masonry, he arrived at the firepit and removed the logbook from his trousers. He drove it into the opening at the bottom, storing it alongside the hidden Polaroid. Using a small, sharp flint, he carefully scratched his initials into the rough surface of a brick.

His hands trembled, but the need to mark this moment, to leave a hidden trace of his actions, kept him focussed. Placing the brick back in its place to conceal the evidence behind it, he stepped back and hid behind a tree. He scanned the firepit and the dark space inside it. No one would think twice to look inside it, or about what lay behind the loose brick. To anyone else, it was just part of the decaying structure. To him, it was the key to everything, the one clue he left behind. After his escape, he would notify the police of the initialled brick so they could uncover the logbook and photo.

With the men now closing in, he had to try and outfox them. To achieve this, he needed to lead them away from the firepit to keep the evidence safe. He ran deep into the forest, dodging in and out of trees. He stopped and leaned against a wide, mottled trunk, where his left foot became tangled in the spaghetti-like outgrowths. His gaze cut to the right: shadows between the trees ghosted towards him.

Shaking his foot loose, he took off again, going from tree to tree, stopping and starting, one to the next. The chase had become a game of hide-and-seek.

He leaned around the trunk.

Two agents stepped into the foggy moonlight.

And now he was running again. Running for his life.

His head start was wearing thin; his legs were numbing, and his lungs burned with every breath. But giving up wasn't an option. He didn't have the athletic edge to outrun them, so his only chance was to outsmart them.

Ahead was an oak tree with a short, stout trunk and low sagging branches. He reached for the nearest branch and tried to pull himself up. He heard the dogs, the drumbeat of their paws, their heavy breaths. One pounced on his leg and pulled him from the tree. He landed square on his back and was quickly swarmed by several dogs, their vicious, amber eyes glowing in the dark.

One sank its teeth into his arm. He almost fought himself loose, but another dog bit his hand and left teeth indentations pooled with blood. A moist, snapping snout brushed over his lips and nose, silencing his cries.

An agent appeared, towering above the dogs. He walked up to Dr. Fletcher and stamped on his face as if squashing a bug. It broke his nose, and blood gushed down his chin.

Another agent kicked him in the mouth, leaving many teeth lying in a reservoir of blood at the back of his throat.

The agents then hoisted Dr. Fletcher to his feet. "Going somewhere?"

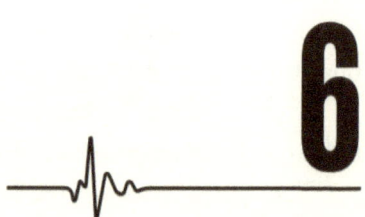

6

"What's in the briefcase?" asked Julia, already under the duvet.

Bryan climbed into his side of the bed, carefully tucking the briefcase by his bedside. Before arranging himself beneath the duvet, he coughed into his fist. "I've had it all week, and you're only asking me now?"

"I've hardly seen you, and whenever I do see you, you're all uptight. And it's only just occurred to me you've hardly let go of it."

"I'm looking after it for someone."

"Who?"

"A friend." He rolled over to avoid making eye contact. He didn't lie well. It was a white lie. But still a lie.

"What friend?"

"You don't know him."

"What's inside it?"

"I don't know, he wouldn't tell me."

"Why does he want you to look after it? I don't think I understand."

"Go to sleep, will you."

Julia rolled up to Bryan and threw an arm across his chest. She liked to cuddle, to feel his warmth flow into hers. They hadn't been intimate in a while, and neither had managed to weave the topic into conversation. Not talking about it made it seem acceptable and normal. The last six months had been the toughest of their twelve years of marriage, compounded by stress that rendered sex undesirable. So when she ran her hand across his stomach and slowly down towards his pelvis, he was completely unprepared.

"Julia?"

"What?"

He paused. "I'm not in the mood."

She stroked his thigh.

"Julia?" He took her hand and pushed it away.

"Fine!" She rolled over. Then she rolled back. "Actually, it's not fine. What are we doing here?"

Bryan sighed. "Do we have to talk about this now?"

"Yes."

"My interview's tomorrow evening. Can we talk after that, after you get home from work?"

But Julia wouldn't let it go. She listed the issues in their relationship. She complained about his attitude around the house. She accused him of not caring about her enough. She brought up the ever-mounting debt and that he had serious trust issues. Bryan listened but said nothing. Once she had finished with her tirade, she rolled to her side of the bed and turned her back on him.

All night, Bryan lay awake in the darkness, listening to the teenage rebels outside shouting, laughing, causing a public nuisance. His eyes were glued to the digital clock by his bed, watching the minutes crawl by. The more he tried to sleep, the more his thoughts circled back to tomorrow's interview.

Julia left for work earlier than usual the next morning to show her anger, and by the time he arrived for his interview, he'd hardly slept. Briefcase in hand, he entered the Beaufort Hotel, a modern four-star accommodation full of middle-class patrons and businesspeople wearing expensive suits. No sooner had he sat down on an armchair than someone said, "Dr. Morgan?"

Bryan looked up. "Yes, that's me." He stood and reached out to shake the hand of a man in a black suit, who didn't reciprocate the gesture.

"Come, there's a car waiting outside."

Bryan frowned. "The interview isn't here?"

"Follow me!"

A black Land Rover with darkened windows was illegally parked on the road. A second black-attired man guided him to the car. A CI agent, he assumed. He looked like a physically imposing man, making Bryan hold back slightly. When the door opened, he saw another agent in black sitting beside the far door. Bryan got in and shimmied across the seat.

The second agent climbed in, squashing up to Bryan and forcing him to move into the middle. The agent from the hotel swung into the passenger seat, and the driver floored the accelerator. They flew over a speed bump, upsetting everything in the boot. By the time the car reached the second speed bump, Bryan's heart was racing. What followed was easily the most uncomfortable ride of his life.

"No need to be nervous," said the agent in the front.

"Easy for you to say. Can you tell me where we're going, please?"

"The airport."

Bryan felt a building pressure at his temples. "We can't go there by car?"

"Not unless you want to travel throughout the night."

"Where are we going?"

"It's a short flight. We'll be there before you know it."

Clearing security at the small airport, an agent had a word to the staff at one of six check-in desks. Then they headed to the only gate in the terminal, descending a large passageway leading to the airfield and a small jet on the damp asphalt with its engines warming up.

Bryan saw the pilot blocking the private jet's doorway. He was easily six foot six, and his lean build made him look even taller. His face was long and narrow, giving him a puppet-like appearance, and his hair was nearly all grey, so thin his scalp showed clearly through the strands. Several badges were sewn into his green jumper for services rendered to the Royal Air Force, including one that read Squadron Leader, evoking memories of his father, an RAF pilot of the Tornado fleet.

"Evening," said one of the agents.

The lanky pilot winked. "Aye."

Bryan boarded ahead of the four agents and located a seat, immediately impressed by the luxurious cabin. The seats had a white leather base with decorative silver steel inserts on the armrests and the finest Italian leather on the backs. He placed the briefcase under his seat.

The agent who had greeted him inside the hotel took the seat adjacent to him. "You look pale," he said.

Bryan smiled nervously. "I have a fear of flying."

He nodded. "I know. Hold out your hand."

Bryan complied.

The agent dropped a white pill onto his palm. "It works wonders. Trust me."

"What is it?"

"A natural medication for flying anxiety."

He handed Bryan a flask of water.

Bryan put the pill on his tongue and chased it down with the water.

"You know that you're more likely to die in a motorcycle accident than on an airplane, right?"

Bryan glanced out the window. "Phobia is phobia. Fear is fear. Unfortunately, logic plays no part in the way our minds are programmed for some emotions."

"Minds can be reprogrammed."

Bryan pursed his lips. "One day maybe."

The pilot's voice boomed from the intercom in a Scottish accent. "John Wells, at your service, the world's number one pilot, and your captain for this evening. The flight will take *blah blah blah*, and the weather is expected to be *dum diddly dum*. Don't forget to buckle up."

Two of the agents laughed softly.

Catching their grins through the open cockpit door, the charismatic captain continued, "God help Britain if she had no Scots to think for her."

He then manoeuvred the jet into position and stopped to await take-off approval. When it arrived five minutes later, the jet surged forward along the runway.

On lift-off, Bryan sat rigid in his seat, his fingers curled around the armrests.

The agent in front of Bryan leaned round. "Can I ask you a question?"

Bryan struggled to get air into his lungs.

The agent passed him a paper bag. "Breathe into this."

He sucked the air out of the bag repeatedly, settling his breathing, and stared nervously through the window into the void of night.

"So, Dr. Morgan, I have a question for you. What's your take on AIDS?"

Bryan was still fixated on the window, trying to regulate his breathing. "What do you mean?"

"Well, in your experience, what's your view on the virus in terms of trajectory and cures?"

Bryan puffed out his cheeks, releasing a long, slow breath. "Seeing as I'm a medic, *was* a medic, I should be optimistic. But I don't see a cure being produced in our lifetime."

"What makes you say that?"

"Every ten seconds of every minute of every day, there's a new HIV infection. In 1985, HIV cases among women were around seven per cent. This year, it has reached something like eighteen per cent, which, ironically, is the result of new HIV infections in women worldwide in marriages or in long-term relationships with primary partners. It has been several years since the first outbreaks in America, and we're no closer to finding a cure now than we were back then. We don't know anything about it other than it's a serial killer. We don't even know where it originated."

"I thought it came from an African monkey?"

He was distracted by a flashing light outside his window. Lightning? Another plane, flying too close? No, it was just the light at the tip of the wing.

"Sorry, what?"

"An African monkey. That's where it originated from."

"That's baseless speculation, not credible fact. There are a hundred theories, the sooty mangabey, or green monkey from Western Africa, being one of them. It was thought polio vaccines played some role. Unlawful experimentation by the government and a suspected vaccine program gone wrong, too. Nobody knows. We may never know."

Bryan had attended a seminar five years ago for medical professionals to understand the issue on a deeper level. The seminar, conducted by the Working Party and funded by the Newman Foundation, looked at the medical professional's role in society, education, training, and general practices. The guest speakers included a junior doctor, a lawyer, a nurse, and numerous other professionals. It was the speech given by the junior doctor that had really struck a chord. She talked about the epidemic from a scientific point of view and quoted her father, one of the top medical researchers in the country. According to the junior doctor, scientists did not believe a cure was on the horizon or that one could even be expected by the end of the twenty-first century. And that no reliable techniques for accurately forecasting the epidemic's long-term trajectory currently existed.

"Basically, what you're saying is, in a hundred years, we may or may not be close to finding a cure?"

"Exactly. In the meantime, we are assuredly heading for a humanitarian catastrophe."

"They used to say that about malaria, one of the leading causes of death worldwide."

Bryan's eyebrows dipped with surprise. "More than half of the population resides in vulnerable areas, and malaria kills two million people a year, with Africa being the hardest hit continent, causing death in infants more than any other age group. Malaria has been around for many thousands of years, and we are still no closer to finding a cure."

"But there *is* a vaccine. SPf66 is on the cusp of getting approved by countries all over the world."

"I believe there's a lot of controversy still surrounding the vaccine."

"Controversial or not, it's immunogenic and has a high efficacy rate."

Bryan shook his head. "There have been numerous trials involving thousands of infants, and while there have been some positive results, there is no evidence the SPf66 can be used successfully for protection against malaria."

"It's true that the trials done in Africa and South America were inconclusive. But it has been considered safe by some institutions and offers reasonable protection with less than six per cent adverse reactions. So, there you have it."

It wasn't worth the hassle of debating with him, so Bryan left it there. He yawned, put his hands in his blazer pockets, and pulled the two halves together.

The jet's climate-control system had evidently packed up, and the cabin was filled with super-cooled air.

Bryan, exhausted from his lack of sleep last night, resisted closing his eyes for as long as possible, but eventually let the darkness take him.

7

Bryan jerked awake, finding himself in a suffocating darkness. Panic surged through him the moment he realised something covered his head—a thick hood, pressing down on his face, trapping him in a humid cocoon. He instinctively tried to lift his hands, but they wouldn't budge. A sharp pain bit into his wrists as he strained against the cable ties securing them to the cold, metal arms of a chair. Around him was silent, and it made his pulse race as he struggled to make sense of where he was and what was happening. He wracked his brains to recall his last memory. *The hotel. The car ride. The private jet.* What had happened after that?

Suddenly, the hood was removed. His hands were cut free. If he wanted to, he could stand. But he was too paralysed to move, and the bright shining light that met his face blinded him as effectively as the hood that had concealed him.

Squinting into the light, he saw two figures emerge from the shadows. They took up positions on either side of him. They stood motionless, their hands clasped in front of them, watching him in silence.

Another man detached himself from the dark corner of the room. At his approach, Bryan held his breath. Fortyish and very good-looking, the man wore a grey tweed suit and showed hints of silver at his temples, calm and distinguished. Bryan waited for him to speak. But then he was gone, and a skinny man with a round face and acne scars took his place. He wore glasses and a green baseball cap and carried a stack of folders in his hand. He placed them on the table next to his computer.

Bryan's legs trembled. "Who are you?"

The man wordlessly connected galvanometers to Bryan's fingertips, the most porous part on the body. He secured a blood-pressure cuff onto his upper arm that was linked to a tube that ran to a polygraph machine. Two pneumographs filled with air were fitted around his chest and abdomen.

The man returned to his chair opposite Bryan, looked at his papers, checked the analogue and instruments, and cursed under his breath.

While he tinkered with his equipment, Bryan wondered what time it was. It was impossible to estimate how long he had been unconscious, but he stole a look at his watch. The interview had been at six. He'd arrived on time. It was now eleven. Was it evening or morning?

He circled back to the flight and recalled the conversation with the agent about the trajectory of AIDS and their debate over the effectiveness of a potential malaria vaccine, SPf66. Beyond that, his memory was blank.

"State your name," said the man.

"Bryan."

"Full name."

"Bryan William Morgan. What is this?"

"Please answer yes or no from this point forward."

The polygrapher didn't raise his eyes once and kept them concealed beneath his cap.

"Who's in charge here?" asked Bryan.

"Are you thirty-five years old?"

Bryan hesitated and looked around the dark room. "Yes."

"Is it 1992?"

"Yes. What is all this? What's going on?"

Bryan shifted, terribly uncomfortable. With the hard chair. With the situation he found himself in. With the intimidating men in the room.

"Are you married?"

"Yes."

"Are you gay?"

"I'm married. I just said."

"Answer yes or no."

"No."

"Are you a religious man?"

"No."

"Have you ever stolen money?"

"No."

"Have you ever broken the law?"

This was ridiculous. It was Bryan who usually performed psychoanalysis on people, probed with questions, scrutinised their replies and exchanges, and assessed their mannerisms, body language, eye contact, and personality. Not the other way round. "No."

The polygrapher pulled his hat even lower to avoid eye contact. A shy person. Probably an only child whose parents thought his shyness showed politeness, but more underlying issues existed underneath the surface. Something he didn't want people to discover about him. A dark secret. A nasty truth. Polygraphic analysis meant he could hide behind a desk and deflect attention onto others. No friends. No family of his own. Not much in the way of a social life. All work, no play, creating a false sense of self-importance.

"Have you ever leaked confidential information of any kind?"

"No."

"Have you ever leaked confidential patient information to your wife before?"

He sighed. "No."

"Do you consider yourself trustworthy?"

"Yes."

No seismic movement in the needle meant no deceptions had been identified so far, and the man hadn't made any notes either. It made Bryan no less unhappy with the situation.

"Have you ever turned your back on someone asking for help?"

Bryan's throat tightened. For a moment, his heart picked up in tempo. The polygraph machine wavered. He swallowed hard, trying to keep calm, but the memory of Michelle Locke flashed in his mind: her face, the desperation in her eyes, the moment he discovered she had thrown herself out of his office window. His mouth went dry. "Yes. No... I mean, not really, no." The machine responded with the needle twitching and the smooth, unbroken line spiking erratically, tracking his inner conflict with brutal betrayal.

"Yes, or no?"

"No."

"Have you ever cheated on your wife?"

"Seriously?"

The handsome man in the grey suit sparked a cigarette in the darkness, illuminating his face. He cracked his knuckles, distracting the polygrapher momentarily.

"Have you ever cheated on your wife?"

"This is ridiculous! No."

"Has she ever cheated on you?"

"No."

"Have you ever lied to your wife?"

"I'm not answering that."

"Have you ever lied to your wife?"

Bryan sighed, thinking about the briefcase. "You people made me lie to—"

"Yes or no?"

"Yes."

The polygrapher traded looks with the man in the suit. "Do you often lie to your wife?"

Bryan remained mute.

"Do you often—"

"Skip it!" said the man smoking in the corner.

The polygrapher took off his glasses and laid them on the table. He pinched the bridge of his nose, then put his glasses back on.

"Where were we? Okay, have you ever done any kind of volunteering?"

"Yes."

"Of a medical nature?"

"Yes."

"Were you a medic in the Royal Army Medical Corps?"

"Yes."

"And you provided first-aid emergency care to all British Army personnel and family?"

"Yes."

"The only frontline experience you have is during the war in the Falklands where you treated wounded soldiers?"

"Yes."

"Not just British soldiers. You also treated enemy soldiers. The Argentinians, even though they were trying to kill our people. Is this correct?"

"People are people. They deserve the same treatment and respect. You see a man in agony on the ground, you're not going to leave them."

"I asked if it was correct. It requires a simple yes or no answer."

"Yes."

"Is this where you met Flymo, real name Bob Edwards?"

"Yes."

"You left the Royal Army Medical Corps because you did not want to go back into a hostile environment. Correct?"

"Yes."

"Are you a coward?"

"No."

"Did you also leave the RAMC because of your marriage to Julia?"

"Yes."

"Not because you were a coward."

"Few medical professionals would do their work in the type of environment I put myself in."

A silence descended upon the room for most of a minute.

"Now, did you get a PhD in Psychology at Cambridge in 1986?"

"Yes."

"You chose this profession because of the number of war veterans you witnessed suffering from psychological trauma. Is that right?"

"Yes."

"Did you publish a book called *Depression: A Detrimental Disease*?"

"Yes."

"Did it have nationwide success?"

"Define success!"

The polygrapher paused and adjusted his glasses. "Have you always demonstrated a sustained commitment to patient well-being?"

"Yes."

"Throughout your working life, have you demonstrated a commitment to the values and goals of your employer and adhered to the code of conduct at all times?"

"Yes."

"Are you open-minded about advances in medicine, no matter how eccentric they may seem?"

Bryan hesitated. "Yes."

The polygrapher looked at his colleague once more. "This is the final question. Why do they sterilise needles for lethal injections?"

Bryan straightened in his chair. "Is this a joke?"

"It's a question. Please answer!"

Bryan sat back smugly and folded his arms. "I can't, it doesn't require a yes or no response."

"Okay, I'll rephra–"

"Enough!" The man in the grey suit traded places with the polygrapher, who quickly gathered all his paperwork and made himself scarce.

His dark eyes were hungry and powerful, his expression shrewd and sophisticated. Gracefully chewing a piece of gum, he leaned back in his chair. "Funny, no one seems to know the answer to that."

Bryan chose to keep his lips sealed.

The man's face hardened as he glanced at the polygraph results. "Congratulations, Bryan."

"On what?"

"You passed." He stood and circled the table. "Let's get you unplugged, shall we?"

"What is this? Who are you?"

"I'm the vice president of this establishment. Don't look so worried. The catering staff, the maintenance crew, cleaners, technicians, security officers, doctors, biologists, agents, even the executive board members all completed these polygraph tests. You don't think you're *that* special, do you?"

Bryan's voice was shaky. "I don't understand."

"You've done nothing wrong. You're not a victim here. The polygraph test is just standard procedure."

As amicable as this man seemed, the bottom line was he had been mistreated and made to feel fear by the intimidation tactics.

"Come on!" He said it like he was taking a friend to the pub.

Bryan followed the vice president out of the dark room into a bright corridor that extended to the horizon and reeked of disinfectant.

"Where am I?"

"My name is Kane Spence. As I said, I'm vice president here. I apologise for how you were brought in, but in about five minutes, you'll appreciate why."

"What is this place?"

"All in good time. Please, follow me. Someone is dying to meet you."

8

Ten feet of rich, crimson carpet led the way to an imposing door with a gleaming brass plaque that showed the words *Presidential Office*.

Bryan hesitated for a moment before entering at the vice president's behest. The room was lavish, but its opulence did little to soften the cold atmosphere. Behind a large, ornate mahogany desk sat a man who barely acknowledged Bryan's presence. He remained fixated on the papers in front of him as though a visitor was a routine disruption in his day. He was in his mid-to-late sixties, his age showing in the deep creases of his face while his frown lines etched so deeply into his pale skin that they extended all the way up to his bald scalp. His collared shirt and a flamboyant silk waistcoat, embroidered with swirling patterns, strained against his bulk and added a touch of arrogance to his appearance.

Perhaps his most distinguishing feature was a black patch covering his right eye, lending him a more menacing air, as if years of physical and political battles had shaped the man he'd become. There was something distinctly Churchillian about him.

Without so much as a word, he flicked his remaining eye towards Bryan, a calculating look that seemed to measure him in an instant. His eye flicked again, this time at a chair at his desk he wanted Bryan to take.

Bryan sat, feeling dwarfed by the majestic desk and its intimidating occupant as the vice president stood obediently to one side.

The old man leaned forward onto his elbows. "Scientists often misjudge the potential of technological advancements. In 1895, Lord Kelvin famously declared that heavier-than-air flying machines were impossible. Most scientists once deemed cloning impossible, yet significant progress has been made. You see, technology has no real limits or boundaries."

Bryan ran his eyes around the office, which lived up to its presidential status. The corporate atmosphere clashed with the exotic details: ornate pillars, rich tapestries, satin curtains, and gleaming mahogany finishes. Lavish cabinets lined the walls, showcasing a collection of ornate trinkets, plants, and an impressive array of first edition books. Among them sat an antique-looking candelabra. The room's main source of light came from an acrylic aquarium nestled between two cabinets, its halogen bulbs casting a glow over the brightly coloured fish that swam inside.

Kane cracked his knuckles, pulling Bryan's focus back to the old man, who continued speaking. "The first generation that will see out the next century is already here. They are our young children. Among them are individuals who will see the twenty-second century, even the twenty-third, when cures for every disease are readily available in local pharmacies. Those people will one day walk beneath new stars and skies. People whose lives and worlds will grow beyond the imagination of science-fiction."

Bryan didn't know what to say, so he said nothing. He was still shaken by the events leading to this encounter. He still couldn't wrap his head around the situation in which he found himself.

"My name is Thomas Smolensk, founder and president. You're currently standing in a subterranean facility, about five hundred feet beneath the surface. What we're doing here – saving lives, improving them, and pushing humanity towards groundbreaking achievements – is worthy of a Nobel Peace Prize. And if the laws change, you might just become part of that legacy."

Bryan had two insistent thoughts. For one, receiving the Nobel Peace Prize was no easy accomplishment. Since 1901, it had been awarded for sustainable development, democracy and peace, banning and clearing of anti-personnel mines, and eliminating nuclear weapons from international politics. His second concerned the president's comment about revising the law. It implied the foundation was not yet legal, meaning it wasn't subject to audits, inspections, and financial reporting.

"What exactly *is* this foundation?"

"You are inside the world's first human cryonics facility."

Bryan needed a moment for it to sink in. "You mean you freeze people?"

"We are in the business of saving lives and restoring full health, something that conventional medical technology can never guarantee, unfortunately. We specialise in preserving individuals at extremely low temperatures when they cannot be treated and cured by conventional medication or surgery. Tissue preserved at the temperature of liquid nitrogen doesn't deteriorate. And memory, personality, and identity are safely stored in the structure and chemistry of the brain."

"I'm quite certain the damage caused by freezing human tissue, and particularly the brain, is irreversible."

"Well, you're wrong, Dr. Morgan. Just as Lord Kelvin was wrong about flight. It has already been done. I was the world's first cryonics patient, suspended in a nine-foot stainless steel cryostat for forty-nine years. Cryonics saved my life. In return, I have dedicated this life to doing the same for others."

Bryan was quiet once more, absorbing the information. "Forty-nine years?"

"I went into cryopreservation in 1919."

Bryan had so many questions, he didn't know which to ask first. "You were alive in the early nineteen hundreds?"

"Actually, I was born in 1873."

"You're having me on, right?"

"Is it so hard to believe?"

"It's hard to imagine."

"Is it? Really?"

"Science is nowhere near close to achieving this."

The president cocked an eyebrow.

Bryan paused. "Walt Disney was frozen after his death. Why hasn't he been brought back?"

"Wrong again. That Walt Disney was cryopreserved, not *frozen*, is untrue. The great man was cremated and interred at the world-famous Forest Lawn Memorial Park Cemetery in Los Angeles."

Bryan's eyes widened in surprise.

"At the end of the day, no amount of vitamins, minerals, or exercise can stop the natural decline of the body. No one is immune to ageing and disease. However, there are ways to prevent premature death from a deadly disease or virus. We have no religious, political, or social agendas whatsoever. We welcome any person with a terminal illness, whether they are Christian, Jewish, agnostic, conservative, democratic, young or old, American, European, Asian, or African. And when all else fails and death does occur, there's cryopreservation as a last resort."

"What do you mean?"

"There are three ways to have closure at the end of your natural life: burial, cremation, and cryopreservation."

Bryan disagreed. The thought of being frozen to the core forever was an absurd idea. Where would people be stored? The cost would be outrageous, and what would be the point?

President Smolensk had more to say on the matter. "The human body is a work of art. It should never be destroyed. Preserving a body in liquid nitrogen offers the possibility of revival in the future, contingent on scientific advancements, of course, when we can reverse ageing. For now, illnesses that are difficult to treat and cure, where time is critical, we need the ability to press pause on life itself. With medical science developing at a relentless speed, the next generation stands a feasible chance of immortality. And I intend to be there for it."

Bryan stuck out his bottom lip. "Your eye: does it have anything to do with why you were–"

"Preserved? Yes, I had a tumour growing behind my eye. In 1919, there were no medical solutions. I was forty-six and determined to survive. With the help of my mother and my twenty-eight-year-old son, we carried out research and spoke to top medical professionals of that era. One of them knew of a secret research facility in Liechtenstein where Europe's finest medical minds congregated. I spent months searching for the facility, determined to find it. Back then, Liechtenstein was still reeling from the aftermath of World War I. Europe was too preoccupied with the chaos and recovery to care about some off-the-grid facility. My mother and I believed in the science, so we invested everything. I volunteered for the procedure myself, knowing I had nothing left to lose. When I went under, freezing human tissue had been perfected, but the process of reanimation, that is bringing someone back from cryogenic preservation, was still a mystery. That was the gamble I took, entering an unknown future with no guarantee I'd ever wake up. It wasn't easy. The project was expensive, fraught with risks that could have bankrupted my family as we funded all the research. Fortunately for us, the biologists we hired managed to break through. But it came at a steep cost. While I was preserved, my mother passed away. To this day, I don't know where or how she died. But the hardest sacrifice was giving up my son. I missed his entire adult life. By the time I woke, he had lived his full span, and I could do nothing but stand by as he took his final breath. Watching him die of old age in his bed—it was the cruellest irony of all. With a few more years, I might have been able to preserve him."

Bryan understood the deep pain of losing a parent, a void that never truly faded. But the thought of losing a child was beyond comprehension, an unimaginable heartbreak.

"And the eye?"

"The operation had to be postponed for nearly fifty years, during which my body was preserved in a cryostat. Eventually, I lost my eye to melanoma, a large T3 tumour. Now, I only have one eye. But I'm alive, and one day, the world will have the same choices I had: between life and death, sacrifice and survival."

He was an inspiring individual; that was one of Bryan's first impressions of the old president. If teaching was about passing on one's life experiences, this old man could fill a few textbooks.

9

A painting of old London, its colours softened by age, sat under the warm light of a parchment lampshade mounted on the wall. Nearby on the same wall, a row of certificates and medals were framed and inscribed in German, telling tales of achievements long past. Bryan's eyes wandered from the wall to the president's side, where an antique grandfather clock stood, its grandeur pulling his focus.

"A fan of old clocks, Dr. Morgan?" President Smolensk asked, pointing with a finger mottled by age spots.

"My family used to own one when I was young. It was a noisy, old thing, but worth a lot of money as a collectable. Until it broke."

"This is a rare nineteenth-century, late-empire ormolu in a patinated gilt bronze clock case."

Bryan nodded. "It's beautiful."

"It's a bloody eyesore. The only reason I keep it is because it's been passed down through family generations."

Bryan shrugged. "Tells the time at least."

The president leaned forward. "Did you know that a deep, raspy cough can often signal a terminal illness?"

The question threw Bryan, making him cock an eyebrow. "I'm not so sure about that."

"The most common cough is caused by a cold, and they come and go like pimples. When the cough is not associated with a cold, it's almost always terminal. Pneumonia, disease of the lungs or windpipe or bronchial tubes, or Legionnaire's disease. Fifty years ago, we wouldn't have known this. Now we have the means to delay these awful illnesses and offer a comprehensive and permanent solution to the problem."

"If cryonic methods are so revolutionary and save lives, why hasn't it been approved by the Department of Health and the government?"

Kane removed his chewing gum and dropped it in the bin. "The developed world has a long history on human rights and personal liberties, and anything to do with dead bodies has all sorts of daft legal rules. Euthanasia is a perfect example. The ethics have always been in question. Some governments have a religious conformist attitude to the rites of the dead, and these bureaucrats try their best to impose their will on the public. They forget millions of human embryos have already been cryopreserved by immersion in liquid nitrogen, revived, brought to term, and are as able as any newborn baby, healthy and happy in body and soul."

Bryan glanced over at the bookshelf and spotted a book entitled *Freezing Time* by Thomas Smolensk.

"Is that your book?"

President Smolensk glanced at the shelf. "A contribution to society, my gift to the people," he said, his voice carrying a mix of pride and quiet conviction. "The book breaks down the science behind cryonics in simple, accessible terms, but it goes further. It dives into the humanitarian implications, the ethical questions we should be asking. Some might see it as indirect marketing, and maybe it is, but my real hope is that it will shift the way the world's elite view this technology. One day, when they understand both the science and the moral responsibility, they might see cryonics as more than simply a fringe idea. They might see it as a chance to extend life and reshape the future."

"Has it been successful?"

"Not as successful as your book on depression. A very insightful read. There are roughly 70,000 copies in circulation around Europe, mostly in public libraries."

"Impressive!"

"Someday, the world will understand cryonics is a gift from God. Someday, medical science will be able to repair any damage to the human body, including senile debility. It's a matter of when, not if. The leading threat to humans in life is death. Nobody can ever be free so long as there is death, and we cannot upgrade the basic quality of life *because* of death. Once death has been eliminated, and we attain immortality, anything will be possible."

Bryan nodded. "What about the effects on the population when the cured are released into society?"

"Population growth is inevitable, with or without cryonic predecessors. You only have to look at statistics. In 1900, the population was about one and a half billion. Ninety-two years later, and today the planet is home to six billion, and it will continue to soar. As more and more cures are discovered for fatal diseases, the need for cryonic preservation will rapidly decrease, and life expectancy will increase of its own accord. It will result in overpopulation, anyway. Even so, there is still an abundance of living space on this planet. Despite growing concerns about overpopulation, the facts tell a different story. A recent study revealed Earth has the capacity to comfortably support over one hundred billion people. Think about that: it's more than ten times the current population. The key isn't about running out of space but in using our resources more intelligently. With advancements in sustainable technology, urban planning, and food production, we have the potential to create liveable environments for future generations. It's not just about survival anymore but about thriving, even with vast numbers."

Bryan mulled over the president's words. "And just how many patients here have failed to survive the cryopreservation process?" His tone was laced with curiosity and scepticism. "I mean, how many attempts have ended in death, where the science just wasn't enough to bring them back?"

"In the two decades since the foundation opened, one."

Bryan could barely hide the surprise on his face. "You've been operating this foundation for twenty years?"

The president gave a gentle nod.

"And only one death? That's impressive."

"Not impressive enough."

Bryan nodded slowly.

President Smolensk clasped his hands together. "Now, do you have any further questions, Dr. Morgan?"

Bryan was swamped with information overload, with so many things he wanted to ask that by the time the president extended the invitation to ask, he could not think of one. He smiled instead. "I've got about a million questions, but none I can think of right now."

"Then let's not waste any more time. Welcome to ELF, the Extended Life Foundation."

10

The vice president led Bryan out of the president's office and into a maze of corridors that twisted and turned through the heart of the sprawling building complex. Passageways seemed to stretch endlessly, a labyrinth of sleek, modern design. The floors, polished to a mirror-like sheen, reflected the overhead lighting and meandering lattice of steel beams and connecting struts. The crisscrossing metal framework gave an impression of walking through the inside of a giant, carefully engineered machine.

Kane walked with slow, synchronised steps, effortlessly gliding along the corridor with his hands behind his back.

Bryan found himself taking the edge off his usual pace just to keep level.

"ELF employs approximately three hundred staff, made up of technicians, cryobiologists, biological researchers, and support staff. We have seventy CI agents. And before you ask, CI stands for Cryonic Investigation. Staff live onsite and are always on-call. We offer generous annual leave to compensate for it. They… we, care for more than four thousand patients. In total, there are five levels, not including the ground level. Level five, the deepest, is restricted to all personnel. There's not a great deal down there, anyway, just storage, archives, and our computer servers. Staff accommodation is on levels four, three, and two. There are canteens on every level and communal lounges for the staff to relax, a gym, pool, squash courts, a cinema, and a library. Right now, we are on level one, the largest level. All labs and offices are on this floor."

They rounded a bend and came to another long corridor leading to the lifts.

"The cryopreservation labs are divided into six sectors and are categorised by illness."

They stopped beside a set of double doors labelled *Lab 3: Leukaemia.*

"The patients we store here suffer from various forms of leukaemia, including hairy cell, lymphocytic, and myeloid—both chronic and acute. At present, we have two hundred and eighty-five patients in cryopreservation, but our goal here is to reach full capacity by the turn of the millennium."

Moving on, they climbed a steep metal staircase onto a viewing platform overlooking a different lab, currently a hive of activity.

Bryan spotted a sign stuck to the window reading *Lab 4: Syndromes.*

Vice President Spence noticed Bryan observing the sign. "This lab doesn't include the Acquired Immune Deficiency Syndrome. AIDS has its own section. As I'm sure you can imagine, the AIDS lab is extensive. In here, we have patients suffering from Sly Syndrome, Galactosialidosis, and Hurler and Hunter Syndrome, among others."

Bryan nodded as he stared down at the lab. "Do you do drug development down here?"

"Yes, we do. We also perform genetic research, biological testing, pathology, biochemistry, and fusions. Some of the most prestigious biologists in Europe work at ELF. It's what they live for. Do you know what the world's biggest killer is?"

"I would say cancer."

"One of them, and has been increasing for years. But it's not the leading cause of death. It's chronic lower respiratory infection and heart disease. After that, cancer, malaria, AIDS, diarrhoea, tuberculosis, measles, whooping cough, tetanus, and meningitis. Most have prophylactic vaccines, yet they still manage to kill more than fifteen million people each year. Sad but true."

The vice president had confessed he was neither a doctor, surgeon, nor cryobiologist, but it was clear just talking to him that he'd done his medical homework, enough to earn Bryan's respect.

Further along the narrow landing that bridged over the corridor running beneath, the vice president pointed out a lab that resembled a giant industrial warehouse.

"The cancer lab is our second largest. We have over one thousand cancer patients, ranging from prostate and liver to brain tumours. These patients are beyond the reach of any current effective treatment, even chemotherapy. Most would be dead already had we not taken them in and cryopreserved them. It's sad to think how many terminal cancer patients are out there, just waiting unnecessarily to die."

Bryan peered through the large glass window, his eyes widening as he took in the breathtaking interior of the lab. It was a sight to behold, a futuristic sanctuary brimming with potential. Hundreds of cylindrical containers in impeccably aligned rows shone with newness and a pristine polish, as if freshly unwrapped from a protective covering. A wave of awe and curiosity came over him as he pictured the lives preserved within those containers. They radiated purpose, a promise of hope and possibility that struck a deep chord.

"We call them cryostats. They are made from fibreglass and perlite, a mineral powder that increases insulation by ten per cent. The patients stored inside are kept cold by the liquid nitrogen running through them."

The steel exterior had a waffle pattern that strengthened the hull while the interior was layered in an insulation blanket to protect the module from harsh sub-zero temperatures. A porthole window made of the highest quality optical glass displayed the face of the patient it contained. Hi-tech electric generators that provided power and cooling water, equipped with temperature and humidity gauges, formed the backbone to the cryostats, fed by a series of cables that were rigged up to enormous liquid nitrogen storage tanks.

Still unsettled about how he had been introduced to ELF and the psychometric assessment, Bryan chose to focus on the positives. The facility was undeniably state-of-the-art and world class, equipped with top-range scientific technology and advanced equipment that offered its staff a remarkable environment for research and discovery.

11

"Do you mind if I have a look inside the lab?" asked Bryan, watching as staff members in protective suits detached pipes from the liquid nitrogen storage unit and inspected the hull's integrity.

"Not at this moment," said Kane. "The technicians are carrying out repairs right now." He stepped sideways along the viewing platform and peered down on *Lab 6: Heterogeneous*. "You can look inside this lab if you want. The theme is the same in all labs."

Kane descended the stairs and moved down the corridor towards the lab, scanning his finger at the door. As it clicked open, Bryan stepped inside, with Kane close behind. This lab was smaller than the others they'd seen, yet it held around two hundred cryostats, glowing faintly like stars in a carefully arranged, artificial galaxy. Bryan swept his eyes over the rows of identical cryostats, standing like tall, vertical coffins that cryopreserved people from all walks of life, their differences frozen in time.

"How does it all work?" Bryan asked.

"The patient is injected with a sedative that knocks them out. Blood is removed from their body, which is injected with a cryoprotectant solution that eliminates freezing damage. At such hostile temperatures, molecular motion stops, chemical reactions cease, and metabolic activity grinds to a halt. This means humans at these freezing temperatures can be kept in an unchanging state for as long as necessary; anything from a few years to a few millennia, with zero biological difference. This is followed by further cooling, done slowly using silicone oil, and then long-term immersion into liquid nitrogen at a temperature of -196°C."

Bryan peered over the shoulder of a young cryobiologist at a computer. The screen was full of line graphs and numbers. The man, transfixed on the numerical formulas, barely took his eyes away from the screen.

"Clive here is monitoring the patients. We have a range of illnesses packed into this room, from Multiple Sclerosis, Cystic Fibrosis, and severe asthma to a suicidal schizophrenic and Functional Neurological Disorder. Some patients carry illnesses we cannot yet identify. Oh, and we even have three in here with Sandhoff Disease."

Sandhoff Disease was a rare genetic disorder resulting in progressive deterioration of the central nervous system and was generally hereditary. Knowing the onset of the disorder usually occurred at around six months and death commonly caused by respiratory infections occurred around three years of age, Bryan quickly concluded the patients were infants.

Kane caught the surprised look on Bryan's face. "I know what you're thinking. You're correct. They're sixteen months old. Three bothers. Their mother couldn't bear to watch them die so young, so she sold everything and put all of them into cryopreservation. I believe she works the streets to maintain their place in here, sadly."

"What, you mean prostitution?"

"Yeah."

"Why?"

"Cryopreservation is not cheap. Prostitution can bring in a decent income."

Bryan had counselled several women over the years who had committed themselves to the sex industry for quick cash, and the psychological damage some suffered was everlasting. Michelle Locke was a case in point, a young woman who had turned to prostitution because it was easier than going back to college to earn a qualification, which cost a lot of money and had no immediate financial return. She was the daughter of a high-profile politician, and why her death had garnered such media attention, bringing the police to his door. Once they'd ruled out murder and determined she had killed herself, the news outlets published stories about her moonlighting sex work, embarrassing her father and the government.

Heading back towards the exit, Bryan changed the subject. "And what about you? What brought you here?"

He expected a meaningful answer. He didn't get one.

"It's a bit of a cliché, but if there's one thing I've learned, it's that life is too short," Kane said, glancing at the cryostats around them, his eyes momentarily distant, as if lost in some memory. "People think they have time, but they don't, not really." His tone became more pragmatic. "Cryonics saved the president's life. He sees it as more than just science. To him, it's a calling, like something divine. He talks about it like he's Noah, and this," he gestured towards the rows of frozen, silent capsules, "this is his ark. It's his way of saving humanity, or at least the parts of it he deems worth saving."

Bryan raised an eyebrow, but Kane didn't seem to notice. "But me? I don't really care that much about playing saviour. I'm a businessman, and just want what everyone else wants: wealth, success, security. You know, the basics. The president can keep his grand vision. I'm here to make sure I come out on top when we go public." He gave a half-hearted smile as if it would soften his words. "Survival of the fittest, right?"

Bryan nodded. He couldn't help but wonder about the vice president. Unlike President Smolensk, he wasn't trying to play God so much as he viewed ELF as a lucrative business interest.

"What's the cost to be preserved here?"

"Well, that depends primarily on the illness. As I said, it's quite expensive. Patients or their guarantors can pay upfront or in instalments, or both. The overheads down here are what drive up costs. The cryostats, the labour, the transport, the surveillance equipment, and of course treatment the patients receive when they are reanimated, not to mention the power consumption. The liquid nitrogen starts to boil off from the moment they enter the cryostat and needs to be constantly replenished. Then, when a cure for their illness is available, the patient goes into surgery and receives their treatment. For long-term illnesses, fees can accumulate, and the payee could be forced to fork out for several years. As you can imagine, much of ELF's revenue is generated from our HIV and AIDS patients. Many have been here for years. It may be expensive, but a small price to pay for extended life. I'm sure you can agree."

Bryan's bottom lip jutted out. "I guess so. But where do I fit into all this? I don't have any scientific background, and my knowledge of cryonics is barely enough. Honestly, I'm having a hard time figuring out what I could possibly bring to the table here. And let's not pretend you don't know that I was under investigation for a patient's death while they were in my care."

"When patients come out of cryopreservation, they are disorientated, confused. They suffer from temporary memory loss, which is subjective and unpredictable. Their memory can take anything from a day to a month to return. It can take many weeks, often months, before they understand what they have been through and are mentally stable enough to rejoin the outside world. They require counselling and advice from an expert to help them get through what is often a lengthy rehabilitation. We also need to have trained medics present in the foundation. Accidents can happen, so we need on-call medics."

"Why not employ a more experienced psychologist? One who didn't quit his job when the pressure got too much for him, for example? Why me?"

"Patients develop colds, flu, pneumonia, and infections due to weak immune systems. They require expert medical support. That is why we chose you. Besides, at the height of your game, you were the best in the business. You have won awards for psychiatric excellence locally and nationally, and your name is well-regarded throughout the country, especially for your fieldwork in the Royal Army Medical Corps."

"How do you know that?"

He smiled reassuringly. "We know everything about our staff."

Further along the corridor, they stopped outside a door with a large sign: *Restricted Access*.

Kane stuck his finger on the authentication device and pushed through the door. The smell of straw and animal faeces immediately enveloped them. Dim light shone down on a series of cages palletised on top of one another, four high and ten across. There was movement in the cages.

"You're a man of medicine. I'm sure you appreciate the importance of medical research."

On closer inspection, Bryan saw the top row of cages held rats, ferrets, and lizards. Dogs, cats, foxes, and monkeys lived in the cramped enclosures at the bottom. Some had bulbous growths or were missing fur. Others had lost entire limbs. Some bore gruesome scars on their heads and necks, covered over by multiple blue stitches. Medical research, no matter how vital to human health and longevity, was a topic steeped in controversy, one that most professionals preferred to keep under wraps. The darker side of the medical industry was rarely discussed in public, and for good reason. Behind closed doors, animals were subjected to unspeakable suffering. Their cries always went unheard, their violent convulsions unseen by the outside world. They were confined to cold, cramped metal cages, and treated not as living beings but as disposable tools in the relentless pursuit of human advancement. Each year, millions of animals were burned, poisoned, or otherwise sacrificed in the name of extending human life and enhancing well-being by developing new treatments. Yet, the cost of this progress was something few were willing to acknowledge openly.

"We foster research and development of new drugs in here," Kane said, his tone almost robotic, as though reciting a line he had delivered a thousand times. "But... we've yet to achieve any major medical breakthrough."

As they ventured deeper into the animal compound, the faint scent of woodchips gradually morphed into something far more sinister: a pungent mix of rotting flesh and dirty, matted fur. The awful stench, like roadkill left too long in the gutters after a rainstorm, hit Bryan like a sharp, suffocating wave. Instinctively, he pulled out a handkerchief and pressed it to his nose and mouth, hoping to blunt the foul odour.

A tall man in a lab coat taking notes on a female dog looked up to greet them. "Hey."

The vice president nodded politely. "This is Dr. Bryan Morgan. Could you tell us what you're working on?"

"There's not much exciting happening in here right now." He pointed at the sorry-looking dog. "I'm assessing Daisy's neural impairment after she was deprived of key nutrients. She's a tough old girl, been here the longest, two years next Friday. I'm thinking about maybe throwing a little celebration for her."

Kane put his hand on the researcher's shoulder. "Give her some of your special party drugs?"

The man's feigned laughter barely masked his grudging respect, and Bryan quickly picked up on the subtle signs of someone trying not to step out of line. The glint of fear in his expression, rigid posture, and restless eyes that couldn't seem to settle told Bryan everything he needed to know. It made him wary.

12

Kane stopped at the crossroads of the corridor and turned to Bryan. "Every year, more than two hundred people meet their end under falling coconuts. Believe it or not, donkeys claim more lives than plane crashes. Then there are the truly bizarre causes of death, like laughing too hard, getting hiccups, even something as simple as going to the toilet. Strange, isn't it? In fact, there are more than three thousand ways to perish. It's unavoidable; death comes for everyone sooner or later. But here's the thing—there *is* a way to cheat it." He paused, a sly grin spreading across his face. "And that's precisely what we do here at ELF. We don't just defy the odds, we outsmart death itself."

As they continued on their way along the wide corridor, they passed a young woman standing alone, absorbed in a document. She wore ripped jeans and a casual jumper that fell to her thighs. Kane glanced back at the off-duty employee. Bryan watched the vice president's eyes travel up her legs, stopping on her behind, actually tilting his head slightly.

Then he snapped back to the moment. "Where… what was I… yeah, the concept of cryogenic freezing is not new, you know. It's been around for over a century. In fact, it has existed for millions of years, just not in a medical pedigree. Insects and small animals such as frogs and fish freeze in lakes all the time and magically return to life in spring. Nowadays, with medical science where it is, viruses, bacteria, sperm, eggs, and embryos can be cryogenically frozen and preserved for indefinite periods."

"And now humans," said Bryan.

He concurred with a nod. "And now humans. As long as it's a disease that does not involve the brain. Once the engine is kaput, it's just like trying to fix a non-waterproof watch at the bottom of a swimming pool."

They stopped at a disk the size of a car wheel embedded in the floor where three corridors crisscrossed. It featured a black starry background with watercolours that resembled a human eye.

"The Eye of God," said Kane, pointing at the insignia. "More commonly known as the Helix Nebula, a series of photo images taken by the Hubble Telescope and the Kitt Peak National Observatory. The Helix Nebula is made up of a trillion mile-long-tunnels of glowing gases."

"What's the significance?"

"The Eye of God watches over those seeking a lifeline. It also represents the president's eye, the first person ever to be successfully cryopreserved."

Once again, Bryan found himself at a loss for words.

"Albert Einstein once said: *There are only two ways to live your life; one is as though nothing is a miracle, and the other is as though everything is a miracle.*' Which do you live by?"

"I don't believe in miracles," said Bryan. "I believe in hard work, intelligence, and a sprinkle of luck."

Kane nodded and continued with the tour.

"So, where are we going now?" asked Bryan.

"I'll introduce you to the chief patient research analyst."

Passing the Security Operations Room, Kane stopped, took three steps back, and pointed through the window at a large, dark space filled with a dozen security monitors hooked up to surveillance.

"The eyes and ears of ELF. The staff is currently on shift changeover. During the day, eight security operators monitor the cameras on a twelve-hour shift. At night, four operators take over."

"What exactly are they monitoring?"

"We have security cameras covering every corner of the foundation. Outside, too. You can never be too careful."

"Who's in charge?"

Kane pointed towards the middle of the room. "See that large man there at the central console? The older gentleman?"

Bryan nodded when he spotted the man, dressed head to toe in black denim. He was broad across the shoulders and waist and casually biting into a banana.

"That's Stefan. We call him the Sheriff. He used to be a security adviser for the prime minister. He's put on a few kilos since then. A mastermind when it comes to ELF's security."

Kane described the Sheriff as the ever-watchful overseer of ELF, sitting in his secluded office like a spider at the centre of its complex web. From his cocoon of surveillance and control, nothing escaped his notice. He knew every detail of what went on: who talked to whom, what people ate for lunch, who arrived late for their shift. Every interaction, every small indiscretion, it all reached him. His grip on the facility was absolute, his eyes everywhere.

Bryan found it unsettling, almost invasive. The place felt less like a research hub and more like a cage, with nowhere to hide from the constant surveillance. But then he reasoned if you did your job and followed the rules, what did it matter if someone was watching?

Further along the corridor, Kane invited Bryan inside the Patient Research Room, where few had access.

"This is where it all begins."

He tapped his finger on top of the authentication pad and the red light turned green.

The room was decked out in hi-tech computer equipment operated by a dozen staff members. The lights were dimmed, the air stuffy from the machinery emitting electrical heat. A map of Liechtenstein with annotations and scribbles all over it hung on the wall. Someone had even drawn a phallic image in the top right corner. Bryan raised an eyebrow.

Kane immediately introduced Bryan to April, the chief analyst, a woman in her mid-thirties with sharp eyes and a determined look. Her role at ELF was crucial as she oversaw all patient research, ensuring every detail was documented and analysed. But her influence stretched far beyond. Kane explained that April was also on the executive board, giving her a voice in the organisation's most critical decisions. What made her even more indispensable was her background. April was a professional computer hacker, skilled in navigating the most secure systems. She had comprehensive access to most hospitals across Europe, a secret network allowing her to pull data on any patient. In fact, she could retrieve information on everything from the patient's medical history to their home address. Diagnosed illnesses, treatment regimens, medication prescriptions, private notes from doctors. Nothing was ever off-limits. Through this extensive data collection, April could conduct deep research into every individual considered for ELF's groundbreaking procedures. Her expertise not only ensured the right candidates were chosen but also helped the foundation stay ahead of any potential security threats or legal pitfalls.

Next, Kane pointed at every team member in the room and whispered who they were, but Bryan instantly forgot all their names.

"What exactly are they doing?"

"Ask April."

They approached her at her desk.

"April. This is Dr. Morgan. He has a question for you."

Bryan swallowed the lump stuck in his throat. "I was just wondering what everyone is doing."

"Hacking into hospital patient-database mainframes!" she said. "I'm scanning for any patients with a terminal illness." She tied her hair up into a bun, gave Bryan a cursory size-up, and continued with her commentary. "Despite denials from government and health bureaucrats, patients' medical records in several countries are held on a central electronic database. I have unlimited and undetected access to that database. It's how we select our patients."

"You mean you randomly pick people with illnesses?"

She glanced at him. "You're a bright spark."

Bryan blushed.

"When we identify a potential candidate, the first thing we do is review their medical condition from the report and evaluate their eligibility to become an ELF patient. Then we assess their financial status. If they meet the required criteria, we hand the candidate over to our agents, who conduct a thorough investigation, lasting up to three months, to ensure the individual meets all the necessary conditions to qualify as a future ELF patient."

"Like we did with you," said Kane.

"You followed me around for three months?"

"Six. It's longer for staff."

Bryan was taken aback, unsure of how to react to what he had just heard. He couldn't mask the shock written all over his face.

"It's the same for everyone," Kane continued, his tone steady. "You came through, though. You passed the final test with the briefcase. It was empty the whole time."

"Empty?"

Bryan's mind raced as he tried to wrap his head around the implications of Kane's words. The briefcase had felt so heavy with expectation, yet it had contained nothing at all, a mere illusion designed to test his resolve. He searched Kane's eyes for reassurance, needing to know he wasn't alone in this bewildering journey. "So, everyone goes through this?"

"Yes," Kane replied, nodding. "It's a part of the process. We need to see how you handle integrity, how you react when faced with pressure. It's not just about your abilities; it's about your mindset. You see, all the while you believed the briefcase contained money and important documents, you kept it close to you. It had built-in cameras and microphones. We've been watching you all this week, twenty-four hours a day, to see if you were tempted to tell anyone about your encounter with the CI agent and the job offer. Had you disclosed that, we wouldn't have shown up at the hotel. Congratulations, by the way!"

"Thanks. I think."

"Don't worry, you'll get the sign-on bonus. A promise is a promise."

Bryan nodded and turned back to April at her terminal.

"I still don't understand how you get into the mainframe database."

April swiped her fringe from her face. "Initially, we used a modified version of the original military network, Arpanet, which allowed us to connect through any platform. However, we now operate our own network that utilises the IP protocol developed by Arpanet. For our research projects, we employ supercomputers that are at the forefront of this technology, which has its roots in the sixties. Currently, we have around one million hosts connected, but that number is expected to grow exponentially over the next decade."

"How do you mean?"

Kane put his large hand on Bryan's shoulder. "You know about CERN? The European Institute for Particle Physics in Switzerland? It has just released the World Wide Web this year, and user numbers are growing at a crazy rate."

Bryan watched April's diligent fingers work at warp speed on the keyboard. "What kind of things do you investigate in potential ELF patients?"

"Finances, medical history, criminal records, education, current employment, background, skills, attributes, and the individual's integrity, ethics, and mindset. After three months of assessment, the board members, along with the president, convene to discuss whether or not the candidate should be approached with an offer for a term in cryopreservation. If the candidate receives approval, a CI agent will personally approach them to extend the offer."

After half hour inside the Patient Research Room, Bryan realised he needed to use the bathroom.

Kane guided him out of the room and pointed along the corridor. "Fifth door on the right."

While Bryan headed to the bathroom, Kane went back inside the Patient Research Room to talk with April.

Bryan paced along the bright corridor, passing the first and second doors on his right.

Two engineers crashed through a set of swing doors on his left with puzzled expressions.

Bryan said hello but got no returned salutation.

In the process, Bryan lost count of how many doors he had passed. None had signs on them. He gambled on the next door and stepped into a dark space, where he fumbled for the light switch.

Black lights sputtered on.

As his eyes adjusted to the dim light, he spotted eight cryostats neatly aligned against the far wall. Seven of them stood empty, their glass windows empty and devoid of life. The final cryostat contained a human figure, shrouded in a thin layer of frost. Curiosity piqued, Bryan reached out and touched the surface of the cryostat. In his haste, he pressed a button, and the interior light flickered on. A frozen man lit up in the rounded window. His expression was one of sheer terror, as if he were facing an unseen horror that threatened to engulf him. The man's long, white hair had crystallised into sharp, icy shards, held back by a headband that seemed to struggle against the weight of the frost. The window framed his gaunt face, accentuating the deep lines carved by time and fear. His broken nose hinted at a violent past, and the absence of his front teeth gave him an almost grotesque appearance.

Bryan studied the man's frozen visage with a heart beating faster and faster. He wondered about the circumstances that had led him to this moment; what horrors he had experienced before being trapped in this state. The cryostat felt like a tomb, holding not just the man's body but also the remnants of his suffering and survival forever suspended in time. A mix of curiosity and dread surged within Bryan as he realised he was staring into the eyes of a dead man who was not completely dead.

The door suddenly swung open; the silhouette of the vice president was pronounced in the black light. His eyes fixed on Bryan, and he hurriedly turned off the lights. "What do you think you're doing?"

Bryan noticed while Kane's mouth smiled, his eyes were most assuredly not. "Sorry. I took a wrong turn."

Kane used his finger on the authentication device to lock the room once outside in the corridor.

Bryan felt a strong urge to enquire about the man in the cryostat, but thought better of it. Kane was not someone he wanted to upset or provoke.

13

Perhaps noticing the fear and surprise in Bryan's eyes, Kane softened his tone. "Security is our top priority here, and we follow strict protocols to ensure everything runs smoothly. That door was left unlocked, but I want you to understand it wasn't your fault. Mistakes happen, and we'll figure out how it occurred."

Bryan nodded. "Was that a patient in that room?"

"I'm afraid that's classified." He smiled a brief smile and moved on.

Standing outside Lab 1, Kane continued like nothing had happened, business as usual, his manners civilised and calm. He put a fresh stick of gum in his mouth. "Let me introduce you to Dr. Huber. He embodies scientific dedication like no one else. Truly, he's the heart and soul of this foundation, our most valuable asset, and is one of its founding members. In

1968, when the president woke up after almost fifty years of cryopreservation, Dr. Huber was just twenty-six, leading the research team and overseeing the surgery on the president's eye. He has witnessed more than most could imagine, with stories that would curl your toes. He's an absolute workaholic, barely sleeps. The president dreads the day he retires or passes. He fears the place will crumble without him. But as brilliant as Dr. Huber is, I believe no one is irreplaceable, though he comes about as close as it gets."

He went on to explain that Dr. Huber's early interest in evolution and biology saw him shoot to the highest status in the first years of practice, though his attitude towards biology remained, in some respects, that of an outsider. His first published paper on cancer cell development brought him into the spotlight, opening doors to a position at one of the Max-Planck Institutes for Biochemistry in Munich. The renowned research institute carried a long, stellar tradition of biomedical research in Germany. Many leading scientists over the last century had worked in Germany or had studied at either Heidelberg or Gottingen University in Berlin. Medicine and the life sciences had a long tradition, with researchers making solid ground on drugs and treatments for numerous serious illnesses.

Four hundred scientists, Dr. Huber included, had studied molecular processes in living cells and protein composition. Dr. Huber had dedicated most of his career to building upon modern bacteriology, immunology, and chemotherapy, and he had played a leading role in perfecting cryonic science.

"How does it all work?" Bryan asked. "How do you take a patient from alive to… well, dead."

"Why don't you ask the master?"

He touched the authentication device with his finger and the big, heavy doors parted and swung open to reveal a lab that looked like an enormous warehouse, so vast that Bryan couldn't see to the other side. Hundreds of vertical cryostats in perfect symmetrical lines filled the floor with aisles running between them that stretched to the distance. Each cryostat displayed a patient serial number, and behind every window lay a frozen human face.

Dr. Huber sat on a stool, his eyes glued to his computer as his fingers tapped steadily on the keys. Small and narrow-shouldered, his pronounced stoop curved his spine just like a drawn bow. Dark hair framed the sides and back of his head, encircling his bald crown.

Kane guided Bryan over to him. "How's everything going here?"

"Fine," said Dr. Huber, barely looking up.

"This is Dr. Morgan."

Dr. Huber remained arched over his terminal as he spoke. "And what do you think of our wet lab?" he asked in a deep voice, completely at odds with his small, nerdy stature.

Bryan frowned. "What's a wet lab?"

Dr. Huber looked at him quizzically, his thick glasses magnifying his eyes to twice their size. "Wet labs test and analyse chemicals, drugs, biological matter. In here, we don't handle biohazards at levels BL-2, BL-3, or BL-4, as defined by the Microbiological and Biomedical Laboratories."

Bryan's confusion was evident once again, his expression betraying his lack of understanding.

Dr. Huber's voice, sort of nasal and sibilant, had distinct traces of a German accent. "You are the new cryobiologist, no?"

"No, I'm not."

"This is Dr. Morgan," said Kane. "He's a psychologist. I think you have him mixed up with Dr. Marshall, who starts here tomorrow. Dr. Morgan just wants to know a bit about the deanimation process."

"I see." Dr. Huber turned back to his computer. "What is there to know? We load the patients in liquid nitrogen and reanimate if and when the cure has become available."

"I'm curious to know why their bodies aren't damaged. I was always under the impression ice crystals in the blood damaged cells and organs when bodies were frozen in ice or, in this case, liquid nitrogen."

Dr. Huber glanced at Bryan. "Patients are not *frozen* in liquid nitrogen. They're cryopreserved. Medical science will falsely state the ice crystals in the blood damage the cells and organs. But we've mastered cryopreservation years ago, and it's high time the world knew the truth."

"What truth?"

"About molecular repair technology. The ultra-miniature robots, known as nanorobots, take the choBryanol away from arteries and are genetically engineered to fix DNA damage. Nanotechnology can repair matter on a molecular or atomic scale. Self-replicating nanomachines not only cure the diseases but can also repair any freezing damage. At liquid nitrogen temperature, biological structures needing the repair can be preserved for millions of years without change."

"I see," said Bryan. "Incredible."

"Not really. Since the start of time, amphibians such as frogs and salamanders have survived freezing temperatures where their body water has formed into ice. This is because their livers manufacture ethylene glycerol. And glycerol is the key to survival. In 1773, Benjamin Franklin, the first man to dream of preserving dead bodies for future repairs, studied how the heat from the sun reanimated flies preserved inside a bottle of wine. He dreamed of inventing a similar method of preserving people so they could be recalled to life. Various bacteria encased within ancient salt crystals were successfully revived after being dormant for hundreds of millions of years. These microorganisms were discovered in tiny water pockets trapped inside the salt deposits and dated back to prehistoric times. Literally frozen in time. Reviving these bacteria not only stunned the scientific community, it also expanded our understanding of life's resilience, forcing scientists to rethink the boundaries of life and survival. In recent years, there are children who once were cryopreserved embryos."

Bryan folded his arms. "What I don't understand is when the body dies, the brain is starved of oxygen. Suspension in liquid nitrogen prevents oxygen from getting to the brain, so how does brain damage not occur?"

Dr. Huber spoke while jotting down some figures from his computer in a logbook. "Brain cells do not die even five minutes after circulation stops. In fact, vessels go into spasm, and the blood thickens. Tissue cells are still alive. Biological death is a process, not an event, and the decline of cells in the tissues and the organs takes many hours after the cessation of the heartbeat. To minimise this damage, the patient is treated as soon as breathing has stopped. We administer CPR to the patient and pure oxygen is delivered to the tissues and the brain."

"So, you're saying there's absolutely no freezing damage caused to the body or brain and no effects caused by a lack of oxygen?"

"No, freezing damage is not eliminated one hundred per cent. But damage is not destruction. For example, if you were to break a ceramic bowl, it can be fixed. But if the bowl is put in acid and dissolves, there's no way to retrieve it. The human body is broken but not destroyed. Something that is damaged can be fixed. And that's why nanotechnology is so crucial. Without it, complex repairs just are not possible. Because the nanotechnology removes the ice formation between cells, it eliminates toxic hypertonic solutions. We also add the extra cryoprotectant to prevent any ice crystals from forming. We insert a measured amount in the red blood cells of the patient. This substance acts like antifreeze and stops ice from forming up to ninety-seven per cent. Cryoprotectant turns the water into hardened glass to prevent crystal formation. Just like the amphibians that use glycerol as their cryoprotectant. Whereas other insects and reptiles use sugars as antifreeze."

Bryan realised his mouth was hanging open. "Has anyone awoken with negative side effects because of cryopr–"

"Not anymore! After twenty years of cryopreserving so many patients, we have become experts in what we do. Many biologists still believe the cessation of electrical activity during cryopreservation causes identity and memory loss. They are years behind our research, which we began in the twenties, long before I was even born. Some short-term memory might be lost, but identity and memory are encoded in synapses and connections between the neurons."

Bryan nodded and folded his arms, trying to process all he had heard so far. "Some people in comas for long periods have woken with entirely different personalities altogether. Is it possible for cryonic patients to experience the same change to their personality?"

"Coma patients had their personality altered due to the trauma of the brain or a new perspective, living with active brains while unconscious. Identity of the cryonic patients is embodied in the physiology of the brain. So the personality from childhood to adulthood is not an altered entity, and it continues even with the accumulation of bad experiences. Identity and personality cannot just become something else. Molecule-by-molecule replacement can alter it a little, but not enough to create a new identity."

Dr. Huber escorted Bryan and the vice president to Lab 2 where all the cancer patients were kept. Cryobiologists had just finished repairing the liquid nitrogen storage tank. This lab intrigued Bryan the most. The use of chemotherapy for treating cancer began in the 1940s with the introduction of nitrogen mustards and folic acid drugs as the first effective treatments. These early breakthroughs were revolutionary at the time, offering hope in the battle against a disease that had long been considered untreatable. Even so, what started out as a humble medical experiment quickly evolved into a vast, multi-billion-dollar industry dedicated to drug development to treat cancer. Over decades, researchers explored multiple chemical compounds, developing a range of chemotherapy treatments aimed at targeting and destroying the cancer cells. Despite these advances, chemotherapy remained a double-edged sword. While it had saved countless lives, it was often only a temporary solution, as cancers developed resistance or returned after treatment. Many key principles and limitations uncovered by the pioneering researchers still held true today. For example, chemotherapy's inability to distinguish between healthy and cancerous cells often led to severe side effects, from hair loss to weakened immune systems. This significant challenge had persisted, despite years of progress. Moreover, modern cancer treatment still faced the same challenge of incomplete effectiveness. While some experienced remission, others endured only temporary relief and had to seek new approaches such as targeted therapies and immunotherapy to complement or replace chemotherapy. Still, chemotherapy remained a cornerstone of cancer treatment.

Dr. Huber logged onto another computer terminal. "The world spends too much time and money on making treatment for current illnesses, and not enough on making preventative medicine. What we do here at ELF eliminates the dilemma of which comes first by taking the subject out of the equation, buying us time to invent preventative medicine *and* treatment. That's what makes ELF so unique. Did you know that cancer is as old as the human race? Modernisation and the industrial revolution did not kick-start cancer, contrary to conventional belief. The oldest known human cancer was found written on an Egyptian papyrus in 3000 BC. And the oldest available specimen of human cancer was a tumour found deep inside a woman's head, discovered in the remains of her skull, and she lived during the Bronze Age. A virus causing cancer in chickens was identified in 1911."

"Is that so," said Bryan.

Dr. Huber checked his watch. "I must go to a patient who is arriving… in fact now. Do you have time?"

Bryan looked at Kane, who nodded his approval. "By all means."

14

A female patient of Asian descent entered the room. She was immediately taken to the prep room annexed to the lab and guided onto a steel gurney. While she lay on her back on a waterproof sheet, her clothes were removed, and her genitalia and breasts were covered with a fogged silicone material. She was then wrapped in a white sheet.

"Try and relax," said Dr. Huber, stooped awkwardly over the patient. "I will give you a general anaesthetic to make you sleep. I'll count back from ten."

She smiled bravely. "Will it hurt?"

"It's just like having a long sleep undisturbed by dreams, nightmares, and toilet intervals. I will set the alarm clock for health and happiness." Holding her hand, he smiled kindly with a practiced warmth. It was clear to Bryan that, even after all these years, his passion and dedication to the job had never waned. He lived for it, every single day. When he spoke about the science, his eyes lit up with a brightness that was hard to miss. His voice gained a certain energy, a liveliness that came from deep within. It wasn't just a job for Dr. Huber, it was his life purpose.

Gowned, gloved, and masked, Bryan watched the process unfold with fascination.

"Ten... nine... eight... seven... six..."

The patient's eyes closed.

Dr. Huber faced Bryan. "They always sleep by six. Next time she wakes up, cars will be driving in the sky and tours to the moon will be as common as beach holidays."

Next, Dr. Huber stopped her heart by lethal injection. He pronounced the woman dead and asked his assistant to write up her death certificate.

"What's wrong with her?" asked Bryan.

"Breast cancer." Dr. Huber explained that an ultrasound had led to a mammogram, which led to a biopsy, which came back as Stage 4 cancer. The only viable medical option after that was cryopreservation.

"Is she leaving behind any family?"

"No. She has been a widow for the last three years. She received the death insurance from her late husband, and that's how she can afford her cryopreservation, and she never had children because of ovulation problems, something we could probably fix in the future if she was twenty years younger."

"It doesn't sound like she has anyone to live for."

"She's fortunate. The hardest part about cryopreservation isn't the goodbyes to those you love before death, it's saying goodbye to them when you come back, and they are in *their* graves."

Dr. Huber seemed to take a certain pleasure during the procedure, while Bryan stood mesmerised, watching as the lifeless body was connected to a heart-lung machine to keep her blood circulating while also cooled to just fifteen degrees. With focussed intensity, Dr. Huber held an enormous needle, ready to administer the calcium channel blockers, including nimodipine, crucial in preventing the movement of calcium ions into the heart cells and blood vessels, increasing the flow of oxygen-rich blood to the heart and other vital areas of the body. The process felt both clinical and surreal, as if science were walking a fine line between life and death.

"Why is she put on a life-support machine if you've just stopped her heart?" asked Bryan.

"When a person dies, that is, at the cessation of heartbeat, nearly all the cells in the human's brain may still be alive. At five to ten minutes without oxygen, degenerative processes begin in the circulatory system of the brain. You know, blood agglutinations and vascular spasms. The same for the internal organs. Why do you think people sign over their organs after death?"

"The exact moment of death does not immediately affect all cells, tissues, and organs," said Bryan.

"Correct. And it's the same with the brain."

"Really?"

Dr. Huber nodded and adjusted his glasses. "Yes, really. After many hours at room temperature, though, arachidonic acid from membranes and lactic acid produced by anaerobic metabolism is released, increasing tissue acidity. In twenty-four hours at room temperature, the brain starts to dissolve. Just like the ceramic bowl, there's no retrieving it once that process is in motion. That is why patients get put on a heart-lung machine, and why we must cool the patient as quickly as possible. Oxygen is pumped around the body while it's in the cooling process, and it delays degeneration of the tissues, cells, organs, and brain. Manual CPR only provides one-third of the total circulation, but a heart-lung machine can provide up to two-thirds the circulation needed for oxygenation."

"Yes, that makes sense," said Bryan.

Holding another enormous syringe, Dr. Huber said, "We now inject her with blood thinners and radical inhibitors to prevent the damaging effects of the free radicals."

The patient was lifted from the gurney and put inside a square tub. Flowing ice water was administered from a squid-like device held by the assistant and was concentrated around her head, neck, groin, and underarms.

"This process cools the patient quicker than ice bags or an ice bath. It's quicker when applied to a broad surface. She will be ready for blood washout and the organ preservation solution thirty-five minutes from now. For larger patients, it can take longer, up to an hour."

Dr. Huber led Bryan back into Lab 1, where they talked more about the science.

The vice president, meanwhile, left to make an urgent call.

By the time he returned, the assistant called Dr. Huber for stage two of the cooling process.

Bryan saw a temperature monitor beside the heart-lung machine that read 283 K. "What temperature is that?"

"10°C. Each ten-degree reduction in temperature cuts the metabolic rate in half."

Kane elaborated. "We don't use Centigrade or Fahrenheit here. We use the Kelvin Scale. The K stands for Kelvin."

"Yeah, I just find Centigrade easier to relate."

Dr. Huber continued. "The blood is now replaced with a saline solution to stop the tissues shrinking or swelling, and ensures organ preservation. The solution is a physiological imitation of the blood but without the complicated clotting properties. Shortly after that, I'll add the cryoprotectant as I explained before to stop the ice formation crushing the cells. You know, even during the most precise microsurgery, the surgeon's scalpel cuts through thousands of living cells. It moves billions of molecules out of position. In theory, every surgical procedure is in fact an extremely violent act. Unlike nanotechnology, which makes mostly scientific repair. After an operation, the body's molecular machinery automatically places things back in the right position."

Dr. Huber had to manipulate the brachiocephalic trunk, the carotid, and the vertebral arteries and cannulate them on both the right and left sides. He carefully used a scalpel to make a precise incision in the jugular vein, then followed with a pair of forceps to gently pry open the tissue. This allowed the patient's blood to drain smoothly through slender tubes into a sealed containment tub.

"Now that the metabolic rate has dropped, and oxygen-carrying water has increased, the patient no longer needs her blood. We'll label and store this for her until she is returned to this world."

Dr. Huber massaged his eyes beneath his glasses. "We're finished. Perfusion and cooling have been completed. We'll now take her to the bassinet of silicone oil for the next stage."

Bryan was about to ask what it entailed when Dr. Huber continued.

"Silicone oil cools fast and remains in liquid state for up to 173 K. Or -100°C."

Bryan followed Dr. Huber into another room, where he saw a deep-sized insulated tub filled with silicone oil cooled with dry ice. Now naked apart from the affixed silicone cups, the woman's body was hoisted with a winch attached to a hammock-like stretcher and carefully lowered into the bath, twenty inches deep. Bryan watched the woman's bloodless, white corpse sink in the ice-cold silicone oil. Bubbles popped on the surface.

Having closed a lid over the body where it would remain for the time it took to reach the temperature of dry ice, Dr. Huber carefully removed his gloves and placed them on the table. "In three hours, we will place the body into a cryostat, which operates the same as a thermos flask with a double wall insulating the interior. Liquid nitrogen freezes a body so rigid it cannot bend. She'll be hard like a surfboard by the end. After this process, the final body temperature will be 77 K, or -196°C, and not one degree under or over. From that point, all we need to do to maintain core temperature is top up the liquid nitrogen because it slowly boils off."

"What happens if there's a power cut?"

"The cryostats do not rely on solely electricity, so there's absolutely zero risk of premature warming if we ever have a power problem."

"What do they run on?"

"Fuel-operated generators. They can make the cryostats run for seventy-two hours in the absence of electricity."

Bryan followed Dr. Huber to an enormous temperature-controlled storage room. "And how does the revival process work exactly?"

Dr. Huber shelved the patient's blood with hundreds of other labelled containment tubs. "Reanimation is performed by repairing the damage caused by the lack of oxygen, the cryoprotectant toxicity, and thermal stress to the bones using nanotechnology to regenerate the tissues."

It occurred to Bryan that perhaps the world wasn't ready for cryonic healthcare. Future generations might reject their predecessors assimilating back into a society in which they did not belong. Humans were supposed to die to make room for the next generations, maintaining a smooth and fair life cycle. On the face of it, ELF had nothing but good intentions, providing hope to the hopeless, health to the unhealthy, and life to the lifeless. The medic in him accepted ELF for what it was: a world-class, life-saving institution.

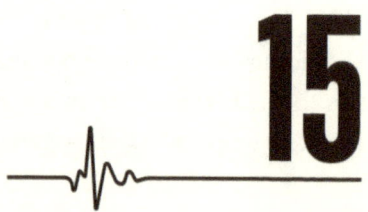

15

At the end of the orientation, several hours after his arrival, Bryan returned to the president's office. He sat in the chair opposite President Smolensk, who had his back turned facing a painted canvas. He stopped to wipe his brushes and blew gently onto the canvas, then swivelled, removing the monocle from his left eye.

"What do you think, Dr. Morgan?"

"It's a beautiful landscape. Is that Venice?"

"About the foundation?"

Bryan managed a smile, despite his fatigue. "I'd be lying if I said I wasn't impressed."

"Escaping mortality is a powerfully seductive fantasy and something everyone dreams and hopes for. The problem with hospitals is that even when a new ward is built or a wing is refurbished, improving the strained welfare systems, it's often too little, too late. Governments allocate such small sums to upgrade facilities, but this creates a backlog of renovations, extensions, and upgrades, leaving countless patients stuck in limbo, waiting for critical surgeries or treatments. Down here, things are different. There's no endless waiting in a conscious state. Our patients don't endure repeated visits for the same advice. They come in sick but hopeful, and when they leave, they are healed and grateful. The long stretch of time between their arrival and recovery is simply a welcome break from the debilitating illnesses that plague them."

"What about their families and friends?" asked Bryan. "I couldn't think of anything worse than being separated from the people I love for thirty, forty years."

"Which is more heartbreaking? Separation from friends and family for decades, or separation lasting forever because of death? But don't be disillusioned. Cryopreservation is not for everyone. You would be surprised to learn just how many people choose to take their chances rather than wake up in an unfamiliar future. It's why we must be selective, carefully choosing people who trust and believe in medical science and who have forward-thinking minds."

President Smolensk scooted his chair across the floor to a cabinet to retrieve his monocle case, which was next to a well-chewed briar pipe.

Bryan scanned the office and spotted a black and white portrait of a gentleman with a white beard and dressed in a waistcoat under a blazer.

"Is that your father up there?"

The president glanced over at the painting. "That's Lord Kelvin. He was a British mathematician and physicist born in Belfast in 1824. He spent most of his adult life working at

Glasgow University until he died in 1907. Lord Kelvin was the first person to develop the theory of the absolute scale of temperature. His diligent work with Carnot's cycle led to the second law of thermodynamics, the law which explains that heat cannot spontaneously pass from one object to another without energy in some form or another being transformed or lost. In the mid-nineteenth century, Lord Kelvin came up with the temperature scale, measured in degrees Kelvin. The freezing point of water is 273 K, and the boiling point is 373 K. The zero point of Kelvin is considered to be the absolute lowest possible temperature of anything in the universe. I'm sure you're aware of absolute zero, Dr. Morgan."

Bryan nodded.

"Lord Kelvin believed it was inconvenient to measure negative values when calculating temperature, so he invented the Kelvin Scale for its logic and suitability. Only scientists use the Kelvin Scale, while Centigrade and Fahrenheit Scales are used throughout the world in our daily lives. But all three temperature scales are connected through the triple point of water. At this temperature, water vapour, liquid water, and ice co-exist simultaneously. The Kelvin Scale measures extreme hot and cold temperatures such as liquid nitrogen and liquid helium. Nitrogen condenses to a liquid at 77 K and helium at an incredible 4.2 K. The surface of Pluto, for example, is 53 K, and the temperature of the sun is at almost 6,000 K. These are but a few examples of how practical the Kelvin Scale is in scientific terms."

"Was he world-renowned?"

"Not a man of history, are you. In the scientific world, yes, and he was knighted in 1866 by Queen Victoria. He was buried in Westminster Abbey next to Sir Isaac Newton. If you ever visit Botanic Park in Belfast, you'll see a large lifelike statue in his honour."

Bryan made a superfluous gesture to show his intrigue. He wasn't much of a history buff, but certain historical facts caught his interest.

"It is said there are only two certainties in life: death and taxes. Our continued success here revolves around proving this statement obsolete. At ELF, we avoid death, and we do not pay taxes."

His comment raised a pertinent question from Bryan. "If nobody knows about ELF, how does the staff manage to hide their salaries from the government? Surely tax evasion has come into question at the government level?"

"Let me be clear here. We don't evade tax, and we are not in the business of hiding anything. We operate independently from other organisations. Employees are paid monthly, and all transactions go through our bank in Balzers."

"Balzers? Isn't that in Liechtenstein?"

"Your geography is better than your history, Dr. Morgan. Our staff can access their income whenever they need it. The bank uses strict privacy and security measures, ensuring that all transactions are untraceable, so they don't have to worry about taxes or the Inland Revenue. It's all above board."

ELF transactions went through an international bank in Balzers, adept at managing sizable, attention-grabbing cash accounts while showing little interest in their origins. As an offshore financial centre and tax haven, Liechtenstein was an ideal choice, offering banking regulations considered even more secure than those of neighbouring Switzerland.

It was evident from Bryan's interactions with President Smolensk that he was of considerable wealth. His opulent lifestyle spoke volumes; his wealth afforded him both the comfort and luxury most could only dream of. With his vast resources, he could wield power that extended way beyond financial means: he could buy power, people, protection, and popularity. Bryan wondered if money served as the driving force behind his actions, overshadowing other motivations. Perhaps it wasn't passion or a desire for recognition that drove him, nor was he influenced by religious beliefs. Instead, a relentless pursuit of wealth that fuelled an insatiable desire for control and dominance. In his world, financial success equated to a measure of respect and authority, and Bryan saw how this wealth sculpted his persona. This perspective gave him pause. It made him consider the nature of ambition and the lengths one might go when motivated by financial gain. The president's character was a reminder that, in some circles, love and compassion took a backseat to power and influence, shaping a reality where morality could be easily compromised for the right price.

"You may be able to avoid tax," said Bryan, "but death will never be avoidable. Delay death, absolutely, but it will get us all in the end."

President Smolensk pursed his lips, partly amused by the suggestion, perhaps even partly insulted.

"So why does cryopreservation remain unsanctioned?" he asked, quickly changing the topic.

"Our proposal to the Liechtenstein Head of State and its Cabinet members was rejected. With advancements in our technology and the promising results from our research, we believed we could secure their support. Even so, they were concerned about the ethical implications and the potential societal impact of cryopreservation. But they will understand

and regret this one day, and ELF will set the benchmark for world health preservation."

They spent the next two hours chatting about Bryan's life, his politics, dreams, ambitions, sacrifices he would have to make, expectations of ELF, and his career goals, compatibly aligned with the job on offer.

The president put his elbows on the desk. "So, I believe we have covered everything? Unless you have anything else you want to ask?"

Bryan stretched his legs and suppressed the urge to yawn, his tiredness catching up with him. "No, I think that's all."

"I hope you see this for what it is. It's an opportunity of a lifetime, guaranteeing you a financially secure future and huge success when we go mainstream. And when it does, the harsh restrictions we all have to bear right now will no longer apply. The question you must ask yourself is are you ready to give up everything you have?"

Bryan saw the pros and cons of accepting the offer and turning it down. President Smolensk and everything he'd seen had been so persuasive, he convinced himself a rewarding future lay within his reach. He just couldn't be sure he would be able to convince Julia of its merits.

"When do I start?"

"You have twenty-four hours to tie up any loose ends."

"Only twenty-four hours?" he replied, his face showing disbelief.

"There's no time to lose. How do you think your wife will take it?"

"Not sure. We're used to being apart. I used to be away for months when I worked as a medic in the Royal Army... why am I telling you this? You know already."

"That was then, this is now."

"Since the break-in at our house, she hasn't been herself, but I'm hoping she will understand that I'll be doing this for both of us."

"Absolutely. Nonetheless, you must never speak of ELF. Not to anyone. It's strictly forbidden. May I recommend you tell her you are working for the government, and that your role is classified? It's what our other employees say. It helps to avoid difficult questions and subsequent lies."

"You claim to know me so well already, you must know I'm not a good liar."

"Then you face your first challenge."

"One last thing," said Bryan. "How do I get back?"

For his answer, President Smolensk nonchalantly held up a black hood. "The same way you came in."

16

Later that day, as dusk approached, Bryan and Julia met by the river at six. This spot held special memories for them; it was where they had gone on their first date and where Bryan had proposed two years later on a bridge. Under it, in fact, on the pavement flanking the river. In their first two years of marriage, they spent every day together and most weekends, until Bryan was called up to the Falklands War in 1982, along with the other medics.

Julia was a few minutes late. She walked towards Bryan with crossed arms, looking anxious and upset. No doubt she had spent a full day worrying over his whereabouts, making it difficult to raise a smile. She tried, but the result was just a weary, fake contortion of the lips.

They met face to face with a mix of caution and awkward pleasure of seeing each other.

"You look lovely," said Bryan.

"Thanks."

They stood in silence, gazing off in a opposite directions, until Julia said, "Are we going to just stand here all night?"

Bryan smiled. "Shall we walk a while?"

He took Julia's hand. He was tempted to wrap his arm around her shoulder or slip it around her waist, like a normal husband holding his wife in public. Instead, he stuck with the hand holding.

Julia asked Bryan a question, but he was distracted, staring at the river without actually seeing it.

"Earth calling Bryan?"

"Sorry, what?"

"I asked you where you were last night."

Bryan's heart sped up. "I'll tell you about it over dinner."

A complex of new restaurants at the river's edge offered a variety of culinary options. Bryan had booked a table in a Spanish restaurant near the window with river views. His stomach churned with nerves as he sat at the table. He knew if Julia didn't warm to an idea right away, she wouldn't warm to it at all. And they had six months of unresolved marital tension to wade through.

The silence between them dragged on as they waited for table service. Bryan fiddled with a serviette, folding the edges over, making mini sculptures.

"So, where did you get to last night?"

He looked up from the serviette. "I was at my interview."

She frowned. "That was yesterday evening. Where were you the rest of the night? I was so worried about you. I almost called the police."

The waitress came over to take their drinks order.

"Red wine," said Julia.

Bryan looked down the wine list and pointed at the most expensive one he could find. "Make that a bottle, please."

"No problem," said the waitress.

When she left, the conversation resumed. "My interview took longer than I expected. And I went to see my mother this afternoon."

Julia rolled her eyes.

"I went to say goodbye. You're right, I do visit her too often. I need to let go. It's time I sorted my life out."

She took his hand. "I'm always here for you. You know that."

He smiled. "Listen, I have good news."

"You got the job!"

He nodded and handed her an envelope.

She tore the seam and reached inside, pulling out a bank card. "What's this?"

"I opened a new account for us. You'll find about twenty grand in there. And that's just the beginning. I've already paid off our outstanding bills, and we are all caught up with the mortgage repayments, meaning the repossession order will be cancelled."

Her mouth fell open. "Is this for real?"

He nodded excitedly. "This is my sign-on bonus. By next year, we should be able to afford to move away and buy a new house outright."

Her bright red lips curved into a rare smile. "So, tell me about this new job."

Bryan wanted to tell Julia the truth. Instead, he used the president's lie and told her he would be working with the government.

Julia's eyebrows shot up, and she blinked rapidly. "The government?"

"Yes."

"Really?"

"Is it so hard to believe?"

Her frown slowly morphed into a smile.

It was the first time Bryan had seen her smile properly all year. Her expression was filled with the honesty and kindness he'd fallen in love with all those years ago.

"What kind of work will you be doing?"

"At this stage, it's a little unclear. All I know is it involves counselling and medical care. Anyway, tonight we celebrate."

They touched glasses when the wine arrived.

Julia enjoyed a long sip and smiled again. "Before I forget, your father tried calling again. I asked him what it was about, but he wouldn't tell me. He said he needed to speak to you in person."

Bryan raised his hand to his forehead. He had learned to never think about his father. Occasionally, he tried, but some automatic reluctance prevented him from doing so. "I have nothing to say to him."

The restaurant had become noticeably more crowded at the dinner-time peak hour, and wonderful seafood aromas teased the air, alerting Bryan to his hunger.

"So, when do you start your new job?"

"First thing in the morning."

"Wow, look at you, Mr. High-flyer. What time do you think you'll be home? I might cook a curry."

Bryan took a long sip of his wine, unable to predict how she would react to the news.

Julia couldn't ignore the change in Bryan's face. "What?"

He stroked her cheek and smiled, but she saw through it. "What is it?"

He withdrew his hand. "Firstly, I want you to know I love you."

"Come on, Bryan. Spit it out!"

"I won't be coming back."

"Tomorrow night?"

"I won't be coming back for a while."

"I don't understand."

"I still get holidays, sixteen weeks per year, but when I'm on duty, I'm on duty permanently. I'll be provided with my own accommodation and meals and stuff."

Julia remained quiet.

"Just think about the money."

She sighed. "What good is money if I don't get to spend it with you?"

"This is a great opportunity, Julia. For both of us. I think I can be happy again. This is just what I need, what I've been looking for."

"There's something you're not telling me."

"I've told you everything I know, which isn't a great deal, I admit."

"Where will you be working?"

Bryan lowered his eyes. "I don't know exactly."

She shook her head.

"I'll call you all the time. You know that."

She said nothing.

"I don't really know what else to say."

"Nothing!" She stood and left the restaurant.

Bryan paid for the wine and left a few minutes after her. He decided to walk home to clear his head. He took an alley leading into a park filled with shapeless shadows. Rounding the corner, he saw a rabble of teenagers spraying graffiti on the wall under a footbridge. One kid kicked a full can of beer and laughed moronically when it skittered across the path and exploded against the wall.

Bryan folded his arms, watching with increasing distaste.

When the lads saw him, they ran off, laughing boyishly and swearing. One skipped backwards and flipped him the finger.

Bryan turned towards the wall, where a mural of swirling psychedelic patterns sprawled across it. His mind drifted to thoughts of the younger generation, their lack in moral values and social responsibility. Twentieth-century Britain seemed to be descending into a cesspit of vandals, thieves, and violent criminals. Graffiti had become an unpleasant stain on society. Councils poured thousands of pounds into scrubbing toilets, park benches, street signs, and transport stations clean, and yet every day, crude markings appeared in his neighbourhood. He was tired of it all. And then it hit him: he was about to leave this crumbling society behind. His eyes settled on the graffiti before him with letters three feet high spelling out *Immortality*.

Bryan's thoughts drifted back to the foundation, where cryobiologists worked tirelessly, creating chemical formulas, manipulating science, pushing the boundaries of medicine, and inching ever closer to achieving what had once seemed impossible—extended life, perhaps even immortality. It was a relentless pursuit, a race against time and nature, and Bryan couldn't help but marvel at the audacity of it all.

The alley was the quickest route home, but Bryan turned back, avoiding the bridge ahead and the potential ambush awaiting him on the other side. He soon found himself back where he started the evening: at the river.

17

Julia was already in bed when Bryan arrived home. It was late, and he had to be up in a few hours. He would leave packing until sunrise and climbed straight under the duvet.

"You leave in the morning, then?" asked Julia.

Bryan flinched. "I thought you were sleeping."

"How can I possibly sleep?"

Bryan could smell alcohol on her breath and spotted an empty Shiraz bottle on her bedside table.

Julia rolled over in a fluid motion and straddled him, her body warm and bare against the cool air. She leaned down, her lips brushing his neck, sending a shiver through him. Her kisses were soft at first before finding his mouth. He tasted the remnants of her lipstick and the rich, lingering flavour of the red wine. The scent of her light, floral, and intoxicating perfume drifted over him, reminding him of the effort she had put into their dinner date. Her fingers slid beneath his shirt, tracing slow, deliberate lines over his skin. She tugged at his T-shirt, pulling it over his head, and he allowed her, the fabric slipping away as easily as his resistance. Her hands moved to his boxer shorts next, peeling them off, and this time, he did not stop her. They lay skin to skin beneath the duvet, their breaths coming quicker as they began to explore each other's bodies. Their gentle touches grew more urgent, and the quiet intimacy between them built with every passing moment.

Bryan was instantly hard, and Julia rolled back on top and took him inside her. He then took her nipple in his mouth, arousing her. Their breathing intensified, bringing them both closer to climax. They rolled over to the other side of the bed, Bryan now on top, still cradled in her arms. He pushed into her hard and deep, and as she approached orgasm, she dug her nails into his chest. He finished, too. He couldn't recall a time when he'd been more consumed by the moment. After all the talking, reasoning, hiding, and the endless squabbling, their physical connection felt more powerful than arguments ever had. It was more rewarding and healing than any words. Their raw, primal urgency tore down walls they hadn't even realised were there, bringing them closer in ways they hadn't imagined possible.

That night, his last in the house, Bryan lay awake thinking about ELF and his decision to join the foundation. He hadn't thought about much else, running through the pros and cons, debating in his head, swinging one way and then the other. He knew deep down it was selfish to take another job that would pull him away from Julia. But wasn't it just as selfish of her to try to stop him? She'd been through a lot recently.

The break-in had shaken her, and the looming financial strain weighed heavily on them both. His brooding, feeling like he was the one being hard done by, only added to their problems. Still, by accepting the job at ELF, he could get them out of the financial mess drowning them, fast. With the money he'd earn, they could turn their lives around, first by moving out of the neighbourhood that had become a constant source of anxiety and into a better home in a safer area. He could make up for the losses they'd inadvertently suffered on the current property and give them a fresh start. But did it really have to be with ELF? Surely there were other well-paying jobs out there that didn't require separation for such long stretches. Yet when he thought about it, he couldn't come up with any alternatives. No job in his field could ever match the financial package ELF offered. The benefits, the salary, they were all unparalleled. Even if he worked two full-time jobs elsewhere, it wouldn't come close to what ELF was willing to pay. It was a harsh reality, but one he couldn't ignore. ELF represented the quickest route out of financial trouble, even if it meant sacrificing more time away from his wife and added another layer of tension to an already strained relationship. But in his mind, wasn't the payoff worth it? The chance to finally escape the constant stress and to give Julia the security and peace she deserved? Still, the nagging doubt did not go away. Something deep down told him not to take the job.

It was growing light when Bryan entered the lounge with his bags all packed. He found Julia staring at the carpet with her chin in her hands. When she looked at him, the heat in her gaze threatened to scald him. "You're going through with it? You're leaving?"

Bryan rubbed his tired eyes. "I have to do this."

Julia rose and walked towards him. She hugged him, and he responded by wrapping his arms around her, stroking her head. He could smell her creamy coconut shampoo, the same product she'd used for years. He would miss it.

Suddenly, she pulled back and, without warning, slapped him hard across the cheek.

Bryan felt the sting in his face burrow down to his skull. "What the hell was that for?"

"You're a coward!" she snapped, her voice trembling with fury. "Always running from your problems. It's why you quit your job, why you changed your last name after your father walked out on you."

"I changed my name because I was adopted," Bryan shot back. "I had no parents."

"Exactly. And now you're avoiding your father because you're too scared to face what you're feeling."

"What kind of father abandons their child? He doesn't even visit Mum's grave."

"Did it ever cross your mind that maybe it's too painful for him? That he can't face it?"

"He couldn't care less about her *or* me."

"It wasn't because he didn't love you that he left. It was his way of dealing with grief."

"You don't know that."

"You've got to let it go."

Bryan could agree he had trust issues, but disloyalty went against his beliefs. He always stood by his morals. "I can't."

Julia's head dropped. "So, he left you, and now you are leaving me. Is that how it works on your side of the family?"

"That's not fair! What choice do I have? If I don't take this job, we'll lose the house."

"Why can't you just get another job?"

"What medical practice is going to want me after what happened? And I'll never receive an offer like this."

There was a moment of intense standoff, and then a black Land Rover pulled up outside.

Julia stood at the bottom of the stairs, watching him zip up his suitcase and gather the remainder of his belongings. "You're abandoning me and our marriage."

"I'm doing this *for* our marriage. For our *futures*."

"Running away solves nothing."

"I promised to fix things, and that's what I'm going to do. I wish there was another way. But there isn't. I hope you can understand this."

"Don't go!" Her voice changed to calmer tones, but her eyes still made him feel like an arsehole.

He shook his head. "I have to do this. It's not just about the money. I need this. I'm nothing without this."

"You're not nothing to me."

He felt an overwhelming wave of guilt that held him back from addressing the core reasons behind his decision to leave. Life had forced him to grow up quickly; he married young and launched his career in the army early, which often meant long stretches away from home, stationed at various military hospitals across the country. He had always led his life filled with purpose and pride. But as he stood there, his emotions pulling him in different directions, he realised it didn't take a psychic to see where his current path was leading him: the drudgery of working another 9-to-5 job with average pay and dealing with the public was enough to drive anyone mad. He couldn't face that working lifestyle anymore. The thought of spending his life in that relentless grind made him feel grey, as if the vibrancy of his youth had already long since slipped away, and the spark that drew him out of bed each day had been extinguished long ago. He needed purpose, to be a part of something bigger. He wanted a life, not an existence, and ELF offered it.

He stood in the doorway with his luggage. "For what it's worth, I'm sorry. I love you with all my heart."

He turned and grabbed his jacket off the stand, draped it over his forearm, and left with tears streaming down his face.

He had already closed the door and was already inside the Land Rover when Julia found her voice and dashed out the front door. "Wait!"

But the Land Rover roared off.

On the final approach to the airport, Bryan took a box of Modafinil out of his pocket. Confident the agents in the front weren't looking, he swallowed a pill quickly and without water.

They pulled up outside the terminal half an hour before the flight was cleared for take-off. Two agents in black suits waited outside the revolving doors.

"Good to go, Dr. Morgan?"

The sacrifices he had made for his career weighed heavily on him, and he couldn't shake the fear he was sacrificing the very thing that mattered most—his relationship with Julia. He let out a long sigh. "Ready as I'll ever be!"

18

The CI agent appeared in the doorway, leaning in slightly. "Dr. Morgan has arrived."

President Smolensk looked up from the stack of papers in front of him, his sharp eye narrowing with focus as he set his pen down carefully. "Send him in."

The door clicked shut behind Bryan as he walked into the office towards the desk.

"Ready to begin?" asked the president.

Bryan pulled out the chair and sat. "I'm ready."

"How did your wife take the news?"

"Not as well as I would've hoped."

Smolensk put his elbows on the desk and laced his fingers together. "There's an irrefutable irony in your wife's middle name."

"What do you mean?"

"Julia Ambrosia Morgan? From the Latin *Ambrosius*?"

Bryan shrugged.

Smolensk raised an eyebrow. "Ah, that's right, you're not much of a historian. *Ambrosius* comes from Greek. It means *immortal*. Quite fitting, wouldn't you say?"

Bryan cast his mind back to the graffiti in the alley the night before, his superstitious nature aroused. "It was meant to be."

"Let's get down to business, shall we? First things first, the contract."

Bryan was given a black leather-bound file with an ornate fountain pen resting on the top. Inside was the contract, thick and heavy, awaiting his signature on the final page. It was so dense he figured it would take him at least a week to read through everything properly. Most of the document focussed on employee integrity. He wasn't permitted to mention the ELF name outside the foundation's walls. And while the job offered flexi-hours, he would essentially be on-call around the clock. The position came with a host of perks including onsite accommodation cleaned daily, free dental and healthcare with regular check-ups, and all meals available on demand, day or night. Buried in the pages was a statement about the cryonics program and its two decades of operation, likely intended to quell any doubts he might have had about the controversial nature of the work. It was all laid out in black and white, an offer almost too good to refuse.

Unsure how his knowledge and skills would need to adapt to this new position and environment, he asked what training he would receive. Smolensk informed him his experience *was* his training and that the keys to the job were congeniality and a willingness to connect with the patient.

"As stated in the contract, all external access is strictly prohibited until you've completed five years at ELF. We offer generous annual leave and encourage all our staff to take full advantage. We don't want burnout sneaking up on anyone. It's counterproductive. Also, let me remind you no literature, documents, or photographs can ever leave the foundation. Security will screen you both when you arrive and when you leave."

"I understand," said Bryan.

"I expect full cooperation from the staff. Incompetence will not be accepted. Excuses, backchat, or disobedience will not be tolerated. Am I clear?"

Bryan smiled to show his understanding. The opportunity to join such a forward-looking organisation was enough to accept the president's terms. He felt working for ELF would fill the void in his life.

Having signed the contract, he left the office and found a CI agent waiting for him in the corridor.

"I'll show you to your office," she said, and handed Bryan a swipe card and identity badge, explaining their purpose as she walked along the corridor. "Your badge must be worn at all times in the foundation. The swipe card provides you with access to the lifts, staffroom, the entertainment rooms, the sports facilities, your apartment, and your office."

After a series of left and right turns along the corridor, she stopped outside an office door, one of many. She pointed at the authentication panel on the wall. "Board members have access to all the rooms, labs, and offices in the foundation by using fingerprint authentication. Everyone else must use their swipe cards, which are renewed annually and are monitored by management."

Bryan pocketed the swipe card. He pinned the ELF badge to his top. It featured the Eye of God insignia with his name and employee number written underneath.

To enter his new office, he swiped the card, and an airlock parted the doors. He took two steps inside the dark, spacious room. A motion-sensor bulb grew bright, flooding the office with light. It was like nothing he had ever seen before and was immediately struck by how medically unofficial it looked. Ostentatious even. It had walnut panelling, tropical plants, and stunning paintings hanging on the walls. A sleek-looking leather sofa sat in the corner. On the other side of the room was a trolley bed with a privacy curtain attached to the wall.

Bryan sat at his desk, inspected his new workspace, sank into the leather swivel chair, and scooted backwards, enjoying his new space.

"Don't get too comfortable," said the agent. "I still have to show you to your apartment."

Inside the lift, Bryan studied a laminated poster detailing the schematics of the foundation. "There's something I still don't understand. How do you make patients disappear from the world for years and then reinstate them in society without raising questions?"

"Patients are legally pronounced dead. We stage a funeral, and people close to the deceased believe it's a genuine funeral. When the patient is reanimated, we arrange a new identity for them."

"How?"

"We have lists of gravesites all around the country. The gravesites belong to newborn babies who died shortly after birth."

"Why babies?"

"Babies who've passed away at such a young age often don't have their deaths officially recorded. We simply match our patients with one of these deceased infants who would have been a similar age, and the patient then assumes their identity."

On level three, the agent guided Bryan past an enormous canteen that served hot and cold meals around the clock. The aromas of freshly prepared food filled the air, drifting through the complex and seeping into the nearby staff apartments.

The agent used Bryan's swipe card to unlock the door to his apartment.

"Your first patient arrives tomorrow morning."

"What time?"

"Between nine and half-past."

"I'll be ready."

The agent walked off, leaving Bryan to step into his new home. The apartment featured a rectangular living room, a separate bedroom with an en-suite bathroom, and a compact, sleek office. There was no kitchen; all food and drinks had to be sourced from the canteen, either dine-in or takeaway. The space was furnished in shades of beige, equipped with every modern convenience and high-end gadget money could buy. The walls were adorned with misty blue and green wallpaper, an intentional touch, perhaps, to mimic nature, compensating for the lack of outdoor access as employees weren't allowed outside until they had completed five years of service.

Bryan spent the first half an hour unpacking his bags and placing his clothes in the drawers and closets. Afterward, he headed to the bathroom and stepped into the shower. The hot water cascaded over him, washing away the days' physical exhaustion, but doing little to ease his guilt. He stood under the stream for twenty minutes, his mind inevitably drifting to Julia. He pictured her at home, perhaps still angry, or worse, bitterly disappointed. No matter how long he stayed under the hot stream, his guilt over the distance he had put between them, both physically and emotionally, remained.

He slipped into comfortable clothes and climbed onto the bed, essentially a rectangular niche in the wall. Hands behind his head and feet crossed, he stared up at the concrete ceiling. A message in big, black letters was written across the concrete and circled.

He stared at the message in ponderous speculation. Who had been bold enough to write it? And why? And what did *find the lie* mean?

19

While travelling through Raipur in India in 1977, a young man named Alexander contracted severe malaria from a mosquito carrying a protozoan parasite. A rapid clinical diagnosis was essential, providing him with time to consider his options. Unfortunately, those options were limited since malaria was an incurable disease. Five months after receiving this grim prognosis, he was approached with an invitation to ELF for cryonic treatment.

After fifteen years in cryopreservation, Alex had spent three hours undergoing reanimation. He awoke with a fever and nausea, his malaria symptoms mimicking the onset of the flu. Temporary muscle paralysis resulting from reanimation had left him confined to the recovery bay. The cryobiologists had spent a further forty-eight hours keeping him hydrated. Now, having been discharged from the recovery bay with full muscle sensation, Alex was ready for the second stage of his recovery: psychotherapy and re-immersion into a society he no longer knew.

The lights slowly and silently shone as Bryan strolled into his new office. He wore a freshly ironed shirt unbuttoned at the top. Ties weren't required. He hated ties and considered them a colonial noose for men. It felt good to be employed again, signalling a crucial turning point in his life. After so long in limbo, the routine of a job brought a sense of purpose and stability that he had sorely missed. The thrill of stepping back into the medical arena reignited his passion for healing and caring for others. Belonging to a team and collaborating with colleagues who shared his dedication would fill him with renewed direction, camaraderie, and belonging. He knew he would revel in the daily interactions with patients, the chance to make a real difference in their lives, and the satisfaction of contributing to a greater cause.

Bryan consulted the notes on his first patient before he arrived and, in doing so, learned he was due for release, even though no cure was available for his malaria. So why had he been brought back? The answer was written in the notes. His monthly repayments had stopped because his father, also his guarantor, had passed away two years ago, and no money was left. Now it was Bryan's job to equip him for the new world, where he would die a lonely orphan due to a failed attempt at cryopreservation.

When Alex arrived, Bryan introduced himself and spent the next half an hour quizzing him to establish his cognition. It included telling the time, simple and complex sums, some geographical and historical trivia, and recalling his personal details.

Bryan looked through Alex's history. "It says you went into cryopreservation in 1977. Did you leave behind much family?"

Alex raised his head slowly. After a long pause, he said, "My father." He looked at his lap. "My girlfriend."

Bryan nodded. "Tell me about them."

Alex recalled how everyone had urged him not to travel to India alone and how devastated they had been when he revealed he had contracted malaria. He deeply regretted not taking the necessary medical precautions before his trip; that decision had effectively derailed his life. He had no illusions about his father's chances of still being alive. At sixty-eight, when Alex underwent cryopreservation, his father had been grappling with his own health issues. As for his girlfriend, she was now fifteen years older than he remembered. Most likely, she was married, a mother now, and happily settled into her family life.

Circling back to Alex's reanimation, Bryan reinforced the complications malaria caused to the immune system, that red blood cells carried oxygen from the lungs around the body but when ruptured, the body's capacity to transport oxygen was severely compromised. He also reiterated he had been fortunate not too many red blood cells had been damaged because he may have become anaemic.

Alex was worried about making a new life under an alias, living alone as someone else with no support network.

Bryan explained it would take a lot of time, but everything would fall into place with his help and guidance, and Alex would learn to live with his illness. He added that many drugs were available on the market to help him soothe the pain and discomfort.

To establish a rapport, the first step in fostering trust and approachability, he briefed Alex on the country's current dire situation, a direct result of the recession. He explained how the decline in the housing market had triggered a surge in repossessions, even mentioning that he had been personally affected by the crisis.

"The pound has just crashed, too. They're calling it Black Wednesday."

Alex showed little interest. "I'm cold. Is that an effect of the malaria?"

Bryan glanced at the thermostat on the wall. "I have the room temperature set at twenty-two degrees." He got up and adjusted the thermostat to twenty-five. "Give it some time to warm up."

Bryan continued to talk about the challenges Alex would likely face and how to deal with them.

In the middle of him speaking, Alex got up and walked off, stopping in front of a mirror. "My face is yellowish."

"That's the malaria; it's still present in your system."

He paused. "I've wasted fifteen years of my life."

Out of professional habit, he gave the usual reassurances, using familiar platitudes to assure Alex everything would be fine. Anything else would only invite negative thinking.

"You have had a traumatic experience. Cryopreservation was always a gamble, but there is still hope. A new vaccine is being trialled in South America called SPf66. It fights malaria, to some extent. Who knows, it may pass the next phase trials and pave the way for a new cure that returns you to full health. In a few years, it might become a fully licensed drug."

Alex stared at his emaciated face in the mirror. "I may not have a few years."

"Try and think positively. First, you must listen to advice. That's a good place to start."

"What advice?"

"You'll need to stimulate your brain. When you can, you must eat lots of fruit and vegetables, and make sure you get lots of vitamins and minerals. You should try herbal extracts, too, like ginseng. Do plenty of physical exercise and try doing puzzles, creative tasks, and memory tests, like opening your cupboard and memorising the contents for two minutes and then testing yourself. You can try writing a list of instructions for simple tasks such as making a cup of tea or getting to the nearest supermarket. Another good memory exercise is to jot things down with your wrong hand or stir two cups of tea at the same time. These are all stimulants for the brain and don't require much effort."

His eyes narrowed. "Fuck this place and your advice!"

Bryan kept his expression as blank as he could. "Let's take a break, shall we? Why don't we reconvene in an hour?"

Alex left the office without saying another word and was escorted back to the recovery bay by a member of staff. But he was back within five minutes, peering around the door. "I'm tired," he said. "Can we meet up this afternoon?"

"Sure, perhaps we can get together at two o'clock?"

He nodded and left.

Since his cryopreservation, Alex had much to learn about the world before he could mentally and physically prepare to reintegrate into society. It had transformed in ways he could not yet grasp, filled with technologies that would likely feel foreign to him. He needed time, a luxury Bryan worried he might not have.

20

Sunny outside. Blue skies. Rain has stopped. Beautiful dawn. Air a bit nippy. Saw a big frog. The weather report came from a veteran cryobiologist, having just returned from his morning stroll, making him the envy of his colleagues at the breakfast table. They hadn't fulfilled their five-year probations. Conversations about the weather were a staple during mealtimes, and for good reason. The longing for sunlight on skin and fresh air in lungs was a shared sentiment among the staff, reminiscent of inmates inside maximum-security prisons. Five years without parole was a daunting sentence, and as they lived and worked, confined by ELF's walls, solitude settled in, an unwelcome precursor to depression. Yet, they had all made the choice to be there. No one had forced them against their will; they were there out of ambition, driven by the shared desire to push the boundaries of science and be part of something major. Had they maybe lived miserable lives on the outside? That seemed doubtful. As Bryan listened in on their lively discussion about the latest weather, he began to realise each staff member had been handpicked for their expertise and resilience. Mental health issues would have raised red flags among the CI agents during their six-month scrutiny. No, these people were sound of mind. In fact, their intelligence and determination shone through as they spoke, revealing not just their commitment to their work but also a shared yearning for the world outside, for life beyond the confines of this spectacular hi-tech prison. The question still remained: what sacrifices had they made to work there? What stories were hidden behind those bright smiles and eager voices?

Bryan was halfway towards biting his tuna sandwich when an attractive woman pulled out a chair next to him and sat down. She put her forearms flat on his table. "Ann Seymour. Doctor. You must be the new psychologist?"

"Bryan. Morgan. Dr. Morgan. Bryan is fine."

Ann was taller than him, her auburn hair a lighter shade, and she was younger. She wasn't beautiful in an obvious way. Her lips were a little too full for his liking, her eyes a little disproportionate to her other features, but the quirks added up to a face that was not only attractive but fascinating. Her lab coat was undone, and she wore a loose-fitting blouse that exposed some cleavage.

"Missing the outside yet?"

"It's only my fifth day."

"Feels like a month already, right?"

Bryan shrugged. "I don't know. I like it here."

"Let's see how long that lasts." She smiled. "I can't wait for Christmas."

"Have holidays booked, do you?"

"Me and half the people in here. It's the only time of year they allow lots of staff to take holidays at the same time. The president is a traditionalist and happens to be a huge fan of Christmas. The foundation goes into a sort of hibernation in the Christmas week. Will you be going home for it?"

"I hadn't thought about it, to be honest. But yes, I will."

"Did you leave any family behind?"

"My wife."

"Parents? Children?"

"No kids, and my mother died when I was fourteen."

"Sorry to hear that."

"I was adopted by another family."

"What about your dad?"

"Long story."

"What was it like growing up with adoptive parents?"

"They were nice. But after a year living with them, when I was fifteen, my stepmother died. She got hit by a car."

"Jesus! Are you cursed or something? I'm sorry, that was insensitive."

"It's okay. I've asked myself that question many times, believe me. I can be quite superstitious. Anyway, I was raised for a year by my adoptive father, who was so depressed that he ended up kicking me out. By the time I was sixteen, I was self-sufficient, got a job, and lived alone until I started uni. That's where I met Julia, my wife."

"And now you're here, away from all the troubles of life above ground. Away from your wife." She pursed her lips.

Bryan looked at his plate, trying not to blush. "What do you do here?"

"I'm a cryobiologist in the syndromes lab."

"How long have you been here?"

"This is my second year. I used to specialise in outdoor science, but it's far too competitive. I found myself constantly underpaid just so I could get work. In here, I save thousands a year."

Bryan took a bite of his sandwich, suddenly missing Julia and their mealtimes together.

Ann drank some tea, and he studied her broken fingernail and the skin on her hands, cracked and dry. She wore bright red lipstick and dark eyeliner, carelessly applied. If he had to compliment her, it would be on her natural beauty, not her cosmetic application. Self-maintenance was an unmet need in these confined settings. A confident individual, he deduced. Intimidated by no one. Popular in high school. The centre of attention. Lots of friends, mostly male. Disconnected from them down here. In this for the money and the experience. Ambitious and assertive. Unlikely to hang around long.

She sipped her tea. "How's your malaria patient doing?"

"Short-fused. He doesn't show much emotion. I'm trying to get him to open up. It's going to take weeks, maybe even months."

"How did he take the news?"

"About his father's death?"

"That he hasn't been cured."

"Well, he hasn't been cured because his father died. He was the guarantor. Alex wasn't overly surprised. Said he had always struggled with his health and drank too much, but he didn't know where all the money had gone."

"There's a rumour going around that they've raised the price of cryopreservation, and more and more guarantors are defaulting on their repayments."

"Can they do that, just put up the price?"

"Who is going to stop them? No one knows this place even exists."

"I guess so."

Ann scratched her head, looked around the canteen, and whispered, "I heard another rumour."

"What rumour?"

"That they have manufactured a cure for HIV and AIDS here in this building, and not one patient has received it."

"Do you believe it?"

"It's actually not a new rumour. Apparently, they created a cure four or five years ago, but they refuse to use it because they'll lose half their patients. If they *were* cured and sent back out into the world only to discover people were still dying of AIDS, it could blow the lid on ELF and what goes on here. With ELF being the manufacturers, nobody knows it exists, including the staff."

"If that's true, how do you know?"

"There's no smoke without fire."

Bryan liked Ann. She was straightforward and down-to-earth, a refreshing change from the platitudes he normally encountered during first meetings. But he didn't want to hear negative opinions about the foundation so soon after starting. From now on, he resolved to keep his colleagues at arm's length, uncertain about whom he could trust. Was Ann just another integrity test devised by management to determine if he had defiant tendencies? The more he thought about it, the less certain he became; he couldn't tell whether he was being assessed or manipulated, and that ambiguity made him wary. In this environment, where everyone had hidden motives, he knew he had to tread carefully.

Completing his first month at ELF, Bryan had settled into a comfortable routine that felt almost second nature. He rose at six, enjoyed breakfast at seven, and was at his desk by half-past, ready to kick off the workday. Typically, he wrapped up his tasks by six and would swing by the canteen for dinner on his way home. In this short time, he had also discovered more about himself; he realised he struggled to relax and always kept his guard up.

While he appreciated many aspects of working at ELF, there were things that bothered him. For one, he often found the president and senior staff to be arrogant, their demeanour dismissive at times. He also harboured lingering doubts that refused to fade. Management's hushed conversations with CI agents were frequently held behind closed doors, stirring up rampant rumours. The unsettling image of the cryopreserved man with the battered face in the private room, coupled with the vice president's reaction, only deepened his suspicions. Despite these concerns, he had to admit that, professionally, it was a fantastic place to work. His doubts started to dissipate, especially when he received his first paycheque, a tangible reminder of his reason for joining and a step towards financial security.

As the weeks wore on, Ann emerged as his sole friend. Problem was, she turned him on. He had to tell himself it was fine to be attracted to other women, providing he didn't do anything untoward. It made him feel no less guilty. To avoid his feelings developing into something more serious, he kept in limited contact with her. He attended to his patients and ate his meals alone in his room most days. He read lots. One book per week. The library had a wide range of fiction, which he gobbled up. And much of his time was spent with Alex. It wasn't easy to pull the troubled patient out of his tormented thoughts, but Bryan was beginning to see some progress. He showed glimpses of his spirit and personality and was even smiling again, despite the random meltdowns.

After six weeks, he was released and returned to society with a new identity to live out his days.

It was midnight on the first Monday in November when he found himself missing Julia more than ever. Just having her around to talk to and confide in. The sacrifice had been made; it was too late for regrets. His memories inexorably returned to the morning of his departure. He had left her on bad terms. There had been no time for any proper goodbyes. It had been so hurried and unceremonious. He had spoken to her a dozen times since his arrival. He wanted to call her now, yearned to hear her sweet voice, even though he knew from experience that it tended to make her decide she was missing him, even when she had accepted he would be gone for extended periods.

On the public telephone in the canteen, Bryan dialled his home number. The call diverted to the answering machine, so Bryan hung up. There was no way for her to return the call, and he had nothing worth recording, so he tried a second time, and was about to hang up again when she answered.

"*Julia speaking.*"

"It's me. You okay?"

"Doing all right. How are you?"

Julia went on to explain that she had been terribly busy, her words flowing quickly, as if trying to fit in everything she wanted to say in a limited timeframe.

Bryan didn't pick up on the strained tone in her voice at the time. He was too caught up in the whirlwind of his new job. Little did he know that, in the future, he would realise his mistake.

21

Bryan crushed the report into a ball and tossed it into the bin in frustration. He rolled his shoulders, sensing the tightness building up in them. Mostly done with the patient progress report, he glanced at the clock. Smolensk expected it on his desk before nine that evening. But before he could send it off, he needed to fix a few typos and trim out some unnecessary lines.

Recycled by a complex water management system, heavy rain caused the internal pipes to groan with the pressure put through them, a further distraction. It was taking him longer than anticipated to adjust to the subterranean lifestyle, and he struggled to make a conscious effort to positively marshal his thoughts. Perhaps he would feel more settled once he had a steady stream of patients and he could immerse himself more in his work.

He hand-delivered the report to Smolensk's office with five minutes to spare and stopped at the canteen on his way home, craving a hot drink. The canteen was empty, except for a single table occupied by a group of cleaning staff in their overalls.

Ann stood at the drinks machine in leggings and a figure-hugging top after a session at the gym, outlining her dazzling figure. Her damp hair hung in a sexy tangle at her shoulders.

Torn between tea and coffee, he opted for a hot chocolate from the machine and walked over to Ann.

"Good workout?" he asked.

Ann glanced up from her tray. "Oh, hi. Yeah, five miles on the treadmill. Would kill for a massage right now."

The image of her lying naked on a massage table, covered in oils and small towels, flashed through his mind before guilt took over and he banished the thought.

Heading towards a free table, Bryan and Ann passed an unclaimed tray of food at the end of the counter, which Bryan almost knocked with his hip.

"I've thought a lot about what you said about ELF and its AIDS treatment. Let's say, for argument's sake, they *did* have a cure. Why not sell it? They would make a killing."

Ann spoke through the vapour curling from her cup of tea. "Questions would be asked. The world would demand to know where it was manufactured. Remember, everything that happens down here is illegal. Yes, saving lives is noble, but how we save lives is against the law. They would only seek approval for the treatment if cryopreservation was officially sanctioned by the government."

"Do you think that will ever happen?"

"Not in a million years."

"Why not?"

"It's basically a question of ethics. When it comes down to parliamentary votes, the majority will always vote against it."

"So, you're saying the AIDS cure, if one does exist, may never be released because of politics?"

"Exactly. My advice to you is reap the financial benefits and leave the politics to management."

Bryan nodded. "I'm not saying I believe the rumour, but if it *did* turn out to be true…"

They both pondered it in silence.

Bryan sipped his hot drink. "Who was the psychologist before me? Who did I replace?"

"Dr. Fletcher. Funny you ask. He's the one who told me about the AIDS cure. Just a few days before you joined. Was absolutely convinced. Some people thought he had gone mad. Me included."

"Did he quit?"

"He just stopped showing up for work, never told anyone he was leaving, which is very strange, considering he worked here for ten years. Even stranger is he had just been promoted. He told me he was going to be working in the research and development field of neuropsychology, with a heavy focus on the complexities of brain-behaviour relationship. His purpose was to help the foundation to gain deeper insights into how neurological processes influenced behaviour, emotions, and cognitive functions. By studying cognitive impairments like memory loss, attention deficits, problem-solving difficulties, and the like, ELF hoped to develop more effective treatment methods. His research would aid in improving the lives of individuals suffering from brain injuries, neurodegenerative diseases, and other conditions that affect mental functioning. It was a role that combined his passion for neuroscience with the drive to make a real-world difference. Then, just before you started working here, he vanished without even saying goodbye."

"Was he depressed or something?"

"Like I said, his behaviour had become very strange, and everyone thought he was going mad, especially in the last few weeks."

"How so?"

"Just distant and edgy, like paranoid sometimes. He just completely detached himself from the staff. He would sit on his own at mealtimes and ignore everyone."

"What did he look like?"

"Thin, early fifties, longish white hair. He was a smart man, a mathematician, and a puzzle fanatic, always had his head buried in some kind of puzzle book. He loved anagrams and coded messages."

Bryan paused to think. "I think I might have seen him. In a cryostat."

Ann paused. "Why would he be in a cryostat?"

"Maybe he fell ill? That would explain why he was acting strange before he disappeared. Maybe he had no choice but to go into cryopreservation and wanted it kept secret."

"That makes sense. He was a proud man. I can imagine him keeping his health a secret. Which lab was he in?"

"It wasn't a lab. It was in a small room near the bathroom on the same level as the labs."

"I don't know of it."

Bryan shrugged. "Maybe it's reserved for staff only."

Ann stuck out her bottom lip. "Could be."

"One thing that struck me as odd, though; his face was all beaten up."

"How so?"

Bryan nodded. "Bruises. His nose looked broken, and he was missing some front teeth."

"Maybe he had a fall. If he was terminally ill, which would be the only reason he would go into cryopreservation, he was surely weak and fragile."

Bryan nodded, feeling more at ease about the situation. It made sense and explained why Kane had reacted that way. He must have tried to protect Dr. Fletcher's privacy. But this was counterbalanced by another, uneasy thought.

"Did he occupy the apartment I'm currently staying in by any chance?"

"Yes, he did."

"It must have been him who wrote *find the lie* above my bed, then."

"Sounds right. Like I said, he was the one who spread the rumours, saying ELF was full of lies and deceit. Find the lie is probably another one of his riddles. Anyway, I think I'm going to crash. I can hardly keep my eyes open. Night."

Bryan stayed, reflecting on the conversation he had just had with Ann. She loved to gossip, and every time they spoke, she eagerly launched into one of her gossip sessions. He worried she might spread the details of what he had seen in the private room, and feared those rumours would come back to bite him.

"Are you going upstairs?"

Bryan turned and saw one of the chefs staring at him. "Me?" he asked, pointing at himself.

"Yes. Can you take this tray up to Dr. Huber in lab one?"

He pointed at the tray of food Bryan had almost knocked off the counter. "He was supposed to collect it forty minutes ago. Would you mind?"

Bryan smiled. "Sure."

On level one, Bryan approached the AIDS and HIV lab and found the door wouldn't respond to his swipe card, so he knocked for a time and waited until a cryobiologist opened it.

"Room service!" he said with a smirk. "Can you pass this to Dr. Huber, please?"

The cryobiologist scowled and crossed her arms. "Do I look like a waitress to you?"

His smile faded. "Can I deliver it to him, then?"

She stepped aside and allowed him to enter.

"Where can I find him?"

She pointed right. "He'll be over by the utility room."

Strolling along the aisles, Bryan swung his head left and right as if crossing a road, observing the dead faces behind the cryostat windows. The tantalising smell of the lasagne on the tray reminded him of Julia's cooking. Just the thought of the cheesy layers and chunky mince made his mouth water.

Bryan spotted Dr. Huber at a terminal, his body hunched over the keyboard. "Evening, Doc."

He glanced up from his computer. "On the bench, please. And address me as Dr. Huber, *not* Doc!"

"Sure. Sorry. By the way, I think the food's gone cold."

"I prefer it cold."

Bryan smiled in his attempt to keep his tone mild. "You're welcome. Enjoy."

He chose a different route back, zigzagging between the numerous cryostats. With such few staff members on duty,

Bryan browsed the entombed patients, their unfamiliar faces frozen in their small windows like a wax museum of horror figures.

Each one was a victim of the HIV epidemic, either in the acute stage, chronic stage, or the final stage: AIDS. A term in cryopreservation had halted the HIV infection in its tracks, and they might one day walk away cured. Still conflicted after hearing ELF had life-saving AIDS medication at its fingertips and the patients were not receiving it, Bryan figured Ann was hardly the most trustworthy person; he didn't know whether he believed a word she said. And what was not confirmed as fact could not be regarded as truth.

The cryostats were nothing short of a medical miracle, a vessel operating outside the laws of time and transporting the occupants into the future. He stopped beside Cryostat 1109. It contained a massive man of about sixty. His skin and hair were frosted with ice, and his large, round face accentuated a look of hope. The next patient along was almost identical, yet there was a certain sameness to all the frozen faces around him. Every face bore the stillness of time, suspended in an eternal moment.

As he moved further down the row, one figure stood out: a pretty woman encased in cryostat 0016. Her pale face was illuminated by the bright interior light, contrasting against the darkened backdrop of the cryostat. The light cast a soft glow around her, accentuating the delicate features that remained untouched by time. He estimated she was about thirty-five, just like him. He stared at her ice-encrusted hair, pinned back by a headband, the frost giving it a shimmering appearance. Her bloodless lips were slightly parted, but there was a serene expression on her face, as if she were merely sleeping rather than frozen in a state of suspended animation. It struck him how peaceful she looked, embodying a stillness that seemed to transcend the cold metal of her surroundings. The sight was both haunting and beautiful, and he felt an inexplicable connection to her, a longing to understand the story behind her frozen expression, the life she had lived, and the reasons that had led her to this chilling state.

Someone smashed a glass. It echoed around the lab.

Bryan turned towards the noise, momentarily startled. As he pivoted back to the woman in the cryostat, something in his brain clicked into place. He studied her features again, examining the details more closely. Her mouth and eyes were sealed shut by the layers of ice, and he noticed a small mole beneath her bottom lip, a subtle detail that somehow made her become more human, more real. The sight of it stirred something deep within him—a familiarity that he couldn't quite place. As he leaned closer, he caught his reflection in the glass overlapping hers, their faces entwined. It seemed a perfect fit, like two pieces of a puzzle that had finally found their match. For a moment, he felt an uncanny connection to her, as though their lives were somehow linked. The longer he gazed at her, the stronger the pull became, as if she were silently calling to him from beyond the veil of ice.

Thoughts and memories clicked into overdrive as reality took hold. Tears filled his eyes, and he quickly blinked them away. His heart raced like a jackhammer, pounding against his ribs, and a wave of nausea rinsed through him. He pulled a biro from his top pocket and wrote 0016, the patient number, on his palm, dutifully underlining it like he did in his patient reports. He turned and bolted along the aisle, weaving in and out of the cryostats as he made his way to the distant door.

He passed a workbench and accidentally knocked a tray of 100ml dippers, which crashed to the floor.

Bursting out of the lab, Bryan sprinted towards the lifts and pressed the level three button. The ride felt agonisingly slow, and as soon as the doors opened, he bolted down the corridor to his apartment. Once inside, he collapsed beside his desk and buried his face in his hands, the tears flowing freely as he struggled to contain the flood of grief.

Eventually, exhaustion took over, and he cried himself to sleep, his head resting heavily against the cool surface of the desk.

Sometime later, he didn't know when, he awoke in a fog of confusion. He blinked to clear his vision, realising where he was and what had woken him: someone was banging on his door.

22

"You wanted to see me?" asked Bryan. He tried not to look as anxious as he felt, but the muscles in his shoulders went rigid with tension.

The door closed with a resonant, ominous click.

Vice President Spence dragged a chair across the floor and sat leaning forward. His intense gaze unsettled Bryan.

President Smolensk leaned back in his chair and folded his arms, giving Bryan a demonic stare through his hawk-like eye. "There was an incident in lab one earlier. Would you care to explain?"

How simple everything had been just a few hours ago, when his biggest decision was whether to drink tea or coffee. Now he faced a far more difficult choice: which lie to tell, all while trying to conceal the fact he was a terrible liar. Sharing his eye contact between the president and vice president, he took a deep breath and said, "I was looking at the patients in the cryostats, and I came across a bit queasy. I think the thick window glass strained my eyes, and the distortion made me feel dizzy. I have always been prone to motion sickness. For instance, if I put on someone else's glasses with thick lenses, I have to take them off immediately because they make me feel sick. Anyway, that's what happened... with the glass; I had to run back to my apartment to throw up. I barely made it in time."

President Smolensk looked unconvinced. "Who is Helen Mansfield?"

Bryan felt a lump materialise in his throat at hearing her name. One, because he hadn't heard it for many years. Two, because it confirmed the woman was indeed his biological mother, the one who had been snatched from his life when he was just fourteen years old. His memories flooded back: the fragments of laughter, soft whispers, and the warmth of her embrace. He would have recognised her face anywhere; it was engrained in his mind. The small mole beneath her bottom lip was unmistakable, a tiny detail he'd often traced with his fingers in his memories. Suddenly, it all made sense. ELF had taken his mother away from him, and the void it created had shaped his entire existence. It was the reason he often felt empty at night and lost during the day. Bryan now grappled with a mix of rage, sorrow, and the unquenchable desire for answers. It fuelled a fire within him, igniting a determination to uncover the truth about her disappearance and the impact it had made on his life. Now was not the right time. His mind was a vortex of confusion, his mind in conflict with his heart, and he knew he had to play his hand carefully in front of his employers, whose frowns intensified.

"I'm sorry, I don't—"

Smolensk cut in vehemently. "What were you doing in the lab?"

"A chef asked me to take a tray of food up to Dr. Huber. I said yes. Did I do wrong?"

Smolensk looked at the vice president and back at Bryan. "Dr. Huber knows he must collect his own food. We've told him enough times."

"I apologise if I caused any trouble."

"How did you get inside the lab?"

"One of the cryobiologists let me in."

A drawn-out silence made Bryan look away with guilt and shame, even though he had done nothing wrong.

"Let me be very clear, Dr. Morgan," said the president with a firm, unwavering tone. "Our employees are carefully handpicked for a reason. As you've seen first-hand, we have a rigorous selection process in place to ensure only the most suitable candidates are brought on board. We would never hire any individuals who have relatives or friends involved in cryopreservation. It's imperative to maintain a professional distance in this place."

He paused for a moment, letting the weight of his words settle. "We can't let emotion compromise our work, can we? This is not just about individual feelings or connections; it's about the integrity of the entire operation. Every decision we make here must be rooted in objectivity and scientific rigour. Emotions can cloud judgment, lead to biased decisions, and ultimately jeopardise the delicate work we do. Our mission is too critical to allow personal relationships to interfere."

The president's fierce stare emphasised the seriousness of the situation. "We deal with life and death here every day. The stakes are incredibly high, and we cannot afford any lapses in professionalism. The cryopreservation process commands a clear mind with focussed intent. Anyone with emotional ties to the patients would pose a risk to our mission."

He leaned slightly closer. "I trust that you understand the necessity of this policy. It's not meant to be punitive, but rather to protect the integrity of our work and the lives that depend on it. We have to maintain a sterile environment, free from any distractions or complications that could arise from personal connections. That's the only way we can ensure our research and procedures remain ethical and effective."

Bryan nodded. "I under–"

"I have staff members going through your records as we speak. If Helen Mansfield is related to you in any way, your employment will be terminated since it undermines company policy and can compromise decision-making. Until then, you leave me no choice but to place you on suspension."

Bryan tried to still his shaking hands.

President Smolensk paused a moment, his single eye on Bryan as if boring through him. "Funny, you were a medic during the Falklands War. You must have seen a lot of terrible things. Who would have thought a frozen face could make you feel so… giddy."

"Like I said, it wasn't the face. It was the glass. I'll know better next time not to look into the window for too long."

"There won't be a next time."

Bryan nodded again. "Understood."

Smolensk shut down. "Close the door on your way out."

Bryan rose from his chair and left the office.

Once Bryan closed the door, Smolensk turned to Kane and said, "I want them brought here, starting with the chef who asked him to bring the food to Dr. Huber. Check the cameras to find out who it was."

Kane nodded. "And Dr. Morgan?"

"I want him kept under twenty-four-hour surveillance!"

23

Back in his apartment, Bryan sat on his bed and removed his mother's photo from his wallet. It had been years since he last looked at it, yet it was always there, a memory he couldn't face but couldn't let go of either. As he studied her familiar features, his breath caught in his throat. Tears broke, leaving tracks of grief across his face. But now, underneath all that resurfaced pain, there was a spark of hope. She was dead. But not gone. She could still live. How had she contracted HIV? Or was it full-blown AIDS? She had been so full of life. How could it have ended like this?

Though his birth certificate read Bryan Mansfield, he had adopted the surname Morgan years ago. It was a defiant move, a way to spite his father, to cut ties with a man he wanted no part of. But in doing so, he'd unknowingly renounced a piece of himself. The hurt from all those years ago still ran deep and cut to his core. It was one thing to lose a mother to illness, but to have your father then walk out was a double whammy. His adoptive parents had provided him with a roof over his head and food on the table, but never the love he had needed. Over time and with maturity, Bryan's resentment towards his father had softened, his anger dulled by years of reflection. But that didn't erase the hurt or justify what his father had done. In the most traumatic moment of Bryan's life, when his grief consumed him as a teenager, his father had walked away, leaving Bryan to navigate the pain alone and barely bothering to call. The silence still stung, a wound that had never quite healed. But now he knew the truth. Staring at his mother's face, casting aside his family name was as if he had betrayed her memory. He carefully folded the photo and slipped it back into his wallet.

The discovery in Lab 1 had altered his understanding of the past, and he had to unravel, sort, and rebuild the narrative to make sense of it. Where to begin? His mother had gone into cryopreservation twenty years ago. She had been there this whole time. She had been buried, not in the ground but in a cryostat deep *beneath* the ground. He recalled her funeral. It had been faked, a carefully constructed lie. He remembered the casket, flowers, mourners dressed in black, weeping as if they were saying their final goodbyes. The casket had been empty. How many had known the truth? The grieving had seemed real, but the burial was nothing more than a ruse to maintain the illusion of death. In reality, her body had been transported under cover to ELF where doctors and scientists trusted their technology would advance far enough to revive her, to bring her back. She was dead. But not dead. She could live again once a cure for AIDS became reality. And now, it was. Dr. Fletcher had discovered it. Was that why he had ended up inside a cryostat, his body battered, his nose broken, his teeth missing? Had he been beaten to keep him silenced and the truth concealed, so the president and his cadre of cryobiologists could continue to swindle citizens out of their money and deprive them of life-saving medication?

And what about his father's role? He had let Bryan believe his mother was dead, complicit in the cover-up. He must have known. He must have been hopeful of a cure. Bryan's years in the Royal Army Medical Corps had given him an education far beyond what his father could have understood. He had trained in large-scale trauma care, worked in humanitarian crises, and attended countless conferences where he learned about diseases like AIDS in detail. His father couldn't have known what Bryan knew. But that didn't absolve him from keeping the truth hidden all those years.

Ann had been right all along. Cryonics, she had argued, would never receive government approval. It was too radical, too unnatural, to ever gain widespread support. Society just wasn't ready for such a profound disruption to the natural order. People were supposed to die. That was the way of life, the cycle everyone accepted. Birth, death, and everything in between was part of the human experience. Freezing people in time to defy the finality of death went against the essence of nature. No matter how advanced science became, most people would refuse to embrace the idea of tampering with mortality itself. Cryonics seemed like an affront to the balance of life, a desperate attempt to cheat death, to rewrite a script that had been written for all living beings since the dawn of time. And while a few, like Bryan, clung to the hope science might offer another chance at life, most couldn't comprehend freezing someone's fate in hopes of a future cure. To them, it was like delaying the inevitable, refusing to accept that death, as painful as it was, gave life its meaning. Ann had seen this resistance clearly, predicting the pushback long before it came. To many, cryonics wasn't about hope or possibility; it was a violation of nature's design, a breach of the cycle that gave order to existence.

Bryan waited for the inevitable knock at his door. Any minute now, the CI agents would learn of Helen Mansfield's past and connect the dots back to him. He was upset with himself for letting his emotions and the situation inside Lab 1 get to him. Now he was suspended, pending termination. The thought of losing his job didn't stir the fear he would have anticipated. In fact, he wasn't even sure he wanted to stay, at least not under these circumstances. Everything had shifted the moment he saw his mother's face. His belief in cryopreservation had turned upside down. It was a wake-up call, a harsh reality check. ELF wasn't offering hope; it was selling a lie. They preyed on the sick and desperate, giving them false promises while lining their pockets. Bryan realised now the organisation wasn't merely about saving lives but exploiting vulnerability, and he could no longer be part of that. It was difficult for Bryan to not act. He was not the type to sit back and watch injustice occur when something could be done about it. But what could he do? He couldn't challenge his superiors. His mother had taught him basic human values as a child. She pressed it upon him to always remain calm and to resolve a problem with a clear head. His father, very much from the school of hard knocks and stiff upper lips, would never agree. He had always believed in the confrontational approach to problems.

Full of mixed emotions, Bryan believed that if you had misgivings about elements of science, you didn't belong in its vicinity. Instinct urged him to allow cryonics to run its course and trust ELF's medical approach. His mother might not live in his lifetime, but at least she could live someday in the future. On the other hand, he just couldn't bear the thought of her waking up in the future to find everyone she had ever loved gone.

Uncertain about what to do next, he paced back and forth across his apartment. Everything was unravelling around him. He'd have done anything for a cigarette at that moment, the familiar burn to calm his nerves. A stiff brandy wouldn't have gone amiss, either. Times such as this warranted something strong to take the edge off.

Bryan finally drifted off around five in the morning, his body giving in to sheer exhaustion. But his sleep was short-lived. An hour later, the piercing noise of a polishing machine buzzed through the corridor, jolting him awake. Groggy and irritated, he opened his eyes. As his vision cleared, he saw the circled message on the ceiling above his bed: *Find the lie.* The words taunted him, staring down like a challenge to uncover the truth Dr. Fletcher had uncovered. His life felt like it had been built on deception, and he was being called to unravel it all. What was the lie? Was it about the cure? Did it concern his mother's death? Did it have links to Dr. Fletcher's sudden disappearance? Everything seemed tangled in a web of secrets, and the truth was buried somewhere deep inside.

He stretched his arms high above his head, trying to shake off the remnants of sleep. But no matter how hard he tried to rationalise the events of the last eight hours, questions filled his mind, and regret crept in like an unwelcome breeze.

He visited the canteen for a coffee to sharpen his mind and help him organise his thoughts. He ran into the chef who had given him the dinner tray. He received an ice-cold stare, but his tiredness and fragile state rendered him impervious. He also failed to register the unfriendly looks, twisted smiles, and venomous whispers from those around him. Only one thing was on his mind. He needed to see his mother one last time before he was expelled from ELF, to say his goodbyes. So what if it landed him in trouble? He was running out of time. Any minute now, a CI agent would arrive to escort him to the president's office, only to be told they had discovered the connection.

A second later, his thoughts were interrupted by another concern that rendered all others meaningless. Would they let him leave? Would they simply drop him back into society, fully aware of what he knew, under such precarious terms? Were they ruthless enough to harm him? There was no higher authority in place to stop them, and he didn't know them well enough to draw any solid conclusions. Worst-case scenarios plagued his mind as he weighed his options, and his stomach felt hideously alive with nerves.

One of the male cryobiologists waved to him. "Morning, Bryan."

Waiting for others to make decisions that would directly affect his future unsettled him, and he considered it essential to prepare for every contingency.

"I said good morning." The cryobiologist waved again.

Bryan looked up at his colleague. "Morning."

His eyes swung left and stopped at an unclaimed tray of food at the counter. Bryan pursed his lips as an idea slowly took shape. He stood, approached the counter, and collected a new tray. He filled it with a variety of breakfast items; a hot plate of eggs and bacon, yoghurt, a banana. He added some cutlery.

Wide awake and fuelled by coffee and determination, he stepped into the corridor and made his way to Lab 1.

24

President Smolensk paced along the corridor and entered the boardroom with an intensity that radiated barely contained menace. The room's thermostat registered high and mirrored his burning rage, because nothing irritated the president more than incompetence. He slammed the door and confronted the board members assembled around a large oval table that could easily seat twenty. Vice President Spence lounged in his chair with one leg crossed casually at the knee, an unwitting target for Smolensk's simmering fury.

The Sheriff sat beside Kane with a jam doughnut sitting on a napkin in front of him. The top buttons on his shirt were undone, exposing his hairless, pink chest, and sweat patches had amassed at his armpits and collar. Due to his surveillance work, the incident in Lab 1 involving Dr. Morgan had come to their attention.

A maid walked around the table, pouring fresh coffee for everyone. She spilled some and quickly mopped it up with a cloth, her nerves making her clumsy. Fortunately for her, the spillage was overshadowed by April's late arrival, earning her a wraith-like stare from President Smolensk.

April had dedicated fifteen years to ELF, overseeing the selection of hundreds of patients. The refined Englishwoman had poured millions of her own money into the foundation, advancing technology and securing her place at the executive table. How she had amassed her fortune remained a mystery, but rumours suggested she had tapped into the vulnerabilities of corporate accounts, exploiting the soft underbelly of online security. Allegedly, she had transferred large sums of stolen money into an account under a pseudonym, using phony identification to withdraw the funds and close the account, all within a single day. In the early eighties, computers were built with a basic set of login information and very little within the virtual ecosystem was password protected. Simple channels for sharing programs via open-access servers and an absence of hacking laws made cyber-trespassing remarkably easy, like walking into someone's house with all the doors and windows open and the alarms switched off. Working for ELF made her vanish from police radars. And by investing her money in ELF, it became untraceable.

Smolensk didn't care where her money came from. April was a rare jewel, the best of the best, with exceptional hacking skills, and he would have done whatever necessary to keep her, including turning a blind eye to her indiscretions. With the World Wide Web recently put in service, she had warned the board hacking was about to become a whole lot easier and more common, insisting on a crucial need to safeguard their computer network by upgrading to top-tier security systems and implementing full encryption.

"Sorry I'm late," she said, sitting opposite the Sheriff.

President Smolensk shut off the air conditioning, and the power wound down to an uneasy silence.

"Where's Dr. Huber?" he asked.

"Unavailable," said Kane.

Seated now at the head of the table, Smolensk pushed his fingers together, the tips whitening as he brought them to his lips. "That's unacceptable. He's the reason we're all here right now. Would someone go and tell him to join us?"

Kane shook his head. "He had a patient to attend to. Said he can't leave."

The maid finished pouring drinks and held up the ceramic pot. "Sir?"

Smolensk waved her away dismissively like she was scum. "What do we know?"

Kane, calm and cool as you like, slipped a stick of chewing gum inside his mouth. "Helen Mansfield is Bryan's biological mother."

The president's eye twitched, and it was tantamount to a volley of expletives in four-letter words. He paused, then told the board too many mistakes had been made, compromising the foundation, and risking everything they had worked hard to achieve. He expressed his utter disappointment in clipped, controlled tones, stating how useless they all were and how crucial it was to select suitable patients and personnel, with zero room for poor judgements. He lost his veneer of control and slammed his fists furiously on the table, causing April's coffee to spill.

"How did this happen?"

Kane was in a daydream, his eyes glazed over, his mouth no longer chewing, his awareness of those around him no more than a sleepwalker.

"Kane!"

He snapped back, his jaws mechanically restarting on the gum. "Sorry, what?"

"How did this happen?"

"There was a major mix-up. It was believed his mother was Felicity Morgan, who died in a car accident years ago. But she was, in fact, his foster mother. Helen Mansfield, his real mother, was admitted to us the year before, December 1972. According to the report, which wasn't very comprehensive, she was one of the first patients here. She worked in a hospital, but it didn't say what her role was or which hospital, and I couldn't find a great deal about her family. But I found out this morning that Helen was a surgeon who had fallen ill after returning from Africa, where she did volunteer work, and was *declared* dead the following year. She left behind her husband, Duncan Mansfield, and her son, Bryan Mansfield."

"Now Bryan Morgan," said the Sheriff, flapping his shirt to draw in cool air.

"That's just wonderful!" Smolensk shook his head slowly. "I'd really love to know who was responsible for this major oversight."

Kane cracked his knuckles twice. "I'll find out."

"April, did you know about this?"

She shook her head. "I wasn't involved in the research on Helen Mansfield. She was before my time. She was one of the first patients here."

"What about Dr. Morgan? Were you involved in that?"

She looked sheepishly at Kane.

"I take full responsibility for him," said Kane.

"Explain."

"It was my decision to employ him. I should have been more thorough. The reports I read were clearly inaccurate."

The Sheriff used his thumb to push half a doughnut into his mouth and finished chewing before speaking. "So, what do we do with him now?"

Kane answered in an even, unflappable voice. "The same as the last time this happened."

The Sheriff licked his lips with a puzzled look on his face.

Kane pressed his fist against his other hand and cracked his knuckles. "Dr. Oswald? The anaesthetist you caught on camera inside a female patient he had just put to sleep?"

"I remember. It's hardly comparable, sexually exploiting a patient and having a family member here, which must have shocked him more than anyone else. I mean, we can hardly blame him for that. It wasn't his fault his mother is a patient here. Maybe his reaction was a little overdramatic, but who can blame him?"

"The result is the same," said Kane. "No matter how you try to mitigate it, we couldn't keep Dr. Oswald here, just as we can't keep Dr. Morgan."

Blowing softly on the surface of his steaming coffee cup, the Sheriff bolted upright. "Wait! You mean you want to… take away his memory?"

"What choice do we have?"

"How does that work again?" asked April.

Kane pointed to the bridge of his nose. "By traumatising the temporal lobes of the brain, affecting the neuroanatomy and fully removing autobiographical memory."

"Good," said Smolensk. "Let's get it done!"

"Seems a bit harsh," said the Sheriff. "He's only been here a short time, and he's doing well. Why not give him a second chance? So what if his mother's here. We're trying to save her life. I see no prob–"

"Not after how he reacted when he saw his mother in the cryostat," said Smolensk. "That's the sign of a man who can't control his emotions. If I can't trust my staff, I can't have them working here." He paused to take a deep breath. "When I questioned him about what happened in the lab, he lied to me. I lose trust in liars."

They discussed it further, each sharing different points of view. Smolensk wanted him gone. April and the Sheriff were happy to offer him a second chance, and Kane was now on the fence.

In the end, they each agreed it was best they find a new psychologist.

The Sheriff slurped his coffee, recoiling from the heat. "What about Dr. Fletcher?"

"What about him?" Kane asked.

"Is he not on the staff anymore?"

"He gave up that privilege when he tried to escape."

April held out her palms. "Why did he try to escape?"

President Smolensk leaned forward. "Because I was going to question him over the logbook, and he knew it. Have we found it yet?"

"No," said Kane. "It's still missing. When we're finished here, I'm heading back to London to search his flat."

Smolensk looked at the Sheriff. "What did you see on the cameras?"

"Dr. Fletcher got in the lifts, even though I had cancelled his swipe card. I tried contacting the guards up at the security checkpoint, but they didn't pick up their radios, so they didn't apprehend him. That's how he got out."

"Can I trust *any* of my staff?" asked Smolensk. How many had let him down? Dr. Morgan. Dr. Fletcher. Dr. Huber. The catering staff. The cryobiologist who let Dr. Morgan inside the lab. The two guards who had let Dr. Fletcher out.

And then there was Nigel Carson. A brilliant mind, Nigel had been a driving force behind many of their initial projects, bringing a level of insight and dedication that was hard to match. His career had been cut short when he was diagnosed with lung cancer, a cruel consequence of years of nicotine abuse. In his absence, he had introduced April to take over as chief analyst, believing she would carry on his legacy while he was in cryopreservation. At first, Smolensk had been sceptical, as he was with all new hires. April was new to the foundation, and stepping into Nigel's shoes seemed like a daunting task. But she quickly proved herself as an asset. With her detailed nature and clinical approach, she exceeded his expectations. Unlike Nigel, who had sometimes been prone to oversight, April approached her work with a rigour both refreshing and necessary. She would never have compiled a profile on Helen Mansfield without conducting such precise, well-documented research, leaving no room for ambiguity. Her thoroughness brought reliability to the team, and her refusal to take short-cuts ensured their work remained credible. April had become an invaluable member of the team, transforming the role of chief analyst into one demanding the highest standards. While Nigel's absence was still felt, he couldn't help but recognise April's presence had ultimately worked out for the best.

"And you're definitely sure Dr. Fletcher wasn't carrying anything?" asked Kane. "The logbook? A bag?"

"No. When the agents caught up with him, they found nothing except his passport and wallet. He was planning to leave the country."

Smolensk snarled. "The longer the logbook floats around, the more likely it is to fall into the wrong hands. That cannot happen. Find it! Consider it a priority. Start by searching all staff apartments again."

"What about Dr. Fletcher?" asked Kane.

"He has been an invaluable asset to the foundation and will continue to contribute to our research and development, albeit in an unconscious state. Please arrange for him to be transported to the testing facility where we can monitor him."

"When are you on leave?"

"From tomorrow. I'll be staying at my holiday home in Scotland for the next fortnight. Is that it for today?"

"We will take care of Dr. Morgan," said Kane. "He won't remember a thing about this place."

The Sheriff put down his coffee cup. "While Kane is in London going through Dr. Fletcher's property, I'll organise another search for the logbook."

The president stood. "Good. Have it done by the end of the day."

25

"You again?" the cryobiologist muttered, clearly displeased to find Bryan standing at the door of Lab 1 again with a tray of food.

He shrugged. "They've got me bringing him his breakfast now, would you believe?"

He didn't stick around for her response and marched into the lab, making his way to the other side carrying the food.

As expected, Bryan found Dr. Huber on duty, fastening a cryo-apron in preparation for the next patient induction. The irony wasn't lost on him. Overwork was detrimental to health, something that he strived to improve in his patients. Workaholics like Huber often used their jobs to mask social awkwardness and their emotional instability. The adrenaline fuelled them, but when it wore off, it left them with irritability and personal discord, the ultimate self-sacrifice.

Perfectionism played its part, too. Over the years, Bryan had helped numerous patients suffering from work-related stress. They lived by rigid to-do lists, cluttered their spaces with Post-it notes, and tried to impose order on the messiness of daily life. Their minds raced even in the dead of night with dopamine flooding their brains while they fixated on trivial matters, unable to escape the cycle. And Dr. Huber was no different, caught in the same destructive loop of striving for control in an uncontrollable world.

"Every time I turn around, you're there!" said Dr. Huber.

Bryan set the tray down on the workbench. "The kitchen asked me to bring up your breakfast."

Dr. Huber arched an eyebrow. "I never eat breakfast this early. The staff knows that. Ten o'clock. It's the same every morning."

Bryan tried to quell his suspicion. "You did mention you liked your food cold. Well, it's cold."

Dr. Huber wasn't buying it. His eyes narrowed, and he crossed his arms. "Why are you *really* here?"

Bryan decided to tell him the truth in a roundabout way. "Okay. The truth is, I wanted to see the lab one last time."

Dr. Huber slowly removed his glasses, scrutinising Bryan with a knowing look. "I see what's happening here," he said in his trademark deep voice. "A board meeting was called this morning. Something about one of our staff having a family member in cryopreservation. They were suspended last night and are about to lose their job. I'm guessing that person is you!"

Bryan's stomach churned. He realised going back there was stupid and immediately regretted acting on such foolish impulse. He showed Dr. Huber the four-digit number he had written on his palm, and in a voice quivering with emotion, said, "My time here's almost up. I wanted to see my mother before I leave." He turned and hurriedly walked away.

At cryostat 0016, he studied her frozen face. He put his hand on the thick, reinforced glass, communicating telepathic thoughts, silently telling her how much he loved and missed her and how sorry he was this had happened.

"Helen Mansfield," said Dr. Huber, slowly walking up to Bryan. "A beautiful woman, one of my favourites. And one of the first patients admitted here. When she first arrived, she had this peculiar immune system failure. HIV and AIDS were unknown at that time, so we placed her in lab six with all the heterogeneous patients. It wasn't until the early eighties that the HIV virus causing AIDS was officially recognised. All the patients now kept in here presented the same symptoms, and after their tissues were examined years later, we realised what was wrong with them and had this lab built."

"What does she have?" asked Bryan. "HIV or AIDS?"

"HIV."

Bryan batted away tears with the back of his hand. "What do you mean, *favourite*?"

Dr. Huber shot Bryan a look, then turned his eyes back to the face in the window. "It's normal to get attached to your patients. Your mother is very special. Like I said, she was one of the first persons here, before AIDS was declared even a worldwide epidemic."

Dr. Huber walked back to his workbench with his hands behind his back.

Bryan followed closely behind, subconsciously balling his hands into fists. "Here's a question. How long would it take you to unfreeze a cryostat?"

Dr. Huber had his back turned. "We do not *unfreeze* the cryostats. We drain away the liquid nitrogen, and the patient is rewarmed and revived, not *unfrozen*."

"How long?"

"Two to three hours. Why?"

Bryan shrugged. "Curious."

Dr. Huber glanced at his watch.

Bryan's eyes darted nervously from side to side, scanning the lab for any signs of movement. He glanced down the aisle, then up at the empty viewing platform, and finally towards the door. The lab was unnervingly quiet. His pulse quickened. He faced Dr. Huber, wondering how to say it and whether to say it in the first place. In the end, he threw caution to the wind. "So, when is ELF planning to go public with the AIDS cure?"

Dr. Huber whipped around. He caressed the back of his neck, his fingers pressing gently against the nerve-rich area in what Bryan saw as a subconscious attempt to lower his heart rate and ease the rising discomfort. Then he folded his arms tightly across his chest, a defensive posture that demonstrated unease. The silence lingered before he let out a forced, awkward laugh, the kind that didn't reach his eyes. It was yet another tell; he was fooling no one. Bryan's question had rattled him, and the layers of discomfort were written all over, no matter how much he tried to mask it.

"What are you talking about?"

"The cure for AIDS. Everyone knows about it. I was just wondering when you think it will be released, so the patients in here can get their lives back. Including my mother."

"Where did you hear that absurd rumour?"

"Everyone's talking about it."

"Are you trying to provoke me? Because it's working."

Bryan saw a large pair of surgical scissors resting on Dr. Huber's workbench. The blades were long, sharp, and carried an inherent threat.

His eyes returned to Dr. Huber. "I'm just saying that—"

"I've heard enough, Dr. Morgan. You don't belong here, and I don't have time for this nonsense. If you'll excuse me, I have work to attend to."

What happened next happened fast.

Dr. Huber turned his back, giving Bryan the opening he needed. In one swift motion, he grabbed the scissors from the workbench and brought them up, positioning the sharp blades against Dr. Huber's throat.

"I want my mother brought back. Now!"

26

The CI agent rummaged through the cluttered utility room, cursing under his breath as he tossed aside wires, tools, loose papers, and old boxes. His identity badge had to be inside here somewhere; it was just on him.

The sudden rise in voices from the lab made him freeze. Slowly, silently, he crept towards the door. When he peered around the frame, his pulse quickened. Dr. Morgan, his face contorted with fury, had a pair of scissors against the throat of Dr. Huber, who had his hands raised in surrender.

The agent's training kicked in. He gripped the handle of his gun and drew it from its holster.

"You're making a big mistake!" shouted Dr. Huber. "You are finished!"

"Shut up and do as I say!" said Bryan. "You're going to have my mother reanimated."

"It's not that simple. You can't just walk out of here with her. She needs time to recover."

"I can wait. For as long as I need to."

"Hands where I can see them!" came a voice from behind.

Bryan spun, reflexes taking over, his hand rising, his arm extending, the scissors driving into the agent's neck. It broke the skin, and blood dripped out, slow at first, until the flow intensified, possibly from a nicked artery. Blood sprayed over Dr. Huber's lab coat and across the workbench.

The agent pressed his hand to his neck, desperately trying to stem the flow of blood. He instinctively checked his hand for blood. It was completely covered, as if he had a red glove on. He clutched his neck once more as his eyes, wide with disbelief and shock, darted around the room and the strength drained from his body. He dropped to his knees with blood cascaded down his pristine suit.

Bryan froze and cupped a hand over his mouth, in just as much shock as the agent and Dr. Huber.

The agent choked as the scissor wound in his neck forced fountains of blood between his fingers. His frightened voice caught, bubbling in his throat with his desperate struggle to breathe against the rising tide of blood.

It drew staff members from all corners of the lab as they gathered around Bryan, their faces stunned and appalled.

Bryan snapped to alertness and grabbed a cloth from the workbench. He applied pressure to the agent's neck to try and stop the bleeding. A red stain rapidly blossomed on the fabric.

Then the agent passed out. Bryan checked his wrist for a pulse. It was very faint, though it seemed to stop the moment he touched it. He stood slowly, shaking his head, and looked at the staff. "I didn't... I'm... what have I done?"

"Is he dead?" asked the female cryobiologist who had let Bryan inside the lab.

Everyone stood frozen, horrified by the sheer amount of blood spreading. Everyone except Bryan. He had witnessed far worse on the battlefields of the Falklands War. Despite his composure, the circumstances were unsettlingly different.

Dr. Huber's jaw went slack. "He's dead!" He looked at Bryan, then back at the agent's seeping neck. Blood flowed dark and thick like motor oil. "You killed him!"

Bryan placed his hands on his head, his fingers gripping his hair as guilt and fear surged through him. His skin prickled with sweat as panic settled in. The stress had been building in him for months, and now it felt like the pressure valve had finally blown wide open, releasing a flood of emotions and impulses he struggled to control. He dragged his gaze away from the dead agent and saw everyone staring at him, gripped by fear.

Bryan held out his arms, the scissors still clasped in his palm. "It wasn't my fault. He came at *me*."

Dr. Huber pointed at the agent. "He's dead!"

"What was I supposed to do?"

"Not kill him!" someone called out as the crowd slowly closed in.

Bryan sprang into action. He bent down and grabbed the agent's gun. As he stood, he swung it from one staff member to the next, forcing them to back off. Then he turned and ran to the door. Ensuring it was electronically locked, he dragged a heavy pedestal in front of it. He slipped a broom between the two door handles. He had the lab in lockdown. No was getting in or out. He made a quick circuit of the lab, rounding up the staff using the gun as a scare tactic, and stood them all against the wall. Then he turned the gun on Dr. Huber. His hand was shaking. He steadied it with his other hand. "Do it now!"

"You really want me to bring her back?"

"Do I not look serious enough to you?"

Dr. Huber looked at his colleagues lined up against the wall and slowly walked to his computer. He began typing, his fingers moving quickly like a pianist playing a fast-paced tune. Menus flashed in and out of the screen as his nimble fingers initiated the reanimation process. It filled with numbers and calculations scrolling so fast they were unreadable.

"What's happening?" asked Bryan.

"Starting reanimation. As you wanted."

One minute stretched to two.

Two stretched to five.

Bryan was startled by a series of banging noises coming from the door. He hesitated for a split second before rushing to the source of the noise, his mind filled with possibilities.

When he reached the door, the banging continued, louder and more urgent. Bryan peered through the narrow window. Outside, a mob of CI agents had gathered, their faces tense with alarm. Some shouted orders, others frantically tried to force their way inside the lab, pushing and shoving the door as they scrambled for access. Their presence sent a wave of panic through Bryan. The lab was already a powder keg, and now, with the agents trying to break in, the situation was on the verge of exploding. He knew he had only minutes to act, but his mind was a blur of indecision.

When Bryan returned, Dr. Huber said, "They're here!" with a smug confidence. "It won't take them long to get in, you know."

Bryan cleared his throat and spoke with the slightly loud, slightly rushed voice of someone on the verge of panic. "I just want my mother to have her life back. That's all. They have to understand that."

"What about the dead agent?"

Bryan swung his head left and right as though he had lost something and was searching for it. "It was… an accident. I never set out to kill anyone."

"Makes no difference."

He knew Dr. Huber was right, but he was too far down the rabbit hole. He'd become a hostage-taker and a murderer. What had propelled such foolish violence? It was as though someone had thrown a switch, and reality had gone haywire.

He loosened a button on his shirt to assist fresh air into his lungs.

"Dr. Huber, do not let that woman out of the cryostat."

It was the voice of President Smolensk coming from an intercom speaker affixed to the wall.

"I'm not in charge right now!" shouted Dr. Huber.

"Dr. Morgan. Put the gun down and unlock the door! Let's talk about this."

It suddenly dawned on Bryan that the president, watching everything unfold through the surveillance cameras, had seen the agent lying lifeless in a pool of blood by the workbench.

Soon enough, everyone, from management to security to housekeeping, would know.

27

Standing at the window on the fourth floor of the office block, Julia gazed at London's sprawling concrete abyss. The city's towering buildings stretched out beneath a hazy sky, and the sun's embers shimmered faintly across the muddied waters of the Thames. On the inside, the sun's warmth filtered through the glass, gently warming the office. Julia stood still, letting the sunlight caress her as she watched the city pulsate from afar. She felt every bit of her thirty-two years, and when she caught her reflection in the window, she forced a smile, but the faint lines at the corners of her mouth betrayed her. It struck her how long it had been since she had last genuinely smiled. Between a turbulent marriage to an absent husband and a stagnant career at a boutique biotech outfit, pregnancy was the last thing she needed. She missed Bryan terribly. She had always been resolute in her decision to avoid becoming a dependent wife, valuing independence and self-sufficiency. She believed that a healthy partnership meant neither partner should feel constrained or limited by the other's expectations or needs. In her view, true love meant supporting each other's freedoms and ambitions, and not sacrificing personal dreams for the sake of the relationship. But in recent months, she had failed to live up to this belief. It was hard to admit she had played a part in her husband's decision to leave.

Geoff from accounting appeared with two full glasses of champagne, but Julia was too caught up in her thoughts to notice him.

"JR Biotech Corp calling Julia?"

His voice snapped her out of her reverie. She looked him in the eye and forced a weak smile. "Sorry, Geoff, in another world."

He passed her a glass of champagne.

"No, but thank you. I really should be getting back to the celebrations."

"Wait!" He grabbed her forearm when she turned to leave. "How about I take you out on a cruise along the river tonight? My treat."

"Not tonight."

He adjusted his ponytail and smiled. "Tomorrow then?"

"I don't think that's a good idea."

"Why not?"

"I'm married, you know that."

"And where is this so-called husband?"

She sighed audibly. "I'm going back to the party."

"I'm sorry, that was uncalled for."

Julia glanced back over her shoulder as she walked away. "Apology accepted."

Back in the office where the champagne breakfast took place, Julia rejoined her colleagues, who were buzzing with excitement. The atmosphere was lively, filled with animated conversations and laughter while they celebrated their recent achievements. JRBC had taken a significant risk by investing in advanced computational biology tools, specifically designed to eliminate any false leads during the initial phases of drug discovery. This bold move was a strategic response to the growing pressure of a shrinking product pipeline, and it had clearly paid off.

As Julia looked around the room, she could see the pride on everyone's faces. The company had not only managed to streamline its processes but had also attracted new contracts with reputable firms in the industry. These partnerships were a testament to their innovative approach and dedication to staying at the forefront of pharmaceutical research. Music in the backdrop and the sound of clinking glasses filled the air as Julia's colleagues toasted to their success and shared sense of accomplishment, bringing them closer together. To Julia, whose role as a secretary felt peripheral to the achievements being celebrated, the festivities held little significance for her. As her colleagues toasted to their success and shared excited chatter about future projects, she found herself standing on the outskirts of the celebration.

Someone touched her on the shoulder. She swung round and saw it was her boss. "Champagne?"

She smiled. "I'm good."

He cocked his head slightly. "Everything okay?"

"Of course. Great event. Everyone seems to be enjoying themselves."

"This is a big win. We should do this more often."

Julia smiled and excused herself. She wormed through the crowd, making slow progress for the far door in the corner. By the time she broke out on the other side, she had been tapped on the back and shoulder and hugged by almost half the people in the room.

She headed straight to her office to collect her handbag, and when she saw the telephone, picked up the receiver and dialled. It rang four times before it was answered.

"I need to see you," she said. "Meet me in an hour at the Embankment. Usual place."

Julia arrived five minutes early, standing by the side of the road with the Thames gently flowing behind her. While she waited, she saw a group of school children in uniform nearby. They laughed and playfully shoved each other as they strolled down the path, their carefree energy stirring a pang of envy in her. It was already eleven o'clock, far past school start time, making it clear they were skipping classes. Their defiance of routine only deepened Julia's longing for the kind of freedom they seemed to enjoy. Life used to be so simple, she pondered.

Then she saw his familiar face among the pedestrians. He waved from distance, ducking in and out of the crowd as he headed towards her.

Out of nowhere, a black Land Rover swerved erratically towards the kerb and screeched to a halt in front of her. The suddenness left Julia frozen in place. Before she could react, the door swung open and two men leaped out.

Without a word, they lunged at her, grabbing her roughly by the arms. A hand clamped tightly over her mouth, stifling the scream that rose in her throat. Panic surged through her, and she began to thrash wildly, furiously kicking at their legs and twisting her body in every direction. Her nails dug into their skin as she clawed at them, trying to inflict some damage, to leave even the faintest mark. But they were much stronger, and her efforts were futile as they lifted her off the pavement with alarming force, her feet barely touching the ground as they dragged her towards the Land Rover and threw her onto the back seat before slamming the door shut.

The interior was cold and dark, and the smell of leather and smoking rubber filled Julia's senses as the Land Rover surged forward with a loud wheelspin.

28

Word spread like wildfire through the halls of the foundation. Panic and shock ricocheted from one lab to another, growing louder with each retelling. Within minutes, the entire staff had learned about the incident unfolding in Lab 1.

Drained by the drama, his lack of sleep, and the stress of taking another man's life, Bryan considered his next move.

The CI agents amassed outside attempted to break down the door, a solid obstacle with reinforced glass windows. This would take some heavy machinery or explosives that would risk damaging the cryostats. Still, it wouldn't be long before they found a way in.

Onlookers jostled for space along the viewing platform, watching with interest until Bryan found a panel of switches that activated an automated blind, covering the window and obscuring their view.

Inside the lab, Dr. Huber complained to Bryan.

Outside, the CI agents yelled at him.

In the Security Operations Room, watching through the cameras, President Smolensk waited impatiently for an end to all this.

Bryan realised it was reckless to pursue the salvation of his mother under such looming threats and with the odds stacked against him. The outcome could only be disastrous. He had no choice but to abort the mission. He had to get out. Now.

"How much longer will this take?"

Dr. Huber faced his monitor. "Small amounts of liquid nitrogen are extracted from the cryostat. Then the body will be warmed one degree at a time. After that, I need to give her back her blood and revive her by injection."

"I asked how long!"

"Two hours. But she won't be able to walk right away. She'll need time to recover. It can take anything from hours to days."

He didn't have hours or days. He barely had minutes.

The CI agents would break down the door any minute and come storming in. He knew he didn't stand a chance. He wasn't trained to fight, let alone take on a team of battle-hardened agents who operated outside the law and carried guns. His training was in saving lives, not ending them. The idea of murder was something he never could have fathomed, and now he'd just committed one.

Clearing his mind of external distractions, he focussed on getting out of the situation he had made for himself. First, he herded the cryobiologists to a storage room and manoeuvred the padlock hanging from the door handle into position.

Escape was his only option. He had to move upward. Up led to freedom. Up meant a chance to reach his home, his wife, the life he once knew. For a fleeting moment, he even convinced himself his old life could still be salvaged, that everything could somehow return to the way it was.

Rounded, galvanised air ducts travelled across the lab's high ceiling. The vent cover grilles led to a web of horizontal and vertical shafts. A tall stepladder was propped against the wall.

"Where do these air ducts lead to?"

But Dr. Huber was engrossed in his monitor, too busy bringing his mother back into the world, and didn't hear him. Not wanting to distract him from the complex procedure, he dragged over the stepladder and climbed to the top rung. He probed at the grille, realising it was too narrow to fit a grown man.

He descended the ladder and ran to Dr. Huber. "Stop the reanimation!"

"Excuse me?"

"I want you to stop reanimation."

"That's the first sensible thing you've said all morning."

"Is there a way out of here?"

Dr. Huber pushed up from the desk. "The same way you came in."

"There must be another way."

"I wouldn't tell you if there was."

Bryan pointed the gun at Huber's heart in an apologetic way. "Then forgive me, but you are no use to me."

Dr. Huber raised his hands. "Wait! There's a fire escape in the utility room. I'll show you to it. Just… just promise not to shoot."

Bryan lowered the gun, annoyed he'd been forced to call his bluff.

Dr. Huber launched into a quick summary of a tunnel that led out of the foundation as he led Bryan into the utility room, where a large sink, benchtop, and rows of shelving filled the wall, packed with abandoned biological equipment, multiple boxes, and random junk. He pointed to a tall unit on the back wall. "Behind the unit is a door. It opens to a tunnel about half a mile long. No one other than the board members know about it."

"Where does it lead to?"

"I don't know. Nobody's ever used it."

"Pull the unit back!"

"It's heavy, I need help."

"Just do it!"

Hunched over with his awkward stoop, Dr. Huber inched the unit back slowly, dragging it one way, then the other, in his struggle to pull it back from the wall.

Bryan cautiously peered around the edge of the unit. His eyes landed on an old door that looked as if it hadn't been touched in years, if at all. The hinges were thick with rust, almost corroded beyond use, and the metal frame was warped. Dust had collected at the base, undisturbed, and cobwebs clung to the corners, confirming how long it had been since anyone had passed through.

Bryan hesitated. The door seemed forgotten, possibly a dead end, but it was his only chance. He could hear the distant sound of agents pounding the door. He didn't have the luxury of time. Despite the door's decrepit appearance, it might be his only escape.

"Open it!"

Dr. Huber applied his weight to the door.

It slowly opened, revealing a dark void beyond.

"I'll be coming back for my mother. And I will have the police with me."

"You're going to prison!"

Bryan didn't have time to worry about the price he had to pay for murdering the agent. Once the police had dismantled the foundation and his mother was safe and free, they would receive his confession in writing.

Dr. Huber raised his glasses. "Let me guess. A couple of months before you were offered the job here, someone you know died."

Bryan frowned. "What are you talking about?"

"The police thought it was you but didn't have enough evidence to convict. You're innocent. I know, the president knows, but the police, they weren't so sure."

"Just… shut up!"

"True story this. But everyone who joined ELF in the last twelve months was on the scene when a suicide involving a person they know occurred. Some would call it a coincidence. The president calls it insurance."

For a moment, he was elsewhere, six months ago, at his office window, staring into the car park. Michelle Locke lay face down on the cold concrete, a pool of blood spreading around her head. Her limbs were bent at unnatural angles, broken in ways that made it hard to look. The piercing scream of a passerby echoed through the darkness. The wail of sirens approaching soon grew louder. The medical centre became awash in red and blue flashes. Her sudden death had not been symptomatic of depression or self-harm. He had seen enough potential suicides to recognise the signs. Michelle had never fitted that profile. During the six sessions they had shared, he had uncovered her frustrations—behavioural issues, a quick temper, hatred for her politician father, and deep resentment for her job in the sex industry. But not once had it seemed hopeless. He had believed in her potential for change. The community engagement program he had recommended to help her navigate these struggles, to rebuild her life, had given her hope. The scene of her death felt like a brutal betrayal of everything they'd worked towards.

"The president hasn't shown you the evidence that will land you in prison. My guess is you'll see it when the police knock on your door."

"You're lying!"

"Am I?"

Bryan saw a torch next to some duct tape on the shelf. He used the tape to bind Dr. Huber's wrists behind his back. He shoved a sponge from the sink in his mouth, used some more of the tape to seal it, and then taped him to the shelf unit.

He was exactly where he wanted to be, at the start of the long tunnel, when a voice boomed from the intercom. But he ignored it, took the torch, and retreated into the tunnel.

"Dr. Morgan, listen very carefully. We have your wife, Julia, and are prepared to do whatever it takes to save Dr. Huber's life."

Dr. Huber heard it, but Bryan had already fled.

29

The abandoned factory rose three stories. Its cracked windows and crumbling walls gave it a haunting, forgotten look, while its sagging roof threatened to collapse at any moment. Deemed unsafe to the community, the building had been condemned, with demolition scheduled for early next year, marking it as another relic of the past soon to vanish from the city.

Julia inhaled sharply through her nose as the black hood was ripped from her head. Her hair clung damply to her scalp, and her flushed cheeks burned. Tape bound her wrists tightly behind her back, and another strip that sealed her mouth also stretched around the back of her head. Her wide, frantic eyes studied the grimy walls and rusted beams of the dilapidated room, and her senses were heightened by the grip of fear.

A pigeon flapped high above in the struts. Julia looked up, glimpsing its tapered tail as it scarpered through a crack in the corrugated roof, dislodging a mixture of dust and fibres that rained down.

A throat cleared behind her, and she snapped her head around, but the captors remained hidden. Turning forward again, she watched as two women in sleek black suits emerged silently from behind a translucent tarp that divided the room from a section of rusted machinery. They moved with grace and took up positions either side of her.

A tall, attractive man appeared before her with a refined, commanding presence and mature, striking features. Dressed in a grey tweed suit, he casually chewed gum, leaving a faint trail of mint in the air. In one swift move, he pressed his fist into his hand and cracked his knuckles.

Then a knife with a tapered blade, seven inches of shining steel, magically appeared in his grip. One minute his hand was cracking against the other and empty, the next it wasn't. He held it in readiness if not actual threat, and pointed it at her left eye, waving it like a wand.

Her protestations were muffled by the tape.

"I don't enjoy doing this," he said calmly.

He pressed the knife into the rosy flesh of her cheek, just beneath her eye. It punctured the skin. A red tear broke.

He moved it to her neck. "This object is sharper than a sabre. I will use it to cut the tape from your mouth. Scream, shout, moan, or struggle, I'll cut your fucking throat. Do we understand each other?"

Julia nodded with a whimper.

He sliced the tape and unravelled it from her head, tearing out some of her hair.

He circled her chair with smooth, calculated steps before stopping.

She waited.

He knelt in front of her.

She could feel his warm, minty breath on her face when he spoke. "What do you know about ELF?"

She didn't trust herself to maintain composure and speak without breaking, so she kept silent. There was something in this man's movements, the confidence in his voice, making her certain this wasn't his first time. But she couldn't make any sense of it. Was this a case of mistaken identity? Had they kidnapped the wrong woman?

Then the penny dropped. She suspected where the man might be going with this. She thought she knew the reason. These people looked like government employees. "Does this have something to do with my husband? Is he in some kind of trouble? Where is he?"

Bryan had always encouraged her to finish her degree and pursue her dreams of one day becoming a medical researcher, envisioning a future where they could live as two successful, happy academics. He thrived on ambition and saw the world through the lens of goals and achievements. But she wasn't like him. Her drive was softer, more relaxed. She was content with her job as a secretary, and all she ever really wanted was a quiet life, a loving family, and a cosy home. Sometimes, she worried Bryan silently disapproved of her lack of ambition. Medicine ran in his blood: his mother a renowned surgeon, his grandfather a practitioner. It wasn't just a career for him; it was a passion, a calling. His eyes lit whenever she showed even a hint of interest in his work, and she'd feel a pang of guilt knowing she didn't share his zeal. While she admired his dedication, the truth was that her dreams were simpler. And sometimes, she questioned if that was enough for him.

Standing behind her now, the man spoke softly in her ear. His breath tickled her neck. "Answer my question!"

She shook her head. "I don't know what ELF is."

"Do you want to know what I hate more than sodomisers and rapists? *Liars*. And you're lying to me. I wouldn't advise it."

Her mouth turned dry. "I've never heard of ELF, I swear. I don't know what you're talking about."

His face came so close, their noses touched, and she saw into his ice-blue eyes. His contact lenses were like transparent shutters. But something more shimmered deep within those eyes. Ruthlessness, she realised with a shudder.

"Lie to me again, I take your finger. That gives you ten opportunities to tell the truth. After that, I take the toes. Then we'll have to start getting creative."

"I told you, I've never heard of ELF! Please, let me go. You must have the wrong person. I've done nothing to hurt anyone or cause any trouble. Please, I'm pregnant. This is not good for the baby."

He circled her slowly, and she twisted in her seat, trying to keep him in view, afraid of what he might do if he slipped out of sight. But he did slip out of sight. She couldn't see him. She couldn't hear him.

The silence became unbearable.

Seconds later, a searing pain shot through her hand. Loud screams tore from her throat. Through tears, she caught sight of her finger dangling in front of her, the diamond ring still in place, and blood oozed from the stark white of the severed bone.

The man in the grey suit reappeared in front of her. "Shall we try again?"

Drool dripped in thin ribbons from her mouth when she spoke, her words broken by sobs. "I told you, I don't know. Why… are you doing this to me?"

The man suddenly turned to his colleagues, sniffing the air. "You smell that?"

Even the tough-looking women had to pinch their noses. "What *is* that?"

"Smells like… gas," he said.

A fourth man in a black suit charged into the room with a gun up and out. "We need to hurry this up. There's a taxi outside. What the fuck's that smell?"

Julia twisted round and saw a gas cylinder leaning against the wall. Its exterior was dented, and the cap sat loosely on top. Above the cylinder, a wall-mounted unit bore a sign that read: *Fire Blanket.* The door to the unit stood open, revealing an empty interior. Just when the scene seemed concerning enough, a burning cigarette soared through the air and landed dangerously close to the leaking gas cylinder.

Her captors saw the cylinder and the cigarette but were slow to react when a figure burst into the room, arms raised high, gripping an orange blanket that trailed behind them like a cape. They cut across the factory floor and headed in her direction, crashing into her with force and knocking her chair over. She fell, flat and hard, hitting her head on the concrete, while the caped individual fell on top of her.

A deafening explosion erupted, a blinding blue cosmos that filled the air with dust and debris and turned the factory into a gutted, charcoal cave. The ceiling collapsed, and wooden beams and corrugated iron crashed to the floor, engulfing everyone in the room.

30

Blacked-out dome lights ran along the tunnel walls at regular intervals, but Bryan had the torch, and he illuminated the path in intermittent beams of light. It was cool inside the tunnel. A draft carried a damp, earthy scent. The thudding from his synthetic, rubberised heels panicked some rats, which cut across his path and fled into various gaps in the wall.

How much further? Did this lead to a dead-end? Had Dr. Huber tricked him into the tunnel to keep him contained? If it was half a mile in length, he was about midway when the first CI agents entered the tunnel. Their torches flashed, tiny pinpricks in the darkness, alerting him of their presence. He heard the eager keening of dogs, yelping as they were set loose. It wouldn't take long for them to catch up with him.

The ground became steeper and less even, and the gravel underfoot transformed into a set of uneven stone steps. At the summit, he arrived at a steel door with a round handle, much like a submarine hatch, which twisted counterclockwise. Beyond it lay a perfectly square, empty room, featureless and dull and completely sealed off. Thick layers of dust blanketed the floor, while the walls and ceiling were bare, solid concrete, not a single door or window. He was trapped. Dr. Huber had played him.

About to turn back, his torchlight caught the gleam of a steel ladder bolted to the wall. At the top of the ladder was a hatch in the ceiling, resembling a drain cover. He placed one foot after the other on the steel rungs, climbing steadily to the top. His breath was heavy in his frantic attempts to flee the foundation. When he finally reached the last rung, he was met by another hatch, identical to the door below, with the same circular locking mechanism. While he held the ladder with his left hand, his right hand, slick with sweat, gripped the handle and turned it counterclockwise. The metal screeched as the hatch loosened. Summoning all his strength, he pushed the hatch open and hauled himself up, gasping for air as he broke out of the dark, suffocating room below.

As Bryan knelt to close the hatch, a pack of dogs burst into the room, their ferocious barks bouncing off the walls. Moments later, several agents stormed in. The second they spotted him, they raised their guns. Shots rang out. But Bryan slammed the hatch shut just in time, listening as the bullets struck against the metal beneath him. He stood on the hatch, using his weight to block their advance.

He caught his breath and took in his surroundings. Tall shafts rose through a hazy mist around him, and the air was cool, earthy, and sweet, refreshing his soul with every inhale. He realised he was standing in a forest.

The silence informed him the agents had likely retreated back down the tunnel. If he weren't forced to flee, to run the gauntlet for his life, he was certain he would have collapsed from sheer exhaustion.

Julia slid out from under the fire blanket, her ears ringing and popping. She had to push a sheet of corrugated iron off her legs so she could stand. She struggled to breathe, her lungs and throat burning with all the dust and ash in the air. The explosion had scorched everything, including her captors. Their faces were now a grotesque blend of brain and blood, and their smoking corpses lay almost camouflaged amid the rubble. Julia only counted three bodies. The man who had dismembered her was not among them.

She looked at her hand with the missing finger in shock, so deep it made her believe for a moment the hand belonged to someone else, anyone but her. She was alive, and that was what mattered. She turned to the person who had saved her from these people. He crawled out from underneath the fire blanket, pushing aside the bricks and beams that had crashed down upon him.

She threw her left hand over her mouth, then flung her arms around him. "Flymo?"

He reciprocated, albeit briefly. He pulled back and took her hand. "We must get you to a hospital. I have a taxi waiting outside."

Before leaving, he used his handkerchief to staunch the bleeding from her severed finger. As he tied a firm knot, she silently watched him. "How did–"

"Later!" he said. He pulled Julia by the hand, leading her out of the room and down a dark flight of steps. They were halted by a locked door. Instead of a knob, it had a push-down lever, and instead of a bolt, there was a keyhole. But Flymo put his shoulder through it, breaking the hinges, and the door cracked open, giving them access to the car park where Flymo's taxi idled. They climbed in.

"Take us to the hospital!" said Flymo.

The driver didn't respond or even move. Flymo repeated his request but got the same silence. He saw what could only be blood on the dashboard. He stepped out of the taxi and cautiously made his way to the front. It looked like someone had thrown a bucket of red paint over the driver's side. A dark red hole in the man's forehead marked where he had been shot.

"We'll find another taxi," said Flymo, dragging Julia out by the forearm.

"What is it?"

"Let's hurry!"

Hand in hand, they moved quickly through the industrial complex to the main road, where they hailed the first taxi.

"Hospital!" said Flymo. "Put your foot down, mate!"

Julia glanced back at the factory through the rear window, its crumbling structure reminding her of the danger she'd just escaped. She lifted the handkerchief, staring at her mutilated hand in disbelief. The sight of it made her shudder, but her thoughts quickly shifted to Bryan, fearing for his life. What kind of danger was he in? What had he got himself into? She could not imagine because she knew nothing about his work.

Her heart pounded as her hand drifted to her stomach, where a new life grew inside of her. It hit her all at once: her unborn child, her husband's safety, and her hopes and dreams for a future that suddenly seemed so fragile.

Seated at his desk inside the Security Operations Room, the Sheriff scanned the live feed within the foundation. His eyes flicked rapidly from screen to screen, searching for any sign of Dr. Morgan. Twenty minutes ago, he had disappeared into the utility room in Lab 1 with Dr. Huber. Ten minutes ago, he'd been cornered by CI agents, who had breached the main door to the lab and had charged into the utility room with dogs on leashes. Since then, only Dr. Huber had emerged. So where was Dr. Morgan and the CI agents?

The Sheriff leaned forward, feeling the tension tightening his jaw as his fingers drummed against the desk. Something was wrong. Why was it taking the agents so long to apprehend Dr. Morgan?

President Smolensk thundered into the room. A shaken-up Dr. Huber was behind him.

"Switch to external surveillance, right now!" the president barked.

The screens flickered as the internal feed shifted across to external cameras. Different angles of the facility appeared on the monitors displaying views from the extensive perimeter surveillance network. A light morning fog had rolled in and blurred the images, forcing them to squint to make out any discernible shapes in the hazy terrain.

"Enhance camera three on the main monitor!" said the president, his tone sharp with urgency.

The Sheriff swiftly toggled the controls and brought up camera fifteen, which covered the entire north entrance. By adjusting the digital filters to cut through the fog, and fine-tuning the infrared settings, any hidden heat signatures would become detectable. The monitor displayed a sharper view of the area outside.

"There!" said the president. "Focus on that movement."

The Sheriff zoomed in, the camera panning smoothly, the robotic arm responding to his precise commands. Something was out there, barely visible in the fog but still distinct. He increased resolution and shifted to thermal imaging, revealing faint heat sources; someone was in the fog. Applying more zoom, they saw a man standing on a drain cover between the trees.

The president leaned closer to the screen. "Notify field security. And set off the smoke cloak alarm."

Embedded within the grids surrounding the foundation were multiple smoke cloak brackets with plug-in connections. These canisters were programmed to activate when the grids detected movement, releasing a dense white cloud of artificial smoke that would blanket the area. The thick, impenetrable smoke was engineered to disorient and immobilise intruders, leaving them confused and vulnerable, and effectively forcing them into submission. The Sheriff used a remote control to activate the smoke cloak before he radioed the field officers protecting the foundation at various checkpoints, informing them of Bryan's location.

Bryan was just ten strides from the hatch when a sudden wall of thick smoke erupted before him. The acrid haze twisted in the air, and he instinctively used his hands to cover his mouth and nose, fearing the smoke could be toxic. Pulse racing, he set off again through the forest, sweeping his arms to avoid crashing into the nearby trees. He glanced nervously over his shoulder, hearing the agents closing in through the dense fog. When he faced forward, he detected movement in the veil of smoke, causing him to panic.

The first blow came out of nowhere and was a blindside crack to his head, knocking him down. Fists, knees, and feet lurched out of the white smoke from all angles, connecting all over his body.

Something solid struck him with crushing force against his temple. He arched into the pain, his body folding onto the grass as he slipped into unconsciousness.

31

Reporters and a swelling crowd of spectators filled the green across from the casualty bay of the Royal Academy Hospital, anxiously awaiting the arrival of the ambulances. Those who managed to secure front-row spots stood pressed against the metal barriers, their faces bathed in the intermittent glow of flashing police lights. Several officers patrolled the perimeter, maintaining order as onlookers strained for a view, eager not to miss any detail of the unfolding scene. Media cameras on tripods stood poised and ready to document every moment, their lenses trained on the hospital entrance and operators on full alert.

Among them were Meagan and Steve, a well-known duo in media circles, driven by their determination to break the story first. Their eyes remained sharp, scanning the scene, ready to pounce on any sign of movement or distant wail of a siren, ensuring no crucial detail went unrecorded. They were both hungry for that perfect shot, the type the tabloids would salivate over, because overnight a headline story had surfaced, and by Saturday, it would take precedence over all other news.

Sporting his new peroxided haircut, Steve was under a lot of pressure to turn his qualifications into publications. The only article he had managed to publish last month was a small piece on the mistreatment of pheasants, detailing the squalid, inhumane conditions in which they were bred. He had written about the dead, featherless birds scattered among the living, the grubby cages, and the cramped, filthy spaces they were forced to endure. It was a worthy topic, but it had barely made a ripple in the news cycle, and quickly became buried under more sensational stories. This news story, conversely, had the potential to reach every corner of the globe. It wouldn't just overshadow the pheasant article—it would be talked about for generations to come. The sheer shock, combined with the fact it was all true, made it irresistible. If he didn't capture the perfect shot, someone else would, and it would be worth a fortune. Every major media outlet would be clamouring to get their hands on it, desperate to feature the story that could define headlines worldwide. The stakes couldn't be higher. This wasn't about a handful of neglected birds; it was about human lives, real drama. A front-page, career-making kind of story. This was his opportunity to break through. His partner, Meagan, a woman with a constant, cheerful grin, operated on a different wavelength to most reporters. Despite her jolly personality, she was relentless and unflinching in her pursuit of a story, with little regard for boundaries, but she always got results. He had to be more ruthless and daring. Today, he felt ready to take that leap, emboldened by the thrill of the chase.

Steve jingled the loose change in his pocket, a small act that helped ease his tension as he impatiently waited for the ambulances to arrive. It gave him something to do, a way to pass the time while the anticipation built around him. To kill time, he checked his camera's settings and picture quality by snapping a shot of Meagan blowing into her cold hands.

"What are you doing?" Meagan asked.

Steve grinned as he stared at the picture on the preview. "You looked adorable warming up your hands," he teased. "Figured I'd write an article about you as a backup plan, just in case the ambulances don't show up."

"And what's your headline? You need a solid headline."

"I'm thinking… *Blow Queen!*"

She pretended to knee him in the groin in retaliation for the sexual innuendo. "You'll be picking up your teeth with a broken hand in a minute, so you'd better pray the ambulances *do* show up."

No sooner had she spoken than two ambulances, flanked by a convoy of police motorcycles, surged into the casualty bay. As soon as they arrived, the line of reporters and camera operators leaped into action. A frenzy ensued as the media reps scrambled to adjust their equipment, vying for the best angles and snapping photos, eager to capture a moment that could define careers. Bright flashes erupted like fireworks, illuminating the scene just as medical staff burst through the doors of the casualty bay, springing into action. The driver of a satellite-broadcasting van following the ambulances tried to negotiate at a barricade guarded by police officers, who raised their hands, signalling for the van to turn back. Meanwhile, as the journalists engaged the officers with claims of their rights, one climbed through a hatch in the roof and began setting up a camera on a tripod, determined to capture the scene from above.

The moment the media had been waiting for arrived as the ambulance doors swung open.

"Here we go!" said Meagan.

Two men, their identities still undisclosed, were carefully lifted from the ambulances on stretchers and rushed into the hospital. Their bodies lay flat and unconscious, with IV lines attached to their arms, delivering vital fluids as medical teams moved swiftly to attend to them.

The large media presence seemed insignificant next to the sheer number of police officers and paramedics at the scene, underscoring just how important these men had become.

The media just wanted the story.

The medical staff focussed on treating the men.

The police, though, were intent on making arrests.

32

Chief Constable Hughes entered his office and shut the door behind him with a force that rattled the glass. Head throbbing, throat aching, the dull pressure in his sinuses made it hard to breathe. He wiped his nose with a tissue and dropped heavily into his chair. He wasn't a man who found much joy in life, but today it deliberately mocked him. The paperwork stacked on his desk only added insult to injury. Everything irritated him, from the bitter taste of his coffee to the frustrating lack of progress on the carjacking case that had been dragging on for weeks. Even the faint sunlight peeking through the blinds felt like an affront.

And when his mobile rang, he gave that his sternest scowl before picking up. "Hughes."

Stroking his grey-black moustache, he listened carefully to the police and crime commissioner. "It's definitely him?"

When the commissioner finished speaking and hung up, Hughes threw his mobile onto his desk, disrupting everything, including his half-eaten muffin, which toppled and collapsed into crumbs.

Next to the muffin was an unmarked envelope. He tipped the photographs onto his desk, carefully spreading them out for a clearer view. Each image captured a grim scene: Michelle Locke, mid-fall, her body plummeting from an office window, suspended in time by the camera lens. The official ruling had been suicide, but the terror on her face in the photo told a different story. She hadn't wanted to die.

Hughes picked up a photo and held it close to his face, squinting at the blurry figure in the background. The man's face was grainy, but the ginger hair, pink shirt, and purple tie were unmistakably clear, and matched the initial police report describing the clothes Bryan Morgan had worn the day of her death. The envelope itself was as mysterious as its contents. No names, no numbers, no notes, just the damning pictures. Whoever had delivered it wanted to remain anonymous, but their message was clear: look closer.

Hughes stared at the photos, considering the implications. It was hardly the smoking gun he needed. The grainy images might not hold up in court, and they certainly didn't carry the weight of hard evidence such as a DNA match or a signed confession. It wasn't enough to secure an instant conviction, but it was enough to shake things up. Enough to keep Hughes digging, and enough to make Morgan the prime suspect and force the case to be reopened, casting doubt on the original ruling of suicide. Michelle Locke's father being a high-profile politician would only add pressure, making it more difficult for Morgan to escape justice. Whoever had gone through the trouble of delivering the photographs in secret clearly knew something, and it meant Hughes was onto something bigger than he first thought.

He picked up his mobile and buzzed Chief Inspector Hill. "My office!"

The daily paper lay sprawled across Hughes' desk, opened on the headline about the Queen's speech during the annual state opening of Parliament. Delivered to the House of Lords, the speech outlined crime and disorder as the government's primary targets for the upcoming legislative year. The British prime minister had made bold promises, insisting tackling crime was a top priority. Yet, despite the importance of the speech and its sweeping reforms, Hughes had his eyes glued to the lead story: a chilling report about the illegal cryonics facility discovered and dismantled in Liechtenstein's north. The article described the gruesome discovery of human-filled cryostats, frozen bodies stored in secret, waiting for a future where they could supposedly be revived. Details were sparse, but it was enough to spark his curiosity. How long had this operation been running unnoticed? And more disturbingly, who were these people chosen or forced into this suspended existence?

Hughes couldn't help but feel a pang of unease. It wasn't just the macabre nature of the crime that unsettled him; it was the international connections. An operation like this wasn't run by amateurs. It took power, influence, and money. The involvement of Liechtenstein, a tiny country known for its discretion in financial dealings, only deepened suspicion. This wasn't a local crime; it was part of something far larger with the potential to stretch across borders and into the highest echelons of power.

Hughes leaned back in his chair, gazing at the wall where his plaque awards represented the high regard in which he was held nationally, a symbol of his role in shaping one of the most effective police forces in the country. He had climbed to the top, reaching the highest rank, and his white hair only augmented his experience. Deep lines on his forehead spoke of years spent battling crime and bureaucracy, but also hinted at a man who took offence at almost everything he saw. He often complained to anyone standing near him long enough to endure it. Some said he took comfort in his sour moods, as if discontent was a companion he had learned to live with.

Still, his hard work had earned him not only respect but also the best office in the complex, complete with sweeping views of the city. It was a coveted space, a sign of his success, but did little to soften his perpetual dissatisfaction.

Chief Inspector Hill strode in. "What's up?"

Hughes stared out his window. "I just got off the phone with the PCC, who got a call from Hospital Watch. Guess who was admitted overnight?"

The chief inspector saw the photos scattered on his desk. "Bryan Morgan?"

Hughes turned around and smirked. "That's why you're chief inspector."

He shrugged like it was nothing. "Learned from the best."

"All right, I don't need your nose up my arse. Assign an officer to his room at the Royal Academy Hospital. As soon as he's well enough, I want him locked away."

33

The doctor slid her stethoscope into the top pocket of her white coat, her expression unchanged as she confirmed with a nod what she had just said.

Julia's eyes widened in disbelief. She cupped a hand over her mouth, her voice trembling when she said, "How can that be?"

"As I said, we're still waiting for some tests to come back, but it does look as though your husband's quadriplegic. I wish I had better news to share."

Tears welled in her eyes as the news sank in.

"There is… something else."

"What?"

The doctor led Julia to an X-ray box inside a small room and flicked on the light. She placed a black and white image on the screen, showing Bryan's skull. She pointed to an area above his left ear. "If you look carefully, you can just make out a tiny fracture on the temporal bone. We believe he was struck by something hard, like metal or stone. It looks like he copped a blow on the forehead, too."

"I saw his neck was bandaged," said Jodie. "Why?"

"He has a stab wound, but it's not life-threatening."

An hour ago, a neurosurgeon had told her Bryan showed limited reaction to visual, tactile, and auditory stimulation, like an infant searching a vacant room for entertainment. His eyes tracked movement but with no focus, as though looking for something that wasn't there. He didn't respond to touch in a meaningful way, and sounds just washed over him without registering, as though his mind was trapped in a loop, cycling through basic sensory experiences without connecting them to reality.

Julia felt a knot tighten in her chest. The image of Bryan, once sharp and full of life, reduced to a vacant, unresponsive state was too much to bear.

"When can I see him?" she asked.

"Come back tomorrow morning. We'll have a better idea of his condition then."

When Bryan stirred from his drug-induced sleep, his body heavy and feverish, it was with the sensation of having been unconscious for a long time. His throat burned with dryness, and each attempt to swallow took some effort. He opened his eyes, bloodshot and streaked with red lines, like lightning. He tried to move, to raise his arm, but the muscles from his neck down refused to obey. Glancing to his side, he noticed a thin tube snaking down from the bag above and feeding into his right hand. His left hand, conversely, was restrained inside a metal handcuff fastened tightly to the bedrail. Bryan rolled his head. A police officer outside his door stood guard. Looking the other way, he saw a fourteen-carat gold wedding ring with a carved white-gold centre on the bedside table. He glanced at his hand hanging limply from the cuff and saw a ring-shaped groove in the flesh of one finger.

The patient in the next bed lay sound asleep, sheets pulled up to his neck. Long, white hair draped over his eyes, but it failed to hide his brutally beaten face, swollen and purple, making him unrecognisable. His right leg dangled out of the sheets, wrapped in bandages from foot to knee. And his right hand was marked with deep teeth imprints.

On the other side of Bryan's bed sat a teenage girl he did not recognise, but knew the woman beside her was Julia. Her expression morphed from relief to surprise to sadness in the space of five seconds. She had put on a few pounds during the two months he had worked for ELF and had cut her hair short with the trimline just above her shoulders. It looked a shade darker and a lot shinier.

The smile Julia gave him was warm and familiar.

He smiled back. It was weak but conveyed the message it intended.

Julia looked at the young girl. "He's responding," she said with excitement. She took his slack hand in hers. "Hey, you. I missed you."

Her other hand stroked his cheek, one of the rare tender gestures she bestowed on him. He could barely feel her soft hands on his skin. She choked on a sob that sprang from nowhere, erasing her smile. He saw her tears. They usually made him turn away because it also made him cry. Instead, he watched them slide down her cheeks without emotion.

She stood and kissed the top of his head. As she got close, the wrinkles around her eyes lit up under the bright light. The last few months had clearly taken their toll on her. She must have had a tough time in his absence.

Bryan spotted a porter pushing a trolley of resuscitation equipment outside his room. The man wasn't concentrating on what was ahead of him and drove the trolley into the leg of a police officer. A mannequin torso for teaching medical students how to suction blood from a stomach toppled from the lower shelf onto the floor.

The officer, wearing a jacket displaying epaulettes with a laurel wreath surmounted by a crown, suggesting he was high rank, gave the porter an icy stare.

The porter apologised, gathered up the half-mannequin, and sped off with the trolley.

The same officer entered Bryan's room, stopping at the end of his bed. He looked freshly showered and shaved, and the smell of Old Spice oozed from his skin.

He faced Julia and the young girl. "I'm Chief Constable Hughes. I'm going to need some time with your husband."

"He's only just woken up," said Julia. "Can't it wait? This is the first time we've seen him."

He smiled. "Please close the door on your way out."

Julia looked at Bryan, then at the chief constable, then at the young girl. "Let's get a cup of tea."

Once the girls were out of sight, the chief constable made himself comfortable in Julia's warm chair.

Bryan had been admitted to the hospital on Friday. By Saturday, he had taken a bad turn, but his condition stabilised by evening. Hughes had returned on Sunday, though Bryan was out cold from the medication. Now, it was Monday.

"Welcome back," he said. "Do you know what month it is?"

Bryan spoke in a rasping, wounded voice. "November."

"December, actually. A season to be jolly and all that."

There was something sharp about the chief constable's most unpleasant tone.

"What happened to you two?"

Bryan showed his confusion with a very slight frown.

"The man in the bed next to you is Heath Fletcher. You were both rescued inside the cryonics foundation."

Bryan looked again at his roommate. The name *Fletcher* rang a bell.

"What were you doing in Liechtenstein, Bryan?"

Bryan decided to stay silent and stuck to it. He needed time to push through the fog clouding his mind and piece things together. He still had no idea why he was in hospital or why his body refused to follow his commands. Worse yet, as confirmed by the chief constable, he couldn't even recall what month it was. His sense of time, like everything else, felt scrambled.

"Were you ill?"

Bryan frowned.

"Or was it some elaborate attempt to escape from your crimes?"

The chief constable seemed to be testing Bryan, pushing his buttons with every question and comment. His posture was commanding, and it became clear he was accustomed to being in control, used to bending others to his will. His sharp eyes, piercing and intense, evaluated Bryan, searching for any sign of weakness or compliance. There was a confidence in the way he spoke, a certainty that left little room for argument.

His clothes hinted at power, and the way he carried himself suggested he was no stranger to the high-stakes world of law enforcement.

Bryan struggled to gather his thoughts, and felt the man's expectations pressing him, intensifying the fog clouding his mind. This wasn't a conversation; it was a duel of wills.

"I mean, to just disappear like that, leaving your wife all alone. Screams guilty, don't you think?"

What was he talking about? Guilty of what? The sight of his handcuffed wrist and the barrage of questions suggested he was in serious trouble, but he had no idea what he had done to land himself in this situation. Bryan couldn't tell if he should be worried, ashamed, or guilty. He felt nothing at all. The numbness had enveloped him, leaving him in a state of disconnection from the gravity of his situation.

A reporter toting a camera suddenly appeared, framed in the doorway. His ID badge, clipped to his shirt pocket, read Steve alongside the logo of the broadcaster he represented. He adjusted the camera strap slung over his shoulder, a hint of excitement in his eyes when he glanced around the room, taking in the scene. It was clear he was eager to get the scoop on the latest developments.

Bryan watched with passive interest as the police officer guarding the door returned from the bathroom. The reporter snapped at least five pictures before he was tackled by the officer, and two security staff joined in to restrain him.

Steve unloaded a list of his rights as the officers wrestled him along the corridor and shoved him into the lift.

"The country just wants the truth!" he shouted.

When Steve reached the lobby level, he hurried out of the building, clutching his prize tightly. He was blissfully unaware

that what he was about to publish would endanger the lives
of the patients in question.

34

By the time Julia and the girl returned, the chief constable had left, and Bryan was alone, staring at the wall, tyring to make sense of everything. According to the chief constable, he was under arrest for murdering Michelle Locke, and kept referring to some facility in Liechtenstein, cryopreservation, and illegal scientific conduct. Truth was, he remembered nothing, not since... he couldn't even recall when it all went blank.

Julia scooted her chair closer to Bryan, whose hand she held. Her grip was firm but trembling. "Why did you leave me?"

Bryan opened his mouth to speak but didn't. He was lost for words. His throat was dry. He tried to summon his voice, but even that eluded him.

"What happened to you?" Julia's eyes searched his for the answers.

He didn't know. He couldn't know. His mind was blank, and his every attempt to recall the past felt like chasing smoke.

"Why did you have to leave, Bryan?" she asked again, her grip tightening.

Her questions were filled with all the pain she'd carried in his absence.

Why had the money stopped?

Why hadn't he called?

Julia's words, rapid and relentless, came like daggers, and he had no defence. He couldn't remember. Couldn't answer. All he had was silence and a growing sense something terrible had happened, something he couldn't grasp, something just out of reach. The more she asked, the more the void inside him deepened.

As Bryan held her hand, he noticed something he hadn't before—one finger was missing, replaced by a jagged stump. Had it always been deformed like that? Surely, he would have remembered. Or had there been an accident? Something that had happened during the lost time, the period that he couldn't account for? The thought left him unsettled as he could not shake the feeling this was more than just a lost memory.

He stared at the young girl beside his wife, longer than he should, making the girl shift uncomfortably.

"Bryan, this is Sarah-George," Julia said quickly, breaking the awkward tension.

The girl smiled and gave a little wave. "Hi."

Bryan's scowl showed his confusion, and with a strained voice, asked, "Who?"

The girls traded hesitant looks, and the nod Julia gave her was a green light. Sarah-George leaned closer to Bryan and took his hand. "I don't know how to say this, even though it's the only thing I've thought about these past few days. So, I'll just say it…. I'm your daughter…'"

The headline read: *Secret House of God.* The article detailed how the National Police of Liechtenstein had uncovered an illegal underground facility hidden beneath Vaduz. During a raid on the secret site, armed mercenaries fiercely resisted, leading to a violent gunfight. The clash escalated until the entire facility was consumed by fire, claiming the lives of police officers, patients, and staff. The discovery had sparked an outcry in Liechtenstein and had made international headlines. Files and data processing units holding the keys to the facility's history and nature had been seized, hard drives and memory boards on mobiles and computers pulled out, but all were encrypted and impossible to decode. Most of the facility's equipment had perished in the fire.

Julia and the chief constable had shared their sides of events, and the newspaper report corroborated them. Twenty years in cryopreservation. Twenty years, one month, and five days to be overscrupulous. His reanimation had caused him short-term memory loss as well as temporary muscle paralysis, which oddly came as a relief as he had overheard the doctors discussing his paralysis in worried tones, but now he knew it wasn't permanent. It was simply a side effect of being brought back from cryosuspension. Paralysis and memory loss were only short-term effects of the cryo-stasis and not a lifelong sentence. Still, the feeling of helplessness lingered while he waited for his body to remember how to move again.

He also realised that his blood had been drained from his jugular, like siphoning fuel from a tank, an invasive procedure he couldn't remember enduring. This explained the small cut on his neck, hidden beneath the bandage. With movement back in his arms, he absently traced his finger along the deep groove on his forehead, a jagged mark that felt as if a knife had carved a lightning bolt into his skin.

How did anyone begin to comprehend, or even accept, they had been cryopreserved for twenty years? While he had been entombed in some godforsaken cryostat, Julia had given birth to their daughter, Sarah-George. An entire lifetime had passed without him. Julia had asked him why he had left. He understood the question with more context. She was fifty-two. A physical seventeen-year gap now stood between them. Meanwhile, his daughter had spent her first nineteen years on Earth fatherless.

As his memories continued to stream back, he recalled his last phone call with Julia. It had been a difficult conversation. Her voice had seemed distant, distracted. She must have only recently found out she was pregnant. The timing matched up with their last night together before he left to start his job at ELF. He had been gone for two months before his lengthy term in cryopreservation. Why hadn't she told him?

Bryan, now a fifty-five-year-old man inside a thirty-five-year-old body, had never felt a greater sense of failure than at this point.

Julia: *Why did you leave me?*

Sarah-George: *I'm your daughter.*

The doctors: *You have a fractured skull, and the muscles in your body are not responding.*

The police: *Photo evidence proves you killed Michelle Locke.*

The consequent effects of his reckless actions had ruined his life. Smolensk and his rebel army of agents had killed him by letting him live.

He glanced down at the newspaper spread across his lap. His face was plastered across the front page underneath bold, sensationalist headlines. He was the subject of no fewer than the first six pages, a disabled psychologist, bound to a hospital bed by handcuffs, his image displayed for the world to see. His face in the picture was unchanged with his features frozen in youth, untouched by the passing decades. Yet in reality, he was twenty years older, a man out of time, a ghost of the past that no longer fitted into the present. The media didn't know his name yet and had resorted to giving him crude nicknames: *The Ghost of Cryonic Past* and *Future Boy. Ice Man* was the most prominent, reminding him of the maliciousness of the British media, and how utterly disconnected he was from the life he'd once known. But why had he become the centre of attention? Why had he survived? Where were the other four thousand patients? His mother, where was she?

The man in the next bed moaned loudly as he woke, then babbled incoherently for the next ten minutes.

Bryan was eager to ask him questions, but not while he was in such a delirious state.

Finally, after finishing his incomprehensible monologue, the man abruptly turned to Bryan and asked, "Where am I?"

With revived muscle power, Bryan slowly pushed himself up the bed and sat upright, a difficult manoeuvre with his left hand still attached to the bedrail. "Are you Heath Fletcher?"

He opened his mouth, and Bryan saw him use his tongue to probe his teeth, with many missing or reduced to jagged razors. He must have copped a powerful blow to the mouth.

"Who are you?" he asked.

"I think I was your replacement at ELF."

"Where am I?"

Bryan coughed to clear his throat, the effects of smoking still with him, even though, technically, he hadn't smoked in twenty years. "Some London hospital. They found us both in Liechtenstein."

"Who did?"

"Police."

He stared at the ceiling for five, ten seconds. "What are you talking about?"

"We were cryopreserved."

"I don't... I have no... I remember running through the forest and..." He shook his head. "Who are you?"

"Bryan. Morgan. I was your replacement at ELF."

He blinked rapidly. "Replacement?"

Bryan nodded. His memories were flooding back now, vivid and intense. He recalled his interview, his first meeting with the president, and treating his first patient suffering from malaria. He remembered the bond he had formed with Ann and the sexual desire she had stirred within him, but couldn't remember if he had succumbed to his desires.

Then it hit him: he had seen Dr. Fletcher before. Inside a secret room. Inside a cryostat. He also recalled taking over his apartment and the message above the bed.

He snapped his head towards Dr. Fletcher. "Find the lie. What does it mean?"

He looked at Bryan slowly. "... What?"

"You left a message above your bed. It said *find the lie*."

"What lie?"

"That's what I'm asking you."

He frowned as he stared at the ceiling. "What happened to me?"

Bryan started to remember more names. Pity he couldn't

recall a meaningful fact or anecdote about his colleagues: Dr. Huber, Dr. Seymour, the Sheriff, April, President Smolensk, Kane.

Memories of the AIDS lab flooded his mind. The vast, sterile room where he had killed an agent. The details came back in fragments: the cold glint of the cryostats, the sharp scent of chemicals, the way the agent had crumpled to the floor when Bryan accidently plunged a pair of scissors into his neck. But strangely, he felt nothing. No guilt or fear, just a hollow detachment, as if the entire event existed in some cruel dream, separated from the reality he now inhabited.

A doctor put his head around the door before sauntering off, stealing glances through the window.

"Liechtenstein?" asked Dr. Fletcher.

"What?"

"You said Liechtenstein."

"That's where the foundation was operating, and where they found us."

"No, that can't be."

"That's where they found us."

"Why were we in Liechtenstein? It doesn't make sense."

"Why do you say that?"

"Liechtenstein was only a small foundation, the first of its kind. About one hundred citizens were cryopreserved there, mostly from Liechtenstein. It had only one lab of cryostats. I worked at the main foundation with more than four thousand patients cryopreserved across six labs. My memory's a mess, but I know it wasn't in Liechtenstein."

Bryan was rendered momentarily speechless. "There's a second foundation?"

Dr. Fletcher nodded.

"Where?"

"Right here in England."

35

Bryan's recovery progressed rapidly, astonishing the doctors. What they had anticipated would never happen happened in a matter of hours. His muscles regained full sensation, and he could even wriggle his toes, monumental movements after his previous immobility. His limbs tingled incessantly, as though waking up after a long, numbing sleep, bringing a mix of relief and discomfort.

He hadn't slept for almost two days, his mind too wired to even contemplate it. Every time he almost felt himself go, his mind teased with a new memory, forcing him to work to fully retrieve it.

Dr. Fletcher had explained the labs had been rigged with explosive devices, a precaution in case the foundation ever came under attack. "In the event of a siege, the president did not want any loose ends," he had said grimly. "Now we are survivors, and that makes us people who know too much." He'd paused, then added, "It would be wise to start thinking about leaving the country."

Bryan had absorbed the severity of his words. Smolensk had gone to extreme lengths to protect his life's work, and now they had become ELF's greatest threat. Bryan realised the danger they were in was more immediate than ever. But when he had asked Dr. Fletcher where this information came from, the answer was chilling. He had stolen the company logbook, a record of everything ELF had tried to hide. It was why he had been condemned to cryopreservation, an act of punishment and protection. The president couldn't afford to lose him, but neither could they risk setting him free with all he knew. His knowledge of the logbook's whereabouts also explained his stark warning. They weren't just running from ELF; they were running for their lives.

Dr. Fletcher had then made a statement that caused his blood to run cold. He was eighty per cent sure the foundation in Liechtenstein was the site of the human experiments. He didn't elaborate on the specifics, but he hinted at something far more sinister, stating this was how ELF had managed to perfect cryopreservation in the first place.

Dr. Fletcher also said the logbook contained information about a drug called HNV1, a revolutionary treatment capable of curing AIDS. This wasn't just a theoretical breakthrough; HNV1 had the potential to change the landscape of medicine entirely. It could effectively treat HIV *and* other long-term infections, including Hepatitis B and C, and also Tuberculosis. The enormity of HNV1's capabilities was staggering. Bryan's mind was swamped with questions: How many lives could be saved? What had the foundation sacrificed in its quest for such a powerful cure? The fact this drug existed and was tied to inhumane experiments should have sickened Bryan, but he felt nothing. After all, it was a game-changer, but it came at an unimaginable cost. The dark reality of their situation sank in: he and Dr. Fletcher were entangled in a web of corruption, greed, and moral compromise, spelling dire consequences for everyone involved.

Not everything in the logbook contained incriminating content, but plenty did. When Bryan had asked him where the logbook was, he had said, "Firepit."

"Where's the firepit?"

Like a malfunctioning robot, he had suddenly looked up at the ceiling and whispered, "Find the lie. Find the lie."

Bryan had asked him *what* lie?

Fletcher had blanked him after that.

Bryan had later asked him where ELF was. Fletcher didn't know, only that it was somewhere in southern England.

The foundation in Liechtenstein, he now understood, was only the sister foundation of ELF. And they held the key to unearthing big brother and unlocking its dark secrets.

Later that evening, the lights on their wing went out, and emergency backup lighting came on in the corridor. It raised instant red flags with Bryan.

This was the first sign of danger.

The second was when the window in the adjacent room suddenly shattered with a deafening smash, causing shards of glass to rain down and scatter over the floor like crystal blades.

Bryan bolted upright and looked towards the door. The officer guarding his room rushed from his post to investigate the incident. Bryan's pulse quickened as he caught a glimpse of the officer's movements in the window reflection of his door. Struggling to see him in the dim light coming from the backup lights, he watched as the officer bent down to pick up a rock and leaned out of the broken window, peering into the car park below to search for the culprits. Who'd thrown the rock? Was it just a random act of vandalism, or something more sinister? Was this unexpected act simply a warning or a distraction? Whatever the reason, he was acutely aware their situation had become increasingly dangerous.

While the officer remained out of sight and away from the door, Bryan wondered what his next step was. First, he tried to squeeze his wrist out of the handcuff, even believing it was possible until he almost tore his skin. He needed a tool to break it open or at least try and weaken the hinges. Craning his neck to peek into the corridor, he noticed an axe locked inside a glass cabinet, intended for fire safety and emergency preparedness. He contemplated how he might get his hands on it when the porter suddenly stopped his trolley just outside the door to tie his shoelace. The trolley was stacked high with resuscitation equipment; presumably staff training had just concluded.

Bryan was about to ask the porter for assistance when the young man looked up from his task and walked into the room with the broken window. He watched as the officer and the porter conversed. He heard a police radio crackling.

He needed to act quickly before it was too late. He swung his legs out of bed, placing his bare feet on the freezing floor. His knees almost buckled from weakened muscles. Steadying himself against the bedframe, he searched for a way out of the trap he now found himself in. He flicked the brakes on the wheels with his heels and dragged the bed towards the door. On his knees, he rummaged through the porter's trolley, desperate to find some kind of weapon or a tool that could help him escape the handcuffs restraining him. From his low position, he glimpsed through a gap in the equipment at two men wearing black entering the corridor through the fire door, which bathed them in the light from the fire exit sign. They moved quickly in his direction along the corridor. Dread filled him when they pulled out guns and attached silencers. In that moment, he recognised them for who they were: CI agents, sent to eliminate him.

He froze as the men closed in. Every instinct screamed at him to move, to escape, but he was paralysed, not by fear but by the immovable bed hanging off his wrist. First, the men entered the adjacent room. Bryan heard them approach the porter and police officer. A series of gunshots erupted, almost silent thuds in the confined space. Bryan stood and flattened himself against the wall, listening, knowing he needed to act swiftly because his survival depended on it.

Without quite knowing what to do, he wheeled the bed back into its rightful place. He arranged his bedding to aid in his disguise and hid beneath the sheets just before the men entered his room, relying on the darkness to keep him hidden. He kept still and stopped breathing as though the act made him invisible, but his heart pounded so hard he could feel it rippling through his entire body.

While one of the agents flattened the window blinds while the other aimed his gun at Dr. Fletcher, who opened his eyes seconds before the agent pulled the trigger: two shots in his chest, a third into his brain. Skull fragments and white hair caked in blood burst all over his pillow.

The agent then turned the gun on Bryan, whose head was visibly sunken into the pillow. The bedsheet was pulled up to the eyes, and his handcuffed wrist poking out of the bedsheet attached to the rail was unmistakable.

Another three shots were discharged.

Two in the chest. One in the head.

Thud. Thud. Thud.

The dark room lit up in a series of flashes.

Blood instantly blossomed on the sheets of both beds.

The agents turned and hurriedly left the room.

36

Explosions echoed in his mind, distant but relentless, while gunfire cracked like thunder, mingling with the haunting wail of screams. Flymo squeezed his eyes shut, willing the noise to stop, but it persisted, a violent soundtrack that refused to fade. He shook his head, trying to escape the torment as he sat inside his old Jaguar, listening to the engine wheezing like an old man struggling for breath.

Switching off the ignition, he got out and locked the door. He turned and faced the Royal Academy Hospital, looking up at its tall windows that glowed with clinical light. With a deep breath, he approached and stopped just short of the entrance, standing beneath a streetlamp, feeling the chill of the evening air.

Just then, two men wearing black suits rushed out of the hospital, splitting off to avoid a collision with Flymo. They jumped into a black Land Rover and sped away with a brief but startling squeal of tyres.

Flymo hadn't set foot inside a hospital in over a decade. The smells and sounds were too close to memories he'd spent years burying. He hesitated outside the entrance, staring at the hospital's towering glass façade. His pulse quickened. Could he even face it? The mere thought of walking inside made his chest tighten. Memories of explosions rocking the air, gunfire shattering the silence, and screams that were loudest of all, filled the spaces in his mind. He clenched his fists, his body stiff with the tension of a man at war, not just with his past but with himself. He could turn around, leave right now, and no one would blame him. But that wasn't how this worked. There was no running from what waited inside those hospital walls.

The cold wind tugged at his long coat as he moved closer to the hospital. The automated doors whirred open, as though inviting him into a place where his nightmares would run riot. Flymo paused for a moment on the threshold, his reflection barely visible in the glass. He didn't recognise the man staring back. The moment the doors parted, the medical environs hit him. Inside, everything was too bright, too clean, too quiet. This wasn't the battlefield, but somehow, it seemed equally as dangerous.

"It's a fucking hospital!" he whispered.

The old lift rattled as it ascended from within its musty darkness. Reaching the third floor, Flymo wended his way along the corridor, beyond the supply rooms and radiology department, heading to the north wing. The corridor in Ward E was flooded. Vast patches in the ceiling loured over three black buckets on the floor, collecting the floodwater. Wet-floor signs stood on either side of the puddles while a cleaner mopped up and an electrician worked beside him, rewiring a busted light.

At the end of the corridor, Flymo found Bryan's room. A trolley stacked with medical supplies and equipment stood haphazardly in front of the doorway, as if abandoned in a rush. Flymo hesitated only briefly before shoving it aside and stepping into the room. The blinds were drawn, and all the lights were turned off. A faint glow from the hallway barely illuminated two beds in the room. He could the see unmoving shapes of Bryan and another patient, both appearing to sleep beneath their covers. He stood still for a moment, debating whether to leave and perhaps return tomorrow. Everything looked peaceful, and he didn't want to disturb the fragile quiet. But as his eyes adjusted to the darkness, he noticed dark stains on the sheets of both beds. On closer inspection, he was both beds had holes torn into the sheets, and the white fabric was soaked in blood. Ominous pools, darkening the linens like ink spreading across paper.

Flymo froze, his body locking up as though paralysed. His hands began to tremble uncontrollably, his fingers twitching with memories he couldn't suppress. The room around him blurred, but his mind was sharp, dragging him back into the thick of it. He could imagine jagged shrapnel marks scarring the walls, bullet holes punched into concrete, bodies piled high with blood pooling beneath them. Explosions roared in his ears. Gunfire snapped through the air. Piercing screams that filled the room. He was back, trapped in a nightmare that had never truly ended.

With a deep breath, he drew back the sheets. He was dead. He had seen enough gunshot victims in his life to know for certain. Bullet wounds to the chest and head would do it. His long, white hair was matted with dried blood, and his mouth hung open in a final, silent scream, exposing shattered teeth. But it was his brown eyes, wide with terror, that told the story. He had known his end was upon him, the inevitability of his own death, frozen in that last moment of fear. Flymo pulled the sheet over the body, covering his face out of respect.

He circled to the next bed with a tightened chest. Bryan's cuffed hand was slack in the cuff attached to the bedrail, and his hair was a mess on the pillow. Even before he pulled the cover back, he knew the truth. His old friend was gone. It didn't take a sharp eye to read the scene. The bullet holes in the sheets and the thick pools of blood denoted fatal wounds. It was obvious. The grim evidence told him all he needed to know.

With a heavy heart, Flymo braced himself and pulled back the sheet. He blinked while his mind scrambled to catch up, almost forcing him to do a double take. Then the realisation dawned. It wasn't Bryan lying in the bed but a mannequin torso, punctured by bullets and leaking red-hued liquid soup, a blood substitute, from its plastic chest. The head, which looked real enough and had a realistic brown wig, had a hole in its forehead. The bottom half of the trick body was made up of pillows.

Movement under the bed made Flymo back away with a startled fright. He gently raised the bedsheets and ran his eyes down the arm handcuffed to the bed to find Bryan cowering underneath. Flymo couldn't decide what shocked him more: the fact he was still alive, or that he hadn't aged a single day since he last saw him two decades ago. Time had left him completely untouched.

"Help me up!" said Bryan.

Flymo, his pale face still showing his utter shock, reached for his arm and pulled him to his feet. "What the fuck?"

Bryan pointed at the door. "There's an axe in the corridor. Get it!"

Flymo froze, too shocked to move or speak.

"Quick!" said Bryan. "They might be back."

Flymo spun on his heel and strode out of the room, his pulse racing. He spotted the cabinet and, without hesitation, slammed his elbow into the glass. The pane shattered with a sharp crack. He ran his eyes along the empty corridor. Where were the staff? He pulled the axe from its stowage, gripping the handle tightly.

Bryan pulled the handcuff chain taut, aligning it parallel with the rail and letting it rest on top.

Flymo raised the axe above his head, while Bryan turned away and braced himself.

He struck the chain, cracking it in half.

It left a ringing in Bryan's ears. He winced and shook his wrist, then massaged it with his other hand before looking at Flymo. "Get me out of here!"

Flymo guided Bryan into the corridor. His bare feet were clumsy, his senses slow, but Flymo wrapped his arm around Bryan's shoulder and assisted along, almost dragging him away from the room.

They passed the officer and porter in the opposite room, their bodies twisted on the floor, execution-style.

Bryan and Flymo took the fire stairs to the lobby, picking up speed the further they descended.

Two police officers loitered over by the drinks machine, chatting about an attractive nurse who had just passed them, laughing at their own crude jokes. They never noticed Flymo and Bryan slip out of the hospital.

37

—√—

"Mate, what the fuck is going on?"

The hospital faded into the distance, a few miles behind them. Flymo, normally an erratic driver, navigated the streets of London with surprising caution, adhering to every speed limit.

Bryan was still in his white hospital gown, barefoot, with a bandaged neck and a broken cuff clinging to his wrist. He let out a dramatic huff. "Where to begin?"

"What happened back at the hospital? It was an absolute bloodbath."

Bryan took a deep breath. "Reporter published my photo in the newspaper."

"And that's a problem because…?"

"They knew where to find me."

"They? The people you worked for in Liechtenstein?"

"Yes, but not in Liechtenstein."

"What do you mean?"

"There's another facility, here in England."

Flymo glanced at Bryan, scanning him from head to toe, still trying to comprehend his sudden presence after all these years. "What the fuck happened to you?"

Bryan stared out of the window. "I tried to escape. I don't recall anything after that."

"Escape? Wasn't this supposed to be your dream job?"

"My mother's in there."

Flymo's jaw dropped. "She died, what forty years ago?"

"She's alive, sort of."

Flymo joined the carriageway and took the old Jaguar up to seventy, still obeying the speed limit.

"All I remember is running up a dark tunnel. I don't know where. I don't know why. Next thing I know, I'm in hospital and it's the future."

"Why did they do that? Freeze you?"

"I don't know. As punishment?"

"Punishment for what?"

"I don't know."

"Why did they try and kill you in the hospital then?"

"You're asking a lot of questions."

"I'm concerned for my mate, that's all."

"We pose a risk to the foundation."

"We?"

"The dead man you saw in my room."

Flymo frowned. "So, police found you in Liechtenstein, what, like frozen in a coffin?"

Bryan manually wound down his window. Fresh, winter air gushed in. "I don't know the details."

Five consecutive sneezes exploded from Flymo's mouth. "Well, it's good to have you back."

Bryan zoned out while Flymo changed down through the gears at a roundabout. "I need to get my mother out of there. I'll kill them all, I don't care."

"Steady on, Rambo. She must be there for a reason."

"She has HIV."

Flymo paused. "Does your father know?"

Bryan nodded. "He knows. But he's living on empty hope. The foundation has developed a cure for AIDS. They've had it for twenty-five years, but they won't fucking use it."

Flymo had never heard Bryan use profanities before. Not once. Threatening to *kill*? To wipe them *all* out? It felt entirely out of character for him. The threat seemed hollow, merely a byproduct of his frustration. The Bryan he knew was deeply empathetic, someone who forged genuine connections with others. He loved intensely and loathed just as fiercely. It was all or nothing with him. He certainly didn't *kill*. He wasn't the type to even resort to violence. This wasn't the Bryan Flymo remembered. He suspected whatever had happened at the foundation had changed Bryan irrevocably. Yet, something about the situation felt off; he was holding back, reluctant to reveal the full truth. A dark secret lurked beneath his veneer. Dirt under his fingernails.

"Why not?"

"The foundation operates illegally. The president wants to go global but can't. If they share the cure with the world, the foundation will be compromised."

Since leaving the hospital, they had passed three police patrol cars, forcing Bryan to slide lower in his seat. He was a fugitive, and half the country was probably looking for him. How did real criminals on the run keep their cool?

"Where are we going?" Bryan asked, breaking the silence between them.

"My house."

"You live in London."

"Not anymore. I bought a place in the countryside about eight years ago. Nice and quiet."

Flymo pulled out his mobile phone and dialled someone with a single button click.

Bryan couldn't help but admire its thin, compact design and sleek functionality. Only wealthy people could afford to own a mobile, and he pondered Flymo must have done well for himself. Presumably, he resided in some grand mansion with multiple rooms and flashy swimming pool. It was the kind of opulent lifestyle he had always chased with luxuries he yearned for.

"Hey, it's me. Guess who's in my car?"

"Is that Julia?" Bryan whispered.

Flymo pressed the mobile against his chest. "I'm going to let her know what's happening."

He kept the call brief and told her they were headed to his house for the night. He also told her to say nothing to the police if they showed up at her door, reassuring her they were fine and had a few matters to sort out.

"What happened to the Viper?" asked Bryan.

"Wrapped her around a tree."

"Sounds about right."

Bryan examined the Jag's shabby interior, an understated car for someone pretentious like Flymo. All the panels were scuffed and cracked. The leather seats had lost their shine and smoothness. Many of the dashboard lights were out. The old engine made rattling noises like a chaotic percussion quartet. And it reeked of brake fluid. It seemed at odds with Flymo's personality. Maybe the old Jaguar was a rare model, one that was worth a fortune.

He turned the microscope on his old friend. Like the Jag, he had not aged well. He was almost completely bald and had gained a lot of weight around his middle. His face was heavily wrinkled, savaged by time. It looked different, contorted with enlarged cheeks. Bryan suspected he had undergone plastic surgery. Observing Flymo more closely, Bryan noted how casually he was dressed. This was a man who had once taken pride in his fashion choices, always sporting the latest trends. His jogging bottoms and brown cardigan, which had a large hole at the elbow and looked unwashed, seemed a departure from that persona, as though he were trying to blend into the background. Then again, Flymo was now two decades older. Perhaps he had grown weary of fashion, opting instead for comfort over style. Flymo had been a full-on fitness fanatic who always bought the newest gadgets and drove fancy cars. The joy and vitality and all the luxuries he used to flaunt so openly were gone, and Bryan couldn't shake the feeling there was more beneath the surface, a story waiting to unfold.

"The world's changed," said Flymo.

"Yeah? I wouldn't know."

"Everything has become digital. Business, entertainment, homes. Even the way people look for love. Dating apps and websites are everywhere. Shopping has moved online, and now we can buy anything with a click. Banking, too. It's all at our fingertips, even if we're on the other side of the world. Tourism is digitalised, with virtual tours and online bookings now the norm. In the wake of terrorism, some airports use hi-tech eye scanners to enhance security. It's a different world, with a new kind of madness. There are even these electronic cigarettes for people who want to smoke without smoking. Things are changing so fast. Internet cafés came and went, a flash in the pan. And now, video stores and music shops are barely hanging on. It's hard to keep up with all the constant changes. It feels like everything we knew is being replaced by something we can't quite touch."

"Why?"

"So-called convenience. If you're tech-savvy. Everything is online."

"Online?"

"On the Internet. Trust me, the world's gone mental."

In Bryan's case, the statement was a nasty truth that was difficult to accept and even harder to admit.

38

Flymo's house was far from any grand estate, and certainly not a mansion. In truth, it barely qualified as a country home. Nestled in the middle of the countryside, it might have once been charming, but time and neglect had taken their toll. The wooden porch sagged precariously with rotting, splintered beams. Rainwater dripped from cracked gutter pipes, staining the faded walls below, while rusty metal panels clung to the sides of the house.

The front garden had become an automotive graveyard, littered with the decaying remains of old VW vehicles. Their rusted bodies were little more than skeletal frames, windows shattered, seats ripped out, leaving gaping holes where once people had sat. Tyres were deflated, and grass crept up the wheels, reclaiming the metal carcasses inch by inch. Weeds pushed through the cracks in the earth, weaving themselves through the engine compartments and doors, as if nature was slowly swallowing up the abandoned cars.

"You live here?" asked Bryan incredulously.

"I admit my standards have slipped a little. Well, a lot."

"What happened?"

"I've been attending group therapy for alcoholics for the past eight years. I left the army a long time ago, just couldn't handle it anymore. I do up old VWs instead and sell them for profit. When I can be bothered."

Bryan took a long look at his old friend, noting the toll that illness and time had taken. He was battling a nasty cold, and it showed. He looked awful, worn down in every way. At fifty-nine, he was partially deaf in one ear, and his once sharp green eyes seemed dulled, softer, as if he was under sedation or had overindulged in cannabis. His notorious energy had faded, replaced by a heavy, tired glaze.

"You never married?"

He forced a laugh. "Me? Married? I think we both know I was never cut out for marriage. I've got a dog to keep me company in my old age. Her name's Sally."

They climbed out of the Jag and approached the house. Flymo unlocked the creaky front door and gestured for Bryan to step inside. The moment Bryan crossed the threshold, he was hit with a wave of nostalgia, though it wasn't a pleasant wave. The old, floral wallpaper, faded and peeling at the edges, covered every wall and was yellowed with age. The thick, brown carpet underfoot looked worn and stiff, as if it hadn't seen a vacuum in years. The furniture was just as dated, with bulky, mismatched pieces that had been dragged through the decades without a single upgrade. The same sunken armchair, scratched coffee table, and dusty bookshelf lined with ancient knickknacks Bryan remembered from years ago. It was as if nothing had changed in Flymo's world, except the slow creep of time that had left everything, including the house, tired and worn.

"It's been tough on us without you around." He said it as an appeal for compassion.

Bryan raised an eyebrow. "Us?"

"Me and Julia."

Bryan nodded, urging Flymo to elaborate. His eyes held something Bryan couldn't quite place: regret, or guilt.

"She was alone and depressed after you disappeared, not knowing what had happened to you. And she had to raise her daughter alone. It was really tough for her."

He used the word *alone* twice in the same breath. He kept pinching the bridge of his nose. Bryan noticed a subtle droop in his friend's shoulders, the way his hands fidgeted nervously He avoided direct eye contact, glancing at the floor, then out the window, as if searching for an escape or the right words to follow up with. A sign of someone with more to share. Bryan's experience in psychology and many years of knowing Flymo hadn't dulled his ability to read the signs.

"Let's go to my garage," said Flymo. "Get that handcuff off your wrist. I've got just the tool."

Ten minutes later, Bryan walked into the lounge flexing his wrist. He changed into a pair of Flymo's jogging bottoms, a plain shirt, and a knitted sweater, each item a few sizes too big. The shoes and socks fitted fine.

Flymo put the kettle on and brewed some tea, and as they sat together, they tried to remember the last time they had seen each other. After a great deal of back-and-forth, they both recalled playing golf together. They hadn't even made it past the first hole before calling it quits and abandoning the game altogether due to imminent rain.

Bryan talked about his encounter with the CI agent on his way home that day, deconstructing how it had gone downhill from that point on, leading him to this point in time. But he found himself more fascinated by the change in Flymo. Age played its part, but it was more than that. All those years of heavy drinking and the numerous hours Flymo had spent at Alcoholics Anonymous meetings had left a mark. By Flymo's own admission, the years had been turbulent. He spoke about his post-war struggles, recounting stories that almost brought him to tears. A few memories caught in his throat, his voice faltering as emotions surfaced. It was painfully clear to Bryan his old friend was a deeply wounded man, the scars of the past visible not only in his words but in every gesture and every pause.

"So, what's next?" asked Flymo, wiping his eyes when he thought Bryan wasn't looking.

"I need to find the foundation. Dr. Fletcher said it was somewhere in the south."

"That narrows it down. Do you have anything else?"

"The first time they took me there, they drugged me on the plane so I wouldn't know where it was they were taking me. They pretended to give me a pill to settle my fear of flying when it was a strong sleeping pill that knocked me out for about three hours. Before my second flight, the day I started working there, I took Modafinil to counteract the sleeping pill they gave me."

"What does Modafinil do?"

"It's a eugeroic drug for treating narcolepsy. Keeps you awake. I pretended to be asleep to hear what was happening and to find out where they were taking me. The flight took forty minutes. When we landed, I opened my eyes briefly and looked out of the window."

"What did you see?"

"Only forest."

"So, a large forest. In England. Somewhere in the south."

"It's something."

"You're sure it's in England?"

"The president made indirect references to Liechtenstein, fooling me into believing it was where the foundation was. In fact, he was funding the facility in Liechtenstein for cryonic research and drug development but using the one in England as more of a hospital for sick patients."

"Well, whatever happens, I'm here to help. We'll sort this mess out."

Bryan nodded.

Long after Flymo had passed out in his armchair, Bryan found the spare room, but he was too restless to sleep. He swung his feet off the bed onto the carpet and stretched his arms, trying to get some circulation in his joints and muscles. He walked barefoot to the bathroom, soaked a towel in cold water, and pressed it to his face. The coolness brought some clarity, but his thoughts quickly shifted to his neck. Carefully, he unwrapped the bandage, exposing a jagged, scabbed-over lump along his jugular. His fingers traced it lightly, feeling the uneven texture beneath his skin, still swollen and tender. The wound, much like the pain it carried, was far from fully healed.

Downstairs in the kitchen, he opened the fridge door and was greeted by the pungent smell of mouldy cheese. A few half-used jars, a bottle of flat lemonade, and other random items were all that filled the shelves. He rummaged through the cupboards for something stronger. Behind an old cereal box, he found what he was looking for: a bottle of whisky. Flymo had purged the house of alcohol long ago, but he had kept a single bottle tucked away, reserved for an emotional emergency.

Back in the bedroom, he sat at the window looking out and drinking whisky. He didn't want to drink so much as he needed something to help him sleep. The feeling of failure burned his lungs with each breath. He had a teenage daughter. Everyone had aged. Life had moved on without him. All the careful counselling he had given at the foundation and all the advice meant to help others reintegrate into society felt utterly meaningless to him. Nothing could prepare someone for the shock of coming back to life and confronting a new reality. The trauma of facing a world that had carried on while he had been frozen in time was too much to bear.

Sally's barking pulled his attention, and he glanced out the window into the night. In the dim light spilling from the room, he saw Flymo, dressed in old army uniform, walking briskly away from the house. Taking another swig of the whisky, he watched in silence, puzzled by the sight. "Where are you off to?" he muttered under his breath.

Sally trailed closely behind Flymo, barking and bounding in excitement. Flymo paused, pointed back at the house, and without a sound, Sally turned around and darted back, leaving Flymo to disappear into the darkness.

With the whisky warming his veins and instantly making him lightheaded, he staggered across the room, unsteady on his feet. On his way to the toilet, he tripped over a shoebox jutting out from under the bed. It tipped over, spilling photos across the carpet. As he bent down to gather them, familiar faces stared back at him. Julia and Sarah-George appeared in more than half of the photos. His daughter looked about two or three years old. The first few images showed the girls in carefully posed shots, followed by slight variations of the same pose. A younger Flymo beamed in the next photo. The backdrop was outdoors, somewhere sunny, peaceful. His arm was around Julia's neck, and little Sarah-George was crawling between his legs. They were all laughing, the picture capturing a moment of joy that felt impossibly distant. He tried to shake off the pang of jealousy and bitterness twisting in his chest. The image of them as a happy family in his absence filled him with rage and equally with regret.

Trying to shake off the obvious truth staring him in the face, he turned away, grabbing the whisky from the table and taking a long, burning sip. But the pull of what he had just seen in the photos kept dragging his mind back. He glanced down again and spotted another picture, this time of Flymo and Julia kissing. He froze, staring at it. He understood that he had been dead, but in this moment, he almost wished he still was.

Driven by a painful curiosity, he strived to unearth more proof of their affair. He yanked open a chest, dumped the drawers onto the floor, and began tearing through everything he could find. He ripped clothes from hangers, pulled boxes from the back of closets, rummaged through their contents with growing desperation. The shelves, cupboards, and even under the bed. Nothing was off-limits. Between each search, he drank more whisky, his anger and heartbreak fuelling him as he tore the room apart in his search of further evidence.

More than ever, he needed the alcohol. That and a quiet place to dream up his vengeance.

It was late. Julia and Sarah-George were headed up the stairs to bed when the home telephone rang. Julia let the machine take it, anxious it could be the authorities calling, searching for her husband.

"It's me. Bryan. I wonder what you're thinking. What to make of everything?"

Julia was relieved to hear his voice. The police hadn't yet come to the house. She'd seen nothing on the news. It didn't mean he was out of trouble. He had escaped police custody; there would be serious repercussions.

Julia bolted down the stairs into the lounge, reaching for the telephone. As her fingers hovered over it, Bryan's voice came through again, bitter and raw.

"Of all people, why him, why my fucking best friend? And what about Sarah-George? Is she his?"

Julia froze, her hand trembling above the telephone.

Sarah-George, standing nearby, quickly shook her head in confusion. "What does he mean?"

Julia hesitated, her heart thumping. Bryan never cursed. The venom in his words hit her hard. "Pay no attention to him," said Julia. "He's drunk."

Sarah-George's brow furrowed. "What does he mean, am I *his*? He's my father, right?"

Julia's throat tightened. She had dreaded this moment for years, knowing the truth would eventually have to come out. But not like this. Not now. "We need to talk," she said softly, avoiding her daughter's eyes. "Tomorrow. I promise, I'll tell you everything."

Sarah-George nodded.

There was a heavy thud.

"Shit!"

Julia listened to him fumbling with the telephone.

"I've dropped the fucking bottle!"

After that, the line went dead.

39

Flymo crouched low as he moved along the stone wall, then hopped over and ducked down. He lifted his head slowly, just enough for his nose to touch the cold stone. Confirming the area was clear, he darted into the woods. Through the trees, he found the provisional path and soon spotted the outpost. He slipped into the gap between an oak tree and a boulder, where he settled in for the night.

His preparations required some knife-work. Using a nine-inch blade, he shaved down a few branches, stripping away the damp outer layers to make dry firewood. A large ring of pebbles held the ash from previous fires, which he cleaned with a fire brush. With a flick of his lighter, the fire caught. He used the knife to slice open his ration pack and heated the sausage and beans in a saucepan over the flames, eager to eat despite the late hour.

Fed and full, he closed his eyes and waited for sleep to take him. He kept the knife close and hummed a tune to pass the time.

His eyes sprang open, and he stopped humming. Sensing something prowling nearby, he flicked on his torch. "Who's there?"

Sweeping the beam left and right, he examined the dark gaps between the tree trunks. He hadn't brought his firearm. The laws in Britain were too draconian to risk going out into the woods armed. The knife, though, he could justify if push came to shove. Seeing no one about, he turned off the torch, closed his eyes, and enjoyed the silent wilderness, the perfect tonic for his troubled mind.

Life as a soldier had made more sense to Flymo, giving him purpose and power. Manifests, maps, reports, strategies, dead drops, adrenalin. His idealised views on army life had shattered that day in the small Iraqi town. The battle against the militant group had rolled fast, flowing through the war-ravaged streets between damaged buildings. The main street had ended at an intersection, and his unit had surged right. Brute force had overwhelmed the enemy all the way to the children's hospital, heavily under siege and the focal point of the battle. Visibility had been poor. Smog and haze and the windswept Iraqi-desert sands had made it hard to see clearly beyond the hospital windows. But there was no mistaking the frenzied shouts from the children holed up in their rooms.

Guns continued to go off.

Glass shattered.

A stun grenade exploded.

The militants shouted and waved their automatic weapons menacingly in the windows. Their demands were punctuated by the sharp rattle of gunfire in the distance, heightening the tension. Faces hidden behind scarves, they glared at anyone who dared to make eye contact, a clear warning they were not to be challenged.

Fighters on the roof of the five-storey hospital suddenly opened fire on his squad. Bullets pitted against metal, wood, and concrete.

Around him, soldiers dropped like bricks. In the space of thirty seconds, he had lost nine men.

The firing came from all directions.

Flymo took two bullets in the back. A third knocked him over. He scuttled up behind a derelict wall and spun, bringing his gun up, but he had no target in sight.

Search. Listen. Evaluate. Act.

He downed a sniper hiding near a pile of bricks. A single shot through the eye. He killed two militants caught between no-man's-land advancing towards the hospital with precision head shots. He took out another driving a van away from the scene, causing him to crash into a wall.

Once the coast was finally clear, he struggled over to the hospital, dragging one of his legs and leaving a furrowed trail of blood in the dusty road, littered with bodies. He entered the hospital several minutes behind his unit, now engaged in a fierce battle on the second floor. The cloying stench of death met him the moment he entered the foyer, with bodies everywhere. The smell was exacerbated by extreme midday heat. Clouds of flies rose and scattered as he approached, then rapidly returned to the bloody remains.

An explosion tore through the hospital canteen, the blast so powerful it shook the entire building and sent shockwaves through the floor. One of the militants had detonated a suicide vest, obliterating everything around him. Civilians inside were caught up in the blast, their fates sealed in an instant. The canteen was reduced to rubble and twisted metal, kicking up clouds of dust and debris. The cries from survivors echoed throughout the corridors. It would take days to sift through the wreckage and recover what remained.

Among the sound of gunfire, he could hear the children's screams. He knew with clinical detachment he was bleeding heavily from the bullets lodged in his back, saturating his uniform. Struggling to breathe, he kept moving forward, gun raised. A boy appeared in the smoke at the end of the corridor. He ran towards Flymo, holding a weapon in his hand. Flymo shot him in the neck and watched him fold to the floor. He walked up to him and turned the boy over.

Her. A young girl. A child. She had a radio in her hand.

As he reeled away, his mind made the quantum leap from confusion to shock. With suddenness, it caught up with him, the years of ferocious battles, too much killing, and too much death.

Still and silent, like the hushed night around him, Flymo stretched his arms behind his head, sending waves of pain through his body. He stared at the blackness, unable to tell if his eyes were open or closed. He turned his head so he could see his house, a faint pinprick of light in the distance. The light in the spare bedroom was on. Bryan was still awake. Lots on his mind, no doubt. He'd missed his friend, missed the banter, the swapping of stories of their past. How would their relationship change with the age difference?

Flymo bore wounds that cut deep yet left no visible mark. In the grips of depression, he needed help, the kind only Julia could give. Despite knowing she'd never truly felt the same, he still loved her. Their so-called relationship, if it had ever really been one, was long over. But what about Julia? How did she feel about her husband's sudden return? Would she take him back, even with the years and the distance that now lay between them? Could seeing him again stir old feelings, or at least give her closure? Maybe, just maybe, it would push her back into Flymo's arms, rekindling something that had once blossomed between them.

And then there was Bryan. Flymo dreaded even thinking about how Bryan would react if he learned about those few stolen moments Flymo and Julia had shared. They had been brief, but intimate. He knew Bryan would have questions, but Flymo had no intention of answering them. If he found out, he could take those questions to Julia. He wasn't going to have that conversation, not now, not ever.

No doubt Bryan had a million other things on his mind. Flymo had been shocked to hear about Bryan's mother. He had almost offered his condolences, but it seemed trite under the circumstances. He knew how close Bryan had been to his mother. He had once told Flymo he had hardly spoken for the first year after her death, a silence he had not learned to stifle with words. Julia had saved him at eighteen years of age, got him talking and loving again, and brought him back from a dangerous path.

Flymo's gut told him Bryan's plan to track down ELF was doomed. It was reckless; no one could take on an empire like that alone and expect to come out on top. But as much as he saw the flaws, Flymo couldn't ignore the surge of excitement building inside him. He wanted in. After what ELF had done to Julia, savagely maiming her, he was driven by a need for revenge. He'd stop at nothing to make them pay, leaving no stone unturned in his mission to shut them down for good. If he played his cards right, maybe he'd hit the kill switch on the organisation. And maybe, in the process, he could win Julia back.

Flymo rolled his eyes back to his house.

The bedroom light was still on. *Every* light was on.

And then he realised they weren't lights at all.

His house was on fire.

40

"Bryan, wake up!" Flymo shouted, his voice frantic. "Bryan, wake the fuck up, the house is on fire!"

Bryan stirred groggily, still trapped in a haze of sleep and experiencing a pounding headache. As his eyes struggled to focus, he could barely make out anything through the blur. The acrid smell of smoke pulled him awake, compelling him to focus on his surroundings. His eyes locked onto the dense clouds of smoke twisting through the gap under the door. He shot upright, and an empty whisky bottle tumbled off the bed, clanking against the floor. The sour tang of stale alcohol clung to his mouth, and the room swayed, a lingering reminder of his drunkenness. "Did you… say fire?" he mumbled, feeling confused and disoriented.

Flymo, still dressed in army uniform, raised the window. "They've thrown petrol around the house."

"Who?"

"Who do you think?"

Bryan staggered to the bedroom door, concentrating to hear the fire raging on the other side, an almost silent killer with multiple weapons: heat, smoke, obstruction. Opening the door, he saw the fire had already penetrated the outside walls and had spread inside, quickly working its way up to the first floor. Flames sparked and surged, consuming the hallway, climbing the banister, curtains, walls, attaching to anything flammable. Windows cracked and wood popped. Thick, grey smoke blanketed the staircase.

Flymo threw the duvet and pillows off Bryan's bed. "Help me get this mattress through the window."

"What for?"

"We have to jump!"

"What about the fire brigade?"

"It's too late. The house is beyond saving."

Bryan considered other options, one that did not involve great heights, but could not think with such a foggy mind.

They each grabbed an end of the mattress and dragged it to the window. Wrestling with the resistance of the springs, they folded it in half and shoved it through the frame. It dropped outside, landing on its edge with a bounce before falling flat.

"You first!" said Flymo.

Bryan squinted through the smoke, holding his breath as he climbed onto the window ledge, ducking to fit beneath the frame. The drop below made his head spin. It was a risky fall, and a bad landing could mean broken bones, or worse. He'd already been paralysed once this week, and he wasn't keen on a repeat.

He let out a sharp breath and stepped off the ledge. He landed on the mattress with a heavy thud, bending his knees to absorb the impact, then rolled onto the grass. Lying on his back, he looked up and gave Flymo a quick nod, signalling he was unharmed.

Flymo climbed out of the window onto the ledge, ready to jump. He stepped off, waving his arms as though holding an imaginary skipping rope. His landing was nowhere near as smooth, and he hit the mattress awkwardly. Bryan could tell by the way he limped away that he'd hurt himself.

The house was completely engulfed now. The fire had also spread into the garden, skipping and dancing along the dry grass. Some of the VWs had already gone up in flames. One car exploded and soared high into the sky, flipping over before crashing down onto another vehicle, landing roof to roof.

Flymo put his hands on his head, watching as the entire roof to his house caved in and the walls folded neatly down on top of it, kicking up plumes of smoke and sparks that peppered the black sky.

"Sally!"

Bryan had difficulty restraining Flymo from dashing back to retrieve his pet.

"She's gone!" said Bryan, holding onto his friend's arm.

Flymo stopped struggling when he was hit by a sudden blast of heat. Backing away, he watched his house succumb to the flames.

He turned and started walking towards his car. "Come, let's go!"

The silence inside the Jaguar was almost as thick as the smell of smoke clinging to their clothes. Only a hot wash could fully banish the odour. But with the sunrise painting the sky in vibrant streaks of purple and orange, that concern felt minor in comparison.

Bryan began to feel more human as the alcohol slowly wore off. The fire had certainly sobered him up quicker than usual. The fire had also destroyed the evidence of Flymo and Julia's affair, but it couldn't erase the haunting images in his mind. The memory of Julia and Sarah-George smiling beside Flymo stayed with him, tormenting and mocking him in equal measure. Should he bring it up with Julia, or wait for her to initiate the conversation? Did she even want to discuss it? He still loved her, but how had her feelings for him changed over the years? In his mind, no time had passed between them. But from Julia and Sarah-George's perspective, a lifetime had. It was a lot to absorb.

The loss of twenty years.

The daughter he never knew.

A ruined marriage.

Two attempts on his life.

An entombed mother.

A looming police conviction. Michelle Locke's death had come back to haunt him, as President Smolensk had always intended. The old man had him precisely where he wanted, trapped in the grip of his authoritative hand.

Flymo had been quiet for over an hour since his house burned down. Finally, he said, "An eventful night, hey!"

Bryan blanked him. His opinion of Flymo had crumbled, his friendship tainted. He could barely look at him. His mind switched back to locating ELF and his mother, what he now considered his utmost priority. Despite the downfall of the Liechtenstein foundation, ELF remained at large. But where?

And then, out of the blue, proving once again the brain worked in mysterious ways, an idea sailed into his mind.

"Take me to a library!"

41

Renowned as a haven for book enthusiasts and the largest independent library in the nation, the London Library buzzed with students immersed in preparing for their final autumn term assessments before the Christmas holidays. Everywhere Bryan turned, he saw bright-eyed kids with their whole lives ahead of them. Their youthful faces glowed as if they believed they had all the time in the world to chase their dreams. Many had wires coming out of their ears, connected to earbuds or hi-tech headsets, while others were glued to their handheld devices of all shapes and sizes, tapping away at their screens or scrolling through streams of information, absorbed in the digital world.

Society had undoubtedly changed since Bryan's captivity, and he wondered how traditional structures of employment and social interaction had been affected by the unprecedented advances in technology. Flat-screen, touch screen, websites, wireless. According to Flymo, everyone owned a mobile, and the Internet was as common as household television. Now, standing inside this library, he bore witness to it. He recalled Kane talking about the World Wide Web, released by CERN the year he had started at ELF. He had predicted exponential growth and had been right. An entitled generation, perhaps, though he had a lot of learning to do in the digital ecosystem.

"Are you going to tell me why we're here?" asked Flymo, turning ear-plugged heads as he limped between the tables of students, still clad in his army uniform.

Bryan's face remained calm, but his voice was stripped of emotion. "A book."

Flymo ran his eyes over the shelves and the thousands of tomes. "A book."

Into the Anstruther Wing and through to the Main Hall with the Reading Room above it, Bryan admired the grille-floored book stacks. The Anstruther Wing had five floors of book storage, all climate-controlled to safely house its prized collections. 25,000 of the rarest and most vulnerable volumes were kept in this room in recessed cases, accessible by a large, manoeuvrable staircase.

"I can save you a lot of time," said Flymo, and gestured with his finger. "Follow me."

He detoured to the IT lab, claimed a computer, and ran a database search. He talked while he typed, explaining how the library's computer search system was far superior to manual book filing systems. "What's the title of this book?"

When Flymo looked, Bryan was over by the front desk.

"Thomas Smolensk," said Bryan. "Where can I find his book?"

The librarian peered over her spectacles with a stern face. "Do you know the title?"

"I can't remember."

"What's the book about?"

"Cryonics."

"The Science and Technology section's in the corner near the magazines. You know you can do a database sear–"

Bryan marched away, passing Flymo in the IT lab. At the Science and Technology indicator tab, he was greeted by an overwhelming sight: thousands of books on medical science lining the shelves, their spines worn and pages well-thumbed from years of use by curious minds. The entire section reeked of aged paper and ink. Titles on everything from molecular biology to advanced medical treatments filled every shelf, promising answers to life's most complex questions. Among them, tucked away in a far smaller, less conspicuous section, was a modest collection dedicated to cryogenics and cryonic science, fields that were both mysterious and controversial, yet quietly advancing in the underbelly of mainstream medical research.

Bryan moved cautiously between the shelves, scanning the titles. Books held the answers to everything; he had always believed that. Somewhere within these pages, perhaps buried deep in an obscure chapter, lay the information he needed. His thoughts turned to the president's book, an elusive title he struggled to recall, but one crucial to his search. It might be the key, the one that would shed light on the foundation's whereabouts, some hidden giveaway, a subtle hint only a keen eye would catch. Maybe an offhand remark in the text or a coded message between the lines would lead him back to his mother. If there was even a chance it contained a clue, he had to find it. His heart quickened as he rifled through the shelves, hoping this obscure volume could unravel the mystery.

The first book he came across on the topic was entitled *Morals of Mortality*. He flipped through the pages and read the headings and subheadings. The premise concerned escaping mortality. It had occurred in all primitive cultures and modern world religions, according to the author, who wasn't Thomas Smolensk.

The next book on the shelf, *Promoting Cryonics*, was written by an American physics professor. It promoted cryobiology with positive implications for the future of the human race. Though based on thorough research and guesswork, it barely scratched the surface of what Bryan had witnessed first-hand. For a book almost fifty years old, he was somewhat impressed by the author's imagination.

Cryonauts in Ice was the next one to pique his curiosity. The dreamer behind the book illustrated her plans for cryotoriums: huge steel structures built to hold cryonic patients.

"Any luck?" asked Flymo, sauntering up behind him.

"Nope."

"What's this book about?"

Bryan ignored him and pulled out another book entitled *A Far Cry from Cryosuspension*. The author believed in evolution and outrightly rejected creationism. She had done bonafide animal research on perfusing and cooling cryonic patients and claimed for cryosuspension to work, a *transport team* would need to be at a patient's bedside, ready to administer requisite drugs and follow procedures when death was pronounced.

And a bunch of rebel CI agents to cover their tracks.

On page twenty, the image of a patient on a bed wearing a hospital gown with a transport team of cryonic specialists encircling her reminded Bryan of the woman he had seen put to death by injection before her body was drained of blood through the jugular, ending with the unceremonious cooling in silicone oil. It occurred to him, for the first time since he woke up in 2012, that the same set of procedures had been conducted on him while he lay naked and unconscious on a gurney. They had stopped his heart. They had drained his blood. They had drowned him in silicone oil. They had locked him up. They had frozen him. And they had ruined his life.

Bryan returned the book to the shelf and, as he turned to the adjacent shelf, saw what he was looking for.

Thomas Smolensk.

The title on the spine read *Freezing Time.*

Skim-reading the book would take time, so he turned to Flymo and said, "You can go."

Flymo frowned. "You what?"

"I'm going to be a while. You can go."

Flymo held out his palms. "Go where?"

Bryan shrugged. "Up to you."

Flymo folded his arms. "Have I done something to upset you?"

Bryan flipped through the front matter pages, stopping at the acknowledgements and dedication. His eyes darted across the lines, searching for any detail that might jump out at him. Sometimes, hidden in the gratitude and tributes to colleagues and mentors, were the breadcrumbs that led to bigger things.

Find Thomas Smolensk, find ELF.

Smolensk was the potential key to unlocking everything.

Flymo tapped Bryan on the shoulder. He turned.

"Hey, I asked if I've done something to upset you."

"No."

"Then what's with the cold shoulder?"

"I need to concentrate."

Flymo hesitated before walking away to give him space.

With the book still open in his hands, Bryan flipped to the first chapter and began reading. He wasn't just searching for information. He was on a hunt. And time was running out.

Two hours later, when he reached the end of the book, his fingers went lax on the page. His reflexes kicked in: a spike in adrenaline, a tight clench in his jaw, butterflies in his gut. He had just discovered how to find ELF.

42

The River Tay served as a gateway to the Scottish Highlands, acting as both a natural boundary and a significant route for exploration and commerce. Stretching an impressive eighty-six miles from its source in the Highlands to the high tide at its mouth, it was Scotland's longest river, flowing through dramatic scenery, and historically connecting communities, providing transportation, and facilitating trade. Its vastness and beauty, coupled with its importance, made it an essential feature of Scotland's geography and cultural heritage.

Bryan crouched behind a cluster of reeds, watching as a man in a wheelchair fished for grayling along the riverbank. The man wore a round hat and a dark green overcoat that hung just above his shins. A distinctive pirate patch covered his right eye, leaving no doubt—this was Thomas Smolensk. Despite the motorised wheelchair, he appeared surprisingly well for his years, though his true age remained a mystery. It was well over a hundred and spanned three centuries.

Bryan watched as the man drove his wheelchair down a narrow path towards a large glass house perched on concrete stilts complete with a wrap-around veranda, a rather modest structure for someone of this man's wealth and ego. He rolled onto a mechanical platform that lifted him smoothly to the deck before he steered his way inside the home, leaving the door open.

Bryan approached the house with cold determination and summoned the platform by pushing a button. As he waited for the platform to descend, he looked around to make sure he was alone. To get his way, he would have to abandon his rational mind for a darker one, but he was prepared for every possibility.

The platform stopped and Bryan boarded. It rose to the upper level, where he disembarked and crossed the deck to the open door. He found Smolensk out of his wheelchair and pouring himself a morning scotch in the large living room, staring out at the mountainous countryside through floor-to-ceiling windows.

When he turned, he looked only slightly surprised to see Bryan standing in the doorway. He hesitated, taking a half-second to match the face to a name. Without saying a word, he turned back to the window and sipped his drink, before finally saying, "I admire your persistence, Dr. Morgan. How did you find me?"

"Does it matter? You know why I'm here."

Sunlight streamed through the window, glinting off the old man's bare scalp. "You want revenge."

"I'm not like you."

Smolensk turned and faced Bryan. "You came here to kill me. At least be honest with yourself."

"Like I said, I'm not like you. I'm no killer."

"The family of the agent you murdered might disagree."

"That was self-defence."

"Don't make excuses. You were going to kill Dr. Huber. With a pair of scissors if I remember correctly. But the agent stopped you. It cost him dearly. Admit it, you're a murderer!"

"Says the man who orchestrated Michelle Locke's death."

"The foundation always comes first. It's more important than you or I. Its value transcends the life of any individual. We introduced an insurance program a year before you came along to protect us from potentially rogue staff. Look what happened. You went rogue. You have to look at the bigger picture. It's like war. Hundreds die so millions can live."

"It's nothing like war! You're in no position to talk about war. You have no idea what war is like. Your views on life are not only misguided but contradictory. You destroy lives as much as you save them. There's nothing noble in that. You're a fraud and a murderer, and that cancels out any good ELF does."

"ELF has been running successfully for over forty years. It's a bit late for a lecture on what's right and wrong. And you of all people have no right to accuse anyone of murder."

Something inside Bryan boiled over. His face turned red. "Where's ELF?"

Smolensk reached for the bottle of scotch and topped up his glass. "You'll never get your mother out."

"You ruined my life!"

"You broke the rules. You broke the contract. You killed an agent. What about *his* life?"

"You take in patients and give them false hope, knowing you have the HNV1 cure on standby. You're taking money from innocent people and giving them nothing in return. My father included. I won't let you get away with it, you fuck!"

President Smolensk smiled. "You feel it, too."

"Feel what?"

"Inside you there's a fire, smouldering like a piece of coal. Aggression, bitterness, rage. I can see the hatred pouring out of you as we speak. I wasn't always like this, you know. I used to be pleasant, well-mannered, respectful, patient. I never lost my temper. But when I woke up in that room in Liechtenstein in 1968, those human qualities were gone, frozen out of me. Deanimation requires immersion in sub-zero conditions, and it left me cold, literally and emotionally. And now you. It took me years to regain even the appearance of respectability, Dr. Morgan. But it was a lesson worth learning. You'll have to do the same."

Bryan shook his head disbelievingly.

"You feel resentment towards people, even the ones you love. Your morals haven't changed at all. You still believe in fairness and helping others. You care about people, but inside you are filled with cold and anger, and lack compassion and empathy. Am I right?"

An icy dread came over Bryan. "If I'm resentful of those I love, it's for good reason. The underlying cause still points at you and your fucking foundation."

"Cryobiologists have always worried about the effects of cryopreservation on the brain. Memories before preservation are always lost. It's known in the industry as cryo-amnesia. Damage to synapses and dendrites also affects memory and personality. Occasionally, it has caused permanent memory loss or dementia. The middle sections of the brain, which are primitive and where rage, fear, and sexual feelings originate, are almost always affected by the sub-zero temperatures and, at the moment, are beyond repair. These emotional defects are what is stopping ELF from becoming legally sanctioned, simply because the world would become an angry, emotional catastrophe. That is what has happened to you, Dr. Morgan. We've suffered the same injustice."

Bryan's denial was offset by the nerve Smolensk had just struck. "Tell me where the foundation is!"

"And why would I sell out my own foundation?"

"Then have my mother cured and let her live."

"Cured. Huh. There is no cure."

"You're lying!"

"Enough of this rubbish."

"Tell me where it is!"

"Get out of my house!"

"I'm not leaving until you tell me."

"I'll call the police."

A dangerous spark flashed in Bryan's eyes. "You're not calling anyone."

Smolensk looked at the sky. "They'll be here any minute."

"Who?"

"Agents. They're flying me back today."

"Then you'd better talk fast."

"We can play this game of verbal chess for as long as you like."

Bryan sighed. "I'm no killer, but I'll take your life if you force my hand."

President Smolensk topped up his class and added a cube of ice. "I would die to protect the foundation. Like I said, it's bigger than you and me. You can do whatever you please with that syringe you're trying to hide behind your back. But I'll tell you nothing."

Smolensk was no fool. He knew that by injecting air into the body, the cause of death would be unexplainable. As the air bubbles circulated the four heart chambers, the capillaries would be too narrow for the bubbles to pass through. This would quicken respiration, creating an airlock and causing the body to shut down. Forensic scientists would only discover the true cause of death if they took an X-ray of the body, an uncommon practice in post-mortem procedures, especially when the victim was an elderly man. An autopsy would fail to uncover any trace of the bubble in his system since cutting open the body would instantly release it from his blood, and the evidence would vanish in the air. Therefore, a heart attack would most likely be listed on the death certificate.

"You certainly know things about the human body, Dr. Morgan. We need people like you."

The way he said it, with a mock smirk on his face, set off an alarm in Bryan's mind. "Why did you send Dr. Fletcher and me to Liechtenstein? Was it to use us as subjects for your experiments?"

"Like I said, we need people like you. Who better than a couple of traitors?"

Bryan's eyes narrowed. "What did you do to us?"

"You'd rather not know."

Bryan stepped forward, the syringe tight in his fist, rage building, patience diminishing. "Tell me where ELF is!"

"No!"

"Now!"

"Never!"

Bryan pulled back the piston, filling the syringe with air. "You've got ten seconds."

Smolensk had slowly and discreetly moved towards his coat stand, where he reached behind and retrieved his rifle, complete with a mounted scope on the top. "This is a licensed gun. And you're an intruder."

He discharged a shot, and the rifle jerked in his hand.

Bryan dived out of the room as a bullet whizzed through the door and out of an open window into the surrounding hills. He scrambled behind the wall.

The moment he stood, Smolensk was upon him, pointing the rifle at his head.

"I guess that's life, Dr. Morgan. You never know when it will end."

A gust of wind sucked the veranda door shut.

It startled the president, who glanced over his shoulder, distracted into thinking someone else had arrived. Perhaps he thought Bryan had an accomplice.

Bryan lunged, capitalising on his concentration lapse. He pushed the rifle away with his left hand and drove the syringe into the old man's neck with his right. A fleeting sense of déjà vu rinsed through him as the image of the scissors driving into the agent's neck flashed in his mind.

The syringe pierced the artery wall, and Smolensk let go of the rifle, dropping it to the floor as he clutched his neck.

Bryan held him as his knees gave and he slid to the floor.

Smolensk's breathing grew quick and shallow, and as he turned his eye to Bryan, a genuine fear gripped him. "There's something I have to…"

"Tell me where!" said Bryan.

"Your… father."

The president's pupil dilated into a black saucer and his eye rolled back, but he wasn't dead. He was still breathing.

"What about my father?"

He returned to consciousness, his eye opening with a look of desperation. "Cryopreserve me! I beg you!"

"Did you never watch James Bond?" asked Bryan coldly. "You only live twice."

Smolensk fell still, a quizzical expression spread across his face. Now he was dead.

43

Bryan's rage had already peaked and was starting to subside. He had committed murder and felt no guilt. He would do it again if he had to. What surprised him most wasn't just the lack of remorse but the absence of any feeling at all. There was none of the horror he'd felt the first time he accidentally took a life, nor the peace or satisfaction he thought revenge might bring. This raised a red flag. Smolensk had told him cryopreservation had frozen basic human qualities out of him, leaving him devoid of empathy and compassion.

Technically, Bryan was back to square one, with no clue where to find ELF. His patience had waned, his anger taken over, and now his only lead lay in the middle of the hallway with his arms by his side, growing just as cold physically as his cryosuspension had left him emotionally. His left eye had a fixed stare.

Bryan knelt beside him, raised his eye patch, and stared at the hollow, dark crater where the eye had been. Technology and medical standards had come a long way during the four decades since Smolensk's surgery. Advances in microsurgery, tissue regeneration, and artificial implants might've restored what was lost. In today's world, medical professionals might have saved his eye, sparing him the indignity of wearing that patch. But time had never really been on Smolensk's side.

Bryan stood up with urgency. Finding ELF was all that mattered. It had to be soon. He had CI agents and the police on his tail, both desperate to track him down and remove him from society or existence, depending on which outfit reached him first. He began his search in the studio. A half-finished landscape on a wooden easel with a blue tarpaulin underneath it stood in the centre of the room. The president's delicately executed artwork, which depicted the River Tay during sunset, impressed him.

Going room to room, he searched every draw, cupboard, and surface, searching through all his paperwork. He returned to the hall and checked the president's pockets, opened his wallet, and hunted for a business card or something with an address. What had the old man wanted to say about Bryan's father? How had he been relevant in all this? Was it merely a coincidence that his father had tried to contact him before he joined ELF? What had they done to him in Liechtenstein? What experiments had they carried out?

He left the house, bitterly disappointed. He had wasted time and killed the only person who could unlock the secret to finding ELF. No one had seen him enter; no one saw him leave. As he reached the river, he paused and glanced back at the house. A thought struck him: he had unfinished business.

So he sprinted back to the house and went inside, making his way to the president's lifeless body. He might have been dead, but he still held the only key to ELF: his fingerprint. Senior management had exclusive access to all the foundation's most secure areas, protected by fingerprint authentication. Bryan knew this was his only chance. The empty syringe had kept the murder clean, leaving no visible sign of his involvement, no physical struggle. But now, standing over the body, he was faced with a grim decision. Hacking off the president's finger would mean crossing a new line, one that screamed foul play. It would be impossible to hide the brutality of such an act. Yet without it, his door into ELF would remain sealed. The choice between preserving his anonymity or getting closer to the answers he so desperately needed was not really a choice at all. He was so far down the rabbit hole now, turning away would be a futile act.

First, he ducked into the studio to collect the blue eight-feet-squared tarpaulin from beneath the easel and dragged it into the hall. He flattened it out and rolled the body onto it. Next, he snapped on a pair of rubber gloves from the kitchen and grabbed a meat cleaver from the knife rack. He flattened the president's hand on the floor and straightened his index finger, severing it with a precise chop at the base, clean across the bone.

Then it struck him: it could be any one of ten fingers.

Five minutes later, he stood at the kitchen sink, rinsing off eight fingers and two thick thumbs before dropping them into a sealable plastic bag.

You feel it, too.

He washed the cleaver and gloves. He washed the sink. He washed his hands, using his wrist to switch the tap off and avoid leaving his fingerprints as evidence. He went back into the hall and stared at the corpse, thinking about something Flymo had said: *some airports use eye scanners these days*.

ELF prided itself on staying at the forefront of cutting-edge technology. Their security systems were top notch and constantly evolving. Had they upgraded from their advanced biometric data recognition and introduced iris scans? Bryan looked at the president's eye with dark, chilling thoughts. If ELF had progressed to include iris recognition, fingerprints alone wouldn't provide him with access.

He raised the knife, steering it with cold calm towards the still, lifeless eye. Maybe a spoon would be more effective, he thought grimly, for scooping deep enough to sever the nerves and tendons. It was a brutal undertaking, but ELF's systems mightn't yield without his eye. Bryan felt his hand trembling as the knife hovered over the socket, the grotesque reality of what he was about to do sinking in. He hesitated. The man was dead, but the sheer brutality of gouging out his eye having mutilated his corpse was too much, and his grip on the knife slackened. He couldn't do it. It showed him at least he still had a heart and a conscience. As Smolensk had stated, it had taken years to regain the appearance of morality, but hinted it was at least attainable.

With a sigh of frustration and disgust at himself, Bryan wrapped Smolensk's body in the tarpaulin. He'd have to find another way to break into ELF if they had installed biometric authentication. For now, the idea of desecrating the body any further was a line he wasn't willing to cross.

Bryan hoisted the tarp-wrapped body into the wheelchair and pushed it down to the riverbank. He left the transparent bag of fingers on the grass, a chilling reminder of what he'd done. With a grunt, he pulled the body from the wheelchair and slid it into the cold water. Without hesitation, he followed, the icy shock hitting him like a zap of electricity. Letting the invisible current guide him, he took a deep breath and dove, dragging the body towards the riverbed. He manoeuvred it into a dense patch of reeds and quickly added rocks to weigh it down. As the corpse settled, Bryan kicked upward, breaking the surface with a gasp, the cold air filling his lungs. He turned to face the house, his chest heaving, his muscles frozen.

He heard a heavy lashing sound and swung his head from side to side, trying to pinpoint the source. Out of nowhere, a helicopter dropped from the sky and landed on the grass near the house. Three men in black suits jumped out and took the staircase up to the deck, vanishing inside the president's home.

The CI agents were here.

Another agent emerged from the helicopter and headed towards the river, having spotted the wheelchair.

Bryan frantically swam out of the current and worked his way upriver towards the bag of fingers. Clinging to the bank, he anchored his fingertips in the mud, which crumbled under the pressure. Peering over the edge of the bank, he saw the agent was less than fifty metres away, and when he turned his head back to view the house, Bryan sprang out of the water and snatched the bag of fingers.

As he dropped back into the icy water, the riverbank gave way beneath him, sending him tumbling into the current. The force spun him downstream, pirouetting helplessly within the rushing water. Mid-spin, he caught sight of the helicopter and the agent on the bank. Their eyes locked for a split second before the agent drew his gun and began sprinting after him along the river's edge.

The Tay widened, its current gaining strength, pushing him faster downstream. He clutched the bag of fingers tightly as he thrashed against the water, striving to reach the opposite bank. All his limbs grew numb, his circulation slowing as the cold gripped him and his heart pounded, fighting to keep his blood moving. Hundreds of metres from the helicopter and house, the river began to narrow, and the thick brush along its banks slowed his momentum. Desperate, he reached out and grabbed onto a gnarled tree root jutting from the shore, its rough surface biting into his fingers. With a grunt of effort, he hauled himself into a small inlet where the water was much shallower, giving him enough room to stand and manoeuvre. His breath came in ragged gasps as he scanned the area, his mind already turning to his next move.

The current continued to push against his stride as he waded across the slippery mud. At one point, his feet went from under him on the algae-covered rocks, and he staggered to regain his footing. Overcome with fatigue, he reached for the sodden bank. With a grunt of pain and effort, he crawled up the mud, pushing himself out of the water.

A patch of earth exploded in his face where a bullet struck the bank. Another grazed his neck. He turned to see the agent standing on the other side with his gun up and out. The other three agents were now running in his direction, also drawing their guns.

Bryan lumbered into the nearby forest, his waterlogged shoes squelching as they slapped against the damp grass. He bent over and rested his hands on his knees, trying to relieve the stitch that had formed in his side within the momentary serenity and safety of the trees. As he straightened, breathing heavily, he scanned the area.

In the distance, he spotted the agents on the other side of the river walking up and down its banks, searching for a clear shot between the trees. In just minutes, they'd realise the river was impassable and take to the skies, scanning every inch of forest from their helicopter. He turned and headed deeper into the forest. He had only moments to disappear, to lose himself in the tangled undergrowth before their eyes were on him from the air.

44

_/\/\/\/_

A body washed ashore on a mudflat sometime after four in the afternoon. A woman walking her dog along the banks of the Tay stumbled upon a blue tarpaulin partially covering the corpse. The tarp had torn open, exposing an arm with tiny stones and dry mud caught in the downy hairs, and five raw stumps where fingers had once been.

Police carefully moved the body from the mudflat to a grassy knoll, ensuring that no evidence was disturbed in the process. A forensic doctor stepped forward, drawing down the zip of the body bag. He examined the old man's heavyset form for any signs of trauma or wounds, checking every inch of skin for bruises or cuts. He studied the left eye and head, searching for any indication of a struggle and cause of death. Raising the body slightly to inspect the nape of the neck, he noted no abnormalities before lowering it back down with care. The nearby officers stood in silence, their expressions grave as they went through the motions, watching the doctor collect hairs and fibres, placing them into small evidence bags. He retrieved the victim's wallet, documenting its contents. He also took a DNA sample, swabbing the inside of the man's mouth to gather any biological material, including fluid from his tongue. The forensic doctor worked efficiently, knowing after the post-mortem examination, he would have a clearer understanding of what had led to the man's death.

The sun was setting behind the Munro region, bringing a cold mountain shadow over the crime scene as Chief Constable Hughes stepped out of the taxi. He made his way towards a large house built on stilts. The scene, as expected, was chaotic, with Tayside Police working diligently to analyse the area and catalogue evidence. Their focus remained on the abandoned wheelchair beside the riverbank, its wheels slightly sunk into the soft earth, as an officer meticulously dusted the handles and supports for fingerprints

One investigator, a skilled tracker known for her keen eye, was on her knees, following a set of footprints pressed into the grass. She traced the imprints carefully, noting their depth and direction as they led away from what was clearly a set of helicopter tracks. As she moved closer to the river, her focus sharpened, piecing together a story that remained untold. She glanced up occasionally to survey her surroundings and the larger investigation unfolding around her, but her attention was fully devoted to the trail before her.

Dogs had also been deployed, their keen noses leading them towards the river. It seemed like the focal point of the investigation, so Hughes changed direction from the house and followed the bank, passing the officer tracking the prints, enjoying the fresh Scottish air. He filled his lungs with a deep breath. What he considered food for the soul. It brought him a semblance of peace, a brief reprieve from London's smoggy skies and septic streets.

Bryan Morgan turned out to be a much larger challenge than initially anticipated. He had managed to escape from police custody at the Royal Academy Hospital two days ago, aided by an accomplice wanted for questioning in connection with the murder of an officer and a porter. A librarian, the first of three people to report seeing Bryan with an older man posing as a soldier at the London Library, informed Chief Constable Hughes the two men had enquired about a book by Thomas Smolensk in the science section.

Hughes had made his way to the library, eager to uncover any clues that could link Bryan and the mysterious man he'd been seen with. After skimming through the book, he landed on the author's back-page bio. A photograph of the tycoon caught his attention, posed at the River Tay, a place described as his favourite in the UK. The bio noted this was where he spent most of his free time since it served as his holiday home. Intrigued, Hughes had studied the author in the photograph with the backdrop of the river and Munro mountains, trying to establish a connection, wondering about Bryan's interest in the author.

Never had he expected to find himself immersed in an active crime scene, with Bryan now the prime suspect, in his view. Tayside Police didn't know that. Yet. They would soon figure it out. Bryan was elusive, but not smart enough to outwit the police. Hughes hoped the location could provide insight into his plans and reveal his next move.

The officer crawling across the grass suddenly called out to her colleagues. "Over here!"

Hughes spun on his heel and backtracked along the edge of the river, lurking behind the officer in passive observation as Tayside Police rushed over.

"I need an evidence bag," she said.

Hughes peered over her shoulder. Among the reeds was a two-tone 14-carat gold wedding ring with a carved white-gold centre.

The officer put on some gloves and bagged the evidence. She passed it to a colleague. "Get this over to the lab!"

45

Three-eighths of South London had plunged into darkness as a widespread blackout gripped the city, a direct result of the storm's wrath. Torrential rain had triggered severe flooding, turning roads into rivers, while relentless winds tore through neighbourhoods, leaving a trail of destruction. Power lines had been torn from their posts, leaving entire blocks without electricity, and emergency services scrambled to restore order.

Julia peered through the window as the storm lashed the street. She spotted other residents peering anxiously through their windows, illuminated by the occasional flash of lightning as the storm continued to batter the city. She looked just as anxious, but for a different reason. Bryan had been missing for two days, and nobody knew where he was. Flymo claimed he had disappeared from the London Library after reading a science book.

Thunder boomed, shaking the house and rattling all the windows, while rain lashed against them in sideways sheets. Julia had just stepped away from the window when a knock came at the door. She opened it to see Bryan standing there, soaked to the skin and trembling from the cold.

She raised her hand to her mouth. "What are you doing here?" Her eyes darted nervously up and down the road.

"I live here," he said.

She invited him in. "Sorry, that didn't come out the way I meant it."

"I have nowhere else to go," he said as he wiped his feet on the mat. He moved on autopilot, guiding him towards the dining room where Sarah-George stood.

"Where have you been?" asked Julia, following him in.

He shrugged in the manner of a person with no care. "I had to take care of something."

"The police came looking for you. What's going on?"

Bryan saw a towel on the radiator and used it to dry his hair and face. "It's… complicated."

He stepped into the kitchen, and though most of it was familiar, a few changes stood out: a new fridge and matching dishwasher gleamed against the walls, now painted blue. The kitchen had witnessed countless arguments over the years, whether over money or the neighbourhood's declining safety, which, he had noticed on his way there, had since improved. The derelict houses were gone, replaced by sleek new homes and condominiums, complete with neatly manicured lawns and expensive cars parked out front. He presumed that even the teenage rebel gangs had moved on, pushed out by the influx of middle-class families and improved police presence. Property values must have soared.

Through the dining room window, he saw their garden, so immaculately kept it was almost unrecognisable. He saw Flymo's army uniform hung on the washing line, drenched by the pouring rain. He turned to Julia. "Why is—"

Flymo walked into the kitchen dressed in a tracksuit and dabbing the end of his nose with a hanky. Bryan stared at him, unable to adjust to his strange, cosmetically altered face. He found it difficult to remain civil, knowing what he now knew. "What are *you* doing here?"

"His house burned down," said Julia. "He's got nowhere to go."

Flymo shrugged, almost apologetically.

"Haven't you got any friends you can stay with?"

Julia's concerned face turned into a scowl. "Don't be rude, Bryan!"

Bryan shook his head and sat at the table. His return had eased some of the worry, but now the house was fraught with tension.

Flymo remained standing while Julia joined Bryan at the kitchen table. "Where have you been? We've all been worried about you. The police came by yesterday, looking for you."

Bryan wasn't listening. His act of pretending nothing had happened was clearly starting to affect Julia.

She grabbed his arm. "Duncan… your father, he's here."

The news threw Bryan into stunned silence. He shot her a look of disbelief. And then he appeared behind her, framed in the doorway. He was an old man with hardly any hair and thin, pale skin that hung loosely on his bones. Deep-set dark circles shadowed his hollow eyes, giving him a gaunt, weary appearance, suggesting life had long since drained the vitality from his face.

His father had reached the physical maturity of a grown man by the age of thirteen. Even as a child, he was no stranger to hard work, toiling alongside adults on construction sites. Day after day, he had pushed his young body to its limits, lifting heavy loads and scaling treacherous heights, fitting in with the burly tradesmen. But those days of youthful strength and vigour had long since faded, and all that remained was a frail old man who found it difficult to speak. "It's... good to see you, son."

"Why are *you* here?" asked Bryan.

"We need to talk."

Bryan shook his head. "No, we don't."

"Yes, we do."

"I have nothing to say to you."

"Then just listen. At least give me that."

Bryan stared at his father, and when his eyes strayed to Julia, she nodded, informing him it was the right thing to do. He looked back at his father. "So talk."

Flymo made himself scarce while Julia made some tea, allowing them to talk without interruption. By the time she returned with their hot drinks, they had spent five minutes in conversation, making headway in their strained relationship.

"I had to let your mother go," Duncan said. "I couldn't watch her die."

Bryan listened intently, shaping his opinions and drawing conclusions. He relied on his professional instincts to analyse and evaluate his father's perspectives, applying psychological principles to discern whether he truly understood his motives and intentions. His father was neither religious nor atheist, but rather somewhere in between, having placed all his hope and faith in science. Yet, in a surprising turn, he said he had *discovered* God. He had learned to pray and started attending church regularly. After retiring from the RAF, he now worked nights at a welding factory and days as a flight instructor. He revealed that he missed his family more than anything else in the world and had never come to terms with losing them. While church offered some comfort and helped ease his guilt, it was about all it could do.

"Like you, I missed your mother. We all have our crosses to bear."

Mindless platitudes like that wouldn't earn him an ounce of respect.

"Will you get to the point?"

He nodded and wiped the tears from his eyes. "I have something important to tell you. It's about ELF."

46

Duncan talked about his time as an RAF pilot. He explained that, many years ago, when Bryan was still just a young boy, he'd been flying on a routine training sortie over the English Channel when he received a call on the radio to carry out an emergency rescue. A private plane had lost communication and was straying into unpermitted airspace. His Tornado F3, equipped with advanced radar, radio, and tracking equipment, was well-prepared for the challenge ahead.

"Lucky we have nine tons of fuel on board," said Duncan.

His co-pilot, seated behind him, laughed. "Sorry if I don't share your optimism."

"Come on. Think of it as a training drill."

When the Bellanca coasted into view, they manoeuvred the Tornado F3 in front and performed the standard wing-rock greeting.

Duncan had a clear view into the cockpit. A young man sat behind the controls, nervously glancing his way and giving a shaky wave of acknowledgment. Next to him, an older man was slumped in his seat with his mouth hanging open, eyes shut, completely unresponsive. Duncan's stomach tightened. He knew then lost communication was likely the least of their problems.

Behind the two pilots sat a teenager of about seventeen with boyish good looks, nervously looking from the window.

Duncan signalled to the young pilot, no doubt a trainee, to follow them back to the English coast. The Bellanca flew slower than the Tornado was used to, and Duncan didn't know how long the aircraft had been airborne. It could run out of fuel at any moment and ditch into the sea.

Passing overland, Duncan made a series of hand gestures, informing the pilot to begin the descent.

The pilot acknowledged by switching his landing lights on and off, a sign he knew his way around the controls.

From there, they guided the aircraft back to Southampton, one of Britain's smaller airports, where an emergency crew stood by after Duncan had radioed in the emergency.

After forty-five tense minutes of skilful airmanship, the young pilot brought the plane down safely at the aerodrome. The landing, though far from smooth, proved a miracle under the circumstances, as the pilot had been flying blind, deaf, and mute, relying on little more than instinct and sheer will.

Soon, the full extent of the malfunction became clearer. The navigation and communication systems had completely failed, leaving the aircraft with only its altimeter and engines operational. The pilot, still in training, had been thrust into a terrifying situation when his instructor, a seasoned aviator, suddenly suffered some kind of seizure mid-flight, collapsing in his seat and leaving the inexperienced trainee to take over.

The first responders were quick to reach the aircraft. The paramedics rushed to the instructor, who was unconscious, and treated him there on the runway before loading him into an ambulance bound for the hospital. His condition, though stable, remained critical.

Meanwhile, the trainee pilot, visibly upset, was consoled by the paramedics and ground crew. His hands shook as he recounted the harrowing ordeal. Ground staff, knowing how overwhelming such a close call could be, offered words of reassurance and comfort, praising the trainee for showing such composure and bravery under unimaginable pressure.

The teenage boy who had quietly sat at the back of the plane went mostly unnoticed at first. All eyes were on the shaken pilot and the ailing instructor, and he remained in the background, seemingly unaffected.

When the paramedics finally turned their attention to him, expecting shock or distress, he remained composed. Calmly, he assured them he was fine, politely declining a blanket and insisting he didn't need to be checked at the hospital, as if he had simply been a passenger on any other flight, not one to narrowly avoid disaster.

"What's your name?" asked Duncan.

The young boy slowly looked up at him. "Kane Spence."

The brave kid reminded Duncan of a certain Bryan but taller, leaner, and older.

"Is the pilot your father?"

The boy nodded.

"Why didn't you go with him to the hospital?"

"No one asked me to."

A paramedic overheard. "I'm going there now. I can take you."

"Give me your number," said Duncan. "I'll call you in a couple of days to check on you."

Duncan and his co-pilot were awarded commendations for their daring rescue efforts, but the recognition itself was unimportant. The ceremony and the accolades didn't matter. What mattered was the understanding that you never crossed paths with people by chance. Every encounter had a purpose: it was either a blessing or a lesson, but never an accident.

Bryan's eyes were wide open. "Kane Spence?"

"Yes."

"Vice President Spence?"

"He's the president there now, has been for about five years."

Bryan's eyes narrowed. "And?"

His father paused. "How do you think I got you the job at ELF?"

Once more, Bryan was rendered speechless. Even if he wanted to shout, curse, or simply ask why, he couldn't. The shock was too great.

"Weeks after the rescue, I called Kane. He told me his father had passed away in hospital. He had suffered a heart attack on his plane. Since then, he'd become acquainted with a wealthy Polish man who offered him a job. After his father's death, he said he wanted to help the sick. But first, he would go to university, all paid for by the Polish man. We kept in contact, and when I told him my wife was ill, and the doctors didn't know why her health was deteriorating at such a rapid speed, he said he could help me."

Bryan finally found his voice. "How could you?"

"It was a mistake. I persuaded your mother to go under. She didn't want to leave you, said she was willing to take her chances with the illness so she could bring you up, see you grow. I was certain they would find a cure within six to twelve months and pushed her to accept the offer. At the time, HIV and AIDS hadn't been recognised as immune system failure. I only found out she had contracted HIV after it was declared a worldwide epidemic in 1983, or 84, I can't remember. It was more serious than I first thought. I realised there wasn't going to be a cure, probably not in my lifetime, and that I would never see her again. For years, I tried to have her released. I knew I had made a mistake enrolling her for cryopreservation, that your mother would hate herself if she was cured some day and brought back to find us gone. She wouldn't *want* to live."

"So why didn't Kane release her?"

"He just told me he had risked his job and reputation by accepting her in the first place because he knew me and had pulled strings to avoid our connection from being discovered. Said he couldn't just release her without raising suspicion and people asking questions. He kept reminding me there were only two ways a patient could be released. Cured, or if the payments stopped."

"Why not stop the payments then?"

"It's not that simple. The contract I signed clearly stated that only in the event of the guarantor's death could a patient be released prematurely. He said I–"

"Why not kill yourself then?"

Duncan inhaled a deep breath. He glanced at Julia in the kitchen, who pretended to do the dishes with one eye on the sink and one on them.

302

"I did consider taking my own life, almost did, but I was a coward. I couldn't do it. I couldn't leave you both."

"Couldn't leave? Huh, that's rich!"

"Please, let me finish. Kane kept me in the loop with her progress. He always gave me the same answer: *our specialists are working on it day and night.* One morning, he told me they were looking to employ a new psychologist. I thought of you instantly. I told him I knew the perfect person for the job. I never told him you were my son. Because you had changed your surname to Morgan, it was easy. I told him you used to be my psychologist and that you came highly recommended. I told him how good and respected you were in the field, and that your patients spoke highly of you. I told him about your awards and your work in the Falklands War and that you were tough, experienced, and could be trusted to be discreet."

"Why have me work there?"

"I thought maybe you could keep an eye on your mother. It made me feel less guilty knowing you were by her side. It was what she would have wanted."

Bryan slammed his fist into the table, knocking over a pair of salt and pepper shakers. "You selfish bastard!"

"You're right. I tried to call you so many times. I wanted to let you know what I had done. I wanted to tell you about ELF, and that someone was going to offer you a job, and that your mother never died all those years ago. I did try to warn you, but you wouldn't talk to me."

"Yeah, it's my fault!"

An hour passed, and Julia thought things would ease up. They didn't. They only got worse. She asked Flymo to act as peacemaker, but when he saw Bryan and Duncan facing off, he turned and limped away. "Let them battle it out," he said.

"All I can say is sorry," said Duncan.

His paternal instincts took over, and in a bid to bridge the widening gap between them, he leaned forward, attempting to take the reconciliation a step further with a hug. His arms reached out, tentative but hopeful, as though the gesture alone could heal the years of distance and unspoken tension.

But as soon as he moved in, Bryan recoiled. With a sharp breath, he raised his palms in protest, a clear signal to his father to keep his distance.

"Why are you here, now, after all this time?"

"I saw you in the newspaper and wanted to try and put things right between us. I guess I was wrong. This old fool never was one for smart choices."

Defusing tension with self-contempt was a technique he used to gain sympathy over blame, Bryan recalled. It didn't work on him.

"You shouldn't have come."

Duncan looked gravely at Julia and back at Bryan. "Listen, we should leave the country, all of us, and lie low for a while."

Bryan shook his head. "I'm wanted by the police. There's no way I can leave the country. And my passport would have expired years ago."

"You don't need a passport for Wales."

Bryan folded his arms and listened, not totally against the idea, but not sold either. By just being here, in his house, he was an easy target for the agents and police.

"A good friend of mine owns a house on Lake Vyrnwy in the Berwyn Mountains. If we leave now, we should be there before midnight."

47

Flymo drove the Jag out of London and onto the motorway, the city fading behind them as they set off on the long drive towards Wales, a journey that would take four to six hours. The engine made a racket, but inside the car, an introspective silence hung heavy.

Bryan sat in the passenger seat, while Julia sat behind him and Sarah-George in the middle, next to his father. He stared blankly ahead, lost in his thoughts, fitting together fragments of his memories and emotions, searching for answers that his mind had stubbornly locked away. Despite his fatigue, Bryan couldn't bring himself to rest. His need for sleep grew with each passing minute, but his mind was too restless to let him drift off. To make things worse, a throbbing headache had settled in, accompanied by bouts of dizziness. He could tell it was from a lack of sleep, but also the light-headedness that resulted from hunger and the constant movement of the car. His stomach had rumbled for hours, but the discomfort was overshadowed by the sharp, pounding pain in his temples.

The Jaguar wasn't exactly a smooth ride. Every bump in the road jostled its passengers, with the engine's overstated roar growing louder whenever Flymo pressed down hard on the accelerator. As the car sped along the motorway, Bryan closed his eyes, hoping to find relief, but the tension refused to abate. The journey was long and unforgiving, with miles of asphalt and unresolved thoughts stretching out before him.

When he glanced at his left hand, he realised something. His wedding ring was no longer on his finger. It must have slipped off, though he couldn't remember seeing it since… when… the hospital?

It called to mind the old superstition: *the loss of a wedding ring was said to foreshadow a couple's separation*, which reinforced his belief that superstition held more truth than people cared to admit.

Flymo switched lanes to give way to a huge lorry with a shipping cargo container on its trailer hammering along the outside lane. As it passed, water churned up from the tyres, spraying the side windows of the Jag. Flymo hit his horn and cursed the driver.

"Why can't we just tell the police about the foundation?" asked Julia, breaking the silence.

Bryan considered her question with all seriousness, but the answer was simple. "I have no proof. I don't even know where it is."

Julia sighed. "What did you get yourself caught up in?"

Sarah-George added, "This is all a bad dream."

"No," said Bryan. "It's a bloody nightmare!"

They had been on the road for a couple of hours when Flymo noticed the petrol needle slipping into the red zone. Refuelling aside, now was a good opportunity to break up the journey, stop for the toilet, and get some provisions, so he swapped lanes and veered onto the slip road, downshifting into the petrol station.

Julia offered to take over the driving duties.

Flymo declared he was happy to continue.

Within minutes, they were away again with a full tank of petrol and some basic stores.

Duncan went over the accommodation arrangements at the lake cabin, scrupulously laying out every detail, as Bryan remembered him doing throughout his childhood. He spoke about the area, outlining the amenities, the route they would take to get there, even the weather forecast for the weekend. It was clear to Bryan his father was stressing over things that didn't require such intense scrutiny. As he listened, he could not help but notice the furrow in his father's brow and the way his hands gestured animatedly, revealing his tension just beneath the surface.

The cabin, Duncan explained, belonged to an old school friend who hadn't been there in over two years. Duncan was eager to ensure everything was in order. It was more than just a weekend getaway; it was a responsibility he had taken on willingly to help a friend. He planned to inspect the property for any signs of structural damage and general wear and tear after such a long absence. Duncan gave them a rundown of the cabin's features, stating it was nestled in the woods by the lake with a cosy fireplace and plenty of space for everyone.

Bryan heard his father's enthusiasm for the task, even if it was laced with unnecessary worry. While he appreciated his father's thoroughness, he questioned if it stemmed from a deeper need to control the situation, finding some comfort in the familiar routines of planning and inspecting. He had been a controlling husband and father, not violent in a physical sense, but undeniably harsh with his words, always asserting his authority and frequently getting his way. As the man of the house, his word was law, with no room for argument. It hardly came as a surprise to Bryan when Duncan had told him he'd been the one to pressure his mother into accepting the offer of cryopreservation. It was so typical of him. His controlling side had also come to the fore when he had pulled strings to get him the job at ELF, ensuring he would be there while his mother fulfilled her term in cryopreservation. The thought stirred the anger boiling within him.

Bryan saw the roadblock before Flymo. The blue and red sapphire lights sent a flurry of nerves throughout the car as Flymo eased off the accelerator.

Three police cars were parked on the hard shoulder, their lights flashing, while officers had set up a line of orange cones to direct traffic into a single lane. An Audi had rear-ended a van, scattering shards of coloured glass across the motorway. The situation turned out to be more fuss than crisis. Though traffic slowed, it continued to move, and soon the cones were adjusted to reopen all three lanes once more.

They soon crossed the River Severn on the Severn Bridge, and a sign read: *Croeso i Gymru.*

Welcome to Wales.

48

They followed a one-mile trek along a serpentine, narrow lane riddled with cracks and potholes. Dead leaves were plastered to the damp ground, creating a slick layer beneath the tyres. Beyond the reach of the Jaguar's headlights, the winding lane made a sharp turn and disappeared into the trees. Stones and gravel careened up into the undercarriage, and low-hanging branches scratched along the roof. The front end dipped into a pothole, causing muddy water to splash on the windshield.

The cabin appeared in the headlights, and soft rain began the moment Flymo rolled to a stop. He sat for a while, leaving the engine to idle for an extra few minutes before disengaging. The silence brought the car back to life, stirring everyone into motion. Bryan had a positive feeling about the secluded place. A smallholding in the middle of nowhere, intimate in a tree-defined enclosure, allowed them to hide and things to settle.

"Why are we just sitting here?" asked Sarah-George.

"Let's go!" said Flymo.

The cabin, called *Lakeside Venue,* as shown on a block of wood hanging from a wrought-iron bracket nailed to one of the support beams, had a raised deck at the front that sat on its original cornerstones, while the slanted gabled roof was supported by rafters secured with wooden pins.

Bryan grabbed the luggage from the boot and opened the car door for Julia.

"Thanks," she said with a hollow smile.

"It doesn't look like anyone's been here for years," said Sarah-George, tiptoeing across the dead leaves cluttering the deck where a lonely rocking chair faced Lake Vyrnwy.

Flymo and Duncan helped Bryan with the bags and went ahead. Bryan took advantage and held back, waiting for them to enter the cabin before slipping away to the side where a two-metre wire-mesh compost bin stood. He ran his left hand through the compost, reached into his pocket, pulled out the bag of severed fingers, and buried them beneath the mulch. They would be safe there.

Halfway up the steps leading to the deck, still feeling dizzy and nauseous, he suddenly tilted his head and shook it, as if trying to dispel water trapped in his ear canal. The sound of metal scraping against the floor in his mind slowly faded, and he noticed his father watching him with a look of concern.

"You okay?"

Bryan continued up the stairs. "Fine!"

He was the last one inside and closed the door. A panel of switches behind the door failed to bring on the lights.

Julia closed the laced curtains, stained yellow and covered in a dark mould.

The radiator pipes in the downstairs bathroom jutted out through the wooden floorboards. The unit was broken, and chunks of plaster had been torn from the walls and ceiling. Julia accidentally bumped a metal pipe leaning against the wall, sending it sliding and kicking up plaster dust. Once it settled, she tried the toilet and showed her relief when the flush still worked. On her way back to the lounge, she stopped to look at a black and white photo of a man with big, bushy hair.

"That's the owner," said Duncan. "Ted Harcourt-Brown when he was younger. Handsome fellow, he was. Always got the ladies. Never held onto them, though." He ran his eyes around the interior. Cobwebs and dust covered everything. "He wasn't exaggerating when he said this place might be in bad shape."

Bryan found a gas boiler in the cupboard. Disinclined to tamper with old gas units in the dark, he decided to look at it in the morning. Instead, he loaded the granite fireplace with logs from an oval wicker basket, located the fire-starter cubes and a box of matches, and lit both. The fire solved the light problem and slowly warmed the cabin.

Sarah-George opened the front door and peered out.

"What are you doing?" asked Julia. "Close the door!"

"I thought I heard a car pull up."

Bryan rushed to the door and stepped out onto the deck. A path snaked towards the lake, brightened by a full moon, and a small fishing boat bobbed next to a pontoon. The trees looked silver under the moonlight and gently rustled in the wind. It was hard to tell if they were pines, oaks, or chestnuts, but their presence made him feel safe. He turned and put his hand on Sarah-George's shoulder. "It's okay, go inside."

"What is it?" asked Julia.

Bryan closed the door and locked it. "Nothing. Nobody knows we're here."

"I'm going to make some tea," said Julia. "I think we all need one."

Duncan rustled up a bottle of gin and some shot glasses. He poured five drinks.

Julia declined and filled an old saucepan with water, which she suspended above the fire.

Flymo also turned down the drink for personal reasons.

"I don't like alcohol," said Sarah-George.

Duncan tipped the shots back into the bottle. "Doesn't anyone drink around here?"

"You can pour me one," said Bryan.

Over drinks, Duncan kicked off small talk with a lame but fairly amusing joke, garnering soft laughter. The joke led to a question on everyone's mind.

"I cannot understand why you're wanted by the police," said Julia.

"It's complicated," said Bryan. "I'll explain everything in the morning."

Sarah-George found a radio. She toyed with the dials, and it crackled to life. She switched stations: classical music to a political talk show to a news broadcast. The news headlines: a ninety-year-old man in Scotland feared missing had been found dead near his home on the River Tay.

"*The body, identified as missing pensioner Thomas Smolensk, was discovered on mudflats at the River Tay close to his home in Perthshire yesterday. The discovery was made shortly after four o'clock by a local woman, who informed Tayside Police. Officers investigating the scene suspect the murder is linked to Bryan Morgan, who escaped from police custody at the Royal Academy Hospital three days ago.*"

Bryan approached the radio. He reduced the volume and faced the room.

Julia stared at him with unblinking eyes.

His father stood. "Bryan?"

Bryan hesitated to say anything. What could he say? But after a brief pause, he shrugged. "I did what I had to do."

"You mean you killed him?" asked his father.

"Thomas Smolensk was my only chance of finding ELF."

"So ask him questions," said Julia. "Did you need to kill him?"

"It was self-defence. He pulled a gun on me."

Bryan turned the radio up. Perhaps there was more. The evening news became the weather segment, but he was still pondering the lead story. How had he been so careless and stupid? He had worn gloves, used a tarp to avoid any spillage, mopped up the blood, cleaned the weapons, the sink. He had weighed the body down with several heavy rocks, pinning it to the riverbed. He thought he had covered his tracks well. Clearly, he hadn't. He switched the radio off.

Everyone had their eyes on him, filled with questions he couldn't answer to their satisfaction. So he turned his back on them and went into the kitchen. He poured himself another shot of gin and knocked it back in one go before refilling the glass. When he returned to the living room, everyone was in the same positions, having not moved or spoken a word, and the fire lit up their sombre faces.

"What happened in those labs?" asked Julia. "I deserve to know."

Bryan remained mute and knocked back his gin.

"We deserve to hear the truth," she iterated.

Duncan sat back down. "Bryan?"

He owed them the truth. No more small lies or half-truths. Though he despised lying, sometimes the truth was far more painful. So, he kept it simple, avoiding the complexity that came with full honesty. He told them all about the cryonics foundation and the work he'd performed there. He explained how he'd found his mother in the AIDS lab and how he had reacted. He recounted the altercation with the CI agent that accidentally ended in death, and what he could remember of his failed escape. As for his twenty years in cryosuspension, he had no memories, nothing to explain that gap. Finally, he shared what had happened at the River Tay in Scotland, how Thomas Smolensk had ended up dead. He downplayed the murder, offering only a brief version, sparing them the grim details.

Brief or not, by the time he had finished sharing his side of the story, Julia had learned her husband was a killer.

49

Bryan eyed the fishing boat tied to the pontoon. It belonged to Ted, the cabin owner. He searched high and low for the key, rummaging through the kitchen draws and cupboards. He came across a jar on the shelf filled with all kinds of metal junk and dumped the contents onto the counter. Bolts, nails, batteries, coins, and paperclips scattered across the surface. Among the clutter, he spotted a rusty key with a black plastic grip with a ring tag that read *boat*.

Everyone was asleep except Sarah-George, sitting out on the deck staring at the lake.

"Fancy a ride on the lake?" he asked.

She nodded and gave him a weak smile.

He smiled back.

Coatless and cold, Bryan pinched his father's blue parka off the dining chair, while Sarah-George put on her raincoat, raised the hood, and tightened the cords around her neck, disappearing into its bulk.

At the pontoon, they hopped onto the boat, mindful of the gap. Bryan inserted the key in the ignition and turned the engine over. It started on the third attempt.

He steered the boat slowly away from the pontoon, gently pushing through the water as it ventured into the lake. Dark clouds scudded across the sky towards the moon, dotting the silver sheen of the lake with black polka dots. The chilly wind numbed their faces as he accelerated into the middle of the lake.

Sarah-George found an iron ring and rubbed its smooth surface. She then hurled it into the black water, watching the splash make ripples in widening circles.

"It's so beautiful," she said.

"Yeah, great spot."

She pointed at the full moon. "Careful though, all the mad people will be out."

Bryan suppressed a smile. "You're superstitious?"

She smiled. "Not as much as you, so Mum tells me."

"Did you know the word lunacy originates from the word lunar?"

"Is that why all the vampires and werewolves come out? I bet they're watching right now from the trees." She turned her hands and fingers into moving spiders. "Spooky."

"Many medical professionals I once knew believed there were more crazed patients during a full moon than any other time. Nurses and police officers have also reported increased accidents and crimes beneath a full moon. Did you know the moon's gravitational influence over the planet affects ocean tides, and the human body is made of mostly water, so that might help explain the erratic behaviour and altered mental states?"

"I didn't know that."

Bryan looked back at the darkened cabin, belching white smoke from its chimney.

Sarah-George pulled her hood down. "Do you think you and Mum can ever... you know?"

It was a difficult question. He smiled to allay her concerns. "I hope so."

Bryan saw so much of Julia in Sarah-George: the way she moved, the fire in her eyes. It stirred deep regret within him, reminding him of all the things he had never said to her while she grew up. All the advice, lessons, and shared experiences he'd missed out on. He wished he'd been there, guiding her through life as a father should.

"Tell me about yourself," he said.

"What do you want to know?"

Bryan shrugged. "Everything."

She paused and thought. "I'm a churchgoer. I'm even in the church choir. I wouldn't say I'm like a devout Christian. Or a good singer." She laughed self-consciously. "I don't have a boyfriend. Not for religious reasons. I just find boys my age immature and idiotic. Erm, what else? Ah, I'm lactose intolerant, can't eat anything dairy. I'm a mobile phone addict. In many ways, I'm just your average teenager, I suppose. I hate being dictated to. I've had so many big fights with Mum, you wouldn't believe. I have a big circle of friends. They're a crazy bunch. I need to be around people. I hate spending time on my own."

Bryan smiled. "Just like your mother."

"We *are* alike. As much as we fight, we're best friends."

"Glad to hear it. Mothers are the most important people in our lives. You only get one. I lost count of the number of soldiers I couldn't save on the battlefield who asked for their mothers moments before they died. It's instinctive."

"What was she like, my grandmother?"

"One in a million, the most loving woman you could ever meet. She wouldn't hurt a fly. I think it's why she became a surgeon. To fix people. To take away their pain. She could do that with surgical equipment or with just a conversation. She always said the right things, at the right times, with the right tone of voice and her full attention on you. She could make you feel like you were the only person in the world. You'll get to meet her soon."

"I can't wait."

Bryan smiled again and looked out across the lake. "So, do you have any pictures of these crazy friends of yours?"

She showed her mobile and whizzed through a slideshow of snaps, deleting some along the way. Bryan was impressed by the effortless swing of her finger. He explained that photos used to be contained in films with limited capacity, and then you had to take them to a print shop to get them developed and wait for days to get them back. He mentioned it cost a lot of money, even for photos you didn't want or like or were of poor quality.

Continuing through her collection, some of herself, most with her church friends, she stopped at one of Julia smiling.

Bryan stared at it before he recoiled and looked out across the lake.

Sarah-George saw the sadness in him. "Mum went crazy after you left. She told me the other day after you left us that voice message."

"Oh God, did you hear that?"

"Yes."

"I'm sorry, I was drunk."

"It's okay. I can't imagine what you're going through right now."

Bryan nodded and looked down at the boat's instruments in shame. When he looked up, he saw the menacing Vyrnwy Dam wall, standing at one hundred and forty-four feet and looming in the darkness ahead. Several arches made up the bridge with a road that ran along the top. Surplus water spilled over the crest and down the dam face.

"So, what did your mother say?"

"She thought you'd disappeared because you were upset with her. She never expected to see you again."

"Why would she think I was upset?"

"She found all the hidden cameras you set up around the house."

Bryan immediately cut the engine and sat opposite Sarah-George. "What cameras?"

"After you stopped calling, she discovered you'd put tiny cameras around the house. Like in every single room."

"I didn't put cameras in the house. Why would I?"

Sarah-George shrugged.

He knew instantly who had done it. And now, he knew why. Six months before he had been offered the job at ELF, someone had broken into his home. Not someone. CI agents. Nothing had been stolen, nothing was out of place. But now, he knew the truth. Their intention had not been to take but to leave. *Eyes.* Surveillance. Hidden cameras, microphones. It all made sense now. That was how they knew so much about him, even details he had never shared. Every move he had made, every private moment, every conversation with Julia. They had watched and listened to it all, invading his privacy so they could determine what kind of person he was, whether he was a suitable candidate to replace Dr. Fletcher and worthy of a job proposition.

Bryan frowned. "But why did she think I was upset?"

"I've probably said too much already." Her eyes softened, her cheeks pinked up.

"Listen, a lot of time has passed between your mother and me." He tilted his head. "Kind of."

She took a deep breath and let it out as a sigh. "When you started work, you were never around, so she turned to Flymo for comfort, and they... I shouldn't be telling you this."

Bryan said nothing, the pause urging her to continue.

"Well, she thought you had seen them together through the cameras. It's why she thought you had stopped contacting her. She was devastated. Flymo was never as important to her as you were, more of a moral support during a difficult time. That's what she told me a few days ago."

The night sky dulled over; the clouds obscured the moon. Rain seemed imminent.

"We should head back."

"Are you angry with me?"

"No."

"Don't be angry with them. Please. Mum had a really hard time after you left. Don't forget she was abducted, and her finger was cut off because of the company you worked for. And she never got over you leaving."

Tonight had been full of surprises, but this trumped the list. Obviously, he and Julia had lots to talk about.

"Sorry you're caught in the middle of all this."

She smiled and looked down at her feet. "I just want you both to work things out."

"Like I said, it's complicated, but we'll figure it out."

Sarah-George glanced up with a firm and resolute look. "I'm glad you killed that president guy. He deserved it after what he's done to our family. I just want you to know I'm on your side."

Bryan smiled faintly. "That means a lot."

His smile faded when, in his periphery, he saw a car on the mainland. Its headlights dipped and swept over the cabin.

Bryan felt the blood drain from his face. "They've found us!"

"Who?"

Bryan dashed to the wheel, hit the ignition, and gunned the engine, steering towards the pontoon.

"Whatever happens, stay on the boat. Do not get off until I come back for you, understand?"

"Who's found us?" she asked with a worried voice.

Nearing the cabin, Bryan saw the headlights flick off and a shadow emerge from what looked like a Land Rover.

"The werewolves!"

50

When the car pulled up outside, its headlamps flooded the small cabin with harsh, artificial light that swept across the living room. Flymo shifted first as the light broke through his drowsy state. Across from him in the adjacent chair, Duncan stirred almost in sync, his fingers twitching against the worn armrests. Both men had been half-asleep in the warmth of the crackling fire. Now, fully awake, their eyes met, sharing the same unspoken question: who could possibly be arriving at this hour?

Julia appeared on the landing, closing her dressing gown and tightening the belt. She peered down on the living room, and then took the stairs, her face rigid with fear as she rushed to Flymo and Duncan. "Where's Sarah-George?"

They heard a car door close. Heavy footsteps on the deck alerted them to the front door. The handle turned, the door swung open, and a man stood in the doorway. The glow from the diminishing fire was too dim to light up the intruder's face. But Julia's face was sharp and terrified, and even Flymo and Duncan looked afraid.

The intruder stepped into the room, his silhouette blurred by the shuddering glow of the fire, revealing the rifle casually slung over his shoulder. He wasn't particularly tall, but there was a boldness in his stride, the way he moved as though the cabin was public property. His thick boots thudded against the wooden floor with confidence and audacity. Though his face remained hidden, an unmistakable air of authority clung to him.

The moment he gripped the rifle, Bryan charged through the door, leaped onto his back, and wrestled him to the floor.

Flymo bolted over and pinned the intruder's arms while Bryan had him in a headlock on his back.

"How did you find us?" Bryan yelled.

"Leave him alone!" said Duncan on his approach. "That's Ted. He owns this cabin."

Bryan loosened the grip he had on the old man's neck and let him go.

Somehow, Ted climbed to his feet unharmed. He bent over, picked up his fishing rod bag, and flung it back onto his shoulder.

Duncan assisted his old friend into the living room and delivered him to the armchair. Ted looked rattled and needed a moment to catch his breath.

"Been trying to reach you all night," he said in a quivering voice. "Couldn't get through on your mobile."

Duncan checked and saw the lack of signal on his mobile, with no unread messages or missed calls. "What's up, Ted?"

"The gas boiler, forgot to warn you about it."

"What's wrong with it?"

"The gas control valve, it's got gas pressure settings that are too high. Inaccurate gas pressure can cause it to produce dangerous carbon monoxide. If that happens, the boiler leaks, and you could all be in danger. I forgot to warn you before you left."

"You drove all this way just to tell us?"

"What choice did I have?"

Duncan put a hand on Ted's shoulder. "Thanks, old fella. At least stay with us tonight. I've got gin."

"Thanks. I'll be back shortly. See if I can't get this bloody gas going for you." He stood and slowly walked towards the door, glancing back at the guests before leaving.

Bryan also left the cabin, right behind Ted, and ran down to the boat to collect Sarah-George, still cowering behind the controls. They returned together after two minutes.

Sarah-George pulled down her hood and ran into Julia's arms, hugging each other tightly. Julia kissed the top of her head.

Ted returned at the same time, saying he had got the gas flowing and all he had to do was switch on the boiler in the cupboard, which he did. He tested the stove, smiling when a ring of blue fire erupted.

But Bryan was distracted by the sound of the front door closing. He looked around the room, into the eyes of Julia, Sarah-George, and Flymo. His father was missing.

Bryan found him leaning against a tree and smoking thirty metres from the cabin. Held in the same hand as the cigarette was the gin bottle.

"Didn't know you smoked," said Bryan.

Duncan turned, expelling a lungful of smoke. "Probably a lot we don't know about each other." He took a long drag and blew the smoke high into the air. "Can't sleep either?"

"Can't remember the last time I slept well."

"Don't try too hard. You've just had twenty years of it."

"Thanks for the reminder." Bryan shook his head. "What happened to her?"

"Your mother? In 1970, she did six months of volunteer work in Zaire, now called the Democratic Republic of Congo. You were, I think, twelve or thirteen at that time. Do you remember?"

"Yes."

"At a hospital in Zaire, she dropped a hypodermic syringe containing fresh blood infected with HIV. The needle pierced her plimsoll and broke the skin on her foot. Of course, at the time, HIV wasn't known, and she thought little of it."

Bryan accepted the gin from his father when he passed it and drank some. "How do you cope? On your own, without her?"

"I miss your mum every single minute of every single day. I have no money. I live in a tiny, rundown flat in the city. I had to sell our house because I needed the money to continue paying for her preservation. Believe me, if I could turn back the clock…"

This was a scenario Bryan had imagined before, sharing a drink and a smoke with his father, listening to stories about his life and family. This was not quite the conversation he had envisaged. For a man in his late seventies, his father was still strong of mind and in full possession of his senses.

"How did ELF not know that she was my mother?" asked Bryan. "They watched me for six months. I visited her grave every month. They had cameras inside my house. They must have heard me talk about her. Why fucking hire me if having employees with family ties to patients was against company policy?"

"Perhaps they weren't as thorough with their onboarding as they were with other new employees because you were my recommendation. One possibility. My guess is they got your real mother mixed up with your foster mother, whose deaths occurred at similar times. Also, your mother's name is barely visible on her gravestone, so they would have assumed that it belonged to your foster mother."

"You've seen Mum's grave?"

"You're not the only one who visits her every month."

Bryan pinched a cigarette from his father, who lit the tip using his cigarette. He took a deep drag and blew the smoke out the side of his mouth, the familiar taste tickling his tongue. "Feels good to smoke again."

"Gave up, did you?"

"A few months… twenty years ago."

Duncan fixed his cloudy, aged eyes on his son. "For what it's worth, I'm glad Thomas Smolensk is dead. The man had it coming!"

51

Thunder cracked, the rain pounded relentlessly on the cabin roof, and the wind shook the windows. Julia pulled back the curtains and gazed out. The downpour had swallowed the trees, and the darkness outside was so deep, it was as if the glass had been painted black.

Unable to sleep, she left Sarah-George alone in the queen bed and went downstairs. She opened the fridge and found a mouldy turnip and an out-of-date mayonnaise jar on the shelf. Their shopping bags hadn't been unpacked yet. She poured herself a glass of water and stared out at the miserable night as the rain continued to pelt the cabin.

Despite the storm raging outside, Duncan's deep, steady breathing rattled through the cabin. Ted slept next to him on the rug under a blanket near the fire, somehow unaffected by Duncan's snoring.

She saw her husband sitting in a rocking chair in front of the fire, his legs crossed casually at the knee, hands upturned on his lap, just staring at the flames.

"What are you doing up?" she whispered.

"Haven't been to sleep yet."

Julia walked into the living room where it was warmer. "Why not?"

"Too much on my mind."

"That makes two of us."

Bryan knew his wife well enough to know her heart was a churning, emotional mess; fear of the future and their lives; guilt over her affair; anger towards ELF; concern because he had killed and was wanted by the police. He had admitted not one terrible murder but two.

"We have lots to talk about," said Bryan.

"Can we talk in the morning?"

He rocked in his chair with quizzical, unblinking eyes on her. "It *is* morning."

"You know what I mean."

He stopped rocking. "You and Flymo?"

Julia paused, clearly taken aback by his words. "Not now. It's been an awful night."

"Is Sarah-George mine?"

"Of course. I only slept with Flymo once."

"That's all it takes to make a baby!" He was surprisingly calm, just stating a fact.

Julia massaged her eyes with the heels of her hands. "She is yours, okay? You don't need to worry."

But Bryan wasn't okay. He had trusted her for as long as he'd known her, and that trust was now broken. He asked more questions about Flymo, carefully checking her answers.

There were things he needed to know, things he had to make her admit.

"Can we talk about it in the morning?"

Bryan threw a couple of logs on the fire. "What happened to your finger?"

She raised her hand. "After you left, I was abducted by a group of people in black suits, which made me think they had to be government. And that's how I knew it was tied to you because you said you were working for them."

"CI agents."

"They threatened to kill me."

"Why?"

"They wanted information."

"About what?"

"They asked what I knew about ELF."

"Did they hurt you?"

She reiterated her disfiguration by holding up her hand. "What does it matter now? It was twenty years ago."

"Did they?"

"They would have if Flymo hadn't saved me."

"Flymo?"

"I arranged to meet him at the Embankment in London. But just as he arrived, a car pulled up and snatched me off the street. They took me to some old, derelict factory, but Flymo followed them in a taxi, so he knew where to find me."

The logs ignited, crackling and sputtering in the fireplace like the neurons in Bryan's brain when he pictured Flymo and Julia together. Yet he kept her talking. He wanted it all out in the open. He could tell she was worn down and just wanted to return to bed, but he wouldn't let her go. He was good at that, good at choosing the right questions. They hadn't done much sleeping between them, and the more they talked, the more Julia came awake.

"You shouldn't have left me," she said. "You're to blame for this whole mess, not me." She broke down. "You pushed me away! I had no one. Flymo was the only one there for me."

Thunder cracked, close and unexpected, causing Julia to flinch.

Bryan looked at his father, still snoring blissfully in the chair with his arms across his chest. "Let's go outside."

They left the cabin and stepped out onto the deck. Bryan tapped the finicky dome light in the ceiling, trying to make it come on. He rested his hands against the wooden balustrade and gazed out across Lake Vyrnwy through the heavy rain.

"I never stopped loving you," said Julia. "We were going through a difficult phase in our marriage, but I always felt we would overcome it. Even when you stopped calling me. After a few months, I knew you weren't coming back. And here we are, twenty years later."

Bryan craned his neck to look at her, studying the lines around her eyes. Every time the age gap came up, the reality of their situation became harder to ignore.

"I blamed myself, you know. I thought it was because of my affair with Flymo."

"Bit late for guilt," he said, relocating to the rocking chair and putting his feet up on the balustrade.

Her lips tightened. "I *am* sorry. I hope you can one day forgive me."

He gave her a vacant look.

She came towards him, a few hesitant steps at a time. She snapped her fingers. "Bryan?"

His unresponsiveness looked like a blatant snub at first.

"Bryan?"

He continued to stare blankly, as if observing Julia from behind a thick pane of glass, deadening all sound and blurring his view.

"If you're going to be like this, I'm going to bed."

Bryan closed his eyes, not as some empty gesture to make a point, but because it happened beyond his control, as if his body had switched to autopilot. For a moment, he remained oblivious to everything around him, as though his spirit had drifted from his body.

As Julia walked away in protest, the sound of her fading footsteps drew him back to reality. "What were we talking about?"

Julia stopped and turned. She slowly walked back to him. "Bryan, what is it? You're scaring me."

A man emerged from the forest and started up the steps towards the cabin.

Julia's hand flew to her chest. Taking frightened backward steps, she tensed as her eyes locked on the dark figure. Her heart rate accelerated further when she saw they were holding a knife.

"Who's there?" Julia called out.

Bryan had jumped up from the rocking chair, looking just as rattled.

As the man moved closer and stepped into the light from the dome above, they saw it was Flymo. His hair and army uniform were soaked. "Hey," he said.

"What the hell are you doing?" asked Julia.

"Nothing," he said, his eyes shifting between Bryan and Julia, adding to the tension. The awkward silence dragged on before he finally said, "Goodnight" and went inside.

Julia shook her head and removed her hand from her chest. "What is going on around here?" She turned to Bryan. "Listen, I'm going back to bed. I want to talk more, but not now. In the morning. Okay? Goodnight."

Bryan waited five minutes, giving Julia time to settle into bed before he went back inside. In the kitchen, he unscrewed the gin bottle and poured what remained into his glass. His insomnia had become an issue, clouding his mind and making it hard to have a meaningful conversation. Whatever he'd said to Julia earlier had clearly upset her. He had always believed sobriety was supposed to bring clarity and focus. How many patients had he warned about the effects of alcohol abuse and how it damaged brain cells and disrupted neurotransmitters? For Bryan, the opposite rang true. He couldn't sleep without it. He needed the alcohol to blunt the pain in his head.

He finished his drink and left the cabin, making his way through the forest, flanking the lake. The rain had eased, but the path became deeply rutted with enormous puddles and slippery bogs. A strong breeze whistled an unheralded tune through the trees, and a wild animal scampered by as Bryan paid attention to his footing. Finally, he dropped to his knees and pressed his forehead against the sodden ground. He was a man stripped bare of defences, his anguish spilling out into the wet earth. His breath came in ragged bursts, releasing the sorrow he could no longer contain. For some time, he stayed put, a forlorn figure in the dark, pouring out his soul onto a world that gave nothing back. And in that desolate stillness, he realised no one was coming to save him.

52

Bryan opened his eyes, momentarily disoriented until it struck him he'd finally slept, even for just a few hours. For a moment, he was alone, but then the door opened, and Julia appeared holding a steaming pot of tea.

"Thought you might like a brew, sleepy head." She made her way to the bed, setting the tray down on a low table, and opened the moss-green velvet curtains. Bryan turned his head as sunlight streamed in.

"Ted did some fishing in the lake early this morning and left shortly afterwards," she said. "We've all eaten breakfast. We thought it best we let you sleep a while longer."

"What time is it?"

"Ten. I was worried about you last night. You zoned out when we were talking. Are you okay?"

He raised an eyebrow. "Nothing a cup of tea won't cure."

She smiled. "Come down when you're ready."

Stretching the sleep out of himself, Bryan walked to the window and admired the panoramic lake view, a glistening bowl with the dam on the far side. A momentary distraction from his problems. How could he fix things with Julia, and did he even want to? He suspected the love she once had for him was now gone, eroded by time and absence. Twenty years was a long stretch for any relationship, but theirs had been particularly scarred. And his recent murderous deeds cast a dark shadow over whatever bond they had left. How could she ever look at him the same? Memories of their life together surfaced. The early days, filled with laughter and hope. The quiet moments they had shared when words weren't needed, when each other's presence was enough. While those images replayed in his mind, they felt distant, almost as if he were watching someone else's life. The love that once anchored him to her was like a relic from a past he no longer belonged to. Was it even possible to close the enormous gap between them? Maybe it was better to let it all slip away.

Everyone was at the kitchen table, making chit chat. Julia laughed at something his father said. Her laughter was one of her most charming virtues and stripped the years from her, reminding Bryan of the teenager he had first met and fallen in love with. She looked up when he entered the room.

He braced himself and made a point of acting composed as he sat down with his cup of tea.

"We were just trying to figure out how we can find ELF," said Duncan. "Where do we even start?"

Bryan felt a warmth spread through his chest as he sipped the tea, hoping it would help clear his mind and steady his thoughts. He had encountered only setbacks since his term in cryopreservation. And yes, he had no leads. The one thing he knew for sure was that ELF had to be exposed. They held the HNV1 cure, and it was long past time they used it to save the millions still suffering from the disease. By doing so, he could bring his mother, and two thousand others locked away from their families, back from the dead. It would put an end to the money draining from his father and the thousands of others pouring fortunes into false hope for their loved ones. And it would prevent the CI agents from coming after him and his family, securing their safety and freedom.

Julia shared a concerned look. She looked at everyone else around the table in silence. She gave Bryan another look, this one of disappointment. In him?

"We'll figure out something." Bryan banged twice on the kitchen table with his knuckles. "Touch wood."

Flymo smiled. "Still superstitious then."

Bryan fixed him with an icy stare. "Still here then."

Flymo stopped smiling.

"Bryan!" said Julia.

Tension filled the cabin; not for the first time.

"What exactly are we looking for?" asked Duncan.

Bryan yawned. "A large building in the south of England, surrounded by fores–" He stopped speaking, as if a plug had been pulled from his head.

An explosion of pain filled his sinuses, and a blinding light struck the corners of his skull. Brightly dancing stars swarmed his vision. It was so intense he clutched his head, writhing like a man undergoing hideous torture. He tried to excuse himself from the table, but fell sideways off his chair, knocking his father's parka off the back. A piece of folded paper slipped out of one of the pockets.

Everyone rushed over to help him up, lifting him back onto his chair.

Bryan removed his hand from his head as the light and accompanying pain receded.

"What just happened?" asked Julia.

"Are you okay?" asked Sarah-George.

Bryan blinked and settled. "I'm fine."

"You're not fine!" said Julia.

"It felt like someone was sticking a knife in my head."

"We should get you to a hospital."

Bryan lowered his head. "It's not the first time." As if his life wasn't in dire enough straits, he now had these seizures to deal with. "I'll be fine."

Flymo was about to speak when his mobile phone rang. Straining as he rose from the table, a reminder that he was no longer young, he excused himself and stepped out onto the deck.

Bryan reached under the table and grabbed the paper that had slipped from his father's parka. He unfolded it, revealing a header with a logo featuring the Queen's crown. The words *Royal Air Force* and *Brize Norton* were inscribed on the ribbon beneath it.

Flymo returned, a smile beaming on his face. "That was my neighbour. He lives a mile down the road from me. He found Sally. She's safe and well."

"Oh, thank God!" said Julia. She stood and hugged him.

Bryan watched with no reaction. He slowly turned to his father, gripping the letter tightly in his hand. "What's this?"

His father took it in his hands, pulled his reading glasses from the top pocket of his shirt, put them on, and read the text. "An invitation to celebrate the seventy-fifth anniversary of Brize Norton Airfield. It's for all current and former RAF members."

"Are you going?"

He lowered his head. "No. I won't know anyone."

His father had worked every hour he could find, driven by a singular purpose: to keep his wife alive. By surrendering her to ELF and throwing himself into two jobs just to afford her cryopreservation, he had eased people out of his life and shut them off. That included his fourteen-year-old son, once the centre of his world. It had left him drowning in his own loneliness and despair.

For the first time, Bryan felt a pang of empathy, a crack in the hardened armour he had built over the years. He could see how his father's desperation had forced him to sacrifice everything for a glimmer of hope, no matter how slim. In that brief moment, he felt a shared understanding of how love and fear could drive someone close to the edge. He approached his father, put his arms around his neck, and pulled him close. His father's shoulders shook with silent sobs throughout their embrace.

Julia and Sarah-George both teared up just watching this unexpected moment unfold.

Bryan pulled back and, with little emotion showing on his face, nodded. "I understand now."

Duncan looked like he had things to say, but he was too emotional to speak.

Bryan held the invitation up. "I think I know how to find ELF."

53

Brize Norton, the UK's largest RAF Station, was the nerve centre of the RAF's air transport capabilities. It had recently reopened with a resurfaced runway and new ground lighting and equipment, installed to meet the Category II operation standards. The service marked the seventy-fifth anniversary and honoured the personnel and civilians who'd lived, worked, flown, fought, and died in the RAF since the airfield opened in August of 1937 as a training ground for airborne forces. It also featured a tribute to the people who died in World War Two.

Duncan reported to the entry control before entering the airbase via the main gate. He explored the wide variety of aircraft, but it was the Hercules and Harriers that captivated him the most. The power and versatility of these machines left him in awe, stirring memories of past adventures in the skies. Roaring over vast stretches of untouched countryside had been one of life's greatest joys. The freedom of the open air and the rush of G-force speeds were unmatched, leaving a thrill he could never forget. These days, grounded by the passage of time, he felt the absence of those moments deeply. He longed for the exhilaration, the endless possibility, and the peace he found soaring above the hurt that awaited constantly below.

At a refreshment stand, he got himself a lemonade and strolled in and out of the tents. Many people had dressed up for the occasion. Some wore their RAF uniforms, old and new. Fathers played with their children, laughing and fooling around, filling him with sadness as he reflected on the fact he had never been a good father. Or husband. He had provided for his family, making sure they were cared for, but he had never showed them how much he loved them. That was his greatest failing, one he regretted more than ever. Bryan had every reason to despise him. What kind of father abandoned their child after they had just lost a mother? Nothing could ever make things right between them.

Something was remorseful about the days and weeks he had invested in trying to persuade Bryan's mother to take up cryopreservation. Almost every day they'd discussed it. And every day her response had been the same: "I won't leave Bryan. He needs his mother. He's just a teenager; teenagers need their mothers."

"You can't mother him if you're dead!"

"I'll take my chances."

"Your condition is incurable, and it's only getting worse. You really must consider cryopreservation. Sooner or later, someone will figure out what this damn illness is and find a cure. They always do. It's just a matter of time. If you don't take up this offer, you could die."

She made a sound that he thought signified agreement.

A fortnight later, a car pulled up to collect her. She had no bags. No belongings. She had removed all her jewellery. The contract was subject to strict rules that governed cryonic patients and their guarantors. Saving her life counted on ELF operating in the shadows. It did not exist. There was no such place.

"Remember, Mr. Mansfield, your wife is dead and gone," said the agent, his tone cold and abrupt as he stood at his front door. "Grieve. Learn to live without her. She's in good hands."

On her way to the car, she looked back, her eyes wild with pain and hopelessness.

He just nodded at her and waved her off like it was no big deal, as if she were going away for the weekend. Inside, he was distraught.

The car disappeared at the end of the road. And that was that. She was gone, out of his life. He dropped like a brick, collapsing in shock on the doorstep. The harsh reality he may not see his loving, beautiful wife again was all too much to bear. Had they made the wrong decision? Had it been better to wait a little longer?

Next on his list of impossible tasks was telling Bryan, but it took a couple of days to pluck up the courage.

"Your mother is gone, and she won't be coming back," he said matter-of-factly.

Bryan's eyes instantly flooded with tears. "Why not?"

"She's been ill for a very long time and couldn't fight the illness. Now she is at peace."

After the funeral, his job quickly became his refuge, the only thing that could keep the overwhelming guilt at bay. The endless tasks and responsibilities at work filled the void left by his grief, giving him no time to dwell on what he had lost or what he could have done differently. It wasn't merely an escape. The cost of his wife's cryopreservation was staggering, with the monthly payments draining his finances. To keep up with the burden, he had little choice but to find extra work. He buried himself in his RAF duties and began offering pilot instruction to bring in more income, leaving Bryan to fend for himself at home most nights.

Their relationship, already strained, deteriorated further. Occasionally, he would call Bryan to check on him, but the conversations were brief. If Bryan raised no complaints and asked no questions, they had nothing to talk about. There was so much left unsaid, but neither had the energy or the will to bridge the widening gap. Work demanded all his attention, and Bryan grew more distant over time. Weeks turned into months. The calls became less frequent until one day, they stopped altogether. He told himself it was fine. Bryan was old enough to take care of himself, and the boy never asked for much. It wasn't until social services contacted him when he realised how deep the divide had grown. Bryan had requested adoption. The news hit him hard. His own son, and the only family he had left, sought a new life with a different family, a choice that made a bold statement.

These memories brought the pain and guilt rushing back. His wife's departure had changed everything, leaving his life lonely and fragile and full of regret.

"Are you okay?" asked a lady with a large hat.

Duncan wiped his eyes. "Yeah, just being a silly, old fool."

She smiled. "Nothing wrong with that."

He smiled and moved along. He had intended to mingle, make friends, start dialogues, and find out who was important, who knew the man he had come there to find, but he changed his mind and worked his way back to the entrance, where he approached the gate attendant.

"Excuse me, I'm looking for someone. Thing is, I'm not sure they've checked in yet. Could you check your list?"

The attendant smiled. "Sure, what name?"

"Captain John Wells."

The attendant ran his finger down the guest list, scanning the names while Duncan waited. He worried the man hadn't turned up. Maybe he had a disciplinary record with the RAF and had been discharged. He may have died of old age. Like Duncan, he may not have known anybody there and decided not to attend.

The attendant's finger stopped on the page. He looked up at Duncan. "He checked in an hour ago. You should find him near the main terminal, with the 101 Squadrons."

54

Bryan and Flymo sat in the Jaguar parked on Black Bourton Road. The silence between them had lasted twenty minutes. Flymo shifted in his seat, glancing at Bryan every now and then, as though waiting for a signal to break the quiet, but he never spoke. His foot tapped restlessly on the floor, but his face remained calm, giving nothing away.

Several Panavia Tornado GRs roared overhead, executing breathtaking manoeuvres that left the spectators inside the base in awe. Cheers and applause erupted as the jets streaked across the sky, their power and agility on full display.

Flymo's foot stopped tapping against the floor. He rolled up his window to shut out the noise of the flyby and turned to Bryan. "Let's talk, shall we?"

Bryan kept his eyes on the road. "We have nothing to talk about."

"I think we do."

Bryan shook his head. "No, Flymo. We don't!"

Flymo was a good man at heart and had always been a loyal friend, but sleeping with his wife was a line that he had knowingly crossed.

Flymo put his hand on Bryan's shoulder. "Listen–"

Bryan glared down at his hand.

Flymo recoiled, taken aback. "Mate, either we resolve this now, or we don't resolve it at all."

Something in his tone grated on Bryan. With so much he didn't want to talk about, finding anything to say felt nearly impossible. "There's nothing *to* resolve."

"You think I don't respect you, that I wouldn't hesitate to stab you in the back."

It hadn't been what Bryan was thinking at all. It was that he expected more from a lifelong friend.

"Mate, let's face it, I was there because you weren't."

Used to Flymo's impatience to resolve a conflict, Bryan knew that arguing changed nothing, gained nothing, and led to nothing but more conflict, so he climbed out of the Jaguar and walked away.

You feel it, too.

As much as he tried to ignore Smolensk's words, he kept hearing them in his mind, fighting against his resistance to believe they were true.

Approaching entry control, he found his father standing near the gate. "Any luck?"

Duncan turned and walked over to the fence. "He's here. I just asked the gate attendant. Not sure what to do now."

"Do you still have the invitation?"

"I had to hand it over. I have a visitor's pass."

"Get me in and I'll help you."

Bryan joined the queue, waiting with his hands pocketed while his father had a word with one of the attendants. When he reached the front, he was granted provisional entry and given a pass on a lanyard.

Together, they headed deeper into the airbase. A parade marched along the runway with large crowds cheering on the sidelines. Base Hangar had been cleared of all aircraft, and technicians had set up a stage with lighting for bands to play later that evening.

"Where are we going?" asked Duncan, following Bryan, who seemed to know where to head.

"Lost and Found."

A Blackburn Beverly raced by, marking fifty-one years since the formation of the Falcon Parachute Display Team. It was the same aircraft used during their historic first jumps. Six parachutists soared through the sky, performing various acrobatics while trailing vibrant-coloured smoke from their boots.

"The Falcon Parachute Display Team," Duncan said with a smile. "They've been delighting crowds all over the world for more than fifty years."

"Fascinating," said Bryan without a single upward glance. He peeled away and strolled into the Lost and Found tent where attendants surrounded by anxious parents checked off their lists and spoke into a public-address system.

Bryan found a free attendant. "We are looking for John Wells. Can you put a shout out for him?"

"Under what name?"

Bryan paused. "Just say an old friend."

"I need a name."

Bryan looked at his father, then back at the attendant. "The thing is my father is an old acquaintance. They served together forty years ago. He really wants to surprise him."

The attendant looked at his father and nodded. He picked up a microphone. "Could Mr. John Wells report to Lost and Found in front of the Air Terminal? Mr. John Wells to Lost and Found. Your friend is looking for you." The message was transmitted to every corner of the airbase through the address system.

The attendant pointed to the left side of the tent. "Please wait over there if you don't mind."

The smell of sizzling sausages from the barbeque in the neighbouring tent encompassed them, making Bryan realise how hungry he was. He had lost a few pounds since waking in the future, having lost all desire to eat.

After an anxious ten-minute wait, a tall, thin man walked into the Lost and Found tent. He had a thick, grey-bronze moustache and an RAF broach pinned to his suit pocket. The top buttons on his shirt were undone, and his grey chest hair spilled out of the gap.

Bryan recognised his long, narrow face instantly. "That's him."

Duncan slowly walked over to greet him. "John!"

The man stared at him with an incredulous look. "Aye. Do I know you?"

Duncan gave him a firm, gentlemanly handshake. "You don't remember me?"

John frowned. "Did we serve together?"

Duncan sipped his lemonade. "I was a technician. I used to service your aircraft."

"I've dealt with a million technicians in my lifetime."

Duncan nodded. "Are you still with the RAF?"

"Nay."

"Miss it?"

"Aye and nay. Sorry, but I don't remember you. Are you sure we've met?"

"John, right? John Wells? I'm Martin Smith. It's been a few years, I admit. Almost thirty, actually."

"Really?"

"We worked together in the eighties."

His face showed he was unconvinced. "That so? I don't remember. Memory's like a sieve these days."

"Tell me about it. I forgot my wife's birthday last week."

He laughed half-heartedly.

"Still doing any flying?"

"Not so much. Not many want to hire an old pilot these days."

"Retired then?"

"Semi-retired. A few associates still call on me for charter flights."

"High-profile celebrities, or just the regular rich bastards? You know, the type who wouldn't piss on you if you were on fire."

"Whoever pays the most. You know, I'm pretty good at remembering faces. Forgive me, but I don't recall you." John looked at his watch. "I'd better get back to my group."

"Wait, you were a squadron leader, right?"

"Aye."

"There's a photo of the squadrons of our era inside the terminal. We're both in it, standing next to a Tornado F3. I saw it when I was in there earlier. That's when I recognised you, and why I put a shout out."

"That so?"

"Come, I'll show you."

Duncan led John through the airbase, weaving in and out of the crowd while Brayn followed, watching closely from a distance in case there was trouble.

When they entered the terminal, which was off-limits to all visitors and therefore empty, he waited outside. This was Duncan's only chance to find out where ELF was located. He couldn't afford to show his face and jeopardise it.

By design, the terminal was functional and utilitarian with official military insignia and hanging banners. The lights were off, making it hard to see clearly. They passed the car rental shop and a row of vending machines that provided adequate light to help them see. Duncan stopped beside the children's play area in the waiting lounge.

"Where's this photo then?"

Duncan paused and swung his head to the left and right, ensuring they were alone. He pulled a small flick knife from his pocket, serrated on one side, razor-sharp on the other. He put it at John's neck with a shaky hand and forced him inside the play area.

John's eyes expanded as he backed away, stumbling over a rocking zebra. His long legs flailed helplessly in the air.

Duncan was quick to pounce, leaning over him, pushing the pointed blade into his neck. "Tell me where the cryonics foundation is!"

John frowned, struggling to find his voice right away. He swallowed hard. "What are you talking about? What are you doing?"

"You worked for a man named Thomas Smolensk. The company was called ELF. You piloted a private jet for him and his staff at least twenty years ago. I want to know where that company was based."

"Aye, that may be true, but I never had direct contact with anyone called Thomas Smolensk. They always contacted me through an intermediary whenever I was needed."

"Tell me where it is!"

"I flew all over the country. I don't recall."

"A destination in the south of England. Surrounded by forest. I want to know its name and location. I swear I'll kill you if you don't tell me."

"But–"

"You've got three seconds!"

John stared into Duncan's old, crazed eyes.

"Three."

"Ease up, will you? I don't know anything."

"Two."

He hesitated. "How can I–"

"One."

"Okay, I'll tell you! Just… back off a bit."

Duncan eased back the blade but left it poised at John's neck, listening carefully as he revealed ELF's location.

55

President Spence had experienced a lifetime of hardship and loss; his existence was shaped by the cruel realities of life and death. From his very first breath, death had made its mark after his mother died on the birthing table bringing him into the world. It was an omen, perhaps, that death would become a constant companion in his life.

As the president of ELF, he had seen many people come through the doors with the hope of preserving themselves for a future beyond their natural lives. But every person had to face an undeniable truth: before they could be preserved, they had to die. Cryopreservation required a sacrifice, a leap into the unknown, and that involved ending their current life.

For Kane, he had long stopped seeing the beauty or joy in living. Life was fleeting, a brief moment of struggle and pain, and death was its inevitable conclusion. He had learned to accept that truth early on. It no longer frightened him. Nor did it inspire any hope. Death was just a door that he'd come to know well and was no more significant than the one he had walked through the day he was born.

By seventeen, Kane had already given up on life. He had inherited almost nothing from his late father, who had died of a heart attack piloting a plane while Kane sat helplessly in the back. Afterward, lacking any direction or purpose, he let himself sink into London's gritty underworld. The first time he crossed paths with Thomas Smolensk, Kane was a shadow of himself, dressed in filthy clothes, his belongings crammed into a suitcase with a broken handle. Thomas Smolensk was the son of Boleslaw Smolensk, a Polish immigrant, nephew of a political leader, and also vice president of Kredyt Bank in Poland. Their meeting would change the course of Kane's life, though at the time, he had no idea just how much.

The wealthy businessman had found Kane sleeping in a dumpster in a dark London alley. Struck by the young man's pitiful state and in an unusually charitable mood, Smolensk offered him a hot meal at a nearby restaurant. As they talked, Smolensk confessed that Kane reminded him of the son he had left behind in 1919 when he underwent cryopreservation, which ultimately led to more questions and a deep discussion. Both men were adrift, having lost their families, and it soon became clear that they had found an unexpected bond in their shared loneliness.

Moved by this connection and no longer having his own child, Smolensk decided to take Kane under his wing. First, he offered him a room at Windermere House and began guiding him towards a new purpose, encouraging him to study neuroscience and human biology. In doing so, Smolensk gave Kane a fresh start, sparking a transformation that neither could've predicted.

Kane was nurtured into a determined, goal-driven man. He attended the Royal Holloway University of London and proved himself reasonably intelligent, sharp, and streetwise. He embraced education with a natural curiosity and a renewed interest in life. While at university, he immersed himself in as many activities as possible, and when pushed, he could turn out a more than passable tune on the guitar.

Kane snapped back, allowing his memories to recede as he stared at the coffin on the grass mantle beside the grave. Dressed in his finest suit, he stood with his arms at his waist and legs slightly apart. He had attended the ex-president's inquest last week, but the coroner's assessment had returned inconclusive.

"He was a good man," said the CI agent, standing just over Kane's shoulder and speaking into his partially deaf ear, the one missing its top. "We will avenge his death. I promise you."

Kane slowly turned, hardly in the world's best mood to begin with. "He was like a father to me, but let's face it, he was not a good man. Still, he was a visionary and a fierce advocate for global health. That was his mission, what drove him, what gave his life purpose. But his death…" Kane shook his head, unable to continue.

Thomas Smolensk had gone to great lengths to ensure the world could sustain good health. In return, his demands had been simple and modest: if he were to die prematurely, take cryopreservation all the way and make history. In doing so, credit his family name and have him immortalised by interring him in a cryostat.

"At least he's at peace now," said the agent.

The words were meant to comfort, but they only fuelled Kane's growing frustration. He clenched his fists and cracked his knuckles to release the tension. He stretched his mouth as his left hand moved restlessly through his beard. "Peace? He's probably turning in his grave right now. His cryopreservation was everything to him, and he's been denied it. You're right about one thing. He will be avenged."

Thomas Smolensk had always been outspoken about the use of cemeteries. With population growth in cities, he argued that local parish graveyards were becoming overwhelmed, unable to handle the rising number of burials in such limited space. What concerned him even more were the public health risks. Medical scientists had already warned about the dangers of burying the deceased in overcrowded urban areas, fearing contamination could pose a serious threat to the living. And now, after all the suffering Smolensk had endured to bring cryopreservation to the public, he would be buried the old-fashioned way, in the ground, surrounded by red satin lining and varnished rosewood as opposed to liquid nitrogen and stainless steel. Inside his will, explicitly and comprehensively outlined, he'd left precise instructions for his cryosuspension. He had gone so far as to personally select the cryostat and have it engraved with his own specifications.

Nevertheless, Kane had opted to bury him. How could he possibly preserve the ex-president? His pale, bloated body had been sliced apart during the autopsy, and both his hands had been turned into permanent fists. There was no coming back from the mutilation. Nanotechnology could do wonders, but not with the extent of damage his body had endured. He would never live again, and placing him inside a cryostat was pointless; it would only immortalise a grotesquely modified figure. It wasn't the way to honour ELF's founder.

After the minister closed the service with a prayer, and a choir boy sang the final song, Kane turned to the CI agent, his lips drawn back from his teeth. "Find Dr. Morgan!"

56

Flymo glanced at the GPS route planner glued to the top of the dashboard and adjusted its position. "What's the name of this place again?"

Bryan had his head against the window, watching the dark, barren countryside roll by. "Windermere House."

Cruising down the deserted road in the dead of night, the old Jaguar shuddered and creaked, filling the interior with a racket: air filters whistling, a high-pitched whine from a worn seal, the dry, rhythmic clatter of tappets. Not exactly the most conspicuous for a covert mission, especially against an outfit willing to go to any extreme to protect its legacy. Success here required them to move unseen and unheard.

His father had warned him that seeking truth and justice was the kind of pursuit that got people killed. Yet, despite his better judgment, and with some persuasion from his father, he had agreed to let Flymo join him. Flymo was a man who never overestimated his skills or underestimated the risks.

For most of the journey, Bryan and Flymo sat in silence, barely exchanging a word. Bryan was content to be lost in his own thoughts. There had been a time when he and Flymo could banter for hours, effortlessly filling the gaps with easy conversation. But now, connecting with the older version of Flymo felt like hard work. Flymo had left the army, claiming he was done with military discipline and protocols. That was the official story. But his erratic behaviour and restlessness pointed to something deeper. Post-war stress was written all over him.

Bryan's book, *Depression: A Detrimental Disease*, was the product of exhaustive research and his first-hand experience, having worked closely with traumatised war veterans at their lowest points. They endured symptoms like reliving traumatic occasions, avoiding certain people and places, mood swings, persistent reminders, flashbacks, insomnia, loss of interest in once-enjoyable activities, and a disconnect from themselves. Trauma often left them jumpy, startled by even the smallest triggers.

"What's with the long trips into the woods?" asked Bryan.

It took Flymo almost twenty seconds to answer. "I killed a young girl by mistake in a children's hospital in Iraq during battle. She was trying to escape from a militant group, and I shot her. She didn't even have a gun. Going into the wild helps me break down my choices and make sense of where my life is now. I had to leave the army. I just couldn't do it anymore. But here's the part I can't figure out: I really miss it. That's another reason I like being in the forest. It keeps me connected to that life. Because after I quit, I lost myself and who I was, felt like I had no purpose, and became irrelevant. I felt like my skills were going to waste, and didn't know what I wanted anymore. It left me totally confused. I turned to alcohol, hoping it might help, but it only made things worse."

"I assume you've had counselling."

"Yeah. The quacks are no help. No offence."

Bryan said nothing. He looked down at the map he had laid across his lap and changed the topic to one he thought might reignite Flymo's thirst for action. "Windermere House must be surrounded by three hundred acres, at least. Maybe more. According to this map, it's mostly forest. We should be able to climb the perimeter walls and use the trees as cover."

"Wait! I thought we were just going to look around. You never said anything about breaking in."

In all fairness, he'd only provided Flymo with a summary of the plan. The finer details had been hashed out with his father. But he had summarised his intentions. He thought he had been clear.

"We talked about this," said Bryan.

"I didn't think we'd actually go through with it."

Bryan shook his head. "You owe me!"

"Hey, I'm only doing this so you'll forgive me."

The rational part of his brain wanted to forgive Flymo, and he really tried, but something more primitive begrudged his indiscretions.

"Forgive?"

"Redemption then."

Bryan snorted a fake laugh.

"Mate, if you want to go in alone…?"

Bryan chose to end the conversation there. This wasn't the time or place to dive into it. They had work to do, dangers to consider, plans to devise. Getting inside ELF would be no easy task. Believing it was even possible was presumptuous and dangerous. But still better than inaction.

Still, Flymo couldn't let it go. "Mate, I refuse to apologise anymore. I've apologised enough. If you're too pig-headed to accept my apology, then you're on your own. I'll drop you off at the mansion."

Bryan was vulnerable to setbacks, and Flymo knew this.

"You're a stubborn man in your old age," said Bryan.

Flymo grinned. "And you're still a superstitious freak."

"You're old. Your face looks weird."

"Could still beat the snot out of you."

Bryan stifled the urge to smile.

"What happened to you in Liechtenstein?"

Bryan admitted what had taken place in the subterranean labs had left him mystified. And, in some way, he didn't want to know. It could only be bad, so he tried to pretend it never happened.

"I honestly don't know."

Flymo changed the topic. "You said about three hundred workers live inside the foundation. But that was twenty years ago. There may be double that now. Do you think you can get in without anyone recognising you?"

"I wasn't there for long. I only met a few people."

"The people who count know your face. The agents tried to kill you, remember? And your face was in the newspaper."

"It's Christmas. Many of the staff will be on their winter holidays. It's the only time of year that management lets the majority of staff take leave at the same time."

"How do you know that?"

"Ann, one of the cryobiologists, told me."

"Twenty years ago," said Flymo. "When it was under the rule of the president you killed. How can you be sure the new president has the same policy?"

"I can't. Let's just hope he's a traditionalist like Smolensk. Besides, it's quarter to three in the morning. Those not taking Christmas holidays this year will be sleeping."

"And security?"

Bryan took a deep breath. "We'll find out soon enough."

He launched into a more detailed rundown of their plan. Having his father's backing had given him a strange, powerful sense of reassurance, providing a support that had long been absent in his life. Photographic evidence was key to ending ELF's lawless conduct. Speed was of the utmost importance, too. It was a lousy plan, in all honesty. Taking ELF on was stupid, even suicidal, but necessary. Bryan knew it wouldn't satisfy Flymo's need to have input and control, although his reaction after Bryan finished sharing the plan took him by surprise.

Flymo began hitting the steering wheel with his palm and smiling. "That's the Bryan I love and remember! The fearless medic from the Falklands, running around the mountaintops ducking bullets helping wounded soldiers. He's back!"

But Flymo's words triggered a flashback to what Thomas Smolensk had told Bryan just before he died.

Middle sections of the brain are primitive.

Where rage, fear, and sexual feelings come from.

Affected by the sub-zero temperatures and are beyond repair.

World would become an emotional catastrophe.

You cannot control your anger.

Bryan dipped his head. "I'm not who I was. I'm not sure I ever will be."

"No shit!" Flymo blew all the air out of his nose. "Mate, if you want me to go through with this, we do it my way. No offence, but you've only completed basic combat training in the army. You aren't trained to deal with dangerous people who would stick a knife in your head, then make a cup of tea. Sometimes, good planning can prove detrimental. Situations change. Instinct and impulse are your best weapons. Let me lead, don't question me. I'll get us in and out. First of all, I'm not as fit as I used to be, and my hip is still sore after jumping from the window. I don't think I can make it over any high walls."

Flymo had been a soldier with legs and arms strengthened from years of endurance. But he was closing in on sixty years of age, overweight and unfit, and had been out of the army for almost a decade. Still, Bryan believed in his capabilities and agreed to the modified plan.

They stopped in a small village at a set of traffic lights.

Bryan scanned the darkened shops, each window adorned with Christmas lights. One storefront displayed its range of guitars draped in tinsel. A blinking security light caught his attention, forcing him to consider the likely security they'd encounter at ELF. How advanced would it be? He rolled down his window for a breath of fresh air, then checked the dashboard clock. Nearly three o'clock.

"How much further?" asked Bryan.

Flymo checked his GPS screen. "We'll be there in half an hour."

57

Flymo pulled into a natural alcove by the roadside, hidden beneath the cover of trees. The narrow, remote country road had been quiet, and Bryan had noticed only one car passing in the opposite direction during the past half hour.

Flymo cut the engine, and they sat quietly, staring blankly ahead. An uneasy pause settled between them as indecision crept in.

"What did you tell Julia about tonight?" asked Flymo.

"Nothing."

"She won't like that."

"I left her a message."

"About coming here?"

"Not exactly."

Flymo jabbed his thumb over his shoulder at the canvas bag on the back seat. "What's in the bag?"

"A pair of black suits I picked up."

"For what?"

"I forgot to mention we're going in disguised as agents."

"Is that so," said Flymo, shaking his head.

They took their time changing into the suits, neither in a hurry to step out of the climate-controlled Jag into the chilly night. The damp weather was horribly reminiscent of his first visit to ELF all those years ago, though from his perspective, it was only two months past and still vivid in his mind.

Pacing along the solid stone wall, Flymo halted with the uncertain gait of a soldier trapped in a minefield. He turned and ran back to the Jag, leaving Bryan alone and confused.

He returned with two golf clubs. "Can't go in unarmed."

"Golf clubs? Really?"

Flymo shrugged. "Got any better ideas?"

Bryan cocked his head. "Give me the nine iron!"

They continued along the wall with their clubs by their sides, glancing behind them, on alert for cameras and other surveillance tech.

"We can forget about climbing these walls," said Flymo. "They're alarmed. Don't touch them."

Bryan had also seen the warning signs on the wall. The entire site was a potential hotbed of security traps, so they had to exercise caution.

On approach to the main gate, a wall-mounted camera pivoted in their general direction.

"Get down!" said Flymo.

A sturdy tree cast a broad shadow over the perimeter wall, shrouding the area from the streetlight. They moved into the darkness, blending effortlessly in their black suits. Only ten metres separated them from the gate.

"How will we get inside the gate with a camera up there?" asked Bryan.

"I don't know," said Flymo.

When the camera swung in the opposite direction, Flymo leaped out of the shade and ran to the gate.

Bryan arrived just behind him and saw a sign on the iron bars declaring the residence *Windermere House*.

A security guard dressed in a black coat with luminous yellow stripes occupied a small booth set back from the gate. A golf cart was parked in front of the booth.

Flymo made a slightly high-pitched barking sound.

"What the hell was that?" whispered Bryan.

"The sound a fox makes," he whispered back.

The security guard came out of the hut and approached the gate.

Flymo and Bryan ran back into the shade of the tree as the camera pivoted once more in their direction.

Waiting until the camera slowly turned away from them, they tiptoed back to the gate. The guard was there, finishing his cigarette. He rested his head against the bars, gazing out. Smoke curled from his lips as he scanned the empty road. On his final drag, he reached through the bars and flicked the cigarette onto the road. Before he retracted his arm, Flymo sprang out from the side and brought the golf club down on his wrist. The sharp crack of bone snapping was unmistakable. Before the guard could react, Flymo struck him over the head through the bars, dropping him instantly.

As the injured guard tried to crawl away, Flymo reached between the bars for his boot and dragged him back until his whole leg was outside the gate.

"Hold his foot," said Flymo.

Bryan grabbed the man's heel with two hands.

The guard, dazed and hurt, didn't put up a fight as Flymo reached into the guard's jacket pocket and pulled out a radio. Another pocket held a remote control for the gate and a gun. He took both.

The guard freed his leg when the gate retracted into the dark grounds, nudging him forward. He crawled away into the bushes, unable to stand up and run but not completely immobilised. When Bryan and Flymo chased into the bushes, they found him passed out and bleeding from his skull.

Flymo closed the gates using the remote and raided the booth, his hands moving deftly as he searched for the key to the golf cart. After a moment, he found it, tucked away in a small drawer. With a satisfied nod, he reconvened with Bryan by the golf the cart. They climbed in and set off along the winding driveway. Ground lights dotted the path at regular intervals, casting pools of light that lit up their surroundings. Driving deeper into the dark complex, the sprawling grounds revealed themselves. When they caught sight of the mansion in the distance, its silhouette imposing against the night sky, Flymo made a quick decision. He veered off the paved path and steered the golf cart into the underbrush, using the trees as cover. The foliage wrapped around them, muffling their stealth approach as they crept closer to the target, with Flymo seemingly in his element of their clandestine mission.

"Like the old days," he said.

Bryan leaned against the dash with both palms. "I don't remember us ever breaking into mansions."

"You know what I mean. This, driving golf carts."

Bryan chuckled. "The last time you drove one of these, you crashed into a sand bunker, I recall."

"Still thrashed you. That was the day I got my first hole in one."

"And last."

Flymo switched off the headlights, slowing their progress as they navigated carefully between the trees. The golf cart bumped along the incline that gradually levelled out. After a short distance, they reached the edge of the forest, revealing a clear view of the eighteenth-century mansion silhouetted against the blackened sky. Its sharply angled roof featured a single, ominous spire that evoked a distinctly Transylvanian Dracula vibe. The sounds of nocturnal birds parroted around them, mingling with the rustle of trees swaying in the wind, creating a scene straight out of a Halloween tale.

Bryan scanned for movement in the windows. The rooms were all black behind the glass. A porch light bathed the front door in a pallid glow.

On foot, they made their way to the mansion, leaving the golf clubs behind as they skirted the edge of the forest to remain hidden. The air felt damp, and water droplets clung to their suit jackets, coating them with a chilly frost.

Bryan noticed a narrow ribbon of gravel in the distance and realised it must be a runway. It would take a skilled pilot like John Wells to execute a precise landing on such a short stretch of asphalt. A helicopter identical to the one he had seen in Scotland sat parked on the grass beside the runway. These discoveries only confirmed what he already knew: they had successfully found ELF.

If Bryan had been paying attention to more than just the landing strip and static helicopter, he might have noticed the steel disk embedded in the ground, which he stumbled over, putting him flat on his front. His stubbed toe throbbed, and waves of pain streaked up his leg. He pulled his knee to his chest and held his foot, sucking air through clenched teeth.

"Let me know when you're done," said Flymo. "I've got all night."

Bryan felt a sense of déjà vu, as if he had been here before. His instincts urged him to focus on what had caused him to stumble. He stood and dug his heel into the long grass.

"What are you doing?"

"I think the entrance to a tunnel is around here. Help me look."

Flymo pivoted his toes on the grass like he was putting out a cigarette. "Where does the tunnel lead to?"

"Inside the foundation. I think my mother is at the other end."

Flymo grunted. "Yeah, because life is that kind."

"I've found it!" said Bryan.

The forest had reclaimed the steel hatch, and Bryan had to tear the grass out to reach the rusty handle. Not that it made a difference. It was sealed. He thought he remembered a locking wheel on the inside, but it may have been just his mind making it up.

When Bryan looked up, he saw a pair of security guards patrolling the mansion. They stayed low and of sight until the guards circled round to the back of the building. With the coast now clear, they broke out of the forest, crossing from grass to gravel, passing a dry, concrete fountain, and hurried towards the mansion.

58

The enormous door was built from solid English oak. Flymo grasped the cool brass knob, and to their surprise, it turned smoothly without so much as a noise. The door swung open silently, and they slipped inside undetected. The air's musty scent hinted that this place saw little foot traffic, serving as a cover to conceal the foundation.

A long hall stretched ahead, and as they moved quietly across the marble floor, passing a spiral staircase that vanished into the blackest black above, the stillness around them grew more pronounced. The darkness thickened until Flymo took his mobile out of his jacket pocket. With a swift flick, the torch beam pierced the dimness, shining a wide cone of light down the hall that picked out the framed paintings lining the walls on either side. Everything was top-notch. He opened doors at random, sweeping the beam into the elegant rooms adorned with paintings and golden gilt mirrors hanging above marble fireplaces. Spaces were filled with outdated furniture and ornate cabinets that spoke of another time, with more hidden areas than a rabbit warren—pantries, alcoves, offices, unexpected cloakrooms, storage.

They moved into the grand hall outfitted in neoclassical architecture with lavish chandeliers dangling from the ceiling. The empty floorspace made every footstep echo, no matter how hard they tried to tread soundlessly.

At first, the enormous fireplace stood like a black hole in the wall with a towering seven-foot frame. But as they drew nearer, they noticed a hidden staircase disappearing gradually down into the pitch-black below.

"Down here," Flymo whispered.

They took the uncarpeted stairs down to the mysterious, dungeon-like basement. A row of halogen lamps sputtered on when they reached the last step, which spread light over the smooth, sandstone walls of a long passageway.

Bryan's heart accelerated. Had they been sprung?

"Motion sensors," Flymo whispered in reassurance as he pocketed the mobile and pointed at a dome-shaped bracket on the wall. They followed the passageway in silence until they reached a right-angle turn. Flymo peered round the wall, sighting two men sitting at a security checkpoint.

Bryan inched his head just beyond the edge of the wall, catching sight of the checkpoint. The lights they had triggered moments earlier had put the guards on alert. Turning back wasn't an option now, even if they wanted to. The only way forward was through the checkpoint.

"Won't they figure out that we are not agents?" Flymo whispered.

"No, there are more than seventy CI agents, and many work off-site. They won't know the difference. We'll be fine."

Unfazed by the presence of security, Bryan approached the checkpoint with steady confidence, his posture calm and assured. Flymo stood closely just behind, mirroring Bryan's confident stride.

Bryan quickly scanned the scene, taking in every detail when he noticed something unusual behind the two officers. It was a portal of some kind, though he couldn't figure out its purpose.

The tension intensified as the men locked eyes, sizing each other up. Bryan silently hoped this wouldn't escalate into a two-on-two confrontation. The ex-president's fingers were in his jacket inside pocket, pressing against his pounding heart as if trying to settle its steady *whomp*.

"Pockets!" said a guard as they approached.

Bryan held out his palms. "I have nothing on me."

The guard glanced at his colleague and back at Bryan with a frown. "Where's your gun?"

"In my apartment."

Flymo took his mobile and gun from his pocket, placing them on the tray.

The same guard looked at Flymo "Seriously? A mobile?"

Flymo shrugged, feigning ignorance.

The second security guard frowned harder than the first. "Unarmed? Mobiles? Playing a dangerous game, aren't we?"

"What's the big deal?" asked Flymo.

The security guards laughed. "Say that to the president, I dare you!"

Flymo smiled. "I won't say anything if you don't."

The guards exchanged glances once more.

"Come on," said Bryan. "It's Christmas. We won't let this happen again."

The second guard pointed at the portal. Its grey, acrylic wall read magnetic anomaly detector, employed with hi-tech digital sensors that scanned for foreign items. "Go on!" he said, waving them through.

Bryan stepped inside the portal, holding his breath as it scanned him. He feared it would detect the severed fingers, but no alarms blared. A green light signalled for him to move forward.

Flymo followed, stepping through the portal without a hitch and emerging on the other side. He turned to the guards. "Can I get my mobile back?"

"You know the rules," said the guard. "Personal phones are not allowed. Only senior management can carry mobiles inside."

"Have a good morning," said Bryan, signalling with a nod to Flymo to follow him to the nearby lifts.

Bryan's relief was evident on his face when he realised the authentication device only required fingerprint verification. Eye-scanning equipment had not been installed, and swipe card technology had been phased out. He reached inside his pocket, retrieved a single finger from the bag, and pressed it firmly against the authentication pad.

A square next to the pad lit up red.

Trying a different finger, he watched it meet the same fate. A quick glance at the security guards revealed they were deep in conversation, their attention elsewhere, which gave him a moment's respite.

Determined, he attempted another finger, but once again, the pad flashed bright red. Frustration accumulated in him as he grabbed the next finger, only for it to slip from his grasp and drop to the ground with a soft thud. Bending down to retrieve it, he stole another glance at the guards, relieved they hadn't noticed his clumsiness.

He pressed the finger against the pad again, but the red light stubbornly persisted.

"Is there a problem?" one of the guards suddenly asked, his attention now on Bryan.

"No problem," Bryan replied, forcing a calmness into his voice, though his heart was anything but calm.

He hastily tried another finger, but the red light flashed again, leaving him to wonder if the ex-president's access had been revoked altogether. Panic threatened to derail his plan. He dropped the redundant finger into his pocket with the others and reached for one more just as the guards began to close in. The square turned red, mocking his efforts.

Finally, with a sense of desperation, he pulled out finger number seven, pressed it against the pad, and this time, the light blazed bright green, accompanied by a reassuring two-tone beep. Bryan faced the guards as the lift doors opened. "Must have oily fingers."

Flymo tilted his head back against the wall the moment the doors closed. "Talk about cutting it fine. I'm not sure my heart can handle that again."

Bryan let out a loud sigh. "They took the mobile."

"They must have had issues in the past. Employees taking photos and videos of secret stuff."

"Without the camera, we can't..."

Bryan squeezed his eyes shut, his facial muscles tightening with all the strength he could muster to repel a blinding, white light. It was followed by a sharp pain that exploded through his sinuses, as if his skull were being split from the inside. The agony was so intense that a guttural howl escaped him, primal and raw, like a wounded wolf. His vision dissolved into a haze of white-hot pain, and a deep, visceral scream tore from him, as if exorcising every morsel of evil.

It took Flymo repeated attempts to bring Bryan back to the moment, shaking him forcefully by the shoulders until his eyes focussed and his convulsions settled.

"Bryan?"

"What?"

Flymo let go of his shoulders and took one step back. "You were having a seizure."

Bryan thrust his hands against the wall, leaned forward, and looked down, taking deep breaths. "I'll be okay."

He desperately wished for this nightmare to end. Julia had always accused him of running from his problems, but there was no escaping from his pain. He couldn't outrun it. His connection to ELF was a constant burden that followed him wherever he went.

You feel it, too, the president's voice repeated in his mind, haunting him with a truth he couldn't deny.

"Your nose!" said Flymo. "It's bleeding!"

Bryan wiped his sleeve across his upper lip, smearing the blood across the fabric. "I'm okay."

Flymo seemed unconvinced. "You should get an MRI or a CT scan. You don't know what they did to you in those labs. When this is all over, I'll take you to the hospital."

"It'll *never* be over."

His wife was old enough to be his mother.

His mother was young enough to be his sister.

His father could have been his grandfather.

Flymo could pass for his father, and his daughter could have been anything from his sibling to his sweetheart. No, it would never be *over*. His time in captivity had warped time, leaving him lost in an unfamiliar and unwelcoming world. He had paid a heavy price and would carry the consequences until his final breath.

Bryan wiped his nose once more on his sleeve and leaned back against the wall, listening as the lift carried them deeper into the core of the establishment. The motion slowed, then stopped. With a soft *whoosh*, the doors slid open.

Ahead, a long corridor reached forward, spanning fifty metres. They emerged from the lift, and Bryan studied their surroundings. The interior had been spruced up with more glass walls and less concrete than he remembered. Further along, a section was under renovation, and they crossed over white sheets covering the floor tiles. All the walls were lined with opaque plastic. A gust of wind channelling through the corridor turned them into translucent ghosts. The changes threw Bryan. After such a brief sojourn at ELF, it was as if he were visiting the foundation for the first time.

Flymo walked ahead and stopped in front of a waxwork head mounted on a column, paying homage to a man. "Who's that?" asked Flymo.

"Thomas Smolensk. He used to be the president. That's the man I killed."

"Looks like a right arse."

Bryan didn't disagree.

They stopped. Their heads snapped to their right upon hearing someone exit a room. A dog barked, but the sound was contained when the door closed.

"Wait here!" said Bryan. "Back in a sec."

Bryan located the room where the dogs were kept and quietly slipped inside, shutting the door behind him. Most of the dogs were fast asleep, except for a forty-five-pound beast that stirred at his presence. It rose to its feet, watching as Bryan pulled out the fingers and casually dropped them into its bowl of dog treats.

Back in the corridor, Bryan scanned his surroundings, his head turning left and right. There was no sign of Flymo. He started down the corridor, eyes darting from door to door as he searched for his old friend. But he found only the hollow silence of the empty facility.

Suddenly, the low, steady hum of electricity faded away, like a massive fan powering down. Bryan froze as the sound evaporated, leaving an unsettling stillness in its wake. Then, in an instant, all the lights blinked off.

59

"*There's no easy way to say this,*" Bryan began, his eyes dropping to his lap, perhaps an indication of his guilt, shame, remorse, or regret. He didn't look up again for almost ten seconds. "*I'm dead. I brought this on myself; everything is my fault. Things didn't turn out like I planned, but that's life, isn't it?*"

Gripping her mobile with both her hands, Julia raised the volume.

"*I wanted to say goodbye in person. I just didn't know how. How does anyone come to terms with the end of their life? I'm afraid I can't explain what's going through my head because I don't fully understand it myself. I do know that I've been stupid and selfish. I am to blame for everything that has happened. My brain snapped inside that foundation, and an innocent man lost his life. As a result, I lost mine. I paid the ultimate price, but then so did all of you. Because of me and my reckless actions, my family has been torn…*"

Bryan looked distracted, as though he had made the video under duress.

Duncan and Sarah-George leaned around Julia's shoulder, peering at the screen.

"*I've disgraced myself, made a mess of everything. Sorry and forgive me seem like such lame words, so I won't use them. To be honest, I don't even know what to say.*"

He stopped speaking, as if the recording had got stuck on freezeframe, even though the seconds in the time bar ticked on. Then he resumed.

"*Sarah-George, we had that one night on the fishing boat. It wasn't enough, but I was happy that I got to know my daughter a little. It was a precious moment. Remember what I said about our mothers and how important they are? Take care of your mother, she's a diamond.*" He smiled. "*And maybe take some singing lessons.*"

Sarah-George choked on her tears, trying not to laugh.

"*As for my father, apologies and forgiveness are not lame words. I see now what you did, what you sacrificed, and why. I want to believe you had no choice, that you had to leave me. I can't forget, and I'll always be sad you weren't a part of my life growing up. But I do forgive you. I have also made family sacrifices, have hurt those important to me, and will go to my grave burdened with regret… just a moment.*"

The video jumped to the next frame, where Bryan had pushed the pause button, probably to compose himself.

"*Time is fragile, and each moment is precious because it's so limited. Make every minute count and always be there for each other.*"

Duncan paced up and down the room and looked again at his watch, noting it was half-four in the morning.

Julia turned to Duncan. "Where did he go? I know he told you."

"It's best you don't know."

"What's going on? Why has he left us this message? Is he in some kind of danger?"

"He told me not to say. For your own protection."

"No! You must tell me! We need to know."

Duncan clutched his chest, his hands trembling as his face turned a deep purple shade. His mouth opened, but no words came out, only strained attempts to speak that caught in his throat. His body convulsed in short, desperate coughs before his legs gave out beneath him. He crumpled to the floor, and his eyes fluttered shut, as if peacefully drifting into sleep.

Julia leaned closer, straining to hear the faint sound of his breathing. She checked his pulse. It was weak and fading.

Sarah-George was already on the phone, urgently calling for an ambulance.

"Wait!" Julia said, looking up at her daughter. "We're in the middle of the Welsh countryside. Ask for a helicopter."

Duncan awoke to the rhythmic thump of helicopter blades slicing through the air, the noise almost drowning out the muffled voices of paramedics surrounding him. A chill swept over him, intensified by the downdraft from the rotors. The paramedics moved with urgency, shouting commands to one another as they raced towards the hospital's automated doors. The world around him blurred as he was wheeled inside, and when the doors shut behind them, a darkness overtook him once more.

When he regained consciousness, thoughts of Helen, his beloved wife, flooded his mind. He could picture her vividly: her curly brown hair, her full lips, and rosy cheeks. Those big, sparkling eyes held a warmth that could melt any heart, and her smile brought joy to people's lives. She wasn't just a good listener; she genuinely cared about understanding people. She had been a devoted wife and a nurturing mother. Desperate to speak to her, to tell her how much he'd missed her all these years, he reached for his oxygen mask and tried to pull it away, but the effort was too much.

A doctor appeared, standing over him and blinking calmly. "You've suffered a massive heart attack, Mr. Mansfield. You are lucky to be alive. You must rest. Try not to speak."

He reached for his mask again, but the doctor stopped him, pushing his hand down to his hip.

"Your heart is wearing out. We may need to implant a defibrillator to monitor your heart rate. We'll know more in a few hours after your electrocardiogram comes back. I suggest you try and rest."

Julia linked her fingers with his and stroked his hair, trying to bring him comfort and peace.

But Duncan was a stubborn old man and tore the mask off his face the moment the doctor left the room.

"Don't do that!" said Julia, reaching to put it back on his face.

He hit her hand away and tried to speak. He clearly had something on his mind, but his consciousness was slipping, blinking blinks that grew longer. "My... phone. Now!"

Julia shook her head. "You're in no state to ca—"

"Get it!"

Then his breath seemed to stick in his throat. He strained, his face turning red, and whispered, "Windermere... H..."

"What?" asked Julia. "Say that again."

But it was too late. He closed his eyes and let death carry him away.

60

Bryan didn't have much time to get what he came for. Every minute that ticked by made his chances slimmer. Without the mobile, gathering evidence was almost impossible. The lack of light made everything feel more dangerous. Alone and in the dark, he knew he was in a knife-edge situation yet again. Where was Flymo? Had he been caught? Or worse, had the old fool wandered off and become lost within the maze of corridors?

Two cryobiologists shining torchlights along the corridor acknowledged Bryan with a nod, fooled into thinking he was an agent. As soon as they turned the corner and vanished out of sight, he went looking for Lab 1. The first door he came across had a lightbox affixed above it. He thought it might lead to an emergency exit, but it was just a backup light. The door was for Lab 4: Syndromes, where Ann worked.

He turned and saw another door opposite the syndromes lab. It had a round window, and the door plaque read Security Operations Room. Illumination from the lightbox penetrated the window. He pressed his face against the glass and couldn't believe what he saw. Six operators with bloody mouths and noses were trussed to their swivel chairs by computer wire. A CI agent lay unconscious on the floor, his hands also tied, and was bound to a support column. A dozen security monitors conveyed black screens, and beneath hung severed wires. The hard drives and the keyboards had been smashed up, and a lone computer mouse dangled from the desk, swaying slightly in the silence.

A black shadow ghosted across the room and suddenly veered towards the door. Bryan backed off as the dark figure neared. The door swung open and crashed against the wall, giving him a fright.

Flymo, proving age was no constraint to brute strength, stepped into light, holding a mobile flip phone. "Let's move," he said. "We don't have long before the alarm's raised."

"*You* knocked the power out?" asked Bryan.

He shrugged. "Who else?"

Bryan shook his head disbelievingly. "I'm glad one of us is enjoying this."

They moved swiftly along the dimly lit corridors. Flymo began recording, holding the phone up in front of his face as they paced forward. They carefully looked through windows into various rooms, squinting in the dim light to spot any signs of life or movement beyond the glass, scanning the door plaques and signs giving directions to the HIV/AIDS lab.

As they approached the steps leading up to the viewing platform overlooking Lab 6, Bryan hesitated and studied his surroundings. He veered right, passing the Patient Research Room, and kept moving, the urgency of their mission driving him forward.

"Do you know where you're going?"

"I think so."

The floorplan likely hadn't changed a great deal. Lab 1 had housed two thousand cryostats and moving them would have been a logistical nightmare. As far as Bryan could recall, assuming nothing else had shifted, Lab 1 was a short walk from the Patient Research Room. Trusting his memory, he followed the route he had in his memory, hoping it would lead him to the right place.

And then he found it.

With the power outage, the electronic door to Lab 1 was left unlocked. Bryan slipped inside and, experiencing déjà vu, dragged a heavy pedestal over to block the door. It felt eerily familiar, as though he'd done this just recently. Which he had. This time, instead of wedging a broom between the handles, he used a mop.

As they slipped into the lab, Bryan snatched the mobile from Flymo's hand. Moving with purpose, he filmed the rows of computers and panned over to the patients sealed within their cryostats. He captured the lab's unnervingly palpable silence, sweeping across the room for a full panoramic before zooming in on some paperwork scattered across a desk.

Turning his attention back to the cryostats, Bryan slowly rotated the camera, capturing the haunting blue light glowing inside each unit shining down on the frozen occupants. The cryostats were now running on backup fuel generators.

Bryan walked quickly past the rows of cryostats until he reached his mother in cryostat 0016. She looked exactly as he remembered, unchanged in twenty years. She hadn't moved a fraction. Her face still looked calm, as if she were listening to soothing music, but the serene expression clashed with the frost coating her features, a layer of ice that made the scene unsettling.

"Is that her?" asked Flymo.

"Yes."

Bryan wiped the sweat from his brow. The steel cryostats generated heat, and the air conditioning had gone offline due to the knocked-out electricity, making the room stifling. He raised the camera to start filming, but his finger accidentally pressed a button, and a sudden flash burst from the camera, flooding the vicinity with a bright white light like a bolt of lightning in the pitch-black of night.

Almost instantly, he saw movement in his periphery. And then he heard a man's voice say, "What's going on here?"

Bryan swung round. The man, wheeling a turbomolecular pumping station used for evacuating liquid nitrogen from the cryostats, wore a blue cryo-apron, gloves, and a thermoplastic mask with a drop-down face shield.

"You?" the man said, his deep voice muffled by the face shield. Bryan's heart skipped a beat. Had he been recognised? The man slowly lifted the shield to his forehead.

At first, Bryan couldn't make out his features in the dim light. But as he stepped forward, the soft blue glow from his mother's cryostat lit his face. The mere sight of Dr. Huber, lurking like a troglodyte in his darkened den, made Bryan's stomach drop. Dr. Huber's bowed shoulders looked like they bore the weight of his own depravity, while his hollow eyes hinted at his constant lack of sleep. The brilliant yet corrupted mind stalked the lab like a blood-starved reptile, stripped of humanity. Sustained by his twisted experiments, he haunted the room day and night, moving through its eerie glow as if it were his personal kingdom.

"How did you—"

Flymo planted a fist on Dr. Huber's jaw, sending the old man to the cold tiled floor in a crumpled heap. On his way down, he collided with the turbomolecular pumping station, which rolled into a nearby cryostat with a loud, crashing thud.

"Was that really necessary?" Bryan asked, wincing.

A cryobiologist, alarmed by the loud noise, rushed over to investigate. Without hesitation, Flymo raised his fists again, his posture radiating his love for violence. He landed a swift punch, knocking the man out cold. Blood dripped from the cryobiologist's nose as he slumped to the floor, unconscious.

Flymo swung his head round. "Send the footage to your father. Quick!"

"How?"

Flymo let out a frustrated sigh and snatched the mobile. "What's his number?"

"I don't know. He programmed it into your mobile."

Flymo hesitated in thought. "I'll have to send it to Julia then."

Bryan nodded. "Know her number by heart, do you?"

Flymo rolled his eyes at Bryan. "Not the time, mate."

Flymo took several minutes, and Bryan became anxious. "Can we hurry this up?"

"There's no coverage down here. I can't get a signal."

Bryan looked over at the door. "We've got what we came for. Let's get out of here and take it to the police!"

"Which way?"

"There's a tunnel in the utility room."

"There's no tunnel," said Dr. Huber, feeling the inside of his mouth and inspecting his fingertips for blood. "It was blocked off after you escaped the last time. I'm afraid you're trapped."

"I don't believe you."

Dr. Huber spat blood to the floor. "See for yourself."

Bryan sprinted to the utility room. He had to force open the door and was met with a hectic jumble of junk that made the space smaller than he remembered. Dust motes floated in the stale air, and the dim light could not penetrate the clutter. Boxes stacked haphazardly spilled their contents to the floor, blending in with old equipment and forgotten tools.

To reach the back wall, Bryan had no choice but to start shifting things around, heaving boxes aside, carving a path as if cutting through a jungle. A cloud of dust erupted, making him cough as he cleared the way.

Flymo stood by the door, the camera still rolling as Bryan waded to the far side. He halted, staring at the white-painted wall. "The tunnel's bricked up," he said, his voice tinged with frustration. He leaned closer, noticing the subtle difference in texture of the bricks where the door used to be.

An alarm blared through the facility, a shrill warning that cut through the silent darkness.

Bryan instinctively raised his hands to his head, a gesture of defeat and despair in his eyes.

"We can fight them," Flymo said confidently.

But Bryan knew the grim reality of their situation. They were outmatched. The threat they faced was more formidable than entrapment. They had guns. They had the advantage of numbers, ready to pounce at any moment. They were trained and ruthless, skilled in combat and merciless in their pursuits.

And most importantly, they had no laws to abide by. They could do whatever they pleased with them without blowback. They had done it once. They would not hesitate to do it again.

Flymo didn't seem to share the same afflictions of doubt. A flare of excitement sparked in him. He missed taking on the enemy and standing on the frontline, risking his life. He longed for a good fight and thrived on violence.

But Bryan had other ideas.

61

A shelving unit spanned one wall inside the utility room, its shelves packed with various glassware. Carboys, beakers, jars, specimen cups, vials, and tubes were haphazardly arranged in rows. On the lower shelf, a high-density polyethylene plastic container sat beside a three-litre dewar of liquid nitrogen, its gauge displaying -196°C.

Without a moment's hesitation, Bryan twisted the lid off the dewar. A vaporous cloud rose from the mouth until the cold mist dissipated. He inserted the pulsation dipstick and carefully siphoned the frigid liquid, pouring the droplets of nitrogen into the plastic container. They hit with a faint sizzle, instantly freezing the surface inside.

Flymo leaned over his shoulder, watching as he gradually filled the container. "What are you doing?"

"Making a bomb!"

"A bomb? You're planning to blow this place up?"

"When the nitrogen warms up, the liquid turns into gas. Hopefully, it'll create a powerful discharge, enough to knock down that wall. The liquid nitrogen will explode in a cloud of freezing steam and ice vapour."

"Since when did you become an explosives expert?"

"I read about it when I was researching the use of liquid nitrogen to treat lesions in the outer layer of human skin."

When it reached about a pint, Bryan stopped and sealed the container tightly. A slight chill radiated through the plastic, reminding Bryan of the dangerous power it held. He stood and faced Flymo. "How can we make this container heat up?"

Flymo saw a sink in the corner of the utility room. He turned on the hot tap and tested it with his fingertips. "That's running hot. Will it do the job?"

Bryan jutted his bottom lip. "It's all we have."

"Are you sure it will work?"

"The nitrogen boils and expands like steam and can fill a volume two thousand times its liquid state, so it should cause a decent explosion."

"The sink's ceramic, though. It will blunt the explosion. We'll have to move it in front of the wall. Shall I do it?"

Bryan shook his head. "No, I'll do it."

Flymo slipped out of the room and crouched behind a cryostat, keeping a watchful eye in the direction of the lab's main door as the alarm blared throughout the building. Dr. Huber and the cryobiologist he had whacked lay motionless on the floor.

Meanwhile, inside the utility room, Bryan positioned the plastic container under the tap and turned on the piping hot water. Within seconds, the liquid nitrogen began to evaporate rapidly, transforming into a dense, mist-like vapour. The gas expanded quickly, building pressure on the container's lid and causing its sturdy exterior to bloat. Bryan let the water run a few moments longer, ensuring the reaction continued, then shut off the hot tap. With the container now dangerously swelled, Bryan carefully and quickly moved it to the base of the wall, positioning it for what was to come.

He dashed out of the utility room, slammed the door, and sprinted towards Flymo. Without missing a beat, he threw himself onto the floor in an overly dramatic dive, landing with a theatrical thud.

Nothing happened.

"That's embarrassing," said Flymo.

"I thought it was going to blow!" said Bryan.

"Go check!" said Flymo.

Bryan climbed to his feet, dusted himself down, and ran back towards the utility room. Just as he was about to open the door, an explosion rocked the room and shook the floor with concussive force. The equipment inside the utility room was transformed into hurtling splinters in a cloud of white vapour that blew the door off its hinges.

Bryan raised his forearms to protect his head and face.

When the dust settled and cleared, he ducked inside the room, flapping his hand as though swatting a fly. The blast had wreaked havoc on the equipment but had only dislodged a few bricks in the wall.

Flymo surveyed the minimal damage. He shoved Bryan aside and drove his foot into the wall, knocking more bricks loose. A final front kick broke through, revealing a darkness beyond and leaving just enough space at the bottom for them to crawl through.

"You go first," said Flymo.

Bryan dropped to his knees and squeezed into the narrow opening, pulling his legs through as he crawled into the space behind the wall. The darkness on the other side was so dense it felt suffocating, making it impossible to see more than a few inches ahead. His breathing quickened, but he remained calm, crouching low and peering back through the hole into the utility room. Flymo's face filled the narrow gap, blocking Bryan's view beyond.

Suddenly, a loud crack split the air. Bryan's heart lurched as Flymo fell sideways, a bullet ripping through his shoulder like a pencil slicing through wet tissue paper.

With Flymo out of view, he saw multiple legs moving in the utility room. Agents, armed and ready, had arrived and had taken Flymo down. But he was not dead. His arm reached through the gap, and his hand held his keys and the mobile flip phone, providing Bryan with one last chance. Then his face appeared over the hole.

"Take it to the police!"

Bryan snatched the mobile and keys. "What about you?"

"I'll hold them off! Go!"

He nodded. "I'll be back with the police."

Bryan bolted up the tunnel, his hands brushing the walls for balance as he took long strides like a man disembarking from a swaying boat. Using the flip phone to light the way, he ran for his life, and this time, he didn't look back.

62

With growing urgency, Bryan gritted his teeth and forced the hatch open, listening to the metal groan under the pressure. He hoisted himself out into the cool night air and scrambled to his feet. He turned and kicked the hatch shut with a heavy thud, sealing the tunnel below.

He looked up at the mansion in the distance, its towering silhouette barely visible against the dark, starless sky. The air was still, and the only sounds were his own laboured breaths and the rustling of leaves in the nearby forest. Moving swiftly, Bryan darted along the tree line. Using the safety of the trees, he crouched behind a thick trunk and peered out cautiously, fixing on the mansion. No lights came on, and there was no movement behind the windows. The lack of activity gave him optimism. He had what he'd come for, and his end goal was almost within reach.

He continued along the forest's edge, ducking, weaving as branches whipped at his clothes and face. The darkness made it hard to see more than a few feet ahead. Then, like a trusted ally, the moon broke through the clouds, casting an eerie glow that lit his path. He sped up, driven by adrenaline as he searched for the golf cart.

He halted behind a tree, seeing someone up ahead, alone and seemingly on patrol. Shifting course, he moved further into the woods until the dense trees opened into a circular field thick with brambles and nettles that clung to his legs as he pressed forward. The uneven ground was littered with chunks of broken masonry and looked like the ancient ruins of some Neolithic settlement, with old stones sticking up like forgotten graves. His pulse quickened at the sound of distant voices cutting through the stillness. They were closer than he thought. He bolted across the grass, scanning for somewhere to hide. He saw a crumbling firepit, its worn stones barely standing, overgrown and forgotten. Without much thinking, he threw himself behind it, pressing low to the cold ground as the voices grew nearer. The firepit had a hollow at its base, just wide enough to hide him. He crouched there, the damp earth cooling his skin as he tried to steady his breathing.

The moonlight flickered in and out as the clouds passed overhead, casting an ever-shifting pattern of light and shade over the ruins. Bryan held his breath, hoping the firepit would keep him hidden.

A memory struck. It came from nowhere. Dr. Fletcher had mentioned something about a firepit. Acting on instinct, Bryan reached inside the hollow. He felt a loose brick. Pulling it out, he saw HF scratched across its surface: Heath Fletcher. Reaching deeper, his fingers touched something smooth. He pulled out a small, sealed book wrapped in clear plastic. His heart leaped, realising it was the missing logbook. He stared at it in disbelief. It was encyclopaedic in size and would take hours to read. Something stuck out of the pages. He opened the plastic bag and pulled out a faded Polaroid photo. The scene it captured was grotesque. Naked patients, their bodies pale and motionless, lay sprawled across dozens of gurneys arranged in symmetrical rows like corpses awaiting autopsy. Cryobiologists stood among them, their faces hidden behind masks, but their indifference was unmistakable. One patient's scalp had been entirely removed, exposing skull and brain in horrifying detail. Glistening tissue caught the light, making the photo even more surreal. A trolley sat beside the patient, cluttered with a disturbing array of tools—scalpels, forceps, and surgical saws, caked in blood. Bloody rags were carelessly tossed across the trolley, adding to the nightmarish scene.

Bryan's stomach twisted. This wasn't cryogenics; it was a twisted form of biological research. He stared at the image in disbelief. The photo told a story of cruelty, of lives discarded like broken machines. The implications were vast. This was damning proof of what was really taking place inside the labs. Forget the footage they had managed to capture. This one image, a snapshot of something far darker than he'd imagined, spoke a thousand words. He slipped the photo back inside the logbook and sealed the plastic bag, knowing whatever secrets behind those mansion walls were far worse than he'd ever feared.

He looked up, listening for voices but hearing none, then dashed back into the forest. After a five-minute search, he spotted the golf cart parked near the forest's edge, nestled between two trees. He started the ignition, activating the electric motor, and flicked the forward switch. Just as he was about to floor the accelerator, he hesitated and jumped out. Something urged him to check the logbook. He had to know. Under the headlamps, he skimmed through the pages, which contained patient numbers instead of names along with notes about certain side effects and fatalities. Vague references to *volunteers* or *donors* were used to mask the source of subjects. It detailed the hidden surveillance used to blackmail staff and outsiders, capturing incriminating conversations and actions. Records of infighting among staff and disagreements over the facility's methods and goals also appeared. Entries described accidents, contamination leaks, and near-disasters, alongside lists of powerful benefactors funding the facility's clandestine research. It also contained escape routes, contingency plans, and records of staff infractions. Dr. Fletcher's name appeared repeatedly. One entry mentioned a colleague accusing him of taking photos in a restricted area, although no evidence ever surfaced to confirm this. The book also described grotesque procedures—lobotomies, human brains frozen and perfused with glycerol before being rewarmed to conduct transplants under carefully controlled conditions.

He read one page out under his breath. "In the beginning, she seemed normal. She responded to instructions, questions, and jokes. On the fourth day, she began to experience cranial discomfort. Unfortunately, after twelve years in a cryostat and following the trans-orbital lobotomy, she displayed a change in emotions. Her moods became increasingly unpredictable. One minute, she was superficially absent, the next volatile and angry. It got worse over time, especially the seizures, leaving her vacant for up to twenty minutes after the episode. Her attention span decreased. At three weeks, she only reacted to stimuli in front of her. She couldn't follow simple rules or solve critical-thinking tasks. In the end, she lost all ability to engage socially with another human being. It's safe to say the trans-orbital lobotomy did not work on this patient."

Bryan felt a stab of alarm at what he had read. Gradually, horrifyingly, realisation dawned. He had undeniable evidence of ELF's existence along with details of recklessly performed neurosurgical procedures, enough to bring down ELF entirely. It was then he recalled Dr. Fletcher telling him the logbook contained information about HNV1, the cure for AIDS.

Bryan glanced up and ran his eyes around him, checking he was alone. He continued skimming over every page of the handwritten reports, each one dated. But two-thirds in, the pages went blank. Flipping back a page, Bryan noticed the last entry was dated September 1992. The exact month and year he'd started work at ELF, and around the time Dr. Fletcher vanished under mysterious circumstances. Dr. Fletcher had occupied his apartment before him, and he remembered the message written on the ceiling of his bed with a circle around it. *Find the lie.*

The message had bothered him since.

What lie?

Dr. Seymour's words tiptoed into his head. *Dr. Fletcher was a puzzle fanatic.*

Bryan thought long, thought hard.

Always had his head buried in some puzzle book. Loved anagrams and coded messages.

Puzzles. Anagrams. Codes.

Find the lie.

The penny suddenly dropped. The answer popped into his head like a blast of music in a horror movie scene.

In the field was a perfect anagram of *find the lie*. It was a clue, intended to guide someone to the logbook's hidden location in the field among the broken masonry. Even the circle drawn around the message held meaning, he realised, signifying the circular clearing where he had stashed the important evidence, which *contained* the lie. *Lies*. In fact, the logbook *was* the lie. Dr. Fletcher had wanted someone to find it should he not make it out of the grounds alive.

Bryan slammed the logbook shut and climbed onto the golf cart. He tramped his foot to the floor and surged forward, weaving between the trees. He cast a glance over his shoulder and to his left and right, checking he did not have a tail. But his hopes of a clean escape were thwarted when two golf carts appeared, their headlights cutting through the tree trunks.

Bryan steered the golf cart out of the forest and onto the driveway, navigating its winding path. The two pursuing carts lagged fifty metres behind him, maintaining the same speed of twenty miles per hour, their maximum potential. Spotting the booth and imposing gate ahead, he snatched the remote control from the seat. Just as he was about to press the open button, the golf cart hit an unexpected bump, launching him out of his seat. The remote control slipped from his fingers and bounced off the steering column before sliding down the front of the cart, landing on the asphalt. The cart's back wheel ran over it.

Bryan slammed on the brake, stopping in front of the gate. He turned to look back. The remote control lay shattered on the driveway, scattered like confetti, while the pursuing golf carts closed in. Just then, a bullet struck his rear wheel, the impact jolting the cart and sending vibrations up through the chassis.

Before he could regain his composure, a second bullet hit the brake lamp, causing it to explode in a shower of sparks and glass. He glanced ahead at the gate, an impossible barrier. He could lead his pursuers on a wild goose chase around the grounds, zigzagging through the trees and bushes, trying to buy himself some time. But how long would that last? Until the golf cart ran out of battery or he ran out of road. Reality quickly sank in: he was trapped.

63

Seated in the back of the limousine, President Spence fiddled with his deformed ear, anxious to reach Windermere House.

"How long?"

"Five minutes," the chauffeur called back, hunched over the steering wheel and speeding along the empty road.

In over forty years, no one had managed to infiltrate ELF. Smolensk had built a system so tight and impenetrable that even the most skilled hackers, spies, and saboteurs couldn't find a way in. He'd taken every conceivable security measure, from video surveillance and staff ID verification to encrypted access protocols, ensuring ELF remained a secure fortress. Smolensk's paranoia meant he had thought of almost every angle from which an attack could come. Almost.

Dr. Fletcher had been the only one audacious enough to challenge the foundation in the past, but his attempt had been swiftly neutralised. Kane had admired his boldness, even if it had cost him dearly. No one else had dared come close. No one, except for Dr. Morgan, who'd been an irritating presence since discovering his mother inside the foundation. Kane had kept an eye on him from that moment on, but he never truly understood the threat the man posed until now.

Kane cursed himself for not realising the reason behind the ex-president's missing fingers. Initially, he assumed it was vengeance for Julia's kidnapping in London, where he'd taken her finger for refusing to admit her knowledge of ELF. Kane had been ready to sever all her fingers, hoping it would force Bryan to surrender himself at the foundation after he'd gone rogue and killed an agent. But the plan had failed—someone had punctured a gas canister and ignited the room, killing his three colleagues and leaving his scheme in ruins. He'd barely escaped before the blast, which left him partially deaf in one ear, with the top half torn off by a shard of shrapnel.

But he had been completely mistaken. Bryan hadn't taken his fingers as an act of vengeance; he had done it to get his hands on the ultimate key: Smolensk's fingerprints. His plan was bold, ruthless, and chillingly effective. With Smolensk's fingers, he could bypass their highest levels of security, walk straight through the fortress doors, and take down everything Kane had sworn to protect. And what better time to act than at Christmas, when most employees were on leave with their families, following a tradition Smolensk had started and Kane had begrudgingly maintained. Next year, that policy would be scrapped. It might make him unpopular, but it was a small price to pay.

Kane had to act fast, or everything was in jeopardy. But every time he called the Security Operations Room, the line wouldn't connect. It just cut off, repeatedly. Desperation set in. He had to warn security about Bryan's plan and stop him before it was too late.

Just before the chauffeur pulled in front of Windermere House, he pushed a button on his remote control to activate the iron gate.

The chauffeur swung off the main road and turned into the driveway, stopping before the gate when a bullet struck the windscreen, showering the dashboard in tiny glass crystals.

Kane instinctively ducked behind the front seat.

A golf cart inside the grounds was parked in front of the gate with an agent behind the wheel.

"Go!" Kane shouted.

The chauffeur didn't respond.

Kane reached out between the front seats and tapped the chauffeur's shoulder. "Go!"

As the chauffeur's lifeless body slumped forward, pressing against the horn in a relentless, piercing blast, Kane caught a glimpse of his face in the rearview mirror and saw a dark red hole in his forehead.

Blocked by the gate, Bryan sat motionless, accepting defeat. As the golf carts closed in and bullets continued to be fired at him, the weight of his failures crushed him. He had failed to expose ELF's crimes against humanity, to free his mother, to save Flymo, and to bring down the institution that had stolen everything from him.

About to step out of the golf cart and raise his hands in surrender, he watched the gate magically swing open. Bryan blinked, barely able to believe his luck. With no time to lose, he pressed the accelerator and sped ahead, veering around a limousine that had just pulled up, its windshield shattered, possibly from a stray bullet meant for him. The horn blared from the limousine, an intimidation tactic to stop him from escaping, but he ignored it and sped past.

Further along the main road, he veered onto the gravel and deployed the brakes. He swapped the golf cart for the Jag and threw the logbook onto the passenger seat. Fumbling, grasping for the car keys, twisting them in his fingers, fitting them in the ignition, and starting the engine, he backed up until he had enough room to perform a U-turn in the alcove. He dropped his foot on the pedal, but the mud churned with the Jag's low-traction tyres and found no purchase. Shifting the gear lever into reverse, he drove back and, with the wheel turned on full lock, accelerated away, leaving the golf carts racing towards him in the middle of the road.

Putting distance between himself and Windermere House, his relief was quickly overshadowed by concern. Thinking, almost obsessively, about the logbook and what he had read, he grappled with a truth he was afraid to confront.

We need people like you, President Smolensk had said. *Who better than a couple of traitors?*

Had they performed a trans-orbital lobotomy on him? He switched on the interior light and examined the corners of his eyes in the rear-view mirror, looking for marks. A lobotomy involved a long, ice-pick-shaped tool being driven through the eye socket and into the skull, targeting the frontal lobe of the brain. By manipulating this section, behaviours could be altered. ELF had been experimenting with ways to correct the negative effects caused by prolonged cryopreservation, trying to find a solution. Until the side effects were resolved, ELF couldn't risk going public with their revolutionary science. In the meantime, they were conducting horrific experiments on the human brain. And he had the Polaroid to prove it.

The road stretched long and straight, and he managed to put some miles behind him. Once he reached an urban area, he intended to locate the nearest police station. Only then would he truly be free from their control. ELF would be shut down, and its HNV1 cure would be confiscated, tested, and, with any luck, approved and made available to the public in time to save his mother and every other person infected with the deadly disease.

Multiple headlights suddenly flared in his mirrors. And in seconds, three luxury Land Rovers surged closely behind him. The old Jaguar didn't stand a chance against the speed and power of the newer Land Rovers. Moreover, every CI agent who'd ever worked for ELF had a history in combat, either in the military or as a personal bodyguard. Some had worked in the police force, others for the government, assigned to serve and protect important diplomats. The men and women were highly trained individuals. It meant their driving skills had been sharpened to perfection and no doubt far exceeded his own.

Bryan drove through a village, the first sign of civilisation since leaving the mansion. One of the Land Rovers pulled up alongside Bryan and nudged the Jaguar. The sound of tearing metal was unmistakable. Bryan swerved off the road and the front wheel grazed the kerb, momentarily throwing him from his seat. He banged his head against the roof. After that, he fastened his seatbelt.

Powering through the bends, straying across the road's designated lines, Bryan ducked down, flinching each time a bullet *whumped* into the Jag. Two more bullets starred the back window, but it didn't shatter. One clattered the radio, and small puffs of smoke rose. It left a burning rubber aftertaste in his mouth.

A Land Rover drew bumper to bumper. It dropped back, then lurched forward, crashing into the Jag. The agent then repeated the manoeuvre, causing both cars to barrel along the road in tandem at sixty miles per hour.

Dropping back, the Land Rover closed the gap again and gave the Jag another strong nudge, propelling it to seventy-five. By the fourth bump, he reached almost eighty miles per hour.

The rear window burst with a thunderous smash, littering the interior with glass fragments. Cold wind buffeted the back of Bryan's head. He hit the brakes, bringing the Jag back to forty miles per hour at a crossroads as the traffic lights ahead changed to red. Instead of stopping, he ran the light. Dark smoke exploded from the rear pipe when he punched the accelerator. He hoped this would give him an advantage, but the Land Rovers also drove through the red light, remaining on his tail.

Bryan made a hard turn into a one-way street running by a school. One of the Land Rovers misjudged the bend and rolled onto its roof, crashing into a wall.

One down, two left.

But Bryan was driving too fast towards the approaching junction and hit the brakes, leaving tyre tracks on the asphalt. The smell of burning brake shoes flooded the interior. He had to complete a series of successive turns to return to the right road but was prevented by a Land Rover that crashed into the back of him, pushing the Jag sideways. Bryan's head slammed against the window with a jarring thud, shooting pain through his skull. Adrenaline surged as he selected first gear and floored the accelerator. He tugged the steering wheel, turning sharply onto the road, the tyres screeching as he sped away.

Speeding towards the junction with the Land Rovers still hot on his trail, their presence a constant threat, Bryan soon approached the end of the road. Just beyond the junction lay a glimmer of hope: a police station.

Police Constable Jones stepped out of the precinct into the courtyard with a cigarette she had every intention of lighting. It had been a long night with eight arrests involving a club brawl between door security and a party of drunks, followed by a teenager caught breaking into a carpenter's van.

Halfway towards lighting the cigarette, she saw a battered Jag heading towards the precinct. It bounced up the kerb, flattened the perimeter fence, and barrelled into the parked police vehicles, squashing them into mangled scrap.

PC Jones dashed into the courtyard and made her way to the Jag. The male driver lay slumped over the steering wheel, unconscious, blood streaming from an extensive gash above his eye. She figured he was probably a drunk who had made a costly mistake by getting behind the wheel. But her second thought, as she surveyed the scene, was that tonight had been hectic enough and all she wanted was a moment to enjoy a peaceful smoke.

64

Chief Constable Hughes peered through the tiny window of the holding cell, his expression a mix of concern and curiosity. Inside, Bryan sat on the bench, visibly shaken and dishevelled, having turned himself in under circumstances that had left the precinct in utter disarray. His eyes had a jaundiced tinge, hinting at exhaustion or some deeper affliction, and a trail of white foam ran from the corner of his mouth to his chin. His head twitched, as if he were being electrocuted by invisible wires. A plaster was taped above his eye to close a gash, while a deep cut marred the bridge of his nose. His face bore further injuries: a swollen upper lip, a bruise underneath one eye, and blood smeared on his left ear, inflicted during the crash.

He let out an unexpected haunting cry, neither the sound of pain nor rage but something more primal, akin to a wolf's howl. It resonated in the small cell, but as the sound faded,

Bryan seemed to settle. He slowly leaned back against the wall, his breath evening out as if everything was normal again.

Hughes had conducted a series of background checks on Bryan. The medic turned psychologist had no police record. Not even a traffic violation. Up until the death of Michelle Locke twenty years ago, he'd been a respectable citizen. Now he faced a sensational murder trial and substantial prison time. On paper, it did not add up.

As the seizure gradually faded and Bryan's body relaxed, his mind began to clear. Glancing around, he realised he was in a holding cell, though the details of how he came to be there were hazy.

Outside his door, he saw Chief Constable Hughes peering through the tiny window of his cell, pinching his moustache thoughtfully. Bryan didn't know how long the chief had been standing there, nor did it matter. He felt detached, as though the world outside the cell was a distant memory. He no longer considered himself a decent man, and not even a good one. Recent events had stripped away any remnants of self-respect he once clung to, leaving behind only a deep-seated loathing for himself and the reckless trail of destruction he had forged. He felt trapped not just in the cell but within the nasty reality of who he had become.

The sound of the door unlocking was followed by Hughes stepping into the cell.

"Look who we have here," he said.

Bryan put his hands over his face and drew them over his head.

Hughes closed the door, and an officer outside locked it. "You look like shit!"

Bryan stretched his arms in front of him and rolled his right shoulder, which ached badly. He could hear the chief constable breathing heavily, as if he'd just sprinted up a steep flight of stairs.

"Do you know where you are?"

Bryan nodded.

"You want to tell me what happened?"

The injuries he had sustained had caused him temporary mental impairment.

"You totalled three police cars in the courtyard. Either you're a terrible driver, or someone was chasing you."

Bryan massaged his eyes with his fingers. "I'm struggling to remember."

"Struggling to remember if you're a terrible driver?"

"Who was chasing me."

"Where have you been hiding these past few weeks?"

Bryan shook his head, trying to recall. He could feel his memory trickling back as the fog in his mind receded. The answers were there, waiting to be plucked from his head. And then, as if propelled by an electric shock, he straightened his posture and looked up.

"They were chasing me."

"Who?"

"Agents. After I escaped from the cryonics foundation."

"What cryonics foundation?"

Bryan stood with urgency. "There's another foundation. It's about twenty or thirty miles from here."

Hughes gestured for Bryan to sit.

Bryan sat on the bench.

"Like the one found in Lichtenstein?"

"What?"

"Like the one in Lichtenstein?"

"Bigger. Much bigger. My friend's in there. His life's in danger."

"You're gonna have to give me more than that."

Bryan poured out everything he knew to Hughes about the foundation and the dark activities occurring underground. He provided a few names, the location of Windermere House, and revealed all he had gathered from the logbook, including the lobotomies and inhumane experiments on people. By the time he finished speaking, Hughes was equipped with all the information he needed to understand the truth and depth of the situation.

"You said you have proof?"

Bryan nodded. "On the front seat of the Jaguar outside. The logbook and a photo. I also recorded some footage on a mobile. It has everything you need."

Hughes' eyes lit up. "Come with me."

He took Bryan by the upper arm and marched him from the holding cell along the corridor. Officers making tea in a small kitchen and talking in soft voices stopped when they saw Bryan and gave him a cold stare.

Outside in the courtyard, a recovery truck cleared away the damaged police cars. The beaten-up Jaguar was isolated in the middle of the car park, where smoke flowed from its engine.

Most of the windows were smashed. The passenger door was jammed, so Hughes slid through the window as smooth and lithe as a snake and grabbed the mobile and logbook off the seat. He shook off the glass and slid back out.

"These I assume?" He held up the book and phone.

Bryan nodded. "The photo's inside the logbook."

Hughes opened it and took the photo out. He studied it for almost a minute. He then spent several minutes browsing the logbook like it were a catalogue.

Snapping the logbook shut, he paced away, took out his mobile, and made a quick call.

When he returned, there was urgency in his voice. "We're sending a team there now, but we're going to need your help. Are you up to it?"

65

Daybreak spread pale streaks of pink and orange light across the sky, with the sun teasing the horizon as the helicopter rose out of the precinct courtyard and pitched forward, sweeping across rooftops. A vista of fields and farms beyond the small town flashed beneath them.

"You look pale," said Hughes, studying Bryan from the adjacent bench. "Not a fan of flying?"

To Bryan's surprise, he felt no anxiety as he looked down at the countryside from high above. His lifelong fear of flying was gone, one positive side effect of damage to the brain's middle regions. Cryopreservation, as Smolensk had explained, impaired rage, fear, and sexual feelings, leaving them beyond repair. He'd already noticed the shift in his emotions, with rage heightened and fear dulled. The absence of sexual urges had yet to reveal themselves. Perhaps confirmation in itself.

Bryan adjusted his headset, straining to hear him over the rotors beating the air. "It's been a rough week."

Nine tactical assault officers, including Chief Constable Hughes, filled the cramped cabin. Each officer was securely harnessed to their seats, bracing themselves for the mission ahead. Dressed in high-grade ballistic vests for protection against gunfire over dark blue uniforms and tactical ballistic helmets, the officers were armed to the teeth, equipped with an array of artillery that included assault rifles, sidearms, and specialised gear, prepared for whatever awaited them on the ground.

The atmosphere buzzed with anticipation and focus, with the officers fixed on the landscape rushing by below as they prepared for the impending confrontation. What drove these people? Did the prospect of a gun battle worry them, or did they get off on the adrenaline effect and gunplay? He felt they were all watching him while pretending not to watch him. In their eyes, he was a criminal.

Guilty until proven innocent.

"What was the deal back at the station?" asked Hughes.

"What do you mean?"

"The episode. The fit."

"I've been having seizures ever since I…"

"Since what?"

"Was a human guinea pig in Liechtenstein."

"Where did you learn that?"

"Thomas Smolensk."

"Is that why you killed him?"

"That was self-defence. He was shooting at me."

Hughes paused, seemingly unconvinced. "Did you cut off his fingers in self-defence, too?"

The chief constable would never understand, and it took any urgency out of having to explain himself. Bryan glanced through the window, closed his eyes, and breathed deeply. He hoped Flymo was okay.

They were ten minutes from Windermere House.

Hughes retrieved the gun from his waistbelt and checked the bullets in the magazine. "Are you sure you're up to this?"

"My friend needs me."

"Show us the way in, then get back to the helicopter. The pilot will fly you back to the station where you'll be safe. Our officers will be waiting for you."

"My mother's in there. I'm not leaving her again."

"I can't let you go in. It might be dangerous."

"I'll only show you in if you let me come too."

Hughes hesitated. He looked at his team. "Fine. As long as you're aware of the risks."

Bryan nodded. "I am."

Flymo had taken down ELF's power and surveillance, but that was almost four hours ago. Was the power still down? Had Hughes paid attention when he had explained just how dangerous these people were? Nine assault officers were no match for an army of highly trained agents.

"Put this on," said Hughes, handing Bryan a bulletproof vest.

He strapped it on, and one of the officers helped with the fastens.

Hughes stroked his tash. "We'll be landing soon."

"We seem outnumbered," said Bryan.

"I have a tactical support unit on its way, and we have the perimeter surrounded."

It put Bryan's mind at ease. "Good."

The helicopter touched down beside a dormant plane on the grass just before eight o'clock. Hughes pushed the sliding door open, and one by one the officers leaped onto the grass, poised for battle, their knees bent and semi-automatics ready.

Hughes grabbed Bryan's arm and dragged him from the helicopter, ducking under the doorframe into a typhoon-like downdraft from the rotor blades.

Hunched forward, they ran and merged into the shadows at the side of the mansion.

The helicopter rose, lowered its nose, and sped over the trees. The dust dispersed, and the area fell silent.

Hughes grabbed his radio and said, "We're in. East side."

They waited, and within minutes, a squad of officers clad in the same dark blue uniforms, tactical ballistic helmets, and ballistic vests assembled.

Bryan counted at least thirty additional assault officers.

Standing with their backs against the wall, Hughes turned to Bryan. "Stay close to me at all times. Clear?"

Flanked by the tactical assault officers, he led the unit to the main entrance under the porch, scanning for agents and other possible traps.

Laden with a carbine and four stun grenades on his belt, the lead officer reached for the front door and nudged it open. The officers raised their weapons and aimed them into the dark, pine-panelled hallway as they swarmed in, their guns roaming left and right in the disconcerting quiet and dimness. They spread out quickly.

"That way!" said Bryan, guiding them along the hallway, beyond the spiral staircase, and through to the grand hall. He took them over to the large fireplace and pointed at the steps leading off into the darkness.

Hughes switched on his police-issue torch. "Let's go!" he said.

Descending the deep staircase, following the torch beam, they swooped into the passageway and deployed along the walls.

Bryan anticipated the automated lights would activate, so when they remained off, it was a positive sign. Without power, ELF's advanced technology and surveillance equipment were rendered useless. The agents would be blind to a police siege, as they had been in Liechtenstein.

But then the hairs on Bryan's neck suddenly rose.

The foundation in Liechtenstein had been wired up with explosives for deliberate self-destruction. It had burned to the ground, leaving the authorities with no ties to those involved and a high body count. Bryan had to now contemplate if they were walking into a ticking timebomb.

In silence, they continued along the darkened passageway. If Hughes feared they would come up against any weapons or explosives or any kind of snare, his fears were allayed by the deserted passageway.

The officers at the front lowered their night-vision optics, seeing everything in green shades. Up ahead were two plastic chairs. Despite the improved visibility, they failed to spot the metal detecting portal for what it was. Their weapons set off the alarm. Red lights on the portal lit them up under a blood-red spotlight.

Moving swiftly in the direction of the lifts, the lead officer tried to open the doors by pushing the button, but nothing happened.

Hughes saw the finger authentication device and turned to Bryan. "The power's out. How do we get in?"

"The labs and lifts run on electricity that comes from a backup generator, in case of emergencies, so I should be able to access the lift." Bryan discreetly reached inside his jacket pocket and fished out the old man's finger. He used his fist to shield the finger and pressed it onto the authentication device, passing it off as his own.

The lift doors opened, and the officers crowded inside.

Bryan pressed level one, and the lift began its descent.

Right before the lift doors opened, the officers readied their weapons, and Hughes touched Bryan on the shoulder. "Remember, stay close to me."

The assault officers had barely taken ten strides from the lift when it all kicked off. One moment, they moved in silent formation, creeping along the corridor; the next, all hell broke loose. Blinding lights and deafening roars filled the corridor. Shadows darted from hidden alcoves, and a sudden, brutal fight ensued.

Bryan froze as the scene exploded into violence around him, unfolding too quickly for him to compute. Something, or someone, hit him in the face. The blow left him bewildered and spinning like a dancer.

Bryan lost sight of Hughes as the officers barked orders at the top of their voices, standard law enforcement strategy aimed at disorientating and overwhelming the enemy. But he was equally disorientated and overwhelmed.

Someone grabbed Bryan by the throat and marched him backwards, crashing through a door into a room. He tripped and fell on his backside but managed to break the fall with his hands. He staggered to his feet, but his arm was caught in a vice-like grip and he was pinned against the wall. A gun was pushed into his mouth. The taste of metal and gun oil was unmistakable as it slid across his tongue towards the back of his throat.

As his vision came back into focus, he traced the hand on the trigger along the arm, all the way to a familiar face.

"You don't know who you're fucking with!" said Hughes.

A sparkle of glee appeared in his cold, menacing eyes. It wasn't that he enjoyed inflicting pain. He revelled in it.

Bryan had strolled into the bear's cave. And like an animal, Hughes had lunged without mercy.

When Hughes took the gun out of his mouth, Bryan spat blood onto the floor. "How much are they paying you?"

"More than they paid you."

Hughes delivered a knee to Bryan's groin, dropping him to the floor. Bryan was no fighter. He'd been a medic, not a soldier. He was the one put on the battlefield to mop up the fight, not cause the mess.

Hughes unleashed a series of blows.

Bryan raised his elbows to protect his face, but Hughes found gaps. One caught him above the eye, and he pressed his hand against the reopened gash above his brow, blinded by his own blood.

There was something unsettling about the chief constable now. Bryan saw an inferno raging in his eyes, right before the final blow that left him semi-conscious on the floor.

Hughes turned to the officers standing at the door. "Take him!"

One lifted Bryan by his hair, another grabbed his arm. They carried him along the corridor, passing the agents he had arrived with. They were all gathered in the corridor and removing their assault gear until they were back in standard black suits, shirts, and ties.

Bryan was thrown into a dark room with glass fish-tank walls, where battery-operated candles flickered realistically in each corner. Blood continued to pour from the gash above his eye. He seemed to be bleeding from the mouth, but it was just excess from his nose.

President Spence entered and hoisted himself up onto a gurney in the centre of the room, where he skimmed through a stack of photos. He was twenty years older than the last time Bryan saw him, and apart from a disfigured ear, he was still a good-looking man with a tidy silver beard.

Kane threw the photos at Bryan, scattering them around him. Through the blood in his eyes, he saw they captured gory images of Thomas Smolensk.

Kane stood and slowly circled Bryan. He moved the way he talked with a kind of synchronised, thought-out precision that cancelled out any element of spontaneity.

"You killed an honourable man," he said. "He was like a father to me. He gave me everything and more. He saved my life. What should I do? Shake your hand under the pretence it never happened? Or honour him by having you killed? Kill *your* father, perhaps?"

Bryan wiped the blood from his nose and mouth. "He's suffered enough."

Kane crouched low. "So did Thomas Smolensk. But that didn't stop you. You robbed him of his glory. After all the turmoil he went through, and I couldn't even grant him his dying wish. He's rotting in the ground as we speak."

Bryan looked into Kane's eyes with defiance. "Where he belongs."

"It is now," said Kane. "And you are where *you* belong. It ends here, I'm afraid. You put up a good fight. I'll give you that. But now you realise that this place is bigger than you or me, and this madness ends today."

He rose and signalled to the agents in the corner of the room. "Have him prepped!"

66

President Spence closed his office door after Chief Constable Hughes walked in. Using the light from his torch, he settled into the chair behind his desk and picked up the phone. "You can turn the power back on now."

Power returned to the foundation instantly. His computer rebooted, the fish tank lights flickered to life, and the wall-mounted lamps glowed brightly.

Kane poured Hughes a vodka and slid the glass across the desk.

"What else do you need from me?" asked Hughes.

"How about the officers at the precinct?"

"Leave them to me."

"Yeah, but what do they know?"

"Nothing. Bryan was concussed when I arrived; he hadn't told them anything."

"What about his wife and daughter?"

"We haven't been able to locate them."

"Keep looking. I don't want them harmed. But if it comes to it, you know what to do."

Hughes pulled out the mobile he'd retrieved from Bryan's car. "I'm sure the Sheriff would like his mobile phone back. I've deleted the footage stored on there. I checked the outbox. Nothing was sent to his wife or anyone else."

"Good."

Hughes handed over the tatty logbook. An old Polaroid stuck out from the pages. "I believe you've been looking for these for several years."

"Twenty," said the president. "I don't know why the old man insisted on keeping a log of everything in this damn book. It's caused nothing but trouble."

Hughes nodded. "So, what happens to Bryan now?"

A fluorescent bulb blazed overhead as the power inside the foundation was finally restored. Bryan scuttled towards the wall, pressing his back against it as if its solidity could shield him from the light. He had a knack for sizing people up with just one glance, reading intentions as easily as he could read their expressions. That was the skill that had made him an exceptional psychologist. But it'd failed him catastrophically. He'd walked right into the constable's trap, seduced by his rugged exterior and hidden sensitivity, which he had mistaken as genuine. How had he misjudged him so entirely? The men in the helicopter hadn't been tactical assault officers; they were ELF agents, disguised to lull him into the mansion. How had they slipped past his defences? Why hadn't he recognised their subtle tells? Was it a side effect of his physically altered mind? The outcome of having damaged cognitive awareness, resulting from a lobotomy? These thoughts unsettled him. Was he really slipping, or had he simply underestimated his opponents?

Half a dozen CI agents lifted Bryan and set him down on the reclining gurney, tying him down using leather restraints with buckles and adjustable straps at his feet, wrists, and waist.

A huge, hulking figure stood over him and circled with soundless movement.

"What's going to happen to me?" asked Bryan, spitting blood to the floor.

"Depends on how well you cooperate."

"Where's Flymo?"

"Your friend?" The man smiled. "Let's just say he did *not* cooperate."

Disgust and anger simmered below Bryan's skin, prickling his flesh sharp and hot.

"Let's not waste any time here," said the agent. "Tell me where it is! All of it!"

"He deserves no mercy," said Kane. "My stepfather may have been a difficult man, but if it wasn't for all the risks he took, we wouldn't be here, utilising breakthrough technology and saving thousands of lives. I mean, just look at him!"

He showed Hughes photos of the ex-president sprawled across an autopsy table, his lifeless form laid bare. His chest was split open, organs exposed, and both his hands had been mutilated beyond recognition.

Hughes looked at one of the ex-president's gruesome face in the bright light of the pathology laboratory. "I tried to have Bryan arrested. I stole his wedding ring from the hospital and planted it at the riverbank in Scotland. Tayside Police should have banged him up. It would have saved us a lot of hassle this morning."

Kane had a strong inkling that more incriminating proof against ELF was out there, hidden away in some obscure file or carefully concealed report or stored within some electronic device. Even if it was only speculation or the faintest trace of evidence, he knew it could be enough to unravel everything if it landed in the wrong hands. He couldn't afford to take any chances, not with the stakes this high. The slightest lead might be all it took for someone to expose ELF's operations, and that was a risk he wasn't willing to take.

"Photos, perhaps?" The agent slapped Bryan around the face. "Correspondence? Messages to family, friends? Did you write something down somewhere?"

Bryan shook his head.

"Tell me where you've hidden it, and all this goes away!"

"I have nothing hidden away," said Bryan, spitting more blood. "You have everything already."

"Not buying it," he said.

The agent fastened small electrodes to Bryan's body. He attached the conductive wires to Bryan's lips, the cold metal making him shiver involuntarily. With the same dispassionate care, he placed electrodes on Bryan's chest, directly over his nipples, where the sensation of metal felt both invasive and surreal.

"Just tell me where it is. Simple. Save yourself from this pain."

Bryan gritted his teeth. "Go *fuck* yourself!"

"Hmm, disappointing!"

A sudden shot of electric current passed through Bryan's body, sending searing heat through his nerves as his muscles involuntarily clenched. He believed he'd reached the absolute limit of his pain, the edges of his consciousness blurring as he endured the relentless assault. His body was already bruised and aching from the brutal pounding Hughes had delivered earlier. But this was a different level. The electricity didn't just hurt; it coursed through him like fire, ripping through every nerve ending, making his bones vibrate beneath his skin. His mind teetered between fight and surrender, desperate for a reprieve that wouldn't come.

Kane clenched his hands together. "I sent agents to kill him. Twice. First at the hospital, where they killed Dr. Fletcher. Then again at his friend's house, which they torched. And somehow, he survived both. He's a fucking Phoenix, rising from the ashes every time. Part of me still wants him dead and buried; I'm sick to death of hearing his name. But… I've decided not to kill him."

"Why not?"

Kane sighed, running a hand through his hair. "Too many have died in here already. And this isn't how my stepfather envisioned this foundation running. Murder contradicts both the nature and ethos of ELF, which is all about extended life. We're supposed to be pioneers in this field, not executioners. If word ever got out about what we've done, it could seriously unsettle the staff and cause a rebellion. It would certainly erode the trust we've worked so hard to build, tarnishing the foundation's reputation." Kane paused as he reflected on the situation. "It's not every day someone volunteers themselves for a project like this. Dr. Morgan will dedicate himself to our cause and help us achieve great things in cryopreservation. I have big hopes for him."

Hughes nodded, understanding the context of his words.

Kane leaned back, his mind racing with possibilities. "We still have a long way to go before we're ready to share this technology with the world. We're on the brink of something extraordinary, and I can't allow my personal feelings to derail everything we have built. It's time to focus on the future, on healing rather than harming, and ensure our vision for ELF aligns with our actions."

Hughes nodded again. "Well, if that's all, I had better be getting back."

Kane stood and shook the chief constable's hand.

As Hughes stepped out of the office and paced down the corridor, a man's haunting screams echoed through the air. A more compassionate person might have paused to offer help or show concern. But Hughes enjoyed his ELF pension too much and made his way to the lifts.

67

Time and hope bled from his grasp, slipping away in a quiet unravelling he could no longer deny. His end was coming. Rather than the knife-edge dread that came with an unexpected demise, it was a slow, creeping resignation. Bryan was at their mercy, powerless against their calculated endeavours. There would be no pardon for him, no leniency for whatever faint spark of humanity he had left. To them, he was only a liability, a variable they could not afford to leave unaccounted for. His body, weakened and wracked by relentless pain, still quivered after hours or torture. They had tried to squeeze information he didn't have from him. The agony burned deep, robbing him of vitality, hollowing him out. Surrender felt like relief, a final reprieve from a life that had now become a perpetual punishment. It would put an end to his infinite troubles, to a mind too fractured to endure much longer. He knew he had become damaged, diminished, and, in some unavoidable way, obsolete. The punishment awaiting him was not undeserved. He had burned every bridge, disappointed everyone who had once believed in him. Perhaps this was the justice he had been running from. As he faced the inevitable, a bitter acceptance settled in him, acknowledging, almost welcoming, whatever punishment awaited.

Bound by the thick, unyielding straps and immobilised by the searing pain in his body, Bryan lay powerless, breathing shallow. He barely registered the agents' movements as they wheeled the gurney from the glass room. Through half-lidded eyes, he glimpsed a plaque bolted to the wall just before they turned and wheeled him through another door into a lab. The letters were blurred, but he could make them out: AIDS/HIV.

Bryan slowly rolled his head back to face the ceiling. For a moment, he was alone, and then Dr. Huber's face appeared above him, his shoulders bowed. Holding a large syringe up to the light, he inspected the fluid inside. Huber's face bore the signs of conflict with a swollen cheek and a cut on his lip. Flymo's handiwork.

"Don't worry," Dr. Huber said in his familiar, resonant deep voice. "I'm not going to kill you. No, you'll live. This century... perhaps the twenty-second. Maybe beyond that. You'll be one of a lucky few in this world to actually see the future."

A wet, sloshing noise drew Bryan's attention. He turned his head weakly to the side. The cryonic bathtub was filling with thick, translucent silicone oil that glimmered under the sterile lights.

"Prepare the cryostat for submersion," Huber instructed one of the cryobiologists.

"What happened to me?" asked Bryan in a weak voice.

"You went rogue."

Bryan paused, struggling to summon any real conviction in his voice. "During those… twenty years?"

"We cryopreserved you."

"Why?"

Dr. Huber strolled around the bed, in and out of range of Bryan's vision, though his voice remained close. "You broke the rules. Contravened the code of conduct. You killed an agent."

"Why freeze me?"

"Dr. Morgan, we do not *free—*"

"Liechtenstein Police rescued Dr. Fletcher and me from the other foundation. What… happened to everyone else?"

"They were all killed in the fire."

"They were in cryostats… they couldn't be evacuated."

"Correct."

"So what about me and Dr. Fletcher? We weren't inside cryostats. Our hearts were already beating. We had our blood before the foundation came… before it came under siege."

"Do you have a point or a question?" asked Huber.

"Why were we not in cryostats?"

Dr. Huber appeared again. He stared thoughtfully in the direction of the cryostats, as if talking to someone else nearby. "For medicine to progress, sacrifice is essential. We can cure terminal illnesses, but what about mental illnesses, which are not terminal? Autism, dementia, schizophrenia… depression. What about brain damage caused by cryopreservation? ELF is evolving all the time. New drugs and treatments in their development stages need to be tested on someone." He faced Bryan. "Does that answer your question?"

"Was a lobotomy performed on me?"

"In the beginning."

"What do you mean?"

"We discovered a long time ago that lobotomies actually are ineffective. We have come a long way since."

Bryan shook his head in confusion.

"We have successfully mapped the human brain and are learning more about the mind and its complex functions. We have tools that allow us to go deep inside the brain while the patient is anaesthetised."

"You opened up my head?"

He smiled. "That's how you reach the brain."

"I don't have scars."

"Nanotechnology is a wonderful invention. Nanorobots repair damage to the body, leaving no skin trauma."

"And?" asked Bryan.

"And what?"

"What happened to us in Liechtenstein?"

"Once the nanorobots had finished their procedure, our cryobiologists studied you, checking to see if surgical changes to your nerve pathways had worked. But before they could confirm, the foundation was attacked. We had thirty staff in Liechtenstein. Most got killed. Some were old friends of mine. A few agents and off-duty medical staff managed to escape in time. But you and Dr. Fletcher were evacuated and taken to a hospital in Vaduz. Once stable, they transferred you to the hospital in London."

When Dr. Huber walked away, Bryan twisted against the straps, fighting to loosen their grip. The agents had left just enough slack, and with a desperate effort, he almost had one hand free. But a violent seizure gripped his body, seizing his muscles. His vision clouded, narrowing to a tunnel of hazy light. His body jerked uncontrollably, and his legs kicked and thrashed as white-hot light exploded behind his eyes, forcing them to roll back.

Agonised screams tore from his throat. A metallic taste filled his mouth as blood poured from his nose and ran down his lips and chin. When the episode passed, his eyes remained wide and wet, locked in a glassy, unblinking stare.

Dr. Huber returned and held up the needle for Bryan to see. "You got lucky, Dr. Morgan. If it was up to me, I would put you down for good. Instead, we shall work on your brain again and attempt to repair the damage. You may become the program saviour. Imagine that. Perhaps you saved a hundred lives during your medical career. But with a successful brain transplant, you may just save a million."

"Transplant," Bryan said faintly.

"That's right. We're halfway there. By applying the same principles of cryopreservation, like maintaining blood flow and oxygenation during the operation to avoid cellular death, we are poised to achieve the impossible. We know how to sever the spinal cord, blood vessels, and other connections, and preventing any damage to the brain tissue while carefully disconnecting the brain from the original body is taken care of by robotics. Reconnecting the brain to the recipient body is just a reverse process of the disconnecting phase. Where we lack expertise and technology is in restoring functionality to the nerve connections, as the brainstem and spinal cord connection govern all bodily movements and sensations. But once we achieve this, the possibilities will be endless. We'll be able to repair spinal cord injuries and cure paralysis. That's the future you'll wake up to, where immobility is no longer a human limitation, and no injury is beyond healing. It's an exciting future, don't you think?"

Dr. Huber found the vein he wanted to inject and pushed the plunger.

Bryan's glare softened, shifting from fury to resignation as the drug coursed through his veins. Darkness crept in from the edges of his vision, further blurring the room around him. His eyes glazed over, and his rage and defiance sank, destined to lie dormant in five gallons of liquid nitrogen.

Within moments, only a narrow sliver of sight remained, a strange limbo, like hovering on the edge of death but fully aware it was imminent. He wondered, with a chill of dread, what kind of society would await him once he resurfaced. Then, slowly, the world faded to black.

Closing the furnace door on level five, the bottommost level in the foundation, Kane stood at the thick-paned window and watched the flames leap to life inside. Heat radiated from the opening, warming his face in the cold basement. A strange satisfaction came over him, watching the logbook crackle as the fire consumed its incriminating content. The flames lit up in green hues as the ink evaporated, and the pages curled and twisted, disintegrating into ash, leaving behind the charred remnants of the foundation's darkest deeds.

Walking away as the furnace settled and cooled, he rode the lifts to level one and headed straight to the AIDS lab. At cryostat 0016, he stopped and looked at the woman inside: Helen Mansfield. Her husband, Duncan Mansfield, was dead. He had suffered a heart attack last week, Kane had learned through his closest sources. It saddened him to think ELF had perhaps played a part in his death.

Five years ago, Duncan had made the choice to switch from monthly instalments to paying upfront on an annual basis. Now that he was dead, Helen Mansfield only had eight months remaining before her term in cryopreservation finally expired because there was no more money. After that, Kane could reinstate her into society or grant a free extension and keep her until they cured her. Duncan had saved his life that day on the plane when his father had suffered a heart attack behind the controls. However, he'd lied about Bryan Morgan when recommending him for employment, and the blowback had been epic in scale, costing the president his life.

Ambivalent about what action to take, he decided that he would sleep on it. He sidestepped to cryostat 0017. Bryan's face was alabaster white, masking the bruising and swelling. His lips were set in a submissive way as if gearing himself up for the future. He had always wanted to be reunited with his mother. Kane had granted him that wish... in a roundabout way. They might meet again in the future one day. They might not. He would decide when the time was right.

Someone called Kane's name over the address system. He gave one last look at Bryan, turned, and left the lab.

EPILOGUE

UK Health Minister Michelle Brown was met with a round of applause from the four hundred media representatives in the VIP hall when she approached the steps, which formed an improvised speaking platform. She'd practiced her speech until it was automatic enough for her to recall.

"Good afternoon, welcome, and of course, thank you for attending such a monumental occasion in the long history of medical science. Since the millennium alone, more and more viruses have emerged, killing millions of people. The SARS viruses, Bird and Swine Flu, and we all remember the Taro Black Death a few years ago, which took the lives of sixteen million people indiscriminately. In the last fifty years, around fifty deadly viruses have emerged. That's one per year, many of which lack any suitable treatments and have no effective prevention or control measures in place."

She paused and looked around the hall. "We have a more existential health threat, and it affects everyone on the planet. The misuse and overuse of antibiotics have contributed to an increase in antimicrobial resistance, seriously threatening drug control strategies against common diseases like tuberculosis, cholera, dysentery, pneumonia, and many others."

The health minister sipped her water and readjusted the mic. "For years, the world has heard rumours about cryonic therapy. Does it work? Are the wheels already in motion? Do we have the technology to cryopreserve individuals for future re-integration? Alongside these rumours are significant moral considerations. Do we want people from the past joining us in the future? Doesn't the world suffer from overpopulation already? Does this throw off the natural order and cycle of life and death? The Extended Life Foundation, ELF for short, has been studying cryonics and developing technology since the late sixties. With the support of the British government, the Department of Health, and the pharmaceutical industry, we're thrilled as we prepare to launch a revolutionary national health program. It is with great enthusiasm that I announce the commencement of cryonic suspension and reanimation."

A roaring round of applause followed.

The health minister waited for the noise to settle before continuing. "The purpose of cryonics is to provide a solution for those who become terminally ill and decide they would like to suspend their lives, hoping that a future cure will be discovered, much like the recent development of a cure for AIDS at ELF."

The crowd applauded again.

"The maximum duration for cryopreservation is capped at twenty-five years. If a cure has not been developed by then, the patient is reanimated to live out the rest of their life. This twenty-five-year period ensures there is no effect on local or global populations; rather, it grants pharmaceutical research organisations crucial time to respond in the event of a sudden mass outbreak, such as with Taro Black Death. ELF offers people a second chance at life. A lifeline. And the man at the helm of this incredible, breakthrough technology, someone who's dedicated his life to turning science-fiction into reality, please welcome ELF President, Mr. Kane Spence."

The applause this time lasted longer. The audience leaned forward in their seats while many stood to show their respect. Cameras clicked and flashed, capturing the moment as the old man made his way to the stage. He paused briefly at the edge of the podium, soaking in the admiration. The warmth from their applause enveloped him, acknowledging his lifetime of achievements and the respect he had earned. As he stepped into the spotlight, his eyes glimmered with a mix of humility and pride.

At the microphone, he took a deep breath, allowing the room to settle. The audience fell into a hushed anticipation, ready to hear the words of a man whose wisdom had shaped many lives.

"Welcome to the future," he said with a smile. "A future where words like incurable, untreatable, and terminal have been relegated to the history books. Where hopeless has been replaced by hopeful, and lifelong has been replaced by long life. This is an extremely proud moment for me. I only wish my stepfather could have been here to witness this. You see, he was the mastermind, the first man in the world to undergo cryopreservation. He had a tumour growing behind his right eye. With financial support from his family, he was suspended, reanimated, and treated for his cancer. At ELF, we offer life in its boldest form. If you're plagued with a serious illness, ELF can save you. We've already cured thousands of people with varying illnesses, and our AIDS treatment is available all around the world, saving millions of lives."

Applause in the VIP lounge erupted once more, resonating with fervour, but Sarah-George had heard enough, and with a brisk command, instructed the television to shut itself off.

"That's it, then," she muttered bitterly. "ELF has gone public, and the criminals who killed Dad thirty years ago… they just get to roam free." She clenched her fists. "God, I'm so angry!"

Julia, quietly observing her daughter's reaction from the other side of the room, approached gently. Her face softened, and she reached out, taking Sarah-George's hand in her own. She squeezed it with the warmth only a mother could convey, as if her touch alone could calm the fury within her daughter. She smiled as if she were privy to some quiet truth. "Maybe it isn't over yet," she whispered, her eyes filled with a depth of certainty that defied explanation. "You know, I have this feeling… deep down, I don't believe we've seen the last of your father. Somehow, somewhere, someday, he'll cross our paths again. And when that day comes, no matter what, we'll meet him with love."

BALLOON: ALTITUDE

An event that could change the course of human history—and possibly end it.

Fable Sky, the world's largest zero-pressure helium balloon, is set to embark on its inaugural flight into the stratosphere. The ambitious space tourism project has been years in the making, requiring detailed planning, the assembly of a highly trained crew, and a small fortune to bring it to fruition.

As the groundbreaking journey into the uncharted stratosphere reaches its climax at 138,000 feet, disaster strikes, shattering the fragile peace below. Alone, adrift, and cut off from communication with flight control, the crew of five faces a perilous race against time, where their survival hangs in the balance.

In this high-stakes adventure, the crew, led by Will, the project leader and captain, must push the limits of their ingenuity, resilience, and teamwork to endure the harsh stratospheric environment and looming catastrophe that awaits them on the ground. Will they reach safety before their oxygen supplies run out?

BALLOON will leave you breathless with its breakneck action and unforgettable characters, set against the backdrop of a world forever changed.

BALLOON: SOLITUDE

Hope begins in the dark. But what if the dark holds a horrifying reality no one is prepared to face?

In the aftermath of a cataclysm that has reshaped society forever, the surviving crew members find themselves cut off from the outside world. Faced with a grim choice — sitting tight and waiting for a rescue that may never come or forging their own path — they look to Will, their balloon captain, and Ariane, the pragmatic NASA research pilot, to lead them forward.

Driven by a shared determination to survive, the crew encounters multiple obstacles and ruthless marauders in their desperate search for a rescue and vital resources. Each member's unique skills and diverse backgrounds prove invaluable and become their greatest assets in this harsh new reality.

Amid escalating tensions, they grapple with the limits of human endurance and the ethical dilemmas that test their humanity. As alliances are strained and trust is questioned, they confront the haunting question: are the greatest threats lurking beyond their shelter, or do dangers lie much closer to home, buried beneath the rubble of their shattered world?

BALLOON unveils a world beyond imagination. Get ready for a journey where crises collide, and the stakes reach new heights.

BALLOON: LATITUDE

In this third and final instalment, will humanity and courage stand between survival and annihilation?

As rations dwindle and graves are hastily dug, time has run out for the remaining crew. Traumatised by recent events but still alive, they must venture out into the unforgiving environment in one last desperate push to survive.

As they journey across the bleak and hostile landscape, they encounter natural phenomena and the constant threat of dwindling supplies. A land of promise awaits, but first impossible decisions must be made, and the crew must be prepared to pay the ultimate price.

At the critical moment, as the line between triumph and catastrophe blurs and the stakes have never been higher, Will must rely on instinct, devise innovative solutions to their dire predicament, and chart their course in a desperate bid for survival as he once again finds himself on a dangerous high-altitude mission. Will they find the freedom they seek? Or will the shadows of deceit consume them before they can soar to safety?

The genre-bending BALLOON trilogy series concludes with high altitudes, high hopes, and high-octane action adventure.

CLOTHO

For those who read between the lines, the new technology was terrifying.

Following a catastrophic terrorist attack that obliterates a prominent transport hub, Nova becomes an unwitting victim, shattering her memory into fragments. The exact circumstances behind the blast remain a mystery, but it has the radical Anti-Tech Movement written all over it.

As she struggles to piece together the remnants of her past, she becomes entangled in a dangerous pursuit against powerful forces that will stop at nothing to suppress the knowledge she possesses, catapulting her into a confused and lonely downward spiral.

When she crosses paths with Arthur, a middle-aged man still reeling from losing his family in the attack, and a homeless boy, Owen, she forms an unlikely bond, and their lives are irrevocably changed. But can she trust them?

Driven by a voracious desire for answers, Nova embarks on a dangerous quest with her unexpected alliances to unravel the truth that lies at the heart of her lost memories. With every step closer to the truth, she realises her forgotten past is entwined with the fate of the entire world, making her a girl who knows too much.

A journey into how technology and best intentions collide, reminding us that some truths are worth risking everything to uncover. Experience this electrifying tech-thriller crammed with mind-bending twists.

ACKNOWLEDGEMENT

It took several individuals to shape this story into a complete novel, and I am indebted to all. I'll start by saluting the kind staff at Alcor in Arizona who took time out of their busy days and obligingly assisted with my research about life extension and the complex science behind cryobiology.

I must thank Craig Titchener for his input in the story's early development. His great aptitude for language and grammar is second to none. Thank you also to Elsa Holland, author of *The Velvet Basement* series, for her wise counsel and invaluable insight. I wish her continued success with her writing career.

Thank you to my wise and wonderful father for his creative perspective and his brutal honesty. I thank my wife for her endless confidence in me and raising no complaints each time I vanished into my writing cave or nipped off to the library to carry out my research. It was a long haul for her, too.

I'd like to express my sincere gratitude to my two talented editors: Camilla Singh and Tom Bazin. First, Camilla, for her dedication to helping me unravel the problems and storylines. Second, Tom Bazin gave his excellent advice and meticulous attention to detail. I wish I had his brain.

I could never have written Lifeline without all these amazing, talented people behind me.

Join the community on
Facebook or subscribe on the
website for the latest news

 @christopherkeithauthor
www.christopherkeithauthor.com

PAGETRIM
BOOK EDIT &
DESIGN SERVICES